UNCONQUERED!

This is the story of a ruthless, blazing and courageous love, a love that flung defiance against the scavengers of human souls.

The time is the Russian Revolution. The place is a country burdened with fear—the midnight knock at the door, the bread hidden against famine, the haunted eyes of the fleeing, the grublike fat of the appeasers and oppressors. In a bitter struggle of the individual against the collective, three people stand forth with the mark of the unconquered in their bearing: Kira, who wants to be a builder, and the two men who love her—Leo, an aristocrat, and Andrei, a Communist.

In their tensely dramatic story, Ayn Rand shows what the theories of communism mean in practice. *We the Living* is not a story of politics, but of the men and women who have to struggle for existence behind the Red banners and slogans. It is a picture of what those slogans do to human beings, what kind of men are able to survive and which of them remain as the ultimate winners.

What happens to the defiant ones? What happens to those who succumb? Who are the winners in this conflict? Against a vivid panorama of political revolution and personal revolt, Ayn Rand offers an answer that challenges the modern conscience.

THIS IS A REPRINT OF THE HARDCOVER EDITION ORIGINALLY PUBLISHED BY RANDOM HOUSE, INC.

WE
THE
LIVING

❖ ❖

AYN RAND

A SIGNET BOOK

Published by THE NEW AMERICAN LIBRARY

SIGNET TRADEMARK REG. U.S. PAT. OFF. AND FOREIGN COUNTRIES
REGISTERED TRADEMARK—MARCA REGISTRADA
HECHO EN CHICAGO, U.S.A.

*SIGNET BOOKS are published by
The New American Library, Inc.,
1301 Avenue of the Americas, New York, New York 10019*

PRINTED IN THE UNITED STATES OF AMERICA

Foreword

I had not reread this novel as a whole, since the time of its first publication in 1936, until a few months ago. I had not expected to be as proud of it as I am.

Too many writers declare that they never succeed in expressing fully what they wished to express and that their work is only some sort of approximation. It is a viewpoint for which I have never had any sympathy and which I consider excusable only when it is voiced by beginners, since no one is born with any kind of "talent" and, therefore, every skill has to be acquired. Writers are *made*, not born. To be exact, writers are self-made. It was mainly in regard to *We the Living*, my first novel (and, progressively less, in regard to my work preceding *The Fountainhead*), that I had felt that my means were inadequate to my purpose and that I had not said what I wanted to say as well as I wished. Now, I am startled to discover how well I *did* say it.

We the Living is *not* a novel "about Soviet Russia." It is a novel about Man against the State. Its basic theme is the sanctity of human life—using the word "sanctity" not in a mystical sense, but in the sense of "supreme value." The essence of my theme is contained in the words of Irina, a minor character of the story, a young girl who is sentenced to imprisonment in Siberia and knows that she will never return: "There's something I would like to understand. And I don't think anyone can explain it. . . . There's your life. You begin it, feeling that it's something so precious and rare, so beautiful that it's like a sacred treasure. Now it's over, and it doesn't make any difference to anyone, and it isn't that they are indifferent, it's just that they don't know, they don't know what it means, that treasure of mine, and there's something about it that they should understand. I don't understand it myself, but there's something that should be understood by all of us. Only what is it? What?"

At that time, I knew a little more about this question than did Irina, but not much more. I knew that this attitude toward

one's own life should be, but is not, shared by all people—
that it is the fundamental characteristics of the best among men
—that its absence represents some enormous evil which had
never been identified. I knew that *this* is the issue at the base
of all dictatorships, all collectivist theories and all human evils
—and that political or economic issues are merely deriva-
tives and consequences of this basic primary. At that time, I
looked at any advocates of dictatorship and collectivism with
an incredulous contempt: I could not understand how any
man could be so brutalized as to claim the right to dispose
of the lives of others, nor how any man could be so lacking in
self-esteem as to grant to others the right to dispose of *his*
life. Today, the contempt has remained; the incredulity is
gone, since I know the answer.

It was not until *Atlas Shrugged* that I reached the full answer to Irina's question. In *Atlas Shrugged* I explain the
philosophical, psychological and moral meaning of the men
who value their own lives and of the men who don't. I show
that the first are the Prime Movers of mankind and that the
second are metaphysical killers, working for an opportunity
to become physical ones. In *Atlas Shrugged*, I show *why* men
are motivated either by a life premise or a death premise. In
We the Living, I show only that they are.

The rapid epistemological degeneration of our present age
—when men are being brought down to the level of concrete-
bound animals who are incapable of perceiving abstractions,
when men are taught that they must look at trees, but never
at forests—makes it necessary for me to give the following
warning to my readers: do not be misled by those who might
tell you that *We the Living* is "dated" or no longer relevant
to the present, since it deals with Soviet Russia in the nine-
teen-twenties. Such a criticism is applicable only to the writers
of the Naturalist school, and represents the viewpoint of those
who, having never discovered that any other school of literature can or did exist, are unable to distinguish the function
of a novel from that of a Sunday supplement article.

The Naturalist school of writing consists of substituting
statistics for one's standard of value, then cataloguing minute,
photographic, journalistic details of a given country, region,
city or back yard in a given decade, year, month or split-
second, on the over-all premise of: "This is what men have
done"—as against the premise of: "This is what men have
chosen and/or *should* choose to do." This last is the premise of
the Romantic school of writing, which deals, above all, with

human values and, therefore, with the essential and the universal in human actions, not with the statistical and the accidental. The Naturalist school records the choices which men happened to have made; the Romantic school projects the choices which men can and ought to make. I am a Romantic Realist—distinguished from the Romantic tradition in that the values I deal with pertain to this earth and to the basic problems of this era.

We the Living is not a story about Soviet Russia in 1925. It is a story about Dictatorship, any dictatorship, anywhere, at any time, whether it be Soviet Russia, Nazi Germany, or—which this novel might do its share in helping to prevent—a socialist America. What the rule of brute force does to men and how it destroys the best, will be the same in 1925, in 1955 or in 1975—whether the secret police is called G.P.U. or N.K.V.D., whether men eat millet or bread, whether they live in hovels or in housing projects, whether the rulers wear red shirts or brown ones, whether the head butcher kisses a Cambodian witch doctor or an American pianist.

When, at the age of twelve, at the time of the Russian revolution, I first heard the Communist principle that Man must exist for the sake of the State, I perceived that this was the essential issue, that this principle was evil, and that it could lead to nothing but evil, regardless of any methods, details, decrees, policies, promises and pious platitudes. This was the reason for my opposition to Communism then—and it is my reason now. I am still a little astonished, at times, that too many adult Americans do not understand the nature of the fight against Communism as clearly as I understood it at the age of twelve: they continue to believe that only Communist methods are evil, while Communist ideals are noble. All the victories of Communism since the year 1917 are due to that particular belief among the men who are still free.

To those who might wonder whether the conditions of existence in Soviet Russia have changed in any essential respect since 1925, I will make a suggestion: take a look through the files of the newspapers. If you do, you will observe the following pattern: first, you will read glowing reports about the happiness, the prosperity, the industrial development, the progress and the power of the Soviet Union, and that any statements to the contrary are the lies of prejudiced reactionaries; then, about five years later, you will read admissions that things were pretty miserable in the Soviet Union five years ago, just about as bad as the prejudiced reactionaries had claimed, but *now* the problems are solved and the Soviet Union is a land of happiness, prosperity, industrial development, progress and power; about five years later, you will read that Trotsky (or Zinoviev or Kamenev or Litvinov or the "kulaks" or the foreign imperialists) had caused the miserable state of things five years ago, but *now* Stalin has purged them all and the Soviet Union has surpassed the decadent West in happiness, prosperity, industrial development, etc.; five years later, you will read that Stalin was a monster who had crushed the progress of the Soviet Union, but *now* it is a land of happiness, prosperity, artistic freedom, educational perfection and scientific superiority over the whole world. How many of such five-year plans will you need before you begin to understand? That depends on your intellectual honesty and your power of abstraction. But what about the Soviet possession of the atom bomb? Read the accounts of the trials of the scientists who were Soviet spies in England, Canada and the United States. But how can we explain the "Sputnik"? Read the story of "Project X" in *Atlas Shrugged*.

Volumes can be and have been written about the issue of freedom versus dictatorship, but, in essence, it comes down to a single question: do you consider it moral to treat men as sacrificial animals and to rule them by physical force? If, as a citizen of the freest country in the world, you do not know what this would actually mean—*We the Living* will help you to know.

Coming back to the opening remarks of this foreword, I want to account for the editorial changes which I have made in the text of this novel for its present reissue: the chief inadequacy of my literary means was grammatical—a particular kind of uncertainty in the use of the English language, which reflected the transitional state of a mind thinking no longer in Russian, but not yet fully in English. I have changed only the most awkward or confusing lapses of this kind. I have reworded the sentences and clarified their meaning, without changing their content. I have not added or eliminated anything to or from the content of the novel. I have cut out some sentences and a few paragraphs that were repetitious or so confusing in their implications that to clarify them would have necessitated lengthy additions. In brief, all the changes are merely editorial line-changes. The novel remains what and as it was.

For those readers who have expressed a personal curiosity

about me. I want to say that *We the Living* is as near to an autobiography as I will ever write. It is not an autobiography in the literal, but only in the intellectual, sense. The plot is invented; the background is not. As a writer of the Romantic school, I would never be willing to transcribe a "real life" story, which would amount to evading the most important and most difficult part of creative writing: the construction of a plot. Besides, it would bore me to death. My view of what a good autobiography should be is contained in the title that Louis H. Sullivan gave to the story of his life: *The Autobiography of an Idea*. It is only in this sense that *We the Living* is my autobiography and that Kira, the heroine, is me. I was born in Russia, I was educated under the Soviets, I have seen the conditions of existence that I describe. The particulars of Kira's story were not mine; I did not study engineering, as she did—I studied history; I did not want to build bridges —I wanted to write; her physical appearance bears no resemblance to mine, neither does her family. The specific events of Kira's life were not mine; her ideas, her convictions, her values were and are.

AYN RAND

New York, October, 1958

❊ *Part One* ❊

I

Petrograd smelt of carbolic acid.

A pinkish-gray banner that had been red, hung in the webbing of steel beams. Tall girders rose to a roof of glass panes gray as the steel with the dust and wind of many years; some of the panes were broken, pierced by forgotten shots, sharp edges gaping upon a sky gray as the glass. Under the banner hung a fringe of cobwebs; under the cobwebs—a huge railway clock with black figures on a yellow face and no hands. Under the clock, a crowd of pale faces and greasy overcoats waited for the train.

Kira Argounova entered Petrograd on the threshold of a box car. She stood straight, motionless, with the graceful indifference of a traveler on a luxurious ocean liner, with an old blue suit of faded cloth, with slender, sunburned legs and no stockings. She had an old piece of plaid silk around her neck, and short tousled hair, and a stockingcap with a bright yellow tassel. She had a calm mouth and slightly widened eyes with the defiant, enraptured, solemnly and fearfully expectant look of a warrior who is entering a strange city and is not quite sure whether he is entering it as a conqueror or a captive.

Behind her was a car overloaded with a freight of humans and bundles. The bundles were wrapped in bed-sheets, newspapers and flour sacks. The humans were bundled in ragged overcoats and shawls. The bundles had served as beds and had lost all shape. Dust had engraved wrinkles on the dry, cracked skin of faces that had lost all expression.

Slowly, wearily, the train pulled to a stop, the last one of a

11

long journey across the devastated plains of Russia. It had taken two weeks to make a three days' trip—from the Crimea to Petrograd. In 1922 the railroads, as well as everything else, had not as yet been organized. The civil war had come to an end. The last traces of the White Army had been wiped out. But as the hand of the Red rule was bridling the country, the net of steel rails and telegraph wires still hung limply, out of the hand's grasp.

There were no schedules, no time-tables. No one knew when a train would leave or arrive. A vague rumor that it was coming rushed a mob of anxious travelers to the stations of every town along its way. They waited for hours, for days, afraid to leave the depot where the train could appear in a minute—or a week. The littered floors of the waiting rooms smelt like their bodies; they put their bundles on the floors, and their bodies on the bundles, and slept. They munched patiently dry crusts of bread and sunflower seeds; they did not undress for weeks. When at last, snorting and groaning, the train rumbled in, men besieged it with fists and feet and ferocious despair. Like barnacles, they clung to the steps, to the buffers, to the roofs. They lost their luggage and their children; without bell or notice the train started suddenly, carrying away those who had crawled aboard.

Kira Argounova had not started the journey in a box car. At the start, she had had a choice seat: the little table at the window of a third-class passenger coach; the little table was the center of the compartment, and Kira—the center of the passengers' attention. A young Soviet official admired the line that the silhouette of her body made against the light square of a broken window. A fat lady in a fur coat was indignant that the girl's defiant posture somehow suggested a cabaret dancer perched among champagne glasses, but a dancer with a face of such severe, arrogant calm, that the lady wondered whether she was really thinking of a cabaret table or a pedestal. For many long miles, the travelers of that compartment watched the fields and prairies of Russia roll by as a background for a haughty profile with a mass of brown hair thrown off a high forehead by the wind that whistled outside in the telegraph wires.

For lack of space Kira's feet rested on her father's lap. Alexander Dimitrievitch Argounov slumped wearily in his corner, his stomach a shelf for his folded hands, his red, puffed eyes half-closed, drowsing, jerking himself up with a sigh once in a while when he caught his mouth hanging open. He wore a patched khaki overcoat, high peasant boots with run-down heels and a burlap shirt on the back of which one could still read: "Ukrainian Potatoes." This was not an intentional disguise; it was all Alexander Dimitrievitch possessed. But he was greatly worried lest someone should notice that the rim of his pince-nez was of real gold.

Crushed against his elbow, Galina Petrovna, his wife, managed to hold her body erect and her book high to the tip of her nose. She had kept her book, but lost all her hairpins in the fight for seats, when her efforts had secured the family's entrance into the car. She was careful not to let her fellow travelers observe that her book was French.

Once in a while her foot felt cautiously under the seat to make certain that her best bundle was still there, the one wrapped in the cross-stitch embroidered table cloth. That bundle held the last remnants of her hand-made lace underwear, purchased in Vienna before the war, and the silverware with the Argounov family initials. She greatly resented, but could not prevent the fact that the bundle served as a pillow for a snoring soldier who slept under the bench, his boots protruding into the aisle.

Lydia, the Argounovs' elder daughter, had to sit in the aisle, next to the boots, on a bundle; but she made it a point to let every passenger in the car understand that she was not used to such mode of traveling. Lydia did not condescend to hide outward signs of social superiority, of which she proudly displayed three: a jabot of tarnished gold lace on her faded velvet suit, a pair of meticulously darned silk gloves and a bottle of eau-de-cologne. She took the bottle out at rare intervals to rub a few drops on her carefully groomed hands, and hid it promptly, noticing the sidewise, yearning glance of her mother from behind the French novel.

It had been four years since the Argounov family left Petrograd. Four years ago Argounov's textile factory on the outskirts of the capital was nationalized in the name of the people. In the name of the people the banks were declared national property. Argounov's safe-deposit boxes were broken open and emptied. The luminous collars of rubies and diamonds, which Galina Petrovna paraded proudly in sparkling ball-rooms and kept prudently locked afterwards, passed into unknown hands, never to be seen again.

In the days when the shadow of a growing, nameless fear descended upon the city, hanging like a heavy mist on unlighted street corners, when sudden shots rang in the night, trucks bristling with bayonets rumbled down the cobblestones, and store windows crashed with a sonorous ringing of glass; when the members of the Argounovs' social set suddenly melted away, like snow drops over a bonfire; when the Argounov family found themselves in the halls of their stately granite mansion, with a considerable sum of cash, a few last pieces of jewelry, and a constant terror at every sound of the door bell—a flight from the city stood before them as their only course of action.

In those days the thunder of the revolutionary struggle had died in Petrograd, in the resigned hopelessness of Red victory, but in the south of Russia it still roared on the fields of civil war. The south was in the hands of the White Army. That army was thrown in disjoined troops across the vast country, divided by miles of broken railroad tracks and unknown, desolated villages; that army carried three-colored banners, an impatient, bewildered contempt of the enemy—and no realization of his importance.

The Argounovs left Petrograd for the Crimea, there to await the capital's liberation from the Red yoke. Behind them, they left drawing rooms with tall mirrors reflecting blazing crystal chandeliers; perfumed furs and thoroughbred horses on sunny winter mornings; plate glass windows that opened on the avenue of stately mansions, the Kamenostrovsky, Petrograd's exclusive thoroughfare. They met four years of crowded summer shacks where piercing Crimean winds whistled through porous stone walls; of tea with saccharine, and onions fried in linseed oil; of nightly bombardments and fearful mornings when only the red flags or the three-colored banners in the streets announced into whose hands the town had passed.

The Crimea changed hands six times. Nineteen twenty-one saw the end of the struggle. From the shores of the White Sea to those of the Black, from the border of Poland to the yellow rivers of China, the red banner rose triumphantly to the sound of the "Internationale" and the clicking of keys, as the world's doors closed on Russia.

The Argounovs had left Petrograd in autumn, calmly and almost cheerfully. They had considered their trip an unpleasant, but short annoyance. They had expected to be back in the spring. Galina Petrovna had not allowed Alexander Dimitrievitch to take a winter fur coat along. "Why, he thinks it's going to last a year!" she had laughed, referring to the Soviet government.

It had lasted five years. In 1922, with a silent, dull resignation, the family took the train back to Petrograd, to start life all over again, if a start were still possible.

When they were in the train and the wheels screeched and tore forward for the first time, in that first jerk toward Petrograd, they looked at one another, but said nothing. Galina Petrovna was thinking of their mansion on Kamenostrovsky and whether they could get it back; Lydia was thinking of the old church where she had knelt every Easter of her childhood, and that she would visit it on her first day in Petrograd; Alexander Dimitrievitch was not thinking; Kira remembered suddenly that when she went to the theater, her favorite moment was the one when the lights went out and the curtain shivered before rising; and she wondered why she was thinking of that moment.

Kira's table was between two wooden benches. Ten heads faced one another—like two tense, hostile walls, swaying as the train rocked—ten weary, dusty white spots in the semi-darkness: Alexander Dimitrievitch and the faint glint of his gold pince-nez, Galina Petrovna, her face whiter than the white pages of her book, a young Soviet official with glimmers of light in his new leather brief case, a bearded peasant in a smelly sheepskin coat, who scratched himself continuously, a haggard woman with sagging breasts, who was counting constantly, hysterically her packages and children; and facing them—two of the bare-footed, uncombed children, and a soldier, his head bent, his yellow bast shoes resting on the alligator suitcase of a fat lady in a fur coat, the only passenger with a suitcase and with pink, glossy cheeks, and next to her the sallow, freckled face of a dissatisfied woman with a man's jacket, bad teeth and a red kerchief on her hair.

Through the broken window, a ray of light came in over Kira's head. Dust danced in the ray and it stopped on three pairs of boots swinging down from the upper berth where three soldiers huddled together. Above them, high over the upper berth, a consumptive young fellow was curled on the baggage rack, his chest crushed against the ceiling, asleep, snoring raucously, breathing with effort. Under the travelers' feet the wheels knocked as if a load of rusty iron crashed and then splinters rolled, clattering down three steps, and another crash and splinters clattering, and another crash and splinters clattering, and over the travelers' heads a man's breath whistled like air hissing out of a punctured balloon; the man stopped at times to moan weakly; the wheels went on clattering.

Kira was eighteen years old and she thought of Petrograd.

The faces around her spoke of Petrograd. She did not know whether the sentences hissed into the dusty air were spoken in one hour, or one day, or through the two weeks in the rocking haze of dust, sweat and fear. She did not remember—because she did not listen.

"In Petrograd they have dried fish, citizens."

"And sunflower-seed oil."

"Sunflower-seed oil! Not real?"

"Stepka, don't scratch your head at me, scratch in the aisle! . . . At our co-operative in Petrograd, they gave potatoes. A bit frozen, but real potatoes."

"Have you ever tried pancakes of coffee grounds with treacle, citizens?"

"Mud up to your knees, in Petrograd."

"You stand in line for three hours at the co-operative and maybe you get food."

"But they have NEP in Petrograd."

"What's that?"

"Never heard? You're not a conscientious citizen."

"Yes, comrades, Petrograd and NEP and private stores."

"But if you're not a speculator, you'll starve, but if you are, you can go in and buy anything you want, but if you buy you're a speculator, and then look out, but if you're not a speculator you have no money for a private store and then you stand in line at the co-operative."

"At the co-operative they give millet."

"Empty bellies are empty bellies with everybody but the lice."

"You stop scratching, citizen."

Someone on the upper berth said: "I'd like buckwheat porridge when I get to Petrograd."

"Oh, Lord," sighed the lady in the fur coat, "if I could have a bath, a nice, hot bath with soap when I get to Petrograd."

"Citizens," Lydia asked boldly, "do they have ice-cream in Petrograd? I haven't tasted it for five years. Real ice-cream, cold, so cold it takes your breath away. . . ."

"Yes," said Kira, "so cold it takes your breath away, but then you can walk faster, and there are lights, a long line of lights, moving past you as you walk."

"What are you talking about?" asked Lydia.

"Why, about Petrograd." Kira looked at her, surprised. "I thought you were talking about Petrograd, and how cold it was there, weren't you?"

"We were not. You're off—as usual."

"I was thinking about the streets. The streets of a big city where so much is possible and so many things can happen to you."

Galina Petrovna remarked dryly: "You're saying that quite happily, aren't you? I should think we'd all be quite tired of 'things happening,' by now. Haven't you had enough happen to you with the revolution, and all?"

"Oh, yes," said Kira indifferently, "the revolution."

The woman in the red kerchief opened a package and produced a piece of dried fish, and said to the upper berth: "Kindly take your boots away, citizen. I'm eating."

The boots did not move. A voice answered: "You don't eat with your nose."

The woman bit into the fish and her elbow poked furiously into the fur coat of her neighbor, and she said: "Sure, no consideration for us proletarians. It's not like as if I had a fur coat on. Only I wouldn't be eating dried fish then. I'd be eating white bread."

"White bread?" The lady in the fur coat was frightened. "Why, citizen, who ever heard of white bread? Why, I have a nephew in the Red Army, citizen, and . . . and, why, I wouldn't dream of white bread!"

"No? I bet you wouldn't eat dry fish, though. Want a piece?"

"Why . . . why, yes, thank you, citizen. I'm a little hungry and. . . ."

"So? You are? I know you bourgeois. You're only too glad to get the last bite out of a toiler's mouth. But not out of my mouth, you don't!"

The car smelt of rotting wood, clothes that had not been changed for weeks and the odor coming from a little door open at the end of the coach.

The lady in the fur coat got up and made her way timidly toward that door, stepping over the bodies in the aisle.

"Could you please step out for a moment, citizens?" she asked humbly of the two gentlemen who were traveling comfortably in that little private compartment, one of them on the seat, the other stretched in the filth of the floor.

"Certainly, citizen," the one who was sitting answered politely and kicked the one on the floor to awaken him.

Left alone where no one could watch her, the lady in the fur coat opened her handbag furtively and unwrapped a little bundle of oiled paper. She did not want anyone in the car to know that she had a whole boiled potato. She ate hurriedly in big, hysterical bites, choking, trying not to be heard beyond the closed door.

When she came out, she found the two gentlemen waiting by the door to retrieve their seats.

At night, two smoked lanterns trembled over the car, one at each end, over the doors, two shivering yellow spots in the darkness, with a gray night sky shaking in the squares of broken windows. Black figures, stiff and limp as dummies, swayed to the clatter of the wheels, asleep in sitting postures. Some snored. Some moaned. No one spoke.

When they passed a station, a ray of light swept across the car, and against the light Kira's figure flashed for a second, bent, her face in her lap on folded arms, her hair hanging down, the light setting sparks in the hair, then dying again.

Somewhere in the train, a soldier had an accordion. He sang, hour after hour, through the darkness, the wheels and the moans, dully, persistently, hopelessly. No one could tell whether his song was gay or sad, a joke or an immortal monument; it was the first song of the revolution, risen from nowhere, gay, reckless, bitter, impudent, sung by millions of voices, echoing against train roofs, and village roads, and dark city pavements, some voices laughing, some voices wailing, a people laughing at its own sorrow, the song of the revolution, written on no banner, but in every weary throat, the "Song of the Little Apple."

> *"Hey, little apple,*
> *Where are you rolling?"*

"Hey, little apple, where are you rolling? If you fall into German paws, you'll never come back. . . . Hey, little apple, where are you rolling? My sweetie's a White and I'm a Bolshevik. . . . Hey, little apple, where. . . ."

No one knew what the little apple was; but everyone understood.

Many times each night the door of the dark car was kicked open and a lantern burst in, held high in an unsteady hand, and behind the lantern came gleaming steel bands, and khaki, and brass buttons; bayonets and men with stern, imperious voices that ordered: "Your documents!"

The lantern swam slowly, shaking, down the car, stopping on pale, startled faces with blinking eyes, and trembling hands with crumpled scraps of paper.

Then Galina Petrovna smiled ingratiatingly, repeating:

"Here you are, comrade. Here, comrade," thrusting at the lantern a piece of paper with a few typewritten lines which stated that a permission for a trip to Petrograd had been granted the citizen Alexander Argounov with wife Galina and daughters: Lydia, 28, and Kira, 18.

The men behind the lantern looked at the paper, and curtly handed it back, and walked farther, stepping over Lydia's legs stretched across the aisle.

Sometimes some men threw a quick glance back at the girl who sat on the table. She was awake and her eyes followed them. Her eyes were not frightened; they were steady, curious, hostile.

Then the men and the lantern were gone and somewhere in the train the soldier with the accordion wailed:

> *"And now there is no Russia,*
> *For Russia's all sprawled.*
> *Hey, little apple,*
> *Where have you rolled?"*

Sometimes the train stopped at night. No one knew why it had stopped. There was no station, no sign of life in the barren waste of miles. An empty stretch of sky hung over an empty stretch of land; the sky had a few black spots of clouds; the land—a few black spots of bushes. A faint, red, quivering line divided the two; it looked like a storm or a distant fire.

Whispers crawled down the long line of cars: "The boiler exploded. . . ."

"The bridge is blown up half a mile ahead. . . ."

"They've found counter-revolutionaries on the train and they're going to shoot them right here, in the bushes. . . ."

"If we stay much longer . . . the bandits . . . you know. . . ."

"They say Makhno is right in this neighborhood."

"If he gets us, you know what that means, don't you? No man leaves alive, but the women do and wish they didn't. . . ."

"Stop talking nonsense, citizen. You're making the women nervous."

Searchlights darted into the clouds and died instantly and no one could say whether they were close by or miles away. And no one could tell whether the black spot that had seemed to move was a horseman or just a bush.

The train started as suddenly as it had stopped. Sighs of relief greeted the screeching of wheels. No one ever learned why the train had stopped.

Early one morning, some men rushed through the car. One of them had a Red Cross badge. There was the sound of a commotion outside. One of the passengers followed the men. When he came back his face made the travelers feel uneasy.

"It's in the next car," he explained. "A fool peasant woman. Traveled between the cars and tied her legs to the buffer so she wouldn't fall. Fell asleep at night, too tired, I guess, and slipped off. Legs tied, it just dragged her with the train, under the car. Head cut off. Sorry I went to see."

Halfway through the journey, at a lonely little station that had a rotting platform and bright posters and unkempt soldiers on both platform and posters, it was found that the passenger coach in which the Argounov family traveled, could go no farther. The cars had not been repaired or inspected for years; when they suddenly and finally broke down, no repairs could help. The occupants were requested to move out speedily. They had to squeeze themselves into the other overcrowded cars—if they could.

The Argounovs fought their way into a box car. Gratefully, Galina Petrovna and Lydia made the sign of the cross.

The woman with the sagging breasts could not find room for all of her children. When the train pulled out, she was seen sitting on her bundles, the bewildered children clinging to her skirt, watching the train with a dull, hopeless stare.

Across prairies and marshes, the long line of cars crawled wearily, a veil of smoke floating and melting into white puffs behind it. Soldiers huddled in groups on the sloping, slippery roofs. Some of them had harmonicas. They played and sang about the little apple. The song trailed and melted away with the smoke.

A crowd awaited the train in Petrograd. When the last panting of the engine reverberated through the terminal vaults, Kira Argounova faced the mob that met every train. Under the folds of shapeless clothes, their bodies were driven by the tense, unnatural energy of a long struggle that had become habitual; their faces were hard and worn. Behind them were tall, grilled windows; behind these was the city.

Kira was pushed forward by impatient travelers. Alighting, she stopped for one short second of hesitation, as if feeling the significance of the step. Her foot was sunburned, and she wore a home-made wooden sandal with leather straps. For one short second the foot was held in the air. Then the wooden sandal touched the wooden boards of the platform: Kira Argounova was in Petrograd.

II

PROLETARIANS OF THE WORLD, UNITE!

Kira looked at the words on the bare plaster walls of the station. The plaster had crumbled off in dark blotches that made the walls look skin-diseased. But fresh signs had been printed upon them. Red letters announced: LONG LIVE THE DICTATORSHIP OF THE PROLETARIAT! WHO IS NOT WITH US—IS AGAINST US!

The letters had been made by a smudge of red paint over a stencil. Some lines were crooked. Some letters had dried with long, thin streaks of red winding down the walls.

A young fellow leaned against a wall under the signs. A crumpled lambskin hat was crushed over his pale hair that hung over his pale eyes. He stared aimlessly ahead and cracked sunflower seeds, spitting the shells out of the corner of his mouth.

Between the train and the walls, a whirlpool of khaki and red dragged Kira into the midst of soldiers' coats, red kerchiefs, unshaved faces, mouths that opened soundlessly, their screams swallowed in a roar of boots shuffling down the platform, beating against the high steel ceiling. An old barrel with rusty hoops and a tin cup attached on a chain bore a painted inscription: "Boiled water" and a huge sign: "BEWARE OF CHOLERA. DO NOT DRINK RAW WATER." A stray dog with ribs like a skeleton's, its tail between its legs, was smelling the littered floor, searching for food. Two armed soldiers were fighting through the crowd, dragging a peasant woman who struggled and sobbed: "Comrades! I didn't! Brothers, where are you taking me? Comrades dear, so help me God, I didn't!"

From below, among the boots and swishing, mud-caked skirts, someone howled monotonously, not quite a human sound nor a barking: a woman was crawling on her knees, trying to gather a spilled sack of millet, sobbing, picking up the grain mixed with sunflower-seed shells and cigarette butts.

Kira looked at the tall windows. She heard, from the outside, the old familiar sound of the piercing tramway bell. She smiled.

21

At a door marked in red letters "Commandant," a young soldier stood on guard. Kira looked at him. His eyes were austere and forbidding like caverns where a single flame burned under cold, gray vaults; there was an air of innate temerity in the lines of his tanned face, of the hand that grasped the bayonet, of the neck in the open shirt collar. Kira liked him. She looked straight into his eyes and smiled. She thought that he understood her, that he guessed the great adventure beginning for her.

The soldier looked at her coldly, indifferently, astonished. She turned away, a little disappointed, although she did not know just what she had expected.

All the soldier noticed was that the strange girl in the child's stocking-cap had strange eyes; also that she wore a light suit and no brassiere, which fact he did not resent at all.

"Kira!" Galina Petrovna's voice pierced the roar of the station. "Kira! Where are you? Where are your parcels? How about your parcels?"

Kira returned to the box car where her family was struggling with the luggage. She had forgotten that she had to carry three bundles, porters being a luxury out of reach. Galina Petrovna was fighting off these porters, husky loafers in ragged soldiers' coats, who seized luggage without being asked, insolently offering their services.

Then, arms strained by the bundled remains of their fortune, the Argounov family descended upon the ground of Petrograd.

A gold sickle and hammer rose over the station's exit door. Two posters hung by its side. One bore a husky worker whose huge boots crushed tiny palaces, while his raised arm, with muscles red as beefsteaks, waved a greeting to a rising sun red as his muscles; above the sun stood the words: COMRADES! WE ARE THE BUILDERS OF A NEW LIFE!

The other bore a huge white louse on a black background with red letters: LICE SPREAD DISEASE! CITIZENS, UNITE ON THE ANTI-TYPHUS FRONT!

The smell of carbolic acid rose higher than all the rest. Station buildings were disinfected against the diseases that poured into the city on every train. Like a breath from a hospital window, the odor hung in the air as a warning and a grim reminder.

The doors into Petrograd opened upon the Znamensky square. A sign on a post announced its new name: SQUARE OF UPRISING. A huge gray statue of Alexander III faced the station, against a gray hotel building, against a gray sky. It was not raining heavily, but a few drops fell at long intervals, slowly, monotonously, as if the sky were leaking, as if it too were in need of repairs, like the rotted wooden paving where raindrops made silver sparks on dark puddles. The raised black tops of hansom cabs looked like patent leather, swaying, quivering, wheels grunting in the mud with the sound of animals chewing. Old buildings watched the square with the dead eyes of abandoned shops in whose dusty windows the cobwebs and faded newspapers had not been disturbed for five years.

But one shop bore a cotton sign: PROVISION CENTER. A line waited at the door, stretching around the corner; a long line of feet in shoes swollen by the rain, of red, frozen hands, of raised collars that did not prevent the raindrops from rolling down many backs, for many heads were bent.

"Well," said Alexander Dimitrievitch, "we're back."

"Isn't it wonderful!" said Kira.

"Mud, as ever," said Lydia.

"We'll have to take a cab. Such an expense!" said Galina Petrovna.

They crowded into one cab, Kira sitting on top of the bundles. The horse jerked forward, sending a shower of mud on Kira's legs, and turned into the Nevsky Prospect.

The long, broad avenue lay before them, as straight as if it were the spine of the city. Far away, the slender gold spire of the Admiralty gleamed faintly in the gray mist, like a long arm raised in a solemn greeting.

Petrograd had seen five years of revolution. Four of those years had closed its every artery and every store, when nationalization smeared dust and cobwebs over the plate-glass windows; the last year had brought out soap and mops, new paint and new owners, as the state's New Economic Policy had announced a "temporary compromise" and allowed small private stores to re-open timidly.

After a long sleep, Nevsky was opening its eyes slowly. The eyes were not used to the light; they had opened in a hurry and they stared, wide, frightened, incredulous. New signs were cotton strips with glaring, uneven letters. Old signs were marble obituaries of men long since gone. Gold letters spelled forgotten names on the windows of new owners, and bullet holes with sunburst cracks still decorated the glass. There were stores without signs and signs without stores. But between the windows and over closed doors, over bricks and boards and cracked plaster, the city wore a mantle of color bright as a patchwork: there were posters of red shirts, and yellow wheat, and red banners, and blue wheels, and red kerchiefs, and gray tractors, and red smokestacks; they were wet, transparent in the rain, showing layers of old posters underneath, growing— unchecked, unrestricted—like the bright mildew of a city.

On a corner, an old lady held timidly a tray of home-made cakes, and feet hurried past without stopping; someone yelled: *"Pravda! Krasnaya Gazeta!* Latest news, citizens!" and some- one yelled: "Saccharine, citizens!" and someone yelled: "Flints for cigarette lighters, cheap, citizens!" Below, there was mud and sunflower-seed shells; above, there were red banners bend- ing over the street from every house, streaked and dripping little pink drops.

"I hope," said Galina Petrovna, "that sister Marussia will be glad to see us."

"I wonder," said Lydia, "what these last years have done to the Dunaevs."

"I wonder what is left of their fortune," said Galina Petrov- na, "if anything. Poor Marussia! I doubt if they have more than we do."

"And if they have," sighed Alexander Dimitrievitch, "what difference does it make now, Galina?"

"None," said Galina Petrovna, "—I hope."

"Anyway, we're still no poor relations," Lydia said proudly and pulled her skirt up a little to show the passersby her high- laced, olive-green shoes.

Kira was not listening; she was watching the streets.

The cab stopped at the building where, four years ago, they had seen the Dunaevs in their magnificent apartment. One half of the imposing entrance door had a huge, square glass pane; the other half was filled in with unpainted boards hastily nailed together.

The spacious lobby had had a soft carpet, Galina Petrovna remembered, and a hand-carved fireplace. The carpet was gone; the fireplace was still there, but there were penciled inscriptions on the white stomachs of its marble cupids and a long, diagonal crack in the large mirror above it.

A sleepy janitor stuck his head out of the little booth under the stairs and withdrew it indifferently.

They carried their bundles up the stairs. They stopped at a padded door; the black oilcloth was ripped and gray lumps of soiled cotton made a fringe around the door.

"I wonder," Lydia whispered, "if they still have their mag- nificent butler."

Galina Petrovna pressed the bell.

There were steps inside. A key turned. A cautious hand half opened the door, protected by a chain. Through the narrow crack, they saw an old woman's face cut by hanging gray hair, a stomach under a dirty towel tied as an apron, and one foot in a man's bedroom slipper. The woman looked at them silently, with hostile inquiry, with no intention of opening the door farther.

"Is Maria Petrovna in?" Galina Petrovna asked in a slightly unnatural voice.

"Who wants to know?" asked the toothless mouth.

"I'm her sister, Galina Petrovna Argounova."

The woman did not answer; she turned and yelled into the house: "Maria Petrovna! Here's a mob that says them's your sister!"

A cough answered from the depths of the house, then slow steps; then a pale face peered over the old woman's shoulder and a mouth opened with a shriek: "My Lord in Heaven!"

The door was thrown wide open. Two thin arms seized Galina Petrovna, crushing her against a trembling chest. "Galina! Darling! It's you!"

"Marussia!" Galina Petrovna's lips sank into the powder on a flabby cheek and her nose into the thin, dry hair sprinkled with a perfume that smelled like vanilla.

Maria Petrovna had always been the beauty of the family, the delicate, spoiled darling whose husband carried her in his arms through the snow to the carriage in winter. She looked older than Galina Petrovna now. Her skin was the color of soiled linen; her lips were not red enough, but her eyelids were too red.

A door crashed open behind her and something came flying into the anteroom; something tall, tense, with a storm of hair and eyes like automobile headlights; and Galina Petrovna recognized Irina, her niece, a young girl of eighteen with the eyes of twenty-eight and the laughter of eight. Behind her, Acia, her little sister, waddled in slowly and stood in the doorway, watching the newcomers sullenly; she was eight years old, needed a haircut and one garter.

Galina Petrovna kissed the girls; then she raised herself on tiptoe to plant a kiss on the cheek of her brother-in-law, Vasili Ivanovitch. She tried not to look at him. His thick hair was white; his tall, powerful body stooped. Had she seen the Admiralty tower stooping, Galina Petrovna would have felt less alarmed.

Vasili Ivanovitch spoke seldom. He said only: "Is that my little friend Kira?" The question was warmer than a kiss.

His sunken eyes were like a fireplace where the last blazing coals fought against slow, inevitable ashes. He said: "Sorry Victor isn't home. He's at the Institute. The boy works so hard." His son's name acted like a strong breath that revived the coals for a moment.

Before the revolution, Vasili Ivanovitch Dunaev had owned a prosperous fur business. He had started as a trapper in the wilderness of Siberia, with a gun, a pair of boots, and two arms that could lift an ox. He wore the scar of a bear's teeth on his thigh. Once, he was found buried in the snow; he had been there for two days; his arms clutched the body of the most magnificent silver fox the frightened Siberian peasants had ever seen. His relatives heard no word from him for ten years. When he returned to St. Petersburg, he opened an office of which his relatives could not afford the door knobs; and he bought silver horseshoes for the three horses that galloped with his carriage down Nevsky.

His hands had provided the ermines that swept many marble stairways in the royal palaces; the sables that embraced many shoulders white as marble. His muscles and the long hours of the frozen Siberian nights had paid for every hair of every fur that passed through his hands.

He was sixty years old; his backbone had been as straight as his gun; his spirit—as straight as his backbone.

When Galina Petrovna raised a steaming spoonful of millet to her lips in her sister's dining room, she threw a furtive glance at Vasili Ivanovitch. She was afraid to study him openly; but she had seen the stooped backbone; she wondered about the spirit.

She saw the changes in the dining room. The spoon she held was not the monogrammed silverware she remembered; it was of heavy tin that gave a metallic taste to the mush. She remembered crystal and silver fruit vases on the buffet; one solitary jug of Ukrainian pottery adorned it now. Big rusty nails on the walls showed the places where old paintings had hung.

Across the table, Maria Petrovna was talking with a nervous, fluttering hurry, a strange caricature of the capricious manner that had charmed every drawing room she entered. Her words were strange to Galina Petrovna, words like milestones of the years they had been parted and of what had happened in those years.

"Ration cards—they're for Soviet employees only. And for students. We get only two ration cards. Just two cards for the family—and it isn't easy. Victor's student card at the Institute and Irina's at the Academy of Arts. But I'm not employed anywhere, so I get no card, and Vasili. . . ."

She stopped short, as if her words, running, had skidded too far. She looked at her husband, furtively, a glance that seemed to cringe. Vasili Ivanovitch was staring into his plate and said nothing.

Maria Petrovna's hands fluttered up eloquently: "These are hard times, God have pity on us, these are hard times. Galina, do you remember Lili Savinskaia, the one who never wore any jewelry except pearls? Well, she's dead. She died in 1919. It was like this: they had nothing to eat for days, and her husband was walking in the street and he saw a horse that fell and died of hunger, and there was a mob fighting for the body. They tore it to pieces, and he got some. He brought it home and they cooked it, and ate, and I suppose the horse hadn't died of hunger only, for they both got terribly sick. The doctors saved him, but Lili died. . . . He lost everything in 1918, of course. . . . His sugar business—it was nationalized the same day when our fur store. . . ."

She stopped short again, her eyelids trembling over a glance at Vasili Ivanovitch. Vasili Ivanovitch said nothing.

"More," said little Acia sullenly and extended her plate for a second helping of millet.

"Kira!" Irina called brightly across the table, her voice very clear and loud, as if to sweep away all that had been said. "Did you eat fresh fruit in the Crimea?"

"Yes. Some," Kira answered indifferently.

"I've been dreaming, yearning and dying for grapes. Don't you like grapes?"

"I never notice what I eat," said Kira.

"Of course," Maria Petrovna hurried on, "Lili Savinskaia's husband is working now. He's a clerk in a Soviet office. *Some* people *are* taking employment, after all. . . ." She looked openly at Vasili Ivanovitch and waited, but he did not answer.

Galina Petrovna asked timidly: "How's . . . how's our old house?"

"Yours? On Kamenostrovsky? Don't even dream of it. A sign painter lives there now. A real proletarian. God knows *where* you'll find an apartment, Galina. People are crowded like dogs."

Alexander Dimitrievitch asked hesitantly: "Have you heard

what . . . about the factory . . . what happened to my factory?"

"Closed," Vasili Ivanovitch snapped suddenly. *"They* couldn't run it. Closed. Like everything else."

Maria Petrovna coughed. "Such a problem for you, Galina, such a problem! Are the girls going to school? Or—how are you going to get ration cards?"

"But—I thought—with the NEP and all, you have private stores now."

"Sure—NEP, their New Economic Policy, sure, they allow private stores now, but where will you get the money to buy there? They charge you ten times more than the ration co-operatives. I haven't been in a private store yet. We can't afford it. No one can afford it. We can't even afford the theater. Victor's taken me to a show once. But Vasili—Vasili won't set foot inside a theater."

"Why not?"

Vasili Ivanovitch raised his head, his eyes stern, and said solemnly: "When your country is in agony, you don't seek frivolous recreations. I'm in mourning—for my country."

"Lydia," Irina asked in her sweeping voice, "aren't you in love yet?"

"I do not answer indecent questions," said Lydia.

"I'll tell you, Galina," Maria Petrovna hurried and coughed, choked, and went on, "I'll tell you the best thing to do: Alexander must take a job."

Galina Petrovna sat up straight, as if she had been slapped in the face. "A *Soviet* job?"

"Well . . . all jobs are Soviet jobs."

"Not as long as I live," Alexander Dimitrievitch stated with unexpected strength.

Vasili Ivanovitch dropped his spoon and it clattered into his plate; silently, solemnly, he stretched his big fist across the table and shook Alexander Dimitrievitch's hand and threw a dark glance at Maria Petrovna. She cringed, swallowed a spoonful of millet, coughed.

"I'm not saying anything about you, Vasili," she protested timidly. "I know you don't approve and . . . well, you never will. . . . But I was just thinking they get bread cards, and lard, and sugar, the Soviet employees do—sometimes."

"When I have to take Soviet employment," said Vasili Ivanovitch, "you'll be a widow, Marussia."

"I'm not saying anything, Vasili, only. . . ."

"Only stop worrying. We'll get along. We have so far. There are still plenty of things to sell."

Galina Petrovna looked at the nails on the walls; she looked at her sister's hands, the famous hands that artists had painted and a poem had been written about—"Champagne and Maria's hands." They were frozen to a dark purple, swollen and cracked. Maria Petrovna had known the value of her hands; she had learned how to keep them in sight constantly, how to use them with the pliant grace of a ballerina. It was a habit she had not lost. Galina Petrovna wished she would lose it; the soft, fluttering gestures of those hands were only one more reminder.

Vasili Ivanovitch was speaking suddenly. He had always been reticent in the expression of his feelings. But one subject aroused him and then his expressions were not restrained: "All this is temporary. You all lose faith so easily. That's the trouble with our spineless, snivelling, impotent, blabbering, broad-minded, drooling intelligentsia! That's why we are where we are. No faith. No will. Thin gruel for blood. Do you think all this can go on? Do you think Russia is dead? Do you think Europe is blind? Watch Europe. She hasn't said her last word yet. The day will come—soon—when these bloody assassins, these foul scoundrels, that Communist scum. . . ."

The door bell rang.

The old servant shuffled to open the door. They heard a man's steps, brisk, resonant, energetic. A strong hand threw the dining-room door open.

Victor Dunaev looked like a tenor in an Italian grand opera, which was not Victor's profession; but he had the broad shoulders, the flaming black eyes, the wavy, unruly black hair, the flashing smile, the arrogantly confident movements. As he stopped on the threshold, his eyes stopped on Kira; as she turned in her chair, they stopped on her legs.

"It's little Kira, isn't it?" were the first sounds of his strong, clear voice.

"It was," she answered.

"Well, well, what a surprise! What a most pleasant surprise! . . . Aunt Galina, younger than ever!" He kissed his aunt's hand. "And my charming cousin Lydia!" His dark hair brushed Lydia's wrist. "Sorry to be so late. Meeting at the Institute. I'm a member of the Students' Council. . . . Sorry, Father. Father doesn't approve of any elections of any sort."

"Sometimes even elections are right," said Vasili Ivanovitch without disguising the paternal pride in his voice; and the warmth in his stern eyes suddenly made them look helpless.

Victor whirled a chair about and sat next to Kira. "Well, Uncle Alexander," he flashed a row of sparkling white teeth at Alexander Dimitrievitch, "you've chosen a fascinating time to return to Petrograd. A difficult time, to be sure. A cruel time. But most fascinating, like all historical cataclysms."

Galina Petrovna smiled with admiration: "What are you studying, Victor?"

"Institute of Technology. Electrical engineer. Greatest future in electricity. Russia's future. . . . But father doesn't think so. . . . Irina, do you ever comb your hair? What are your plans, Uncle Alexander?"

"I'll open a store," Alexander Dimitrievitch announced solemnly, almost proudly.

"But it will take some financial resources, Uncle Alexander."

"We've managed to save a little, in the south."

"Lord in Heaven!" cried Maria Petrovna. "You'd better spend it quickly. At the rate that new paper money is going down—why, bread was sixty thousand rubles a pound last week—and it's seventy-five thousand now!"

"New enterprises, Uncle Alexander, have a great future in this new age," said Victor.

"Until the government squashes them under its heel," Vasili Ivanovitch said gloomily.

"Nothing to fear, Father. The days of confiscations are past. The Soviet government has a most progressive policy outlined."

"Outlined in blood," said Vasili Ivanovitch.

"Victor, they're wearing the funniest things in the south," Irina spoke hurriedly. "Did you notice Kira's wooden sandals?"

"All right, League of Nations. That's her name. Trying to keep peace. I would *love* to see the sandals."

Kira raised her foot indifferently. Her short skirt concealed little of her leg; she did not notice the fact, but Victor and Lydia did.

"At your age, Kira," Lydia remarked pointedly, "it's time to wear longer skirts."

"If one has the material," Kira answered indifferently. "I never notice what I wear."

"Nonsense, Lydia darling," Victor stated with finality, "short skirts are the height of feminine elegance and feminine elegance is the highest of the Arts."

*

That night, before retiring, the family gathered in the drawing room. Maria Petrovna painfully counted out three logs, and a fire was lighted in the fireplace. Little flames flickered over the glazed abyss of darkness beyond the big, bare, curtainless windows; little sparks danced in the polished curves of the hand-carved furniture, leaving in shadows the torn brocade; golden spangles played in the heavy gold frame of the only picture in the room, leaving in shadows the picture itself: a painting of Maria Petrovna twenty years ago, with a delicate hand resting on an ivory shoulder, mocking the old knitted shawl which the living Maria Petrovna clutched convulsively over her trembling shoulders when she coughed.

The logs were damp; a fretful blue flame hissed feebly, dying and flaring up again in a burst of acrid smoke.

Kira sat in the deep, silken fur of a white bear rug at the fireplace, her arm encircling affectionately the huge monster's ferocious head. It had been her favorite since childhood. When visiting her uncle, she had always asked for the story of how he had killed that bear, and she had laughed happily when he threatened that the bear would come back to life and bite disobedient little girls.

"Well," said Maria Petrovna, her hands fluttering in the fire glow, "well, here you are back in Petrograd."

"Yes," said Galina Petrovna, "here we are."

"Oh, Saint Mother of God!" sighed Maria Petrovna. "It makes it so hard sometimes to have a future to think about!"

"It does," said Galina Petrovna.

"Well, what are the plans for the girls? Lydia darling, quite a young lady, aren't you? Still heart-free?" Lydia's smile was not a grateful one. Maria Petrovna sighed: "Men are so strange, nowadays. They don't think of marriage. And the girls? I was carrying a son at Irina's age. But she doesn't think of a home and family. The Academy of Arts for her. Galina, do you remember how she used to ruin my furniture with her infernal drawings as soon as she was out of diapers? Well, Lydia, are you going to study?"

"I have no such intention," said Lydia. "Too much education is unfeminine."

"And Kira?"

"It's funny to think that little Kira is of college age, isn't it?" said Victor. "First of all, Kira, you'll have to get a labor book—the new passport, you know. You're over sixteen. And then. . . ."

"I think," Maria Petrovna suggested eagerly, "that a profession is so useful nowadays. Why don't you send Kira to a medical school? A lady doctor gets such nice rations!"

"Kira a doctor?" Galina Petrovna sneered. "Why, the selfish little thing just loathes physical injury. She wouldn't help a wounded chicken."

"My opinion . . ." Victor began.

A telephone rang in the next room. Irina darted out and returned, announcing aloud with a significant wink at Victor: "For you, Victor. It's Vava."

Victor walked out reluctantly. Through the door, left open by a draft, they heard some of his words: ". . . I know I promised to come tonight. But it's an unexpected examination at the Institute. I have to study every minute of the evening. . . . .Of course not, no one else. . . . You know I do, darling. . . ."

He returned to the fireplace and settled himself comfortably on the white bear's back, close to Kira.

"My opinion, my charming little cousin," he stated, "is that the most promising career for a woman is offered not by a school, but by employment in a Soviet office."

"Victor, you don't really mean that," said Vasili Ivanovitch.

"One has to be practical nowadays," Victor said slowly. "A student's ration doesn't provide much for a whole family—as you ought to know."

"Employees get lard and sugar," said Maria Petrovna.

"They are using a great many typists," Victor insisted. "A typewriter's keys are the stepping stones to any high office."

"And you get shoes, and free tramway tickets," said Maria Petrovna.

"Hell," said Vasili Ivanovitch, "you can't make a drayhorse out of a racing steed."

"Why, Kira," asked Irina, "aren't you interested in the subject of this discussion?"

"I am," Kira answered calmly, "but I think the discussion is superfluous. I am going to the Technological Institute."

"Kira!"

There were seven startled voices and they all uttered one name. Then Galina Petrovna said: "Well, with a daughter like this even her own mother isn't let in on secrets!"

"When did you decide that?" Lydia gasped.

"About eight years ago," said Kira.

"But Kira! What will you do?" Maria Petrovna gasped.

"I'll be an engineer."

"Frankly," said Victor, annoyed, "I do not believe that engineering is a profession for women."

"Kira," Alexander Dimitrievitch said timidly, "you've never liked the Communists and here you select such a modern favorite profession of theirs—a woman engineer!"

"Are you going to build for the Red State?" asked Victor.

"I'm going to build because I want to build."

"But Kira!" Lydia stared at her, bewildered. "That will mean dirt, and iron, and rust, and blow-torches, and filthy, sweaty men and no feminine company to help you."

"That's why I'll like it."

"It is not at all a cultured profession for a woman," said Galina Petrovna.

"It's the only profession," said Kira, "for which I don't have to learn any lies. Steel is steel. Most of the other sciences are someone's guess, and someone's wish, and many people's lies."

"What you lack," said Lydia, "are the things of the spirit."

"Frankly," said Victor, "your attitude is slightly anti-social, Kira. You select a profession merely because you want it, without giving a thought to the fact that, as a woman, you would be much more useful to society in a more feminine capacity. And we all have our duty to society to consider."

"Exactly to whom is it that you owe a duty, Victor?"

"To society."

"What is society?"

"If I may say it, Kira, this is a childish question."

"But," said Kira, her eyes dangerously gentle and wide, "I don't understand it. To whom is it that I owe a duty? To your neighbor next door? Or to the militia-man on the corner? Or to the clerk in the co-operative? Or to the old man I saw in line, third from the door, with an old basket and a woman's hat?"

"Society, Kira, is a stupendous whole."

"If you write a whole line of zeroes, it's still—nothing."

"Child," said Vasili Ivanovitch, "what are you doing in Soviet Russia?"

"That," said Kira, "is what I'm wondering about."

"Let her go to the Institute," said Vasili Ivanovitch.

"I'll have to," Galina Petrovna agreed bitterly. "You can't argue with her."

"She always gets her way," said Lydia resentfully. "I don't see how she does it."

Kira bent over the fire to blow at the dying flame. For one moment, as a bright tongue leaped up, a red glow tore her face out of the darkness. Her face was like that of a blacksmith bending over his forge.

"I fear for your future, Kira," said Victor. "It's time to get reconciled to life. You won't get far with those ideas of yours."

"That," said Kira, "depends on what direction I want to go."

III

Two hands held a little book bound in gray burlap. They were dry and calloused. They had seen many years of labor in the oil and the heat and the grease of roaring machines. The wrinkles were encrusted in black on a skin stiff with the dust of years. There were black tips on the cracked fingernails. One finger wore a tarnished ring with an imitation emerald.

The office had bare walls. They had served as towel to many a dirty hand, for traces left by five fingers zigzagged across the faded paint. In the old house now nationalized for government offices, it had been a washroom. The sink was removed; but a rusty outline with glaring nailholes still drew its picture on the wall, and two broken pipes hung out, like the bowels of the wounded building.

The window had an iron grate and broken panes which a spider had tried to mend. It faced a bare wall with red bricks losing the last scabs of paint which had been the advertisement of a hair-restorer.

The official sat at his desk. The desk had a blotter torn in one corner and a half-dry inkstand. The official wore a khaki suit and glasses.

Like two silent judges presiding behind their spokesman, two pictures flanked his head. They had no frames; four thumbtacks nailed each to the wall. One was of Lenin, the other of Karl Marx. Red letters above them said: IN UNION LIES OUR STRENGTH.

Head high, Kira Argounova stood before the desk.

She was there to receive her labor book. Every citizen over sixteen had to have a labor book and was ordered to carry it at all times. It had to be presented and stamped when he found employment or left it; when he moved into an apartment or out of one; when he enrolled at a school, got a bread card or was married. The new Soviet passport was more than a passport: it was a citizen's permit to live. It was called "Labor Book," for labor and life were considered synonymous.

The Russian Socialist Federalist Soviet Republic was about to acquire a new citizen.

The official held the little book bound in gray burlap, whose many pages he was going to fill. He had trouble with his pen; it was old and rusty, and dragged strings from the bottom of the inkstand.

On the clean open page he wrote:

Name: ARGOUNOVA,
      KIRA ALEXANDROVNA.
Height: MEDIUM.

*

Kira's body was slender, too slender, and when she moved with a sharp, swift, geometrical precision, people were conscious of the movement alone, not of the body. Yet through any garment she wore, the unseen presence of her body made her look undressed. People wondered what made them aware of it. It seemed that the words she said were ruled by the will of her body and that her sharp movements were the unconscious reflection of a dancing, laughing soul. So that her spirit seemed physical and her body spiritual.

*

The official wrote:
Eyes: GRAY.

*

Kira's eyes were dark gray, the gray of storm clouds from behind which the sun can be expected at any moment. They looked at people quietly, directly, with something that people called arrogance, but which was only a deep, confident calm that seemed to tell men her sight was too clear and none of their favorite binoculars were needed to help her look at life.

*

Mouth: ORDINARY.

*

Kira's mouth was thin, long. When silent, it was cold, in-domitable, and men thought of a Valkyrie with lance and winged helmet in the sweep of battle. But a slight movement made a wrinkle in the corners of her lips—and men thought of an imp perched on top of a toadstool, laughing in the faces of daisies.

*

Hair: BROWN.

*

Kira's hair was short, thrown back off her forehead, light rays lost in its tangled mass, the hair of a primitive jungle woman over a face that had escaped from the easel of a mod-ern artist who had been in a hurry: a face of straight, sharp lines sketched furiously to suggest an unfinished promise.

*

Particular Signs: NONE.
The Soviet official picked a thread off his pen, rolled it in his fingers and wiped them on his trousers.

*

Place and Date of Birth: PETROGRAD, APRIL 11, 1904.

*

Kira was born in the gray granite house on Kamenostrov-sky. In that vast mansion Galina Petrovna had a boudoir where, at night, a maid in black fastened the clasps of her diamond necklaces; and a reception room where, her taffeta petticoats rustling solemnly, she entertained ladies with sables and lorgnettes. Children were not admitted into these rooms, and Galina Petrovna seldom appeared in any of the others.

Kira had an English governess, a thoughtful young lady with a lovely smile. She liked her governess, but often preferred to be alone—and was left alone. When she refused to play with a crippled relative of whom the family's compassion had made a general idol—she was never asked to do it again. When she threw out of the window the first book she read about the good fairy rewarding an unselfish little girl—the governess never brought another one of that kind. When she was taken to church and sneaked out alone in the middle of the services, to get lost in the streets and be brought home to her frantic family—in a police wagon—she was never taken to church again.

The Argounov summer residence stood on a high hill over a river, alone in its spacious gardens, on the outskirts of a fashionable summer resort. The house turned its back upon the river and faced the grounds where the hill sloped down gracefully into a garden of lawns drawn with a ruler, bushes clipped into archways and marble fountains made by famous artists.

The other side of the hill hung over the river like a mass of rock and earth disgorged by a volcano and frozen in its chaotic tangle. Rowing downstream, people expected a dinosaur to stretch its head out of the black caves overgrown with wild ferns, between trees that grew horizontally into the air, huge roots, like spiders, grasping the rocks.

For many summers, while her parents were visiting Nice, Biarritz and Vienna, Kira was left alone to spend her days in the wild freedom of the rocky hill, as its sole, undisputed sovereign in a torn blue skirt and a white shirt whose sleeves were always missing. The sharp sand cut her bare feet. She swung from rock to rock, grasping a tree branch, throwing her body into space, the blue skirt flaring like a parachute.

She made a raft of tree branches and, clutching a long pole, sailed down the river. There were many dangerous rocks and whirlpools on the way. The thrill of the struggle rose from her bare feet, that felt the stream pulsating under the frail raft, through her body tensed to meet the wind, the blue skirt beating against her legs like a sail. Branches bending over the river brushed her forehead. She swept past, leaving threads of hair entwined in the leaves, and the trees leaving wild red berries caught in her hair.

The first thing that Kira learned about life and the first thing that her elders learned, dismayed, about Kira, was the joy of being alone.

*

"Born in 1904, eh?" said the Soviet official. "That makes you . . . let's see . . . eighteen. Eighteen. You're lucky, comrade. You're young and have many years to give to the cause of the toilers. A whole life of discipline and hard work and useful labor for the great collective."

He had a cold, so he took out a large checkered handkerchief and blew his nose.

*

Family Position: SINGLE.

*

"I wash my hands of Kira's future," Galina Petrovna had said. "Sometimes I think she's a born old maid and sometimes a born . . . yes, bad woman."

Kira saw her first years of lengthened skirts and high heels during their refuge in Yalta, where the strange society of emigrants from the North, families of old names and past fortunes, clung together like frightened chickens on a rock with the flood rising slowly around them. Young men of irreproachably parted hair and manicured nails, noticed the slim girl who strode down the streets swinging a twig like a whip, her body thrown into the wind that blew a short dress which hid nothing. Galina Petrovna smiled with approval when the young men called at their house. But Kira had strange eyebrows; she could lift them in such a cold, mocking smile, while her lips remained motionless—that the young men's love poems and intentions froze at the very roots. And Galina Petrovna soon stopped wondering why the young men stopped noticing her daughter.

In the evenings Lydia read avidly, blushing, books of delicate, sinful romance, which she hid from Galina Petrovna. Kira began reading one of these books; she fell asleep and did not finish it. She never began another.

She saw no difference between weeds and flowers; she yawned when Lydia sighed at the beauty of a sunset over lonely hills. But she stood for an hour looking at the black silhouette of a tall young soldier against the roaring flame of a blazing oil well he had been posted to guard.

She stopped suddenly, as they walked down a street in the evening, and pointed at a strange angle of white wall over battered roofs, luminous on a black sky in the glare of an old lantern, with a dark, barred window like that of a dungeon, and she whispered: "How beautiful!"

"What's beautiful about it?" Lydia asked.

"Because it's so strange . . . promising . . . as if something could happen there. . . ."

"Happen to whom?"

"To me."

Lydia seldom questioned Kira's emotions; they were not feelings to her but only Kira's feelings; and the family shrugged impatiently at what they called Kira's feelings. She had the same feeling for eating soup without salt, and for discovering a snail slithering up her bare leg, and for young men who pleaded, broken-hearted, their eyes humid, their lips soft. She had the same feeling for white statues of ancient gods against black velvet in museums, and for steel shavings and rusty dust and hissing torches and muscles tense as electric wires in the iron roar of a building under construction. She seldom visited museums; but when they went out with Kira, her family avoided passing by any construction works: houses, and particularly roads, and most particularly bridges. She was certain to stop and stand watching, for hours, red bricks and oaken beams and steel panels growing under the will of man. But she could never be made to enter a public park on Sunday, and she stuck her fingers into her ears when she heard a chorus singing folk songs. When Galina Petrovna took her children to see a sad play depicting the sorrow of the serfs whom Czar Alexander II had magnanimously freed, Lydia sobbed over the plight of the humble, kindly peasants cringing under a whip, while Kira sat tense, erect, eyes dark in ecstasy, watching the whip cracking expertly in the hand of a tall, young overseer.

"How beautiful!" said Lydia, looking at a stage setting. "It's almost real."

"How beautiful!" said Kira, looking at a landscape. "It's almost artificial."

*

"In a way," said the Soviet official, "you comrade women have an advantage over us men. You can take care of the young generation, the future of our republic. There are so many dirty, hungry children that need the loving hands of our women."

*

Union Membership: NONE.

*

Kira went to school in Yalta. The school dining room had many tables. At luncheon, girls sat at these tables in couples, in fours, in dozens. Kira always sat at a table in a corner—alone.

One day her class declared a boycott against a little freckled girl who had incurred the displeasure of her most popular classmate, a loud-voiced young lady who had a smile, a handshake and a command ready for everyone.

That noon, at luncheon, the little table in the corner of the dining room was occupied by two students: Kira and the freckled girl. They were half through their bowls of buckwheat mush, when the indignant class leader approached them.

"Do you know what you're doing, Argounova?" she asked, eyes blazing.

"Eating mush," answered Kira. "Won't you sit down?"

"Do you know what this girl here has done?"

"I haven't the slightest idea."

"You haven't? Then why are you doing this for her?"

"You're mistaken. I am not doing this *for* her, I am doing it *against* twenty-eight other girls."

"So you think it's smart to go against the majority?"

"I think that when in doubt about the truth of an issue, it's safer and in better taste to select the least numerous of the adversaries. . . . May I have the salt, please?"

At the age of thirteen, Lydia fell in love with a grand opera tenor. She kept his picture on her dresser, with a single red rose in a thin crystal glass beside it. At the age of fifteen, she fell in love with Saint Francis of Assisi, who talked to the birds and helped the poor, and she dreamed of entering a convent. Kira had never been in love. The only hero she had known was a Viking whose story she had read as a child; a Viking whose eyes never looked farther than the point of his sword, but there was no boundary for the point of his sword; a Viking who walked through life, breaking barriers and reaping victories, who walked through ruins while the sun made a crown over his head, but he walked, light and straight, without noticing its weight; a Viking who laughed at kings, who laughed at priests, who looked at heaven only when he bent for a drink over a mountain brook and there, over-shadowing the sky, he saw his own picture; a Viking who lived but for the joy and the wonder and the glory of the god that was himself. Kira did not remember the books she read before that legend; she did not want to remember the ones she read after it. But through the years that followed, she remembered the end of the legend: when the Viking stood on a tower over a city he had conquered. The Viking smiled as men smile when they look up at heaven; but he was looking down. His right arm was one straight line with his lowered sword; his left arm, straight as the sword, raised a goblet of wine to the sky. The first rays of a coming sun, still unseen to the earth, struck the crystal goblet. It sparkled like a white torch. Its rays lighted the faces of those below. "To a life," said the Viking, "which is a reason unto itself."

*

"So you're not a Union member, citizen?" said the Soviet official. "Too bad, too bad. The trade unions are the steel girders of our great state building, as said . . . well, one of our great leaders said. What's a citizen? Only a brick and of no use unless cemented to other bricks just like it."

*

Occupation: Student.

*

From somewhere in the aristocratic Middle Ages, Kira had inherited the conviction that labor and effort were ignoble. She had gone through school with the highest grades and the sloppiest composition books. She burned her piano etudes and never darned her stockings. She climbed to the pedestals of statues in the parks to kiss the cold lips of Greek gods—but slept at symphony concerts. She sneaked out through a window when guests were expected, and she could not cook a potato. She never went to church and seldom read a newspaper.

But she had chosen a future of the hardest work and most demanding effort. She was to be an engineer. She had decided it with her first thought about the vague thing called future. And that first thought had been quiet and reverent, for her future was consecrated, because it was *her* future. She had played with mechanical toys, which were not intended for girls, and had built ships and bridges and towers; she had watched rising steel and bricks and steam. Over Lydia's bed hung an ikon, over Kira's—the picture of an American skyscraper. Even though those who listened smiled incredulously, she spoke about the houses she would build of glass and steel, about a white aluminum bridge across a blue river—"but, Kira, you can't make a bridge of aluminum"—about men and wheels and cranes under her orders, about a sunrise on the steel skeleton of a skyscraper.

She knew she had a life and that it was her life. She knew the work which she had chosen and which she expected of life. The other thing which she expected, she did not know, for it had no name, but it had been promised to her, promised in a memory of her childhood.

When the summer sun sank behind the hills, Kira sat on a

high cliff and watched the fashionable casino far down by the river. The tall spire of the music pavilion pierced the red sky. The slim, black shadows of women moved against the orange panels of the lighted glass doors. An orchestra played in the pavilion. It played gay, sparkling tunes from musical comedies. It threw the fire of electric signs, of ringing glasses, of shining limousines, of nights in Europe's capitals—into the dark evening sky over a silent river and a rocky hill with prehistorical trees.

The light tunes of casinos and beer-gardens, sung all over Europe by girls with sparkling eyes and swaying hips, had a significance for Kira that no one else ever attached to them. She heard in them a profound joy of life, so profound that it could be as light as a dancer's feet. And because she worshipped joy, Kira seldom laughed and did not go to see comedies in theaters. And because she felt a profound rebellion against the weighty, the tragic, the solemn, Kira had a solemn reverence for those songs of defiant gaiety.

They came from the strange world where grownups moved among colored lights and white tables, where there was so much that she could not understand and so much that was awaiting her. They came out of her future.

She had selected one song as her, Kira's, own: it was from an old operetta and was called "The Song of Broken Glass." It had been introduced by a famous beauty of Vienna. There had been a balustrade on the stage, overlooking a drop with the twinkling lights of a big city, and a row of crystal goblets lined along the balustrade. The beauty sang the number and one by one, lightly, hardly touching them, kicked the crystal goblets and sent them flying in tingling, glittering splinters—around the tight, sheer stockings on the most beautiful legs in Europe.

There were sharp little blows in the music, and waves of quick, fine notes that burst and rolled like the thin, clear ringing of broken glass. There were slow notes, as if the cords of the violins trembled in hesitation, tense with the fullness of sound, taking a few measured steps before the leap into the explosion of laughter.

The wind blew Kira's hair across her eyes and sent a cold breath at the toes of her bare feet hanging over the cliff's edge. In the twilight, the sky seemed to rise slowly to a greater height, growing darker, and the first star dropped into the river. A lonely little girl on a slippery rock listened to her own hymn and smiled at what it promised her.

Such had been Kira's entrance into life. Some enter it from

under gray temple vaults, with head bowed in awe, with the light of sacrificial candles in their hearts and eyes. Some enter it with a heart like a pavement—tramped by many feet, and with a cold skin crying for the warmth of the herd. Kira Argounova entered it with the sword of a Viking pointing the way and an operetta tune for a battle march.

*

The Soviet official angrily wiped his pen with his checkered handkerchief, for he had made an ink spot on the last page.

"Toil, comrade," he said, "is the highest aim of our lives. Who does not toil, shall not eat."

The book was filled. The official applied his rubber stamp to the last page. The stamp bore a globe overshadowed by a crossed sickle and hammer.

"Here's your Labor Book, Citizen Argounova," said the Soviet official. "You are now a member of the greatest republic ever established in the history of the world. May the brotherhood of workers and peasants ever be the goal of your life, as it is the goal of all Red citizens."

He handed her the book. Across the top of the first page was printed the slogan:

PROLETARIANS OF THE WORLD, UNITE!

Under it was written the name:

KIRA ARGOUNOVA

IV

Kira had blisters on her hands where the sharp string had rubbed too long. It was not easy to carry packages up four floors, eight flights of stone stairs that smelled of cats and felt cold through the thin soles of her shoes. Every time she hurried down for another load, skipping briskly over the steps, sliding down the bannister, she met Lydia, climbing up slowly, heavily, clutching bundles to her breast, panting and sighing bitterly, steam blowing from her mouth with every word: "Our Lord in Heaven! . . . Saint Mother of God!"

The Argounovs had found an apartment.

They had been congratulated as if it were a miracle. The

miracle had been made possible by a handshake between Alexander Dimitrievitch and the Upravdom—the manager—of that house, a handshake after which Alexander Dimitrievitch's hand remained empty, but the Upravdom's did not. Three rooms and a kitchen were worth a little gratitude in an overcrowded city.

"A bath?" the indignant Upravdom had repeated Galina Petrovna's timid question. "Don't be foolish, citizen, don't be foolish."

They needed furniture. Bravely, Galina Petrovna paid a visit to the gray granite mansion on Kamenostrovsky. Before the stately edifice rising to the sky, she stood for a few moments, gathering her faded coat with the shedding fur collar tightly around her thin body. Then she opened her bag and powdered her nose: she felt ashamed before the gray slabs of granite. Then she did not close her bag, but took out a handkerchief: tears were painful in the cold wind. Then she rang the bell.

"Well, well, so you're Citizen Argounova," said the fat, glossy-cheeked sign painter who let her in and listened patiently to her explanation. "Sure, you can have your old junk back.' That which I don't use. It's in the coach house. Take it. We're not so hard-hearted. We know it's tough for all you citizens bourgeois."

Galina Petrovna threw a wistful glance at her old Venetian mirror whose onyx stand bore a bucket of paint, but she did not argue and went down to the coach house in the back yard. She found a few chairs with missing legs, a few priceless pieces of antique porcelain, a wash stand, a rusty samovar, two beds, a chest of old clothes, and Lydia's grand piano, all buried under a pile of books from their library, old boxes, wood shavings and rat dung.

They hired a drayman to transfer these possessions to the little flat on the fourth floor of an old brick house whose turbid windows faced the turbid Moika stream. But they could not afford a drayman twice. They borrowed a wheelbarrow—and Alexander Dimitrievitch, silently indifferent, carted the bundles left at the Dunaevs to their new home. The four of them carried the bundles up the stairs, past landings that alternated grimy doors and broken windows; the "black stairway" it used to be called, the back entrance for servants. Their new home had no front entrance. It had no electrical connections; the plumbing was out of order; they had to carry water in pails from the floor below. Yellow stains spread over the ceilings, bearing witness to past rains.

"It will be very cozy—with just a little work and artistic judgment," Galina Petrovna had said. Alexander Dimitrievitch had sighed.

The grand piano stood in the dining room. On top of the grand piano, Galina Petrovna put a teapot without handle or nose, the only thing left of her priceless Sachs tea service. Shelves of unpainted boards carried an odd assortment of cracked dishes; Lydia's artistry decorated the shelves with borders of paper lace. A folded newspaper supported the shortest leg of the table. A wick floating in a saucer of linseed oil threw a spot of light on the ceiling in the long, dark evenings; in the mornings, strands of soot, like cobwebs, swayed slowly in the draft, high under the ceiling.

Galina Petrovna was the first one to get up in the morning. She threw an old shawl over her shoulders and, blowing hard to make the damp logs burn, cooked millet for breakfast. After breakfast the family parted.

Alexander Dimitrievitch shuffled two miles to his business, the textile store he had opened. He never took a tramway; long lines waited for every tramway and he had no hope of fighting his way aboard. The store had been a bakery shop. He could not afford new signs. He had stretched a piece of cotton with crooked letters by the door, over one of the old black glass plates bearing a gold pretzel. He had hung two kerchiefs and an apron in the window. He had scraped the bakery labels off the old boxes and stacked them neatly on empty shelves. Then he sat all day, his freezing feet on a cast-iron stove, his arms folded on his stomach, drowsing.

When a customer came in, he shuffled behind the counter and smiled affectionately: "The best kerchiefs in town, citizen. . . . Certainly, fast colors, as fast as foreign goods. . . . Would I take lard, instead of money? Certainly, citizen peasant, certainly. . . . For half a pound? You can have two kerchiefs, citizen, and a yard of calico for good measure."

Smiling happily, he put the lard into the large drawer that served as cash register, next to a pound of rye flour.

Lydia wound an old knitted scarf around her throat, after breakfast, put a basket over her arm, sighed bitterly and went to the co-operative. She stood in line, watching the hand of the clock on a distant tower moving slowly around its face and she spent the time reciting mentally French poems she had learned as a child.

"But I don't need soap, citizen," she protested when her turn came, at the unpainted counter inside the store that smelled of dill pickles and people's breath. "And I don't need dried herring."

"All we've got today, citizen. Next!"

"All right, all right, I'll take it," Lydia said hastily. "We've got to have something."

Galina Petrovna washed the dishes after breakfast; then she put on her glasses and sorted out two pounds of lentils from the gravel that came with them; she chopped onions, tears rolling down her wrinkles; she washed Alexander Dimitrievitch's shirt in a tub of cold water; she chopped acorns for coffee.

If she had to go out, she sneaked hurriedly down the stairs, hoping not to meet the Upravdom. If she met him, she smiled too brightly and sang out: "Good morning, Comrade Upravdom!"

Comrade Upravdom never answered. She could read the silent accusation in his sullen eyes: "Bourgeois. Private traders."

Kira had been admitted to the Technological Institute. She went there every morning, walking, whistling, her hands in the pockets of an old black coat with a high collar buttoned severely under her chin. At the Institute, she listened to lectures, but spoke to few people. She noticed many red kerchiefs in the crowds of students and heard a great deal about Red builders, proletarian culture and young engineers in the vanguard of the world revolution. But she did not listen, for she was thinking about her latest mathematical problem. During the lectures, she smiled suddenly, once in a while, at no one in particular; smiled at a dim, wordless thought of her own. She felt as if her ended childhood had been a cold shower, gay, hard and invigorating, and now she was entering her morning, with her work before her, with so much to be done.

At night, the Argounovs gathered around the wick on the dining room table. Galina Petrovna served lentils and millet. There was not much variety in their menus. The millet went fast; so did their savings.

After dinner, Kira brought her books into the dining room, for they had but one oil wick. She sat, the book between her elbows on the table, her fingers buried in the hair over her temples, her eyes wide, engrossed in circles, cubes, triangles, as in a thrilling romance.

Lydia sat embroidering a handkerchief and sighed bitterly: "Oh, that Soviet light! Such a light! And to think that someone has invented electricity!"

"That's right," Kira agreed, astonished, "it's not a very good light, is it? Funny. I never noticed it before."

One night, Galina Petrovna found the millet too mildewed to cook. They had no dinner. Lydia sighed over her embroidery: "These Soviet menus!"

"That's right," said Kira, "we didn't have any dinner tonight, did we?"

"Where's your mind," Lydia raged, "if any? Do you ever notice anything?"

Through the evenings, Galina Petrovna grumbled at intervals: "A woman engineer! Such a profession for a daughter of mine! . . . Is that a way for a young girl to live? Not a boy, not a single beau to visit her. . . . Tough as a shoe-sole. No romance. No delicacy. No finer feelings. A daughter of mine!"

In the little room which Kira and Lydia shared at night, there was only one bed. Kira slept on a mattress on the floor. They retired early, to save light. Tucked under a thin blanket, with her coat thrown over it, Kira watched Lydia's figure in a long nightgown, a white stain in the darkness, kneeling before her ikons in the corner. Lydia mumbled prayers feverishly, trembling in the cold, making the sign of the cross with a hurried hand, bowing low to the little red light and the few glimmers of stern, bronze faces.

From her corner on the floor, Kira could see the reddish-gray sky in the window and the gold spire of the Admiralty far away in the cold, foggy dusk over Petrograd, the city where so much was possible.

*

Victor Dunaev had taken a sudden interest in the family of his cousins. He came often, he bent over Galina Petrovna's hand as if he were at a Court reception, and laughed cheerfully as if he were at the circus.

In his honor, Galina Petrovna served her last precious bits of sugar, instead of saccharine, with the evening tea. He brought along his resplendent smile, and the latest political gossip, and the current anecdotes, and news of the latest foreign inventions, and quotations from the latest poems, and his opinions on the theory of reflexes and the theory of relativity and the social mission of proletarian literature. "A man of culture," he explained, "has to be, above all, a man attuned to his century."

He smiled at Alexander Dimitrievitch and hastily offered a light for his home-made cigarettes; he smiled at Galina Petrovna and rose hastily every time she rose; he smiled at

Lydia and listened earnestly to her discourses on the simple faith; but he always managed to sit next to Kira.

On the evening of October tenth, Victor came late. It was nine o'clock when the sound of the door bell made Lydia dash eagerly to the little anteroom.

"Sorry. So terribly, terribly sorry," Victor apologized, smiling, hurling his cold overcoat on a chair, raising Lydia's hand to his lips and patting his unruly hair with a quick glance in the mirror, all within the space of one second. "Detained at the Institute. Students' Council. I know this is an indecent hour to visit, but I promised Kira a ride around the city and . . ."

"It's perfectly all right, Victor dear," Galina Petrovna called from the dining room. "Come in and have some tea."

The tiny flame floating in linseed oil quivered with every breath, as they sat at the table. Five huge shadows rose to the ceiling; the feeble glow drew a triangle of light under the five pairs of nostrils. Tea gleamed green through heavy glasses cut out of old bottles.

"I heard, Victor," Galina Petrovna whispered confidentially, like a conspirator, "I heard—on good authority—that this NEP of theirs is only the beginning of many changes. The beginning of the end. Next they're going to return houses and buildings to former owners. Think of it! You know our house on Kamenostrovsky, if only. . . . The clerk in the co-operative is the one who told me about it. And he has a cousin in the Party, he ought to know."

"It is highly probable," Victor stated with authority, and Galina Petrovna smiled happily.

Alexander Dimitrievitch poured himself another glass of tea; he looked at the sugar, hesitated, looked at Galina Petrovna, and drank his tea without sugar. He said sullenly: "Times aren't any better. They've called their secret police G.P.U. instead of Cheka, but it's still the same thing. Do you know what I heard at the store today? They've just discovered another anti-Soviet conspiracy. They've arrested dozens of people. Today they arrested old Admiral Kovalensky, the one who was blinded in the war, and they shot him without trial."

"Nothing but rumors," said Victor. "People like to exaggerate."

"Well, anyway, it's becoming easier to get food," said Galina Petrovna. "We got the nicest lentils today."

"And," said Lydia, "I got two pounds of millet."

"And," said Alexander Dimitrievitch, "I got a pound of lard."

When Kira and Victor rose to go, Galina Petrovna accompanied them to the door.

"You'll take care of my child, won't you, Victor dear? Don't stay out late. Streets are so unsafe these days. Do be careful. And, above all, don't speak to any strangers. There are such odd types around nowadays."

*

The cab rattled through silent streets. Wide, smooth, empty sidewalks looked like long canals of gray ice, luminous under the tall lamp posts that swam, jerking, past the cab. At times, they saw the black circle of a shadow on the bare sidewalk; over the circle, a woman in a very short skirt stood swaying a little on fat legs in tightly laced shoes. Something like the black silhouette of a windmill wavered down the sidewalk; over it—a sailor tottered unsteadily, waving his arms, spitting sunflower seeds. A heavy truck thundered by the cab, bristling with bayonets; among the bayonets, Kira saw the flash of a white face, pierced by two holes of dark, frightening eyes.

Victor was saying: "A modern man of culture must preserve an objective viewpoint which, no matter what his personal convictions, enables him to see our time as a tremendous historical drama, a moment of gigantic importance to humanity."

"Nonsense," said Kira. "It is an old and ugly fact that the masses exist and make their existence felt. This is a time when they make it felt with particular ugliness. That's all."

"This is a rash, unscientific viewpoint, Kira," said Victor, and went on talking about the esthetic value of sculpture, about the modern ballet and about new poets whose works were published in pretty little books with glossy white paper covers; he always kept the latest poem on his desk along with the latest sociological treatise, "for balance" he explained; and he recited his favorite poem in the fashionable manner of an expressionless, nasal sing-song, slowly taking Kira's hand. Kira withdrew her hand and looked at the street lights.

The cab turned into the quay. She knew they were driving along a river, for on one side of them the black sky had fallen below the ground into a cold, damp void, and long bands of silver shimmered lazily across that void, streaming from lonely lights that hung in the darkness somewhere very far away. On the other side of them, mansions fused into a black skyline of urns, statues, balustrades. There were no lights in the mansions. The horse's hoofs, pounding the cobblestones, rolled in echoes through rows of empty chambers.

Victor dismissed the cab at the Summer Garden. They walked, shuffling through a carpet of dry leaves that no one swept. No lights, no other visitors disturbed the silent desolation of the famous park. Around them, the black vaults of ancient oaks had suddenly swallowed the city; and in the moist, rustling darkness, fragrant of moss, mouldy leaves and autumn, white shadows of statues outlined the wide, straight walks.

Victor took out his handkerchief and wiped an old bench wet with dew. They sat down under the statue of a Greek goddess whose nose was broken off. A leaf floated down slowly, fluttered around its head and settled in the curve of its handless arm.

Victor's arm slowly encircled Kira's shoulders. She moved away. Victor bent close to her and whispered, sighing, that he had waited to see her alone, that he had known romances, yes, many romances, women had been too kind to him, but he had always been unhappy and lonely, searching for his ideal, that he could understand her, that her sensitive soul was bound by conventions, unawakened to life—and love. Kira moved farther away and tried to change the subject.

He sighed and asked: "Kira, haven't you ever given a thought to love?"

"No, I haven't. And I never will. And I don't like the word. Now that you know it, we're going home."

She rose. He seized her wrist. "No, we're not. Not yet."

She jerked her head, and the violent kiss intended for her lips brushed her cheek. A swift movement of her body set her free and sent him reeling against the bench. She drew a deep breath and tightened the collar of her coat.

"Good night, Victor," she said quietly. "I'm going home— alone."

He rose, confused, muttering: "Kira. . . . I'm sorry. I'll take you home."

"I said I'm going alone."

"Oh, but you can't do that! You know you can't. It's much too dangerous. A girl can't be alone in the streets at this hour."

"I'm not afraid."

She started walking. He followed. They were out of the Summer Garden. On the deserted quay, a militia-man leaned against the parapet, gravely studying the lights in the water.

"If you don't leave me right now," said Kira, "I'm going

to tell this militia-man that you're a stranger who's annoying me."

"I'll tell him you're lying."

"You may prove it—tomorrow morning. In the meantime, we'll both spend a night in jail."

"Well, go ahead. Tell him."

Kira approached the militia-man. "Excuse me, comrade—" she began; she saw Victor turning and hurrying away "—can you tell me please which way is the Moika?"

Kira walked alone into the dark streets of Petrograd. The streets seemed to wind through an abandoned stage setting. There were no lights in the windows. Over the roofs, a church tower rose against floating clouds; the tower looked as if it were swimming slowly across a motionless sky, menacing, ready to collapse into the street below.

Lanterns smoked over locked gates; through grilled peep-holes, night-watchmen's eyes followed the lonely girl. Militia-men glanced at her sidewise, sleepily suspicious. A cab driver awakened at the sound of her steps to offer his services. A sailor tried to follow her, but took one look at the expression of her face and changed his mind. A cat dived soundlessly into a broken basement window as she approached.

It was long past midnight when she turned suddenly into a street that seemed alive in the heart of a dead city. She saw yellow, curtained squares of light breaking stern, bare walls; squares of light on the bare sidewalk at glass entrance doors; dark roofs, far away, that seemed to meet in the black sky over that narrow crack of stone and light.

Kira stopped. A gramophone was playing. The sound burst into the silence from a blazing window. It was "The Song of Broken Glass."

It was the song of a nameless hope that frightened her, for it promised so much, and she could not tell what it promised; she could not even say that it was a promise; it was an emotion, almost of pain, that went through her whole body.

Quick, fine notes exploded, as if the trembling chords could not hold them, as if a pair of defiant legs were kicking crystal goblets. And, in the gaps of ragged clouds above, the dark sky was sprinkled with a luminous powder that looked like splinters of broken glass.

The music ended in someone's loud laughter. A naked arm pulled a curtain over the window.

Then Kira noticed that she was not alone. She saw women with lips painted scarlet on faces powdered snow-white, with red kerchiefs and short skirts, and legs squeezed by high shoes laced too tightly. She saw a man taking a woman's arm and disappearing through a glass door.

She understood where she was. With a jerk, she started away hurriedly, nervously toward the nearest corner.

And then she stopped.

He was tall; his collar was raised; a cap was pulled over his eyes. His mouth, calm, severe, contemptuous, was that of an ancient chieftain who could order men to die, and his eyes were such as could watch it.

Kira leaned against a lamp post, looking straight at his face, and smiled. She did not think; she smiled, stunned, without realizing that she was hoping he would know her as she knew him.

He stopped and looked at her. "Good evening," he said.

And Kira who believed in miracles, said: "Good evening."

He stepped closer and looked at her with narrowed eyes, smiling. But the corners of his mouth did not go up when he smiled; they went down, raising his upper lip into a scornful arc.

"Lonely?" he asked.

"Terribly—and for such a long time," she answered simply.

"Well, come on."

"Yes."

He took her arm and she followed him. He said: "We have to hurry. I want to get out of this crowded street."

"So do I."

"I must warn you not to ask any questions."

"I have no questions to ask."

She looked at the unbelievable lines of his face. She touched timidly, incredulously, the long fingers of the hand that held her arm.

"Why are you looking at me like that?" he asked. But she did not answer. He said: "I'm afraid I'm not a very cheerful companion tonight."

"Can I help you?"

"Well, that's what you're here for." He stopped suddenly. "What's the price?" he asked. "I haven't much."

Kira looked at him and understood why he had approached her. She stood looking silently into his eyes. When she spoke, her voice had lost its tremulous reverence; it was calm and firm. She said: "It won't be much."

"Where do we go?"

"I passed a little garden around the corner. Let's go there first—for a while."

"Any militia-men around?"

"No."

They sat on the steps of an abandoned residence. Trees shielded them from a street light, and their faces and the wall behind them were dotted, checkered, sliced with shivering splinters of light. Over their heads were rows of empty windows on bare granite. The mansion bore an unhealed scar above its entrance door from where the owner's coat of arms had been torn. The garden fence had been broken through, and its tall iron spikes bent toward the ground, like lances lowered in a grave salute.

"Take your cap off," said Kira.

"What for?"

"I want to look at you."

"Sent to search for someone?"

"No. Sent by whom?"

He did not answer and took off his cap. Her face was a mirror for the beauty of his. Her face reflected no admiration, but an incredulous, reverent awe. All she said was: "Do you always go around with your coat shoulder torn?"

"That's all I have left. Do you always stare at people as if your eyes would burst?"

"Sometimes."

"I wouldn't if I were you. The less you see of them the better off you are. Unless you have strong nerves and a strong stomach."

"I have."

"And strong legs?"

His two fingers were held straight while his fingertips threw her skirt up, high above her knees, lightly, contemptuously. Her hands grasped the stone steps. She did not pull her skirt down. She forced herself to sit without movement, without breath, frozen to the steps. He looked at her; his eyes moved up and down, but the corners of his lips moved only downward.

She whispered obediently, without looking at him: "And strong legs."

"Well, if you have strong legs, then—run."

"From you?"

"No. From all people. But forget it. Pull your skirt down. Aren't you cold?"

"No." But she pulled the skirt down.

"Don't pay any attention to what I say," he told her. "Have you anything to drink at your place?"

"Oh, . . . yes."

"I warn you I'm going to drink like a sponge tonight."

"Why tonight?"

"That's my habit."

"It isn't."

"How do you know?"

"I know it isn't."

"What else do you know about me?"

"I know that you're very tired."

"I am. I've walked all night."

"Why?"

"I thought I told you not to ask any questions."

He looked at the girl who sat pressed tightly against the wall. He saw only one gray eye, quiet and steady, and above it—one lock of hair; the white wrist of a hand held in a black pocket; the black, ribbed stockings on legs pressed tightly together. In the darkness, he guessed the patch of a long, narrow mouth, the dark huddle of a slender body trembling a little. His fingers closed around the black stocking. She did not move. He leaned closer to the dark mouth and whispered: "Stop staring at me as if I were something unusual. I want to drink. I want a woman like you. I want to go down, as far down as you can drag me."

She said: "You know, you're very much afraid that you can't be dragged down."

His hand left her stocking. He looked at her a little closer and asked suddenly: "How long have you been in this business?"

"Oh . . . not very long."

"I thought so."

"I'm sorry. I've tried my best."

"Tried what?"

"Tried to act experienced."

"You little fool. Why should you? I'd rather have you as you are, with these strange eyes that see too much. . . . What led you into . . . this?"

"A man."

"Was he worth that?"

"Yes."

"What an appetite!"

"For what?"

"For life."

"If one loses that appetite, why still sit at the table?"

He laughed. His laughter rolled into the empty windows above them, as cold and empty as the windows. "Perhaps to collect under the table a few little crumbs of refuse—like you —that can still be amusing. . . . Take your hat off."

She took off her tam. Against the gray stone her tangled hair and the light tangled in the leaves, glittered like warm silk. He ran his fingers through her hair and jerked her head back so violently that it hurt her. "Did you love that man?" he asked.

"What man?"

"The one who led you into this?"

"Did I . . ." She was suddenly confused, surprised by an unexpected thought. "No. I didn't love him."

"That's good."

"Have you . . . ever . . ." she began a question and found that she could not finish it.

"They say I have no feeling for anyone but myself," he answered, "and not much of that."

"Who said it?"

"A person that didn't like me. I know many people that don't like me."

"That's good."

"But I've never known one who said it was good."

"Yes, you've known one."

"And can you tell me who that is?"

"Yourself."

He bent toward her again, his eyes searching the darkness, then moved away and shrugged: "You're wrong. I'm nothing like what I think you think I am. I've always wanted to be a Soviet clerk who sells soap and smiles at the customers."

She said: "You're so very unhappy."

His face was so close she could feel his breath on her lips. "Who asked you for sympathy? I suppose you think you can make me like you? Well, don't fool yourself. I don't give a damn what I think of you and less what you think of me. I'm just like any other man you've had in your bed—and like any you will have."

She said: "You mean you would like to be like any other man. And you would like to think that there haven't been any other men—in my bed."

He looked at her silently. He asked abruptly: "Are you a . . . street woman?"

She answered calmly: "No."

He jumped to his feet. "Who are you, then?"

"Sit down."

"Answer."

"I'm a respectable little girl who studies at the Technological Institute, whose parents would throw her out of the house if they knew she had talked to a strange man on the street."

He looked down at her; she sat on the steps at his feet, looking up at his face. He saw no fear and no appeal in her eyes, only an insolent calm. He asked: "Why did you do it?"

"I wanted to know you."

"Why?"

"I liked your face."

"You little fool! If I were someone else, I might have . . . acted differently."

"But I knew you were not someone else."

"Don't you know that such things are not being done?"

"I don't care."

He smiled suddenly. He asked: "Want a confession from me?"

"Yes."

"This is the first time I've ever tried to . . . to buy a woman."

"Why did you try it tonight?"

"I didn't care. I've walked for hours. There isn't a house in this city that I can enter tonight."

"Why?"

"Don't ask questions. I couldn't make myself approach one of . . . of those women. But you—I liked your strange smile. What were you doing on such a street at such an hour?"

"I quarreled with someone and I had no carfare and I went home alone—and lost my way."

"Well, thank you for a most unusual evening. This will be a rare memory to take with me of my last night in the city."

"Your—last night?"

"I'm going away at dawn."

"When are you coming back?"

"Never—I hope."

She got up slowly. She stood facing him. She asked: "Who are you?"

"Even if I trust you, I can't tell you that."

"I can't let you go away forever."

"Well, I would like to see you again. I'm not going far. I may be back in town."

"I'll give you my address."

"Don't. You're not living alone. I can't enter anyone's house."

"Can I come to yours?"

"I haven't any."

"But then. . . ."

"Let's say that we'll meet here again—in a month. Then, if I'm still alive, if I can still enter the city, I'll be waiting here for you."

"I'll come."

"November tenth. But let's make it in daylight. At three o'clock in the afternoon. On these steps."

"Yes."

"Well, it's as crazy as our whole acquaintance. And now it's time for you to go home. You shouldn't be out at this hour."

"But where will you go?"

"I'll walk until dawn. It's only a few more hours. Come on."

She did not argue. He took her arm. She followed. They stepped over the bowed lances of the broken fence. The street was deserted. A cab driver on a distant corner raised his head at the sound of their steps. He signaled the cab. Four horseshoes struck forward, shattering the silence.

"What's your name?" she asked.

"Leo. And yours?"

"Kira."

The cab approached. He handed the driver a bill. "Tell him where you want to go," he said.

"Good-bye," said Kira, "—for a month."

"If I'm still alive," he answered, "—and if I don't forget."

She climbed to the seat, kneeling and facing the back of the carriage. As it slowly started away, her hatless hair in the wind, she watched the man who stood looking after her.

When the cab turned a corner, she remained kneeling, but her head dropped. Her hand lay on the seat, helpless, palm up; and she could feel the blood beating in her fingers.

V

Galina Petrovna moaned, every morning: "What's the matter with you, Kira? You don't care if you eat or not. You don't care if you're cold. You don't hear when people talk to you. What's the matter?"

In the evenings, Kira walked home from the Institute, and her eyes followed every tall figure, peering anxiously behind every raised collar, her breath stopping. She did not expect to find him in the city; she did not want to find him. She never worried whether he would come or not. She never wondered whether he liked her. She never had any thought of him beyond the one that he existed. But she found it hard to remember the existence of anything else.

Once, when she came home, the door was opened by Galina Petrovna with red, swollen eyes. "Have you got the bread?" was the first question thrown into the cold draft of the open door.

"What bread?" asked Kira.

"*What* bread? Your bread! The Institute bread! This is the day you get it! Don't tell me you've forgotten it!"

"I've forgotten it."

"Oh, my Lord in Heaven!"

Galina Petrovna sat down heavily and her hands fell helplessly. "Kira, what's the matter with you? She gets rations that aren't enough to feed a cat and she forgets them! No bread! Oh, Lord merciful!"

In the dark dining room, Lydia sat at the window, knitting a woolen stocking by the light of the street lamp outside. Alexander Dimitrievitch drowsed, his head on the table.

"No bread," announced Galina Petrovna. "Her highness forgot it."

Lydia sneered. Alexander Dimitrievitch sighed and got up. "I'm going to bed," he muttered. "You don't feel so hungry when you sleep."

"No dinner tonight. No millet left. The water pipes broke. No water in the house."

"I'm not hungry," said Kira.

"You're the only one in the family with a bread card. But, Lord, you don't seem to think anything of it!"

"I'm sorry, Mother. I'll get it tomorrow."

Kira lighted the wick. Lydia moved her knitting toward the little flame.

"Your father hasn't sold a single thing today in that store of his," said Galina Petrovna.

Lydia's needles clicked in the silence.

The door bell rang sharply, insistently. Galina Petrovna shuddered nervously and hurried to open the door.

Heavy boots stamped across the anteroom. The Upravdom entered without being invited, his boots trailing mud on the dining-room floor. Galina Petrovna followed, anxiously clutching her shawl. He held a list in his hand.

"In regards to this water pipes business, Citizen Argounova," he said, throwing the list on the table without removing his hat. "The house committee has voted a resolution to assess the tenants in proportion to their social standing, for the purpose of water pipes, to repair same, in addition to rent. Here's a list of who pays what. Have the money in my office no later than ten o'clock tomorrow morning. Good night, citizen."

Galina Petrovna locked the door after him and held the paper to the light, in a trembling hand.

Doubenko—Worker—in #12..........3,000,000 rubles
Rilnikov—Soviet Employee—in #13....5,000,000 rubles
Argounov—Private Trader—in #14....50,000,000 rubles

The paper fell to the floor; Galina Petrovna's face fell on her hands on the table.

"What's the matter, Galina? How much is it?" Alexander Dimitrievitch's voice called from the bedroom.

Galina Petrovna raised her head. "It's . . . it's not very much. Go on. Sleep. I'll tell you tomorrow." She had no handkerchief; she wiped her eyes with a corner of her shawl and shuffled into the bedroom.

Kira bent over a textbook. The little flame trembled, dancing on the pages. The only thing she could read or remember was not written in the book:

". . . if I'm still alive—and if I don't forget. . . ."

*

Students received bread cards and free tramway tickets. In the damp, bare offices of the Technological Institute, they waited in line to get the cards. Then, in the Students' Co-operative, they waited in line to get the bread.

Kira had waited for an hour. The clerk at the counter shoved hunks of dried bread at the line moving slowly past him, and dipped his hand into a barrel to fish out the herring, and wiped his hand on the bread, and collected the wrinkled bills of paper money. The bread and herring disappeared, unwrapped, into brief cases filled with books. Students whistled merrily and beat tap steps in the sawdust on the floor.

The young woman who stood in line next to Kira, leaned suddenly against her shoulder with a friendly, confidential grin, although Kira had never seen her before. The young woman had broad shoulders and a masculine leather jacket; short, husky legs and flat, masculine oxfords; a red kerchief tied carelessly over short, straight hair; eyes wide apart in a round, freckled face; thin lips drawn together with so obvious and fierce a determination that they seemed weak; dandruff on the black leather of her shoulders.

She pointed at a large poster calling all students to a meeting for the election of the Students' Council. She asked: "Going to the meeting this afternoon, comrade?"

"No," said Kira.

"Ah, but you must go, comrade. By all means. Tremendously important. You have to vote, you know."

"I've never voted in my life."

"Your first year, comrade?"

"Yes."

"Wonderful! Wonderful! Isn't it wonderful?"

"What's wonderful?"

"To start your education at a glorious time like this, when science is free and opportunity open to all. I understand, it's all new to you and must seem very strange. But don't be afraid, dear. I'm an old-timer here, I'll help you."

"I appreciate your offer, but . . ."

"What's your name, dear?"

"Kira Argounova."

"Mine's Sonia. Just Comrade Sonia. That's what everybody calls me. You know, we're going to be great friends, I can feel it. There's nothing I enjoy more than helping smart young students like you."

"But," said Kira, "I don't remember saying anything particularly smart."

Comrade Sonia laughed very loudly: "Ah, but I know girls. I know women. We, the new women who are ambitious to have a useful career, to take our place beside the men in the productive toil of the world—instead of the old kitchen drudgery—we must stick together. There is no sight I like better than a new woman student. Comrade Sonia will always be your friend. Comrade Sonia is everybody's friend."

Comrade Sonia smiled. She smiled straight into Kira's eyes, as if taking, gently, irrevocably, those eyes and the mind behind them into her own hand. Comrade Sonia's smile was friendly; a kindly, insistent, peremptory friendliness that took the first word and expected to keep it.

"Thank you," said Kira. "What is it you want me to do?"

"Well, to begin with, Comrade Argounova, you must go to the meeting. We're electing our Students' Council for the year. It's going to be a tough battle. There is a strong anti-proletarian element among our older students. Our class enemies, you know. Young students like you must support the candidates of our Communist Cell, who stand on guard over your interests."

"Are you one of the Cell's candidates, Comrade Sonia?"

Comrade Sonia laughed: "See? I told you you were smart. Yes, I'm one of them. Have been on the council for two years. Hard work. But what can I do? The comrade students seem to want me and I have to do my duty. You just come with me and I'll tell you for whom to vote."

"Oh," said Kira. "And after that?"

"I'll tell you. All Red students join some kind of social activity. You know, you don't want to be suspected of bourgeois tendencies. I'm organizing a Marxist Circle. Just a little group of young students—and I'm the chairman—to learn the proper proletarian ideology, which we'll all need when we go out into the world to serve the Proletarian State, since that's what we're all studying for, isn't it?"

"Did it ever occur to you," asked Kira, "that I may be here for the very unusual, unnatural reason of wanting to learn a work I like only because I like it?"

Comrade Sonia looked into the gray eyes of Comrade Argounova and realized that she had made a mistake. "Well," said Comrade Sonia, without smiling, "as you wish."

"I think I'll go to the meeting," said Kira, "and—I think I'll vote."

*

An amphitheater of crowded benches rose like a dam, and the waves of students overflowed onto the steps of the aisles, the window sills, the low cabinets, the thresholds of the open doorways.

A young speaker stood on the platform, rubbing his hands solicitously, like a sales clerk at a counter. His face looked like an advertisement that had stayed in a shop window too long: a little more color was needed to make his hair blond, his eyes blue, his skin healthy. His pale lips made no frame for the dark hole of his mouth which he opened wide as he barked words like military commands at his attentive audience.

"Comrades! The doors of science are open to us, sons of toil! Science is now in our own calloused hands. We have outgrown that old bourgeois prejudice about the objective impartiality of science. Science is not impartial. Science is a weapon of the class struggle. We're not here to further our petty personal ambitions. We have outgrown the slobbering egoism of the bourgeois who whined for a personal career. Our sole aim and purpose in entering the Red Technological Institute is to train ourselves into efficient fighters in the vanguard of Proletarian Culture and Construction!"

The speaker left the platform, rubbing his hands. Some hands in the audience clapped noisily. Most hands remained in the pockets of old coats, under the desks, silent.

Kira leaned toward a freckled girl beside her and asked: "Who is he?"

The girl whispered: "Pavel Syerov. Of the Communist Cell. Party member. Be careful. They have spies everywhere."

The students sat in a huddled mass rising to the ceiling, a tight mass of pale faces and old, shapeless overcoats. But there was an unseen line dividing them, a line that drew no straight boundary across the benches, but zigzagged over the room, a line no one could see, but all felt, a line as precise and merciless as a sharp knife. One side wore the green student caps of the old days, discarded by the new rulers, wore them proudly, defiantly, as an honorary badge and a challenge; the other side wore red kerchiefs and trim, military leather jackets. The first faction, the larger one, sent speakers to the platform who reminded their audience that students had always known how to fight tyranny, no matter what color that tyranny was wearing, and a thunder of applause rolled from under the ceiling, down to the platform steps, an applause too loud, too long, earnest, hostile, challenging, as the only voice left to the crowd, as if their hands said more than their voices dared to utter. The other faction watched them silently, with cold, unsmiling eyes. Its speakers bellowed belligerently about the Dictatorship of the Proletariat, ignoring the sudden laughter that seemed to burst from nowhere, and the impudent sunflower-seed shells sent expertly at the speaker's nose.

They were young and too confident that they had nothing to fear. They were raising their voices for the first time, while the country around them had long since spoken its last. They were graciously polite to their enemies and their enemies were graciously polite and called them "comrades." Both knew the silent struggle of life or death; but only one side, the smaller, knew whose victory was to come. Young and confident, in their leather jackets and red kerchiefs, they looked with a deadly tolerance at those others, young and confident, too, and their tolerance had the cold glint of a hidden bayonet they knew to be coming.

Pavel Syerov bent toward his neighbor, a slight young man with a narrow, consumptive face, and whispered: "So that's the kind of speeches they make here. What a task we have awaiting us! Had anyone dared that at the front. . . ."

"The front, Comrade Syerov," answered the soft, expressionless voice of his companion, "has changed. The external front is conquered. It's on the internal front that we have to dig our trenches now."

He bent closer to Comrade Syerov. His long, thin hands were pressed to the desk; he barely raised one finger and moved it slowly, indicating the auditorium from wall to wall. "On the internal front," he whispered, "there are no bombs, no machine guns. When our enemies fall—there is no blood, no cry. The world never knows when they were killed. Sometimes, they do not know it themselves. This day, Comrade Syerov, belongs to the fighters of Red Culture."

When the last speech had been heard, a vote was taken. Candidates left the room in turn, while others made short speeches about them; then hands were raised, and students standing on tables, waving pencils, counted the votes.

Kira saw Victor going out and heard the speech of his loyal supporter about the wisdom of Comrade Victor Dunaev who was guided by a spirit of understanding and co-operation; both factions applauded; both factions voted for Comrade Dunaev. Kira did not.

"Candidate Pavel Syerov will kindly leave now," the chairman of the meeting announced. "Word is given to Comrade Presniakova."

To the clatter of applause, Comrade Sonia leaped to the

platform, tore off her red kerchief and shook her short, bristling mane of hair with spirited abandon.

"Just Comrade Sonia!" she greeted her audience. "Hearty proletarian greetings to all! And—particularly—particularly to our comrade women! There's no sight I like better than a new woman student, a woman emancipated from the old slavery of dishes and diapers. So here I am—Comrade Sonia—ready to serve you all!" She waited for the applause to stop. "Comrade students! We've got to stand up for our rights. We've got to learn to speak our proletarian will and make our enemies take notice. We've got to stamp our proletarian boot into their white throats and their treacherous intentions. Our Red schools are for Red students. Our Students' Council must stand on guard over proletarian interests. It's up to you to elect those whose proletarian loyalty is beyond doubt. You've heard Comrade Syerov speak. I'm here to tell you that he's an old fighter in the Communist ranks, a Party member since before the revolution, a soldier of the Red Army. Let us all vote for a good proletarian, a Red soldier, the hero of Melitopol, Comrade Pavel Syerov!"

Through the roll of applause, her heavy shoes clattered down the platform steps, her stomach shaking, her broad face open in a huge grin, the back of one hand wiping perspiration from under her nose.

Comrade Syerov was elected; so was Comrade Sonia; so was Comrade Victor Dunaev; but so were members of the green cap faction—two-thirds of the new Students' Council.

"And to close the meeting, comrades," shouted the chairman, "we'll sing our old song, 'Days of Our Life.' "

A discordant chorus boomed solemnly:

> *"Swift as the waves*
> *Are the days of our life. . . ."*

It was an old drinking song grown to the dignity of a students' anthem; a slow, mournful tune with an artificial gaiety in the roll of its spiritless notes, born long before the revolution in the stuffy rooms where unshaved men and mannish women discussed philosophy and with forced bravado drank cheap vodka to the futility of life.

Kira frowned; she did not sing; she did not know the old song and did not want to learn it. She noticed that the students in leather jackets and red kerchiefs kept silent, too.

When the song ended, Pavel Syerov shouted: "Now, comrades, our answer!"

For the first time in Petrograd, Kira heard the "Internationale." She tried not to listen to its words. The words spoke of the damned, the hungry, the slaves, of those who had been nothing and shall be all; in the magnificent goblet of the music, the words were not intoxicating as wine; they were not terrifying as blood; they were gray as dish water.

But the music was like the marching of thousands of feet, measured and steady, like drums beaten by unvarying, unhurried hands. The music was like the feet of soldiers marching into the dawn that is to see their battle and their victory, as if the song rose from under the soldiers' feet, with the dust of the road, as if the soldiers' feet played it upon the earth.

The tune sang a promise, calmly, with the calm of an immeasurable strength, and then, tense with a restrained, but uncontrollable ecstasy, the notes rose, trembling, repeating themselves, too rapt to be held still, like arms raised and waving in the sweep of banners.

It was a hymn with the force of a march, a march with the majesty of a hymn. It was the song of soldiers bearing sacred banners and of priests carrying swords. It was an anthem to the sanctity of strength.

Everyone had to rise when the "Internationale" was played.

Kira stood smiling at the music. "This is the first beautiful thing I've noticed about the revolution," she said to her neighbor.

"Be careful," the freckled girl whispered, glancing around nervously, "someone will hear you."

"When all this is over," said Kira, "when the traces of their republic are disinfected from history—what a glorious funeral march this will make!"

"You little fool! What are you talking about?"

A man's hand grasped Kira's wrist and wheeled her around.

She stared up into two gray eyes that looked like the eyes of a tamed tiger; but she was not quite sure whether it was tamed or not. There were four straight lines on his face: two eyebrows, a mouth and a scar on his right temple.

For one short second, they looked at each other, silent, hostile, startled by each other's eyes.

"How much," asked Kira, "are you paid for snooping around?"

She tried to disengage her wrist. He held it. "Do you know the place for little girls like you?"

"Yes—where men like you wouldn't be let in through the back door."

"You must be new here. I'd advise you to be careful."

"Our stairs are slippery and there are four floors to climb, so be careful when you come to arrest me."

He dropped her wrist. She looked at his silent mouth; it spoke of many past battles louder than the scar on his forehead; it also spoke of many more to come.

The "Internationale" rang like soldiers' feet beating the earth.

"Are you exceedingly brave?" he asked. "Or just stupid?"

"I'll let you find that out."

He shrugged, turned and walked away. He was tall and young. He wore a cap and a leather jacket. He walked like a soldier, his steps deliberate and very confident.

Students sang the "Internationale," its ecstatic notes rising, trembling, repeating themselves.

"Comrade," the freckled girl whispered, "what have you done?"

*

The first thing that Kira heard when she rang the Dunaevs' door bell, was Maria Petrovna's cough. Then, the key turned. Then, a wave of smoke struck Kira in the face. Through the smoke, she saw Maria Petrovna's tear-filled eyes and her swollen hand covering her mouth, shaking with a violent cough.

"Come in, come in, Kira darling," Maria Petrovna hissed. "Don't be afraid. It's not a fire."

Kira walked into the gray fog that bit her eyelids like a strong onion; Maria Petrovna shuffled after her, painfully spurting words and coughs: "It's the stove . . . that Soviet wood . . . we got . . . won't burn . . . so damp you could . . . breed polliwogs. . . . Don't take your . . . coat off, Kira . . . it's too cold. . . . We have the windows open."

"Is Irina at home?"

"She certainly is," Irina's clear, bright voice came from somewhere in the fog, "if you can find her."

In the dining room, the big double-paneled windows had been sealed for the winter; but one small panel was open; a whirlpool of smoke spun around it, fighting the cold fresh air from the street. Irina sat at the table, her winter coat thrown over her shoulders, blowing at her stiff, blue fingers.

Maria Petrovna found a trembling little shadow in the corner behind the buffet and dragged her out. "Acia, say how-do-you-do to cousin Kira."

Acia stared up sullenly, her red eyes and little wet nose showing above the collar of her father's fur jacket.

"Acia, do you hear me? And where's your handkerchief? Say how-do-you-do to cousin Kira."

"How do you do," Acia muttered, staring at the floor.

"Why aren't you at school today, Acia?"

"Closed," Maria Petrovna sighed. "The school's closed. For two weeks. No wood."

A door banged in the fog. Victor came in. "Oh, how do you do, Kira?" he said coldly. "Mother, *when* is this smoke going to stop? How can one be expected to study in this infernal atmosphere? Oh, I don't care. If I don't pass the examinations, there'll be no bread cards for a certain family!" The door banged louder as he went out.

Kira sat watching Irina sketch. Irina studied Art; she devoted her time to solemn research into the ancient masterpieces of the museums; but her quick hand and mischievous eyes produced the impudent art of the newspapers. She sketched cartoons whenever she was supposed to, and at any other time. A drawing board on her lap, throwing her head and hair back once in a while for a swift glance at Acia through the smoke, she was sketching her little sister. On the paper, Acia was transformed into a goblin with huge ears and stomach, riding on the back of a snail.

Vasili Ivanovitch came home from the market. He was smiling happily. He had stood at the market all day and had sold the chandelier from their drawing room. He had managed to get a good price for it.

His smile widened when he saw Kira and he nodded to her cheerfully. Maria Petrovna brought him a bowl of hot soup. She asked timidly: "Would you like some soup, Kira?"

"No, thank you, Aunt Marussia, I've just had my dinner."

She knew that Maria Petrovna had but one bowl of soup left, saved for Vasili Ivanovitch; she knew that Maria Petrovna sighed with relief.

Vasili Ivanovitch ate cheerfully, talking to Kira as if she were his personal guest; he spoke to so few of their guests that Maria Petrovna and Irina did not object, watching anxiously the rare sight of his smile.

He chuckled: "Look at Irina drawing. Here she is, daubing, smudging all day long. Not bad, are they, Kira? The drawings, I mean. How's Victor at the Institute? Not one of the last, I bet. . . . Well, we still have something left. Yes, we still have something left." He leaned forward suddenly over his soup, his eyes sparkling, his voice low: "Have you read the papers tonight, Kira?"

"Yes, Uncle Vasili. What was it?"

"The news from abroad. Of course, there wasn't much in the paper. *They* wouldn't print it. But you have to know how to read between the lines. Just watch it. Just mark my word. Europe is doing things. And it won't be long . . . it won't be long now before . . ."

Maria Petrovna coughed nervously. She was used to it; for five years she had listened to what Vasili Ivanovitch read between the lines of the newspapers about the salvation coming from Europe, which never came. She sighed; she did not dare to argue. Vasili Ivanovitch was grinning happily: " . . . and when it happens, I'm all set to start again where they've interrupted. It won't be difficult. Of course, they've closed my store and taken all the furniture away, but . . ." he leaned close to Kira, whispering, "but I've watched it. I know where they've taken it. I know where it is now."

"You do, Uncle Vasili?"

"I've seen the showcases in a government shoe store on the Bolshoi Prospect; and the chairs—in a factory restaurant in the Viborgsky district; and the chandelier—the chandelier's in the new Tobacco Trust office. I haven't been wasting time. I'm ready. As soon as . . . as soon as things change—I'll know where to find it all and I'll open the old store again."

"That's wonderful, Uncle Vasili. I'm glad they haven't destroyed your furniture or burned it."

"No, that's my luck, they haven't. It's still as good as new. I did see a long scratch on one of the showcases, it's a shame, but it can be fixed. And—here's the funniest thing," he chuckled slyly, as if he had outwitted his enemies, "the sign boards. Do you remember my sign boards, Kira, gilded glass with black letters? Well, I've even found those. They're hanging over a co-operative near the Alexandrovsky market. On one side it says: 'State Co-operative' but on the other—on the other side it still says: 'Vasili Dunaev. Furs.' " He caught the look in Maria Petrovna's eyes. He frowned. "Marussia doesn't believe any more. She doesn't think we'll get it all back. She loses faith so easily. How about it, Kira? Do you think you'll live your whole life under a Red boot?"

"No," said Kira, "it can't last forever."

"Of course, it can't. Certainly, it can't. That's what I say, it can't." He rose suddenly. "Come here, Kira, I'll show you something."

"Vasili," Maria Petrovna sighed, "won't you finish your soup?"

"Never mind the soup. I'm not hungry. Come on to my office, Kira."

There was no furniture left in Vasili Ivanovitch's office but a desk and one chair. He unlocked a desk drawer and took out a bundle wrapped in an old, yellowed handkerchief. He unfastened a tight knot and, smiling proudly, happily, straightening his stooped shoulders, showed Kira neatly tied piles of large, crisp currency bills of the Czar's days. They were large piles; they contained a fortune of many thousands.

Kira gasped: "But, Uncle Vasili, they're . . . they're worthless. You're not allowed to use . . . or even to keep them any more. It's . . . dangerous."

He laughed: "Sure, they're worthless—*now*. But just wait and see. Wait till things change. You'll see how much there is right here in my fist."

"But . . . Uncle Vasili, where did you get them?"

"I bought them. Secretly, of course. From speculators. It's dangerous, but you can get them. It cost me a lot, too. I'll tell you why I bought so many. You see, just . . . just before it happened . . . you know, before they nationalized the store . . . I owed one large bill—for my new plate-glass windows—got them from abroad, from Sweden, no one in town had any like that. When they took the store, they kicked their boots through the glass, but it doesn't matter, I still owe the firm for it. There's no way I can pay now—you can't send money abroad —but I'm waiting. I can't pay it in that worthless Soviet paper trash . . . why, abroad they wouldn't use it in the bathroom. And you can't get gold. But these—these will be as good as gold. And I'll pay my debt. I've checked up. The old man of the glass firm has died, but his son is alive. He's in Berlin now. I'll pay him. I don't like to be in debt. I've never owed a ruble to any man in my life." He weighed the paper bundle in the palm of his large hand. He said softly: "Take one advice from an old man, Kira. Don't ever look back. The past is dead. But there is always a future. There is always a future. And—here's mine. A good idea, wasn't it, Kira, getting this money?"

Kira forced a smile, and looked away from him, and whispered: "Yes, Uncle Vasili, a very good idea."

The door bell rang. Then, in the dining room, they heard a girl's laughter that seemed clearer, louder than the bell. Vasili

Ivanovitch frowned. "Here she is again," he said sullenly. "Vava Milovskaia. A friend of Victor."

"What's the matter, Uncle Vasili? You don't like her?"

He shrugged: "Oh, she's all right, I suppose. I don't dislike her. Only there's nothing in her to like. Just a scatter-brained little female. Not a girl like you, Kira. Come on, I suppose you'll have to meet her."

Vava Milovskaia stood in the middle of the dining room like two luminous circles; the lower and larger one—a full skirt of pink starched chintz; the upper and smaller one—a tangled chrysanthemum of glistening black curls. Her dress was only chintz, but it was new, obviously expensive, and she wore a narrow diamond bracelet.

"Good evening, Vasili Ivanovitch!" she sang. "Good evening! Good evening!" She jumped up, her hands on his shoulders, her pink skirt flaring, and planted a kiss on his stern forehead. "And this is—I know—Kira! Kira Argounova. I'm so glad to see you, at last, Kira!"

Victor came out of his room. Vava repeated persistently that she had come to see Irina, but he knew, as everybody knew, the real object of her visit. He watched her, smiling. He laughed happily, and teased her, and pulled Acia's ear, and brought a warm shawl for Maria Petrovna when she coughed, and told anecdotes, and even forced Vasili Ivanovitch, who sat gloomily in a dark corner, to smile once at a joke.

"I've brought something to show you all," Vava announced mysteriously, producing a little package from her handbag. "Something . . . something marvelous. Something you've never seen before."

All heads bent over the table, over a tiny, round, orange and gold box. Vava whispered the magic words: "From *abroad.*"

They looked at it reverently, afraid to touch it. Vava whispered proudly, breathlessly, trying to sound casual: "Face powder. French. Real French. It's smuggled from Riga. One of father's patients gave it to him—in part payment."

"You know," said Irina, "I've heard that they use not only powder, abroad, but—imagine—lipstick!"

"Yes," said Vava, "and that woman, father's patient, promised to get me—a lipstick, next time."

"Vava! You won't dare to use it!"

"Oh . . . I don't know. Maybe . . . maybe a tiny bit . . . just once in a while."

"No decent woman paints her lips," said Maria Petrovna.

"But they say they do and it's perfectly all right—abroad."

"Abroad," Maria Petrovna sighed wistfully. "Such a place does exist somewhere, doesn't it? . . . Abroad. . . ."

*

Snow had not come; but a heavy frost glazed the mud on the sidewalks, and the first icicles grew whiskers in the mouths of drain pipes. The sky hung clear and green, lustrous with cold glints of ice. Men walked slowly, awkwardly, like beginners learning to skate; they slipped, waving one helpless leg high in the air, grasping the nearest lamp post. Horses slipped on the glassy cobblestones; sparks flew from under the hoofs scratching the ice convulsively.

Kira walked to the Institute. Through her thin soles, the frozen sidewalk sent a cold breath up her legs. She hurried uncertainly, her feet slipping at odd angles.

She heard steps behind her, very firm, resolute steps that made her turn involuntarily. She looked at the tamed tiger with the scar on his forehead. Their eyes met. He smiled. And she smiled up at him. He touched the visor of his cap. "Good morning," he said.

"Good morning," said Kira.

She watched his tall figure walking on hurriedly, his shoulders erect in his leather jacket, his feet steady on the ice.

Across from the Institute, he stopped suddenly and turned, waiting for her. She approached. The high sidewalk sloped down abruply at a steep, frozen, dangerous angle. He offered his arm to help her. Her feet slipped perilously. His strong hand closed over her arm and quickly, masterfully landed her on her feet.

"Thank you," she said.

"I thought you might need help. But then," he looked at her with a faint smile, "I suppose you weren't afraid.".

"On the contrary. I was very much afraid—*this time*," she said, and her smile was an answer of sudden understanding.

He touched the visor of his cap and hurried away through the Institute gates, down a long corridor.

Kira saw a boy she knew. She pointed at the disappearing figure in the leather jacket, and asked: "Who is that?"

The boy looked and made a strange, warning noise with his lips. "Be careful of *that*," he whispered and breathed three dreaded letters: "G.P.U."

"Oh, is he?" said Kira.

"Is he?" said the boy with a long, indignant whistle for an answer.

VI

For a month Kira had not approached the neighborhood of the mansion with a broken garden fence; she had not thought of the garden, for she did not want to see it empty, even before her own closed eyes. But on November tenth she walked toward it calmly, evenly, without hurry, without doubts.

Darkness was coming, not from the gray, transparent sky, but from the corners of houses where shadows suddenly grew thicker, as if without reason. Slow whirls of smoke over chimneys were rusty in the rays of a cold, invisible sunset somewhere beyond the clouds. In store windows kerosene lamps stood on the sills, melting yellow circles on the huge, frozen panes, around little orange dots of trembling fire. It had snowed. Whipped into mud by horses' hoofs, the first snow looked like a pale coffee with thin, melting splinters of sugar. It hushed the city into a soft, padded silence. Hoofs thumped through the mud with a clear, wet sound, as if someone were clicking his tongue loudly, rhythmically, and the sound rolled, dying, down long, darkening streets.

Kira turned a corner; she saw the black lances bowing to the snow, and the trees gathering snatches of cotton in the black net of bare branches. Then, for one second, she stopped, because she was suddenly afraid to look; then she looked into the garden.

He stood on the steps of the mansion, his hands in his pockets, his collar raised. She stopped to look at him. But he heard her and turned quickly.

He walked to meet her. He smiled at her, his mouth a scornful arc. "Allo, Kira."

"Good evening, Leo."

She pulled off a heavy black mitten; he held her hand for a long moment in his cold, strong fingers. Then he asked: "Foolish, aren't we?"

"Why?"

"I didn't think you'd come. I know I had no intention of coming."

"But you're here."

"I awakened this morning and I knew that I'd be here—against my better judgment, I admit."

"Are you living in Petrograd now?"

"No. I haven't been here since that night I met you. We've often gone without food because I couldn't drive to the city. But I've returned to meet a girl on a street corner. My compliments, Kira."

"Who went without food because you couldn't drive to the city?"

His smile told her that he understood the question and more than the question. But he said: "Let's sit down."

They sat down on the steps and she tapped her feet against each other, knocking off the snow. He asked: "So you want to know with whom I'm living? See? My coat is mended."

"Yes."

"A woman did that. A very nice woman who likes me very much."

"She sews well."

"Yes. But her eyesight isn't so good any more. And her hair's gray. She's my old nurse and she has a shack in the country. Anything else you want to ask?"

"No."

"Well, I dislike women's questions, but I don't know whether I like a woman who won't let me have the satisfaction of refusing to answer."

"I have nothing to ask."

"There are a few things you don't know about me."

"I don't have to know."

"That's another thing I want to warn you about: I don't like women who make it obvious how much they like me."

"Why? Do you think I want you to like me?"

"Why are you here?"

"Only because I like you. I don't care what you think of women who like you—nor how many of them there have been."

"Well, that was a question. And you won't get any answer. But I'll tell you that I like you, you arrogant little creature, whether you want to hear it or not. And I'll also ask questions: what is a child like you doing at the Technological Institute?"

He knew nothing about her present, but she told him about her future; about the steel skeletons she was going to build, about the glass skyscraper and the aluminum bridge. He listened silently and the corners of his lips drooped, contemptuous, and amused, and sad.

He asked: "Is it worth while, Kira?"

"What?"

"Effort. Creation. Your glass skyscraper. It might have been worth while—a hundred years ago. It may be worth while again—a hundred years from now, though I doubt it. But if I were given a choice—of all the centuries—I'd select last the curse of being born in this one. And perhaps, if I weren't curious, I'd choose never to be born at all."

"If you weren't curious—or if you weren't hungry?"

"I'm not hungry."

"You have no desires?"

"Yes. One: to learn to desire something."

"Is that hopeless?"

"I don't know. What is worth it? What do you expect from the world for your glass skyscraper?"

"I don't know. Perhaps—admiration."

"Well, I'm too conceited to want admiration. But if you do want it—who can give it to you? Who is capable of it? Who can still want to be capable? It's a curse, you know, to be able to look higher than you're allowed to reach. One's safer looking down, the farther down the safest—these days."

"One can also fight."

"Fight what? Sure, you can muster the most heroic in you to fight lions. But to whip your soul to a sacred white heat to fight lice . . . ! No, that's not good construction, comrade engineer. The equilibrium's all wrong."

"Leo, you don't believe that yourself."

"I don't know. I don't want to believe ar.ything. I don't want to see too much. Who suffers in this world? Those who lack something? No. Those who have something they should lack. A blind man can't see, but it's more impossible not to see for one whose eyes are too sharp. More impossible and more of a torture. If only one could lose sight and come down, down to the level of those who never want it, never miss it."

"You'll never do it, Leo."

"I don't know. It's funny, Kira. I found you because I thought you'd do it for me. Now I'm afraid you'll be the one who'll save me from it. But I don't know whether I'll thank you."

They sat side by side and talked and, as the darkness rose, their voices fell lower, for a militia-man was on guard, passing up and down the street behind the bowed lances. Snow squeaked under his boots like new leather. The houses were growing blue, dark blue against a lighter sky, as if the night were rising from the pavements. Yellow stars trembled in frosted windows. A street lamp flared up on the corner, behind the trees. It threw a triangle of pink marble veined by shadows of bare twigs on the blue snow of the garden, at their feet.

Leo looked at his wristwatch, an expensive, foreign watch under a frayed shirt cuff. He rose in one swift, supple movement and she sat looking up with admiration, as if hoping to see him repeat it.

"I have to go, Kira."

"Now?"

"There's a train to catch."

"So you're going again."

"But I'm taking something with me—this time."

"A new sword?"

"No. A shield."

She got up. She stood before him. She asked obediently: "Is it to be another month, Leo?"

"Yes. On these steps. At three o'clock. December tenth."

"If you're still alive—and if you don't. . . ."

"No. I'll be alive—because I won't forget."

He took her hand before she could extend it, tore off the black mitten, raised the hand slowly to his lips and kissed her palm.

Then he turned quickly and walked away. The snow creaked under his feet. The sound and the figure melted into the darkness, while she was still standing motionless, her hand outstretched, until a little white flake fluttered onto her palm, onto the unseen treasure she was afraid to spill.

*

When Alexander Dimitrievitch's store did good business, he gave Kira money for carfare; when business fell, she had to walk to the Institute. But she walked every day and saved her carfare to buy a brief case.

She went to the Alexandrovsky market to buy it; she could get a used one—and any article that people used or had used —at the Alexandrovsky market.

She walked slowly, carefully stepping over the goods spread on the sidewalk. A little old lady with ivory hands on a black lace shawl looked at her eagerly, hopefully, as she stepped over a table cloth displaying silver forks, a blue plush album of faded photographs, and three bronze ikons. An old man with a black patch over one eye extended to her silently the picture of a young officer in a nicked gold frame. A coughing young woman thrust forward a faded satin petticoat.

Kira stopped suddenly. She saw broad shoulders towering over the long, hopeless line on the edge of the sidewalk. Vasili Ivanovitch stood silently; he did not advertise his purpose in standing there; the delicate clock of bright Sachs porcelain held in two red, frozen, gloveless hands did it for him. The dark eyes under his heavy, graying brows were fixed, expressionless, on some point above the heads of the passersby.

He saw Kira before she had a chance to run and spare him, but he did not seem to mind; he called her, his grim face smiling happily, the strange, helpless smile he had but for Kira, Victor and Irina.

"How are you, Kira? Glad to see you. Glad to see you. . . . This? Just an old clock. Doesn't mean much. . . . I bought it for Marussia on her birthday . . . her first birthday after we were married. She saw it in a museum and wanted it. It and no other. So I had to do some diplomatic work. It took an Imperial order from the palace to get it sold out of the museum. . . . It doesn't run any more. We'll get along without it."

He stopped to look hopefully at a fat peasant woman who was staring at the clock, scratching her neck. But when she met Vasili Ivanovitch's eyes, she turned and hurried away, raising her heavy skirts high over felt boots.

Vasili Ivanovitch whispered to Kira: "You know, this is not a cheerful place. I feel so sorry for all these people here, selling the last of their possessions, with nothing to expect of life. For me, it's different. I don't mind. What's a few knick-knacks more or less? I'll have time to buy plenty of new ones. But I have something I can't sell and can't lose and it can't be nationalized. I have a future. A living future. My children. You know, Irina—she's the smartest child. She was always first in school; had she graduated in the old days she would have received a gold medal. And Victor?" The old shoulders straightened vigorously like those of a soldier at attention. "Victor is an unusual young man. Victor's the brightest boy I've ever seen. Sure, we disagree a little sometimes, but that's because he's young, he doesn't quite understand. You mark my word: Victor will be a great man some day."

"And Irina will be a famous artist, Uncle Vasili."

"And, Kira, did you read the papers this morning? Just watch England. Within the next month or two. . . ."

A fat individual in a sealskin hat stopped and eyed the Sachs clock critically.

"Give you fifty millions for it, citizen," he said curtly, pointing at the clock with a short finger in a leather glove.

The price could not buy ten pounds of bread. Vasili Ivanovitch hesitated; he looked wistfully at the sky turning red high above the houses; at the long line of shadows on the sidewalk, that peered eagerly, hopelessly into every passing face.

"Well . . ." he muttered.

"Why, citizen," Kira whirled on the man, her voice suddenly sharp, querulous, like an indignant housewife, "fifty millions? I've just offered this citizen sixty millions for the clock and he wouldn't sell. I was going to offer. . . ."

"Seventy-five millions and I'll take it along," said the stranger.

Vasili Ivanovitch counted the bills carefully. He did not follow the clock with his eyes as it disappeared in the crowd, quivering against a portly hip. He looked at Kira.

"Why, child, where did you learn that?"

She laughed. "One can learn anything—in an emergency."

Then they parted. Vasili Ivanovitch hurried home. Kira went on in search of the brief case.

Vasili Ivanovitch walked to save carfare. It was getting dark. Snow fluttered down slowly, steadily, as if saving speed for a long run. Thick white foam grew along the curbs.

On a corner, a pair of human eyes looked up at Vasili Ivanovitch from the level of his stomach. The eyes were in a young, clean-shaven face; the legs of the body to which the face belonged seemed to have fallen through the sidewalk, up to above the knees; it took Vasili Ivanovitch an effort to realize that the body had no legs, that it ended in two stumps wrapped in dirty rags, in the snow. The rest of the body wore the neat, patched tunic of an officer of the Imperial army; one of its sleeves was empty; in the other there was an arm and a hand; the hand held out a newspaper, silently, level with the knees of the passersby. In the lapel of the tunic Vasili Ivanovitch noticed a tiny black and orange band, the ribbon of the Cross of St. George.

Vasili Ivanovitch stopped and bought a newspaper. The newspaper cost fifty thousand rubles; he handed down a million-ruble bill.

"I'm sorry, citizen," the officer said in a soft, courteous voice, "I have no change."

Vasili Ivanovitch muttered gruffly: "Keep it. And I'll still be your debtor."

And he hurried away without looking back.

*

Kira was listening to a lecture at the Institute. The auditorium was not heated; students kept on their overcoats and woolen mittens; the auditorium was overcrowded; students sat on the floor in the aisles.

A hand opened the door cautiously; a man's head leaned in and threw a quick glance at the professor's desk. Kira recognized the scar on the right temple. It was a lecture for beginners and he had never attended it. He had entered the auditorium by mistake. He was about to withdraw when he noticed Kira. He entered, closed the door noiselessly and took off his cap. She watched him from the corner of her eye. There was room in the aisle by the door, but he walked softly toward her and sat down on the steps in the aisle, at her feet.

She could not resist the temptation of looking down at him. He bowed silently, with the faintest hint of a smile, and turned attentively toward the professor's desk. He sat still, his legs crossed, one hand motionless on his knee. The hand seemed all bones, skin and nerves. She noticed how hollow his cheeks were, how sharp the angles of his cheekbones. His leather jacket was more military than a gun, more communistic than a red flag. He did not look up at her once.

When the lecture ended and a mob of impatient feet rushed down the aisles, he got up; but he did not hurry to the door; he turned to Kira.

"How are you today?" he asked.

"Surprised," she answered.

"By what?"

"Since when do conscientious Communists waste time by listening to lectures they don't need?"

"Conscientious Communists are curious. They don't mind listening to investigate that which they don't understand."

"I've heard they have many efficient ways of satisfying their curiosity."

"They don't always want to use them," he answered calmly, "so they have to find out for themselves."

"For themselves? Or for the Party?"

"Sometimes both. But not always."

They were out of the auditorium, walking together down the corridor. A strong hand clapped Kira's back; and she heard a laughter that was too loud.

"Well, well, well, Comrade Argounova!" Comrade Sonia roared into her face. "What a surprise! Aren't you ashamed of yourself? Walking with Comrade Taganov, the reddest Communist we've got?"

"Afraid I'll corrupt him, Comrade Sonia?"

"Corrupt? *Him?* Not a chance, dear, not a chance. Well, bye-bye. Have to run. Have three meetings at four o'clock—and promised to attend them all!"

Comrade Sonia's short legs marched resonantly down the hall, her arm swinging a heavy brief case like a knapsack.

"Are you going home, *Comrade Argounova?*" he asked.

"Yes, *Comrade Taganov.*"

"Would you mind if you're compromised by being seen with a very red Communist?"

"Not at all—if your reputation won't be tarnished by being seen with a very white lady."

Outside, snow melted into mud under many hurried steps and the mud froze into sharp, jagged ridges. He took Kira's arm. He looked at her with a silent inquiry for approval. She answered by closing her eyes and nodding. They walked silently. Then she looked up at him and smiled.

She said: "I thought that Communists never did anything except what they had to do; that they never believed in doing anything but what they had to do."

"That's strange," he smiled, "I must be a very poor Communist. I've always done only what I wanted to do."

"Your revolutionary duty?"

"There is no such thing as duty. If you know that a thing is right, you want to do it. If you don't want to do it—it isn't right. If it's right and you don't want to do it—you don't know what right is and you're not a man."

"Haven't you ever wanted a thing for no reason save one: that *you* wanted it?"

"Certainly. That's always been my only reason. I've never wanted things unless they could help my cause. For, you see, it is *my* cause."

"And your cause is to deny yourself for the sake of millions?"

"No. To bring the millions up to where I want them—for my sake."

"And when you think you're right, you do it at any price?"

"I know what you're going to say. You're going to say, as so many of our enemies do, that you admire our ideals, but loathe our methods."

"I loathe your ideals."

"Why?"

"For one reason, mainly, chiefly and eternally, no matter how much your Party promises to accomplish, no matter what paradise it plans to bring mankind. Whatever your other claims may be, there's one you can't avoid, one that will turn your paradise into the most unspeakable hell: your claim that man must live for the state."

"What better purpose can he live for?"

"Don't you know," her voice trembled suddenly in a passionate plea she could not hide, "don't you know that there are things, in the best of us, which no outside hand should dare to touch? Things sacred because, and only because, one can say: 'This is *mine*'? Don't you know that we live only for ourselves, the best of us do, those who are worthy of it? Don't you know that there is something in us which must not be touched by any state, by any collective, by any number of millions?"

He answered: "No."

"Comrade Taganov," she whispered, "how much you have to learn!"

He looked down at her with his quiet shadow of a smile and patted her hand like a child's. "Don't you know," he asked, "that we can't sacrifice millions for the sake of the few?"

"Can you sacrifice the few? When those few are the best? Deny the best its right to the top—and you have no best left. What *are* your masses but millions of dull, shrivelled, stagnant souls that have no thoughts of their own, no dreams of their own, no will of their own, who eat and sleep and chew helplessly the words others put into their brains? And for those you would sacrifice the few who know life, who *are* life? I loathe your ideals because I know no worse injustice than the giving of the undeserved. Because men are not equal in ability and one can't treat them as if they were. And because I loathe most of them."

"I'm glad. So do I."

"But then. . . ."

"Only I don't enjoy the luxury of loathing. I'd rather try to make them worth looking at, to bring them up to my level. And you'd make a great little fighter—on our side."

"I think you know I could never be that."

"I think I do. But why don't you fight against us, then?"

"Because I have less in common with you than the enemies who fight you, have. I don't want to fight for the people, I don't want to fight against the people, I don't want to hear of the people. I want to be left alone—to live."

"Isn't it a strange request?"

"Is it? And what is the state but a servant and a convenience for a large number of people, just like the electric light and the plumbing system? And wouldn't it be preposterous to claim that men must exist for their plumbing, not the plumbing for the men?"

"And if your plumbing pipes got badly out of order, wouldn't it be preposterous to sit still and not make an effort to mend them?"

"I wish you luck, Comrade Taganov. I hope that when you find those pipes running red with your own blood—you'll still think they were worth mending."

"I'm not afraid of that. I'm more afraid of what times like ours will do to a woman like you."

"Then you do see what these times of yours are?"

"We all do. We're not blind. I know that, perhaps, it is a living hell. Still, if I had a choice, I'd want to be born when I was born, and live the days I'm living, because now we don't sit and dream, we don't moan, we don't wish—we do, we act, we build!"

Kira liked the sound of the steps next to hers, steady, unhurried; and the sound of the voice that matched the steps. He had been in the Red Army; she frowned at his battles, but smiled with admiration at the scar on his forehead. He smiled ironically at the story of Argounov's lost factories, but frowned, worried, at Kira's old shoes. His words struggled with hers, but his eyes searched hers for support. She said "no" to the words he spoke, and "yes" to the voice that spoke them.

She stopped at a poster of the State Academic Theaters, the three theaters that had been called "Imperial" before the revolution.

" 'Rigoletto,' " she said wistfully. "Do you like opera, Comrade Taganov?"

"I've never heard one."

She walked on. He said: "But I get plenty of tickets from the Communist Cell. Only I've never had the time. Do you go to the theater often?"

"Not very often. Last time was six years ago. Being a bourgeois, I can't afford a ticket."

"Would you go with me if I asked you?"

"Try it."

"Would you go to the opera with me, Comrade Argounova?"

Her eyebrows danced slyly. She asked: "Hasn't your Communist Cell at the Institute a secret bureau of information about all students?"

He frowned a little, perplexed: "Why?"

"You could find out from them that my name is Kira."

He smiled, a strangely warm smile on hard, grave lips. "But that won't give you a way of finding out that my name is Andrei."

"I'll be glad to accept your invitation, Andrei."

"Thank you, Kira."

At the door of the red-brick house on Moika she extended her hand.

"Can you break Party discipline to shake a counter-revolutionary hand?" she asked.

He held her hand firmly. "Party discipline isn't to be broken," he answered, "but, oh! how far it can be stretched!"

Their eyes held each other longer than their hands, in a silent, bewildering understanding. Then he walked away with the light, precise steps of a soldier. She ran up four flights of stairs, her old tam in one hand, shaking her tousled hair, laughing.

VII

Alexander Dimitrievitch kept his savings sewn in his undershirt. He had developed the habit of raising his hand to his heart once in a while, as if he had gas pains; he felt the roll of bills; he liked the security under his fingertips. When he needed money, he cut the heavy seam of white thread and sighed as the load grew lighter. On November sixteenth, he cut the seam for the last time.

The special tax on private traders for the purpose of relieving the famine on the Volga had to be paid, even though it closed the little textile store in the bakery shop. Another private enterprise had failed.

Alexander Dimitrievitch had expected it. They opened on every corner, fresh and hopeful like mushrooms after a rain; and, like mushrooms, they faded before their first morning was over. Some men were successful. He had seen them: men in resplendent new fur coats, with white, flabby cheeks that made him think of butter for breakfast, and eyes that made him raise his hand, nervously, to the roll over his heart. These men were seen in the front rows at the theaters; they were seen leaving the new confectioners' with round white cake boxes the price of which could keep a family for two months; they were seen hiring taxis—and paying for them. Insolent street children called them "Nepmen"; their cartoons adorned the pages of Red newspapers—with scornful denunciations of the new vultures of NEP; but their warm fur hats were seen in the windows of automobiles rocketing the highest Red officials through the streets of Petrograd. Alexander Dimitrievitch wondered dully about their secrets. But the dreaded word "speculator" gave him a cold shudder; he lacked the talents of a racketeer.

He left the empty bakery boxes; but he carried home his faded cotton sign. He folded it neatly and put it away in a drawer where he kept old stationery with the embossed letterhead of the Argounov textile factories.

"I will not become a Soviet employee if we all starve," said Alexander Dimitrievitch.

Galina Petrovna moaned that something had to be done. Unexpected help appeared in the person of a former bookkeeper from the Argounov factory.

He wore glasses and a soldier's coat and he was not careful about shaving. But he rubbed his hands diffidently and he knew how to respect authority under all circumstances.

"Tsk, tsk, tsk, Alexander Dimitrievitch, sir," he wailed. "This is no life for you. Now, if we get together . . . if you just invest a little, I'll do all the work. . . ."

They formed a partnership. Alexander Dimitrievitch was to manufacture soap; the unshaved bookkeeper was to sell it; he had an excellent corner on the Alexandrovsky market.

"What? How to make it?" he enthused. "Simple as an omelet. I'll get you the greatest little soap recipe. Soap is the stuff of the moment. The public hasn't had any for so long they'll tear it out of your hands. We'll put them all out of business. I know a place where we can get spoiled pork fat. No good for eating—but just right for soap."

Alexander Dimitrievitch spent his last money to buy spoiled pork fat. He melted it in a big brass laundry tub on the kitchen stove. He bent over the steaming fumes, blinking, his shirt sleeves rolled above his elbows, stirring the mixture with a wooden paddle. The kitchen door had to be kept open; there was no other stove to heat the apartment. The bitter, musty odor of a factory basement rose, with the whirling steam of a laundry, to the streaked ceiling. Galina Petrovna chopped the spoiled pork fat on the kitchen table, delicately crooking her little finger, clearing her throat noisily.

Lydia played the piano. Lydia had always boasted of two accomplishments: her magnificent hair, which she brushed for half an hour every morning, and her music, which she practised for three hours each day. Galina Petrovna asked for Chopin. Lydia played Chopin. The wistful music, delicate as rose petals falling slowly in the darkness of an old park, rang softly through the haze of soap fumes. Galina Petrovna did not know why tears dropped on her knife; she thought that the pork fat hurt her eyes.

Kira sat at the table with a book. The odor from the kettle raked her throat as if with sharp little prongs. She paid no attention to it. She had to learn and remember the words in the book for that bridge she would build some day. But she stopped often. She looked at her hand, at the palm of her right hand. Stealthily, she brushed her palm against her cheek, slowly, from the temple to the chin. It seemed a surrender to everything she had always disliked. She blushed; but no one could see it through the fumes.

The soap came out in soft, soggy squares of a dirty brown. Alexander Dimitrievitch found an old brass button off his yachting jacket and imprinted an anchor in the corner of each square.

"Great idea! Trademark," said the unshaved bookkeeper. "We'll call it 'Argounov's Navy Soap.' A good revolutionary name."

A pound of soap cost Alexander Dimitrievitch more than it did on the market.

"That's nothing," said his partner. "That's better. They'll think more of it if they have to pay more. It's quality soap. Not the old Jukov junk."

He had a tray with straps to wear over his shoulders. He

arranged the brown squares carefully on the tray and departed, whistling, for the Alexandrovsky market.

*

In a hall of the Institute Kira saw Comrade Sonia. She was making a little speech to a group of five young students. Comrade Sonia was always surrounded by a brood of youngsters; and she always talked, her short arms flapping like protective wings.

". . . and Comrade Syerov is the best fighter in the ranks of proletarian students. Comrade Syerov's revolutionary record is unsurpassed. Comrade Syerov, the hero of Melitopol. . . ."

A freckled boy with a soldier's cap far on the back of his head, stopped his hurried waddle down the hall and barked at Comrade Sonia: "The hero of Melitopol? Ever heard of Andrei Taganov?"

He sent a sunflower seed straight at a button on Comrade Sonia's leather jacket and staggered away carelessly. Comrade Sonia did not answer. Kira noticed that the look on her face was not a pleasant one.

Finding a rare moment when Comrade Sonia was alone, Kira asked her: "What kind of man is Comrade Taganov?"

Comrade Sonia scratched the back of her head, without a smile. "A perfect revolutionary, I suppose. Some call him that. However, it's not my idea of a good proletarian if a man doesn't unbend and be a little sociable with his fellow comrades once in a while. . . . And if you have any intentions in a bedroom direction, Comrade Argounova—well, not a chance. He's the kind of saint that sleeps with red flags. Take it from one who *knows*."

She laughed aloud at the expression on Kira's face and waddled away, throwing over her shoulder: "Oh, a little proletarian vulgarity won't hurt you!"

*

Andrei Taganov came again to the lecture for beginners, in the crowded auditorium. He found Kira in the crowd and elbowed his way toward her and whispered: "Tickets for tomorrow night. Mikhailovsky Theater. 'Rigoletto.' "

"Oh, Andrei!"

"May I call for you?"

"It's number fourteen. Fourth floor, on the back stairs."

"I'll be there at seven-thirty."

"May I thank you?"

"No."

"Sit down. I'll make room for you."

"Can't. I have to go. I have another lecture to attend."

Cautiously, noiselessly, he made his way to the door, and turned once to glance back at her smiling face.

*

Kira delivered her ultimatum to Galina Petrovna: "Mother, I have to have a dress. I'm going to the opera tomorrow."

"To the . . . opera!" Galina Petrovna dropped the onion she was peeling; Lydia dropped her embroidery.

"Who is he?" gasped Lydia.

"A boy. At the Institute."

"Good-looking?"

"In a way."

"What's his name?" inquired Galina Petrovna.

"Andrei Taganov."

"Taganov? . . . Never heard. . . . Good family?"

Kira smiled and shrugged.

A dress was found at the bottom of the trunk; Galina Petrovna's old dress of soft dark-gray silk. After three fittings and conferences between Galina Petrovna and Lydia, after eighteen hours when two pairs of shoulders bent over the oil wick and two hands feverishly worked two needles, a dress was created for Kira, a simple dress with short sleeves and a shirt collar, for there was no material to trim it.

Before dinner, Kira said: "Be careful when he comes. He's a Communist."

"A Com . . ." Galina Petrovna dropped the salt shaker into the pot of millet.

"Kira! You're not . . . you're not being friendly with a *Communist?*" Lydia choked. "After shouting how much you hate them?"

"I happen to like him."

"Kira, it's outrageous! You have no pride in your social standing. Bringing a Communist into the house! I, for one, shan't speak to him."

Galina Petrovna did not argue. She sighed bitterly: "Kira, you always seem to be able to make hard times harder."

There was millet for dinner; it was mildewed and everyone noticed it; but no one said a word for fear of spoiling the others' appetite. It had to be eaten; there was nothing else; so they ate in silence.

When the bell rang, Lydia, curious in spite of her convictions, hurried to open the door.

"May I see Kira, please?" Andrei asked, removing his cap.

"Yes, indeed," Lydia said icily.

Kira performed the introductions. Alexander Dimitrievitch said: "Good evening," and made no other sound, watching the guest fixedly, nervously. Lydia nodded and turned away.

But Galina Petrovna smiled eagerly: "I'm so glad, Comrade Taganov, that my daughter is going to hear a real proletarian opera in one of our great Red theaters!"

Kira's eyes met Andrei's over the wick. She was grateful for the calm, gracious bow with which he acknowledged the remark.

*

Two days a week were "Profunion days" at the State Academic Theaters. No tickets were sold to the public; they were distributed at half-price among the professional unions. In the lobby of the Mikhailovsky Theater, among trim new suits and military tunics, a few felt boots shuffled heavily and a few calloused hands timidly removed leather caps with flapping, fur-lined ears. Some were awkward, diffident; others slouched insolently, defying the impressive splendor by munching sunflower seeds. Wives of union officials ambled haughtily through the crowd, erect and resplendent in their new dresses of the latest style, with their marcelled hair, sparkling manicures and patent leather slippers. Glistening limousines drove, panting sonorously, up to the light-flooded entrance and disgorged heavy fur coats that waddled swiftly across the sidewalk, projecting gloved hands to throw coins at the ragged program peddlers. The program peddlers, livid, frozen shadows, scurried obsequiously through the free "prof-union" audience, a wealthier, haughtier, better fed audience than the week-day paying guests.

The theater smelt of old velvet, marble and moth balls. Four balconies rose high to a huge chandelier of crystal chains that threw little rainbows on the distant ceiling. Five years of revolution had not touched the theater's solemn grandeur; they had left but one sign: the Imperial eagle was removed from over the huge central box which had belonged to the royal family.

Kira remembered the long satin trains, and the bare white shoulders, and the diamonds that sparkled like the crystals of the chandelier, moving down the orange carpets of the wide aisles. There were few diamonds now; the dresses were dark, sober, with high necklines and long sleeves. Slender, erect in her soft gray satin, she walked in as she had seen those ladies walk many years ago, her arm on that of a tall young man in a leather jacket.

And when the curtain went up and music rose in the dark, silent shaft of the theater, growing, swelling, thundering against walls that could not hold it, something stopped in Kira's throat and she opened her mouth to take a breath. Beyond the walls were linseed-oil wicks, men waiting in line for tramways, red flags and the dictatorship of the proletariat. On the stage, under the marble columns of an Italian palace, women waved their hands softly, gracefully, like reeds in the waves of music, long velvet trains rustled under a blinding light and, young, carefree, drunk on the light and the music, the Duke of Mantua sang the challenge of youth and laughter to gray, weary, cringing faces in the darkness, faces that could forget, for a while, the hour and the day and the century.

Kira glanced at Andrei once. He was not looking at the stage; he was looking at her.

During an intermission, in the foyer, they met Comrade Sonia on the arm of Pavel Syerov. Pavel Syerov was immaculate. Comrade Sonia wore a wrinkled silk dress with a tear in the right armpit. She laughed heartily, slapping Kira's shoulder.

"So you've gone quite proletarian, haven't you? Or is it Comrade Taganov who's gone bourgeois?"

"Very unkind of you, Sonia," Pavel Syerov remonstrated, his pale lips opening in a wide grin. "I can compliment Comrade Argounova on her wise choice."

"How do you know my name?" Kira asked. "You've never met me."

"We know a lot, Comrade Argounova," he answered very pleasantly, "we know a lot."

Comrade Sonia laughed and, steering Syerov's arm masterfully, disappeared in the crowd.

On the way home, Kira asked: "Andrei, did you like the opera?"

"Not particularly."

"Andrei, do you see what you're missing?"

"I don't think I do, Kira. It's all rather silly. And useless."

"Can't you enjoy things that are useless, merely because they are beautiful?"

"No. But I enjoyed it."

"The music?"

"No. The way you listened to it."

At home, on her mattress in the corner, Kira remembered regretfully that he had said nothing about her new dress.

*

Kira had a headache. She sat at the window of the auditorium, her forehead propped by her hand, her elbow on a slanting desk. She could see, reflected in the window pane, a single electric bulb under the ceiling and her drawn face with dishevelled hair hanging over her eyes. The face and the bulb stood as incongruous shadows against the frozen sunset outside, beyond the window, a sunset as sinister and cold as dead blood.

Her feet felt cold in a draft from the hall. Her collar seemed too tight around her throat. No lecture had ever seemed so long. It was only December second. There were still so many days to wait, so many lectures. She found her fingers drumming softly on the window pane, and each couple of knocks was a name of two syllables, and her fingers repeated endlessly, persistently, against her will, a name that echoed somewhere in her temples, a name of three letters she did not want to hear, but heard ceaselessly, as if something within her were calling out for help.

She did not notice when the lecture ended and she was walking out, down a long, dark corridor, to a door open upon a white sidewalk. She stepped out into the snow; she drew her coat tighter against a cold wind.

"Good evening, Kira," a voice called softly from the darkness.

She knew the voice. Her feet stood still, then her breath, then her heart.

In a dark corner by the door, Leo stood leaning against the wall, looking at her.

"Leo . . . how . . . could . . . you?"

"I had to see you."

His face was stern, pale. He did not smile.

They heard hurried steps. Pavel Syerov rushed past them. He stopped short; he peered into the darkness; he threw a quick glance at Kira; then he shrugged and hurried away, down the street. He turned once to glance back at them.

"Let's get away from here," Kira whispered.

Leo called a sleigh. He helped her in, fastened the heavy fur blanket over their knees. The driver jerked forward.

"Leo . . . how could you?"

"I had no other way of finding you."

"And you. . . ."

"Waited at the gate for three hours. Had almost given up hope."

"But wasn't it. . . ."

"Taking a chance? A big one."

"And you came . . . again . . . from the country?"

"Yes."

"What . . . what did you want to tell me?"

"Nothing. Just to see you."

On the quay, at the Admiralty, Leo stopped the sleigh and they got out and walked along the parapet. The Neva was frozen. A solid coat of ice made a wide, white lane between its high banks. Human feet had stamped a long road across its snow. The road was deserted.

They descended down the steep, frozen bank to the ice below. They walked silently, suddenly alone in a white wilderness.

The river was a wide crack in the heart of the city. It stretched the silence of its snow under the silence of the sky. Far away, smokestacks, like little black matches, fumed a feeble brown salute of melting plumes to the sunset. And the sunset rose in a fog of frost and smoke; then it was cut by a red gash, raw and glowing, like living flesh; then the wound closed and the blood flowed slowly higher up the sky, as if under a misty skin, a dull orange, a trembling yellow, a soft purple that surrendered, flowing up into a soft irrevocable blue. The little houses high and very far away, cut brown, broken shadows into the sky; some windows gathered drops of fire from above; others answered feebly with little steely lights, cold and bluish as the snow. And the golden spire of the Admiralty held defiantly a vanished sun high over the dark city.

Kira whispered: "I . . . I was thinking about you . . . today."

"Were you thinking about me?"

His fingers hurt her arm; he leaned close to her, his eyes wide, menacing, mocking in their haughty understanding, caressing and masterful.

She whispered: "Yes."

They stood alone in the middle of the river. A tramway

clattered, rising up the bridge, shaking the steel beams to their roots in the water far below. Leo's face was grim. He said: "I thought of you, too. But I didn't want to think of you. I fought it this long."

She did not answer. She stood straight, tense, still.

"You know what I wanted to tell you," he said, his face very close to hers.

And, without thought, without will or question, in a voice that was someone's order to her, not her voice, she answered: "Yes."

His kiss felt like a wound.

Her arms closed around the frightening wonder of a man's body. She heard him whisper, so close that it seemed her lips heard it first: "Kira, I love you. . . ."

And someone's order to her repeated through her lips, persistently, hungrily, insanely: "Leo, I love you. . . . I love you. . . . I love you. . . ."

A man passed by. The little spark of a cigarette jerked up and down in the darkness.

Leo took her arm and led her away, on perilous ground, through the deep, unbroken snow, to the bridge.

They stood in the darkness of steel vaults. Through the black webbing above, they saw the red sky dying out slowly.

She did not know what he was saying; she knew that his lips were on hers. She did not know that her coat collar was unbuttoned; she knew that his hand was on her breast.

When a tramway rose up the bridge over their heads, the steel clattered convulsively, a dull thunder rolling through its joints; and for a long time after it was gone, the bridge moaned feebly.

The first words she remembered were: "I'll come tomorrow."

Then she found her voice and stood straight and said: "No. It's too dangerous. I'm afraid someone saw you. There are spies at the Institute. Wait for a week."

"Not that long?"

"Yes."

"Here?"

"No. Our old place. At night. Nine o'clock."

"It will be hard to wait."

"Yes, Leo . . . Leo. . . ."

"What?"

"Nothing. I like to hear your name."

That night, on the mattress in the corner of her room, she lay motionless and saw the blue square of the window turn pink.

VIII

In the Institute corridor, on the next day, a student with a red badge stopped her.

"Citizen Argounova, you're wanted in the Communist Cell. At once."

In the room of the Communist Cell, at a long bare table, sat Pavel Syerov.

He asked: "Citizen Argounova, who was the man at the gate with you last night?"

Pavel Syerov was smoking. He held the cigarette firmly at his lips and looked at Kira through the smoke.

She asked: "What man?"

"Comrade Argounova having trouble with her memory? The man I saw at the gate with you last night."

A picture of Lenin hung on the wall, behind Pavel Syerov. Lenin looked sidewise, winking slyly, his face frozen in half a smile.

"Oh, yes, I do remember," said Kira. "There was a man. But I don't know who he was. He asked me how to find some street."

Pavel Syerov shook the ashes off his cigarette into a broken ashtray. He said pleasantly: "Comrade Argounova, you're a student of the Technological Institute. Undoubtedly you wish to continue to be."

"Undoubtedly," said Kira.

"Who was that man?"

"I wasn't interested enough to ask him."

"Very well. I won't ask you that. I'm sure we both know his name. All I want is his address."

"Well, let me see, . . . yes, he asked the way to Sadovaia Street. You might look there."

"Comrade Argounova, I'll remind you that the gentlemen of *your* faction have always accused us proletarian students of belonging to a secret police organization. And, of course, that might be true, you know."

"Well, may I ask *you* a question, then?"

"Certainly. Always pleased to accommodate a lady."

"Who *was* that man?"

Pavel Syerov's fist came down on the table. "Citizen Argounova, do you have to be reminded that this is no joke?"

"If it isn't, will you tell me what it is?"

"You'll understand what it is and damn quick. You've lived in Soviet Russia long enough to know how serious it is to protect counter-revolutionaries."

A hand opened the door without knocking. Andrei Taganov came in. His face showed no astonishment or emotion. Syerov's did; he raised the cigarette to his lips a little too quickly.

"Good morning, Kira," Andrei said calmly.

"Good morning, Andrei," she answered.

He walked to the table. He took a cigarette and bent toward the one in Syerov's hand. Syerov held it out to him hastily. Syerov waited; but Andrei said nothing; he stood by the table, the smoke of his cigarette rising in a straight column. He looked at Kira and Syerov, silently.

"Comrade Argounova, I do not doubt your political trustworthiness," Comrade Syerov said gently. "I'm sure that the single question of one address will not be hard for you to answer."

"I told you I don't know him. I've never seen him before. I can't know his address."

Pavel Syerov tried surreptitiously to observe Andrei's reaction; but Andrei did not move. Pavel Syerov leaned forward and spoke softly, confidentially. "Comrade Argounova, I want you to understand that this man is wanted by the State. Perhaps it's not our assignment to search for him. But if you can help us to find him, it will be very valuable to you and to me—and to all of us," he added significantly.

"And if I can't help you—what am I to do?"

"You're to go home, Kira," said Andrei.

Syerov dropped his cigarette.

"That is," Andrei added, "unless you have lectures to attend. If we need you again—*I'll* send for you."

Kira turned and left the room. Andrei sat down on the corner of the table and crossed his legs.

Pavel Syerov smiled; Andrei was not looking at him. Pavel Syerov cleared his throat. Pavel Syerov said: "Of course, Andrei, old pal, I hope you don't think that I . . . because she is a friend of yours and. . . ."

"I don't think it," said Andrei.

"I'd never question or criticize your actions. Not even if I did think that it's not good discipline to cancel a fellow Communist's order before an outsider."

"What discipline permitted you to call her for questioning?"

"Sorry, pal. My fault. Of course, I was only trying to help you."

"I have not asked for help."

"It was like this, Andrei. I saw her with him at the door last night. I've seen his pictures. The G.P.U. has been searching for him for almost two months."

"Why didn't you report it to me?"

"Well, I wasn't sure it was the man. I might have been mistaken . . . and. . . ."

"And your help in the matter would have been—valuable to you."

"Why, old pal, you're not accusing me of any personal motives, are you? Maybe I did overstep my authority in these little G.P.U. matters that belong to your job, but I was only thinking of helping a fellow proletarian in his duty. You know that nothing can stop me in fulfilling my duty, not even any . . . sentimental attachments."

"A breach of Party discipline is a breach of Party discipline, no matter by whom committed."

Pavel Syerov was looking at Andrei Taganov too fixedly, as he answered slowly: "That's what I've always said."

"It is never advisable to be overzealous in one's duty."

"Certainly not. It's as bad as being lax."

"In the future—any political questioning in this unit is to be done by me."

"As you wish, pal."

"And if you ever feel that I cannot perform that task— you may report it to the Party and ask for my dismissal."

"Andrei! How can you say that! You don't think that I question for a single minute your invaluable importance to the Party? Haven't I always been your greatest admirer— you, the hero of Melitopol? Aren't we old friends? Haven't we fought in the trenches together, under the red flag, you and I, shoulder to shoulder?"

"Yes," said Andrei, "we have."

*

In the year 1896, the red-brick house in the Putilovsky factory district of St. Petersburg had no plumbing. The fifty worker families that clotted its three floors had fifty barrels in which to keep their water. When Andrei Taganov was born, a kindly neighbor brought a barrel from the stair-landing; the water was frozen; the neighbor broke the ice with an ax, and emptied the barrel. The pale, shivering hands of the young mother stuffed an old pillow into the barrel. Such was Andrei's first bed.

His mother bent over the barrel and laughed, laughed happily, hysterically, until tears fell into the dimples of the tiny, red hands. His father did not hear of his birth for three days. His father had been away for a week and the neighbors spoke about it in whispers.

In the year 1905, the neighbors did not need to whisper about the father any longer. He made no secret of the red flag he carried through the streets of St. Petersburg, nor of the little white pamphlets he sowed into the dark soil of crowds, nor of the words his powerful voice sent like a powerful wind to carry the seeds—the flaming words to the glory of Russia's first revolution.

It was Andrei's tenth year. He stood in a corner of the kitchen and looked at the brass buttons on the gendarmes' coats. The gendarmes had black moustaches and real guns. His father was putting his coat on slowly. His father kissed him and kissed his mother. The gendarmes' boots grated the last paint off the kitchen floor. His mother's arms clung to his father's shoulders like tentacles. A strong hand tore her off. She fell across the threshold. They left the door open. Their steps rang down the stairs. His mother's hair was spilled over the bricks of the stair-landing.

Andrei wrote his mother's letters. Neither of them had been taught to write, but Andrei had learned it by himself. The letters went to his father and the address bore, in Andrei's big, awkward handwriting, the name of a town in Siberia. After a while his mother stopped dictating letters. His father never came back.

Andrei carried the baskets with the laundry his mother washed. He could have hidden himself, head and toes, in one of the baskets, but he was strong. In their new room in the basement there was a white, billowing, sour foam, like clouds, in the wooden trough under his mother's purple hands and a white, billowing, sour steam, like clouds, under the ceiling. They could not see that it was spring outside.

But they could not have seen it, even without the steam: for the window opened upon the sidewalk and they could watch only the shiny new galoshes grunting through the mud of melting snow, and, once, someone dropped a young green leaf right by the window.

Andrei was twelve years old when his mother died. Some said it was the wooden trough that had killed her, for it had always been too full; and some said it was the kitchen cupboard, for it had always been too empty.

Andrei went to work in a factory. In the daytime, he stood at a machine and his eyes were cold as its steel, his hands steady as its levers, his nerves tense as its belts. At night, he crouched on the floor behind a barricade of empty boxes in the corner he rented; he needed the barricade because the three other corner tenants in the room objected to candle light when they wanted to sleep, and Agrafena Vlassovna, the landlady, did not approve of book reading. So he kept the candle on the floor, and he held the book to the candle, and he read very slowly, and he wrapped his feet in newspapers, because they were very cold; and the snow wailed battering the window, the three corner tenants snored, Agrafena Vlassovna spat in her sleep, the candle dripped, and everybody was asleep but Andrei and the cockroaches.

He talked very little, smiled very slowly and never gave coins to beggars.

Sometimes, on Sundays, he passed Pavel Syerov in the street. They knew each other, as all children did in the neighborhood, but they did not talk often. Pavel did not like Andrei's clothes. Pavel's hair was greased neatly and his mother was taking him to church. Andrei never went to church.

Pavel's father was a clerk in the corner dry-goods store and waxed his moustache six days a week. On Sundays, he drank and beat his wife. Little Pavel liked perfumed soap, when he could steal it from the apothecary shop; and he studied God's Law—his best white collar on—with the parish priest.

In the year 1915, Andrei stood at the machine, and his eyes were colder than its steel, his hands steadier than its levers, his nerves colder and steadier than both. His skin was tanned by the fire of the furnaces; his muscles and the will behind his muscles were tempered like the metal he had handled. And the little white pamphlets his father had sown, reappeared in the son's hands. But he did not throw them into crowds on the wings of fiery speeches; he passed them stealthily into stealthy hands and the words that went with them were whispers. His name was on the list of a party about which not many dared to whisper and he sent through the mysterious, unseen veins of the Putilovsky factory messages from a man named Lenin.

Andrei Taganov was nineteen. He walked fast, talked slowly, never went to dances. He took orders and gave orders, and had no friends. He looked at superintendents in fur coats and at beggars in felt boots, with the same level, unflinching eyes, and had no pity.

Pavel Syerov was clerking in a haberdashery. On Sundays he entertained a noisy crowd of friends in the corner saloon, leaned back in his chair and swore at the waiter if service was too slow. He loaned money freely and no one refused a loan to "Pavlusha." He put on his patent leather shoes when he took a girl to a dance, and put eau-de-cologne on his handkerchief. He liked to hold the girl's waist and to say: "We're not a commoner, dearie. We're a gentleman."

In the year 1916, Pavel Syerov lost his job in the haberdashery, owing to a fight over a girl. It was the third year of the war; prices were high; jobs were scarce. Pavel Syerov found himself trudging through the gates of the Putilovsky factory on winter mornings, when it was so dark and so early that the lights over the gate cut his puffed, sleepy eyes and he yawned into his raised collar. At first, he avoided his old crowd, for he was ashamed to admit where he was working. After a while, he avoided them because he was ashamed to admit that they had been his friends. He circulated little white pamphlets, made speeches at secret meetings and took orders from Andrei Taganov only because "Andrei's been in it longer, but wait till I catch up with him." The workers liked "Pavlusha." When he happened to meet one of his old friends, he passed by haughtily, as if he had inherited a title; and he spoke of the superiority of the proletariat over the paltry petty bourgeoisie, according to Karl Marx.

In February of the year 1917, Andrei Taganov led crowds through the streets of Petrograd. He carried his first red flag, received his first wound and killed his first man—a gendarme. The only thing that impressed him was the flag.

Pavel Syerov did not see the February Revolution rise, triumphant, from the city pavements. He stayed at home: he had a cold.

But in October, 1917, when the Party whose membership

cards Andrei and Pavel carried reverently, rose to seize the
power, they were both in the streets. Andrei Taganov, his hair
in the wind, fought at the siege of the Winter Palace. Pavel
Syerov received credit for stopping—after most of the treasures
were gone—the looting of a Grand Duke's mansion.

In the year 1918, Andrei Taganov, in the uniform of the
Red Army, marched with rows of other uniforms, from shops
and factories, through the streets of Petrograd, to the tune
of the Internationale, to the depot, to the front of civil war.
He marched solemnly, with silent triumph, as a man walks
to his wedding.

Andrei's hand carried a bayonet as it had fashioned steel;
it pulled a trigger as it had pushed a lever. His body was
young, supple, as a vine ripe in the sun, on the voluptuous
couch of a trench's mud. He smiled slowly and shot fast.

In the year 1920, Melitopol hung by a thread between the
White Army and the Red. The thread broke on a dark spring
night. It had been expected to break. The two armies held
their last stand in a narrow, silent valley. On the side of the
White Army was a desperate desire to hold Melitopol, a
division numbering five to one of their adversaries, and a
vague, grumbling resentment of the soldiers against their
officers, a sullen, secret sympathy for the red flag in the
trenches a few hundred feet away. On the side of the Red
Army was an iron discipline and a desperate task.

They stood still, a few hundred feet apart, two trenches
of bayonets shimmering faintly, like water, under a dark
sky, of men ready and silent, tense, waiting. Black rocks rose
to the sky in the north and black rocks rose to the sky in the
south; but between them was a narrow valley, with a few
blades of grass still left among the torn clots of earth, and
enough space to shoot, to scream, to die—and to decide the
fate of those beyond the rocks on both sides. The bayonets
in the trenches did not move. And the blades of grass did
not move, for there was no wind and no breath from the
trenches to stir them.

Andrei Taganov stood at attention, very straight, and asked
the Commander's permission for the plan he had explained.
The Commander said: "It's your death, ten to one, Comrade
Taganov."

Andrei said: "It does not matter, Comrade Commander."

"Are you sure you can do it?"

"It has been done, Comrade Commander. They're ripe.
They need but one kick."

"The Proletariat thanks you, Comrade Taganov."

Then those in the other trenches saw him climb over the top. He raised his arms, against the dark sky; his body looked tall and slender. Then he walked, arms raised, toward the White trenches; his steps were steady and he did not hurry. The blades of grass creaked, breaking under his feet, and the sound filled the valley. The Whites watched him and waited in silence.

He stopped but a few steps from their trenches. He could not see the many guns aimed at his breast; but he knew they were there. Swiftly, he took the holster at his belt and threw it to the ground. "Brothers!" he cried. "I have no weapons. I'm not here to shoot. I just want to say a few words to you. If you don't want to hear them—shoot me."

An officer raised a gun; another stopped his hand. He didn't like the looks of their soldiers; they were holding bayonets; but they were not aiming at the stranger; it was safer to let him speak.

"Brothers! Why are you fighting us? Are you killing us because we want you to live? Because we want you to have bread and give you land to grow it? Because we want to open a door from your pigsty into a state where you'll be men, as you were born to be, but have forgotten it? Brothers, it's your lives that we're fighting for—against your guns! When our red flag, ours and yours, rises . . ."

There was a shot, a short, sharp sound like a pipe breaking in the valley, and a little blue flame from an officer's gun held close under blue lips. Andrei Taganov whirled and his arms circled against the sky, and he fell on the clotted earth.

Then there were more shots and fire hissing down the White trenches, but it did not come from those on the other side. An officer's body was hurled out of the trench, and a soldier waved his arms to the Red soldiers, yelling: "Comrades!" There were loud hurrahs, and feet stamping across the valley, and red banners waving, and hands lifting Andrei's body, his face white on the black earth, his chest hot and sticky.

Then Pavel Syerov of the Red Army jumped into the White trenches where Red and White soldiers were shaking hands, and he shouted, standing on a pile of sacks:

"Comrades! Let me greet in you the awakening of class consciousness! Another step in the march of history toward Communism! Down with the damn bourgeois exploiters! Loot the looters, comrades! Who does not toil, shall not eat!

Proletarians of the world, unite! As Comrade Karl Marx has said, if we, the class of . . . "

Andrei Taganov recovered from his wound in a few months. It left a scar on his chest. The scar on his temple he acquired later, in another battle. He did not like to talk about that other battle; and no one knew what had happened after it.

It was the battle of Perekop in 1920 that surrendered the Crimea for the third and last time into Soviet hands. When Andrei opened his eyes he saw a white fog flat upon his chest, pressing him down like a heavy weight. Behind the fog, there was something red and glowing, cutting its way toward him. He opened his mouth and saw a white fog escaping from his lips, melting into the one above. Then he thought that it was cold and that it was the cold which held him chained to the ground, with pain like pine needles through his every muscle. He sat up; then he knew that it was not only the cold in his muscles, but a dark hole and blood on his thigh; and blood on his right temple. He knew, also, that the white fog was not close to his chest; there was enough room under it for him to stand up; it was far away in the sky and the red dawn was cutting a thin thread through it, far away.

He stood up. The sound of his feet on the ground seemed too loud in a bottomless silence. He brushed the hair out of his eyes and thought that the white fog above was the frozen breath of the men around him. But he knew that the men were not breathing any longer. Blood looked purple and brown and he could not tell where bodies ended and earth began, nor whether the white blotches were clots of fog or faces.

He saw a body under his feet and a canteen on its hip. The canteen was intact; the body was not. He bent and a red drop fell on the canteen from his temple. He drank.

A voice said: "Give me a drink, brother."

What was left of a man was crawling toward him across a rut in the ground. It had no coat, but a shirt that had been white; and boots that followed the shirt, although there did not seem to be anything to make them follow.

Andrei knew it was one of the Whites. He held the man's head and forced the canteen between lips that were the color of the blood on the ground. The man's chest gurgled and heaved convulsively. No one else moved around them.

Andrei did not know who had won last night's battle; he did not know whether they had won the Crimea; nor whether

—more important to many of them—they had captured Captain Karsavin, one of the last names to fear in the White Army, a man who had taken many Red lives, a man whose head was worth a big price in Red money. Andrei would walk. Somewhere this silence must end. He would find men, somewhere; Red or White—he did not know, but he started walking toward the sunrise.

He had stepped into a soft earth, damp with cold dew, but clear and empty, a road leading somewhere, when he heard a sound behind him, a rustling as of heavy skis dragged through the mud. The White man was following him. He was leaning on a piece of stick and his feet walked without leaving the ground. Andrei stopped and waited for him. The man's lips parted and it was a smile. He said: "May I follow you, brother? I'm not very . . . steady to find my own direction."

Andrei said: "You and I aren't going the same way, buddy. When we find men—it will be the end for either you or me."

"We'll take a chance," said the man.

"We'll take a chance," said Andrei.

So they walked together toward the sunrise. High banks guarded the road, and shadows of dry bushes hung motionless over their heads, with thin branches like a skeleton's fingers spread wide apart, webbed by the fog. Roots wound across the road and their four feet crossed them slowly, with a silent effort. Ahead of them, the sky was burning the fog. There was a rosy shadow over Andrei's forehead; on his left temple little beads of sweat were transparent as glass; on his right temple the beads were red. The other man breathed as if he were rattling dice deep inside his chest.

"As long as one can walk—" said Andrei.

"—one walks," finished the man.

Their eyes met as if to hold each other up.

Little red drops followed their steps in the soft, damp earth—on the right side of the road and on the left.

Then, the man fell. Andrei stopped. The man said: "Go on."

Andrei threw the man's arm over his shoulder and went on, staggering a little under the load.

The man said: "You're a fool."

"One doesn't leave a good soldier, no matter what color he's wearing," said Andrei.

The man said: "If it's my comrades that we come upon— I'll see that they go easy on you."

"I'll see that you get off with a prison hospital and a good bed—if it's mine," said Andrei.

Then, Andrei walked carefully, because he could not allow himself to fall with his burden. And he listened attentively to the heart beating feebly against his back.

The fog was gone and the sky blazed like a huge furnace where gold was not melted into liquid, but into burning air. Against the gold, they saw the piled black boxes of a village far away. A long pole among the boxes pointed straight at a sky green and fresh, as if washed clean with someone's huge mop in the night. There was a flag on the pole and it beat in the morning wind like a little black wing against the sunrise. And Andrei's eyes and the tearless eyes on his shoulder looked fixedly at the little flag, with the same question. But they were still too far away.

When they saw the color of the flag, Andrei stopped and put the man down cautiously and stretched his arms to rest and in greeting. The flag was red.

The man said strangely: "Leave me here."

"Don't be afraid," said Andrei, "we're not so hard on fellow soldiers."

"No," said the man, "not on fellow soldiers."

Then Andrei saw a torn coat sleeve hanging at the man's belt and on the sleeve the epaulet of a captain.

"If you have pity," said the man, "leave me here."

But Andrei had brushed the man's sticky hair off his forehead and was looking attentively, for the first time, at a young, indomitable face he had seen in photographs.

"No," said Andrei, very slowly, "I can't do that, Captain Karsavin."

"I'm sure to die here," said the Captain.

"One doesn't take chances," said Andrei, "with enemies like you."

"No," said the Captain, "one doesn't."

He propped himself up on one hand, and his forehead, thrown back, was very white. He was looking at the dawn.

He said: "When I was young, I always wanted to see a sunrise. But mother never let me go out so early. She was afraid I'd catch a cold."

"I'll let you rest for a while," said Andrei.

"If you have pity," said Captain Karsavin, "you'll shoot me."

"No," said Andrei, "I can't."

Then they were silent.

"Are you a man?" asked Captain Karsavin.

"What do you want?" asked Andrei.

The Captain said: "Your gun."

Andrei looked straight into the dark, calm eyes and extended his hand. The Captain shook it. When he took his hand out of the Captain's, Andrei left his gun in it.

Then he straightened his shoulders and walked toward the village. When he heard the shot, he did not turn. He walked steadily, his head high, his eyes on the red flag beating against the sunrise. Little red drops followed the steps in the soft, damp earth—on one side of the road only.

IX

"Argounov's Navy Soap" was a failure.

The unshaven bookkeeper scratched his neck, muttered something about unprincipled bourgeois competition and disappeared with the price of the three pieces he had sold.

Alexander Dimitrievitch was left with a tray full of soap and a black despair.

Galina Petrovna's energy found their next business venture.

Their new patron had a black astrakhan hat and a high astrakhan collar. He panted after climbing four flights of stairs, produced from the mysterious depths of his vast, fur-lined coat a heavy roll of crinkling bills, counted them off, spitting on his fingers, and was always in a hurry.

"Two kinds," he explained, "the crystals in glass tubes and the tablets in paper boxes. I furnish the materials. You —pack. Remember, eighty-seven tablets is all you have to put into a box labeled 'One Hundred.' Great future in saccharine."

The gentleman in the astrakhan hat had a large staff; a net of families packing his merchandise; a net of peddlers carrying his trays on street corners; a net of smugglers miraculously procuring saccharine from far-away Berlin.

Four heads bent around the wick in the Argounov dining room and eight hands counted carefully, monotonously, despairingly: six little crystals from a bright foreign tin can into each little glass tube, eighty-seven tiny white tablets into each tiny white box. The boxes came in long sheets; they had to be cut out and folded; they bore German inscriptions in green letters—"Genuine German Saccharine"; the other side of the sheet bore the bright colors of old Russian advertisements.

"Sorry, it's too bad about your studies, Kira," Galina Petrovna said, "but you'll just have to help. You have to eat, you know."

That evening, there were only three heads and six hands around the wick: Alexander Dimitrievitch had been mobilized. There had been snow storms; snow lay deep and heavy on Petrograd's sidewalks; a mobilization of all private traders and unemployed bourgeois had been effected for the purpose of shoveling snow. They had to report for duty at dawn; they grunted and bent in the frost, steam rising to blue noses, old woolen mittens clutching shovels, red flesh in the slits of the mittens; they worked, bending and grunting, shovels biting wearily into white walls. They were given shovels, but no pay.

Maria Petrovna came to visit. She unrolled yards of scarfs from around her neck, shaking snow off her felt boots in the anteroom, coughing.

"No, no, Marussia," Galina Petrovna protested. "Thanks, but you can't help. The powder'll make you cough. Sit by the stove. Get yourself warm."

". . . seventy-four, seventy-five, seventy-six . . . What news, Aunt Marussia?" Lydia asked.

"Heavy are our sins," Maria Petrovna sighed. "Is that stuff poisonous?"

"No, it's harmless. Just sweet. The dessert of the revolution."

"Vasili sold the mosaic table from the drawing room. . . . Fifty million rubles and four pounds of lard. I made an omelet with the egg powder we got at the co-operative. They can't tell me they made that powder out of fresh eggs."

". . . sixteen, seventeen, eighteen . . . they say their NEP is a failure, Marussia . . . nineteen, twenty . . . they're going to return houses to owners before long."

Maria Petrovna took a little nail buffer out of her bag and went on talking, polishing her nails mechanically; her hands had always been her pride; she was not going to neglect them, even though she did think, at times, that they had changed a little.

"Did you hear about Boris Koulikov? He was in a hurry

and he tried to jump into a crowded tramway at full speed. Both legs cut off."

"Marussia! What's the matter with your eyes?"

"I don't know. I've been crying so much lately . . . and for no reason at all."

"There's no spiritual comfort these days, Aunt Marussia," Lydia sighed, ". . . fifty-eight, fifty-nine. . . . Those pagans! Those sacrilegious apostates! They've taken the gold ikons from the churches—to feed their famine somewhere. They've opened the sacred relics . . . sixty-three, sixty-four, sixty-five. . . . We'll all be punished, for they defy God."

"Irina lost her ration card," sighed Maria Petrovna. "She gets nothing for the rest of this month."

"I'm not surprised," said Lydia coldly. "Irina is not to be trusted."

Lydia disliked her cousin ever since Irina, following her custom of expressing her character judgments in sketches, had drawn Lydia in the shape of a mackerel.

"What's that on your handkerchief, Marussia?" Galina Petrovna asked.

"Oh . . . nothing . . . sorry . . . it's a dirty one. . . . I can't sleep at night any more, it seems. Seems my nightgown is always so hot and sticky. I'm so worried about Victor. Now he's bringing the strangest fellows into the house. They don't remove their caps in the drawing room and they shake ashes all over the carpet. I think they're . . . Communists. Vasili hasn't said a word. And it frightens me. I know what he thinks. . . . Communists in the house!"

"You're not the only ones," said Lydia and threw a dark glance at Kira. Kira was stuffing crystals into a glass tube.

"You try and speak to Victor and he says: 'Diplomacy is the highest of the Arts.' . . . Heavy are our sins!"

"You'd better do something about that cough, Marussia."

"Oh, it's nothing. Nothing at all. Just the cold weather. Doctors are fools and don't know what they're talking about."

Kira counted the little crystals in the palm of her hand. She tried not to breathe or swallow; when she did, the white powder, seeping through her lips and nostrils, bit her throat with the pain of a piercing, metallic sweetness.

Maria Petrovna was coughing: "Yes, Nina Mirskaia. . . . Imagine! Not even a Soviet registration wedding. And her father, God rest his soul, was a bishop. . . . Just sleeping together like cats."

Lydia cleared her throat and blushed.

Galina Petrovna said: "It's a disgrace. This new love freedom will ruin the country. But, thank God, nothing like this will ever happen to us. There still are some families with some standards left."

The bell rang.

"It's father," said Lydia and hurried to open the door. It was Andrei Taganov.

"May I see Kira?" he asked, shaking snow off his shoulders.

"Oh! . . . Well, I can't stop you," Lydia answered haughtily.

Kira rose, when he entered the dining room, her eyes wide in the darkness.

"Ah! . . . Well, what a surprise!" said Galina Petrovna, her hand holding a half-filled box, trembling, the saccharine tablets rolling out. "That is . . . yes . . . a most pleasant. . . . How are you tonight? . . . Ah! . . . Yes. . . . May I present? Andrei Fedorovitch Taganov—my sister, Maria Petrovna Dunaeva."

Andrei bowed; Maria Petrovna looked, astonished, at the box in her sister's hand.

"May I speak to you, Kira?" Andrei asked. "Alone?"

"Excuse us," said Kira. "This way, Andrei."

"I daresay," gasped Maria Petrovna, "to your room? Why, modern youth behaves almost like . . . like Communists."

Galina Petrovna dropped the box; Lydia kicked her aunt's ankle. Andrei followed Kira to her room.

"We have no light," said Kira, "just that street lamp outside. Sit down here, on Lydia's bed."

Andrei sat down. She sat on her mattress on the floor, facing him. The street light from beyond the window made a white square on the floor, with Andrei's shadow in the square. A little red tongue flickered in space, high in the corner of Lydia's ikons.

"It's about this morning," said Andrei. "About Syerov."

"Yes?"

"I wanted to tell you that you don't have to worry. He had no authority to question you. No one can issue an order to question you—but me. The order won't be issued."

"Thank you, Andrei."

"I know what you think of us. You're honest. But you're not interested in politics. You're not an active enemy. I trust you."

"I don't know his address, Andrei."

"I'm not asking whom you know. Just don't let them drag you into anything."

"Andrei, do you know who that man is?"

"Do you mind if we don't discuss it, Kira?"

"No. But will you allow me one question?"

"Yes. What is it?"

"Why are you doing this for me?"

"Because I trust you and I think we're friends. Though don't ask me why we are, because I don't know that myself."

"I know that. It's because . . . you see, if we had souls, which we haven't, and if our souls met—yours and mine—they'd fight to the death. But after they had torn each other to pieces, to the very bottom, they'd see that they had the same root. I don't know if you can understand it, because, you see, I don't believe in souls."

"I don't either. But I understand. And what is the root?"

"Do you believe in God, Andrei?"

"No."

"Neither do I. But that's a favorite question of mine. An upside-down question, you know."

"What do you mean?"

"Well, if I asked people whether they believed in life, they'd never understand what I meant. It's a bad question. It can mean so much that it really means nothing. So I ask them if they believe in God. And if they say they do—then, I know they don't believe in life."

"Why?"

"Because, you see, God—whatever anyone chooses to call God—is one's highest conception of the highest possible. And whoever places his highest conception above his own possibility thinks very little of himself and his life. It's a rare gift, you know, to feel reverence for your own life and to want the best, the greatest, the highest possible, here, now, for your very own. To imagine a heaven and then not to dream of it, but to demand it."

"You're a strange girl."

"You see, you and I, we believe in life. But you want to fight for it, to kill for it, even to die—for life. I only want to live it."

Behind the closed door, Lydia, tired of counting saccharine, rested by playing the piano. She played Chopin.

Andrei said suddenly: "You know, that's beautiful."

"What's beautiful, Andrei?"

"That music."

"I thought you didn't care for music."

"I never have. But, somehow, I like this, now, here."

They sat in the darkness and listened. Somewhere below, a truck turned a corner. The window panes trembled with a thin, tense shudder. The light square with Andrei's shadow rose from the floor, swept, like a fan, across the walls, and froze at their feet again.

When the music ended, they returned to the dining room. Lydia still sat at the piano. Andrei said hesitantly: "It was beautiful, Lydia Alexandrovna. Would you play it again?"

Lydia jerked her head proudly. "I'm sorry," she said, rising brusquely. "I'm tired." And she left the room with the step of a Jeanne d'Arc.

Maria Petrovna cringed in her chair, as if trying to squeeze herself out of Andrei's sight. When her cough attracted his eyes, she muttered: "I've always said that our modern youth does not follow sufficiently the example of the Communists."

When Kira accompanied him to the door, Andrei said: "I don't think I should call on you, Kira. It makes your family uncomfortable. It's all right, I understand. Will I see you at the Institute?"

"Yes," said Kira. "Thank you, Andrei. Good night."

*

Leo stood on the steps of the empty mansion. He did not move when he heard Kira's feet hurrying across the snow; he stood motionless, his hands in his pockets.

When she was beside him, their eyes met in a glance that was more than a kiss. Then, his arms crushed her with the violence of hatred, as if he wanted to grind their coats into shreds against each other.

Then he said: "Kira. . . ."

There was some odd, disturbing quality in the sound of his voice. She tore his cap off; she raised herself on tiptoe to reach his lips again, her fingers in his hair.

He said: "Kira, I'm going away."

She looked at him, very quietly, her head bent a little to one shoulder, in her eyes—a question, but no understanding.

"I'm going away tonight. Forever. To Germany."

She said: "Leo. . . ." Her eyes were wide, but not frightened.

He spoke as if biting into every word, as if all his hatred and despair came from these sounds, not their meaning: "I'm a fugitive, Kira. A counter-revolutionary. I have to leave Russia before they find me. I've just received the money—from my aunt in Berlin. That's what I've been waiting for. They smuggled it to me."

She asked: "The boat leaves tonight?"

"A smugglers' boat. They smuggle human flesh out of this wolf-trap. And desperate souls, like mine. If we're not caught —we land in Germany. If we're caught—well, I don't suppose it's a death sentence for everybody, but I've never heard of a man who was spared."

"Leo, you don't want to leave me."

He looked at her with a hatred more eloquent than tenderness. "Sometimes I've found myself wishing they would catch the boat and bring me back."

"I'm going with you, Leo."

He was not startled. He asked: "Do you understand the chance you're taking?"

"Yes."

"Do you know that it's your life at stake if we don't reach Germany, and perhaps also if we do?"

"Yes."

"The boat leaves in an hour. It's far. We have to start right away. From here. No time to get any luggage."

"I'm ready."

"You can't tell anyone. You can't telephone any farewells."

"I don't have to."

"All right. Come on."

He picked up his cap and walked to the street, swiftly, silently, without looking at her or noticing her presence. He called a sleigh. The only words he spoke were an address to the driver. The sharp runners cut into the snow, and the sharp wind into their faces.

They turned a corner, past a house that had collapsed; snow-dusted bricks had rolled far out into the street; the ray of a lamp post behind the house pierced the empty rooms; the skeleton of an iron bed hung high somewhere in the ray of light. A newsboy barked hoarsely: *"Pravda! . . . Krasnaya Gazeta!"* to an empty street.

Leo whispered: "Over there . . . there are automobiles . . . and boulevards . . . and lights. . . ."

An old man stood in a doorway, snow gathering in the brim of his frayed hat, his head hanging down on his breast, asleep over a tray of home-made cookies.

Kira whispered: ". . . lipstick and silk stockings. . . ."

A stray dog sniffed at a barrel of refuse under the dark window of a co-operative.

Leo whispered: ". . . champagne . . . radios . . . jazz bands."

Kira whispered: ". . . like the 'Song of Broken Glass' . . ."

A man moaned, blowing on his hands: "Saccharine, citizens!"

A soldier cracked sunflower seeds and sang about the little apple.

Posters followed them, as if streaming slowly from house to house, red, orange, white, arms, hammers, wheels, levers, lice, airplanes.

The noise of the city was dying behind them. A factory raised tall black chimneys to the sky. Over the street, on a rope from roof to roof, like a barrier, a huge banner clicked, fighting the wind, twisting in furious contortions, yelling to the street and the wind:

PROLETAR . . . OUR COLLECTI . . . CLASS WELD . . . STRUG . . . FREED . . . FUTURE . . .

Then their eyes met, and the glance was like a handshake. Leo smiled; he said: "I couldn't ask you to do this. But I think I knew you'd come."

They stopped at a fence on an unpaved street. Leo paid the driver. They started to walk slowly. Leo watching cautiously till the sleigh disappeared around a corner. Then he said: "We have two miles to walk to the sea. Are you cold?"

"No."

He took her hand. They followed the fence down a wooden sidewalk. A dog howled somewhere. A bare tree whistled in the wind.

They left the sidewalk. Snow rose to their ankles. They were in an open field, walking toward a bottomless darkness.

She moved with quiet precision, as one moves in the face of the inevitable. He held her hand. Behind them, the red glow of the city breathed into the sky. Ahead of them, the sky bent to the earth, or the earth rose to the sky, and their bodies were cutting the two apart.

Snow rose to their calves. The wind blew against them. They walked bent forward, their coats like sails fighting a storm, cold tightening the skin of their cheeks.

Beyond the snow was the world; beyond the snow was that consummate entity to which the country behind them bowed reverently, wistfully, tragically: Abroad. Life began beyond the snow.

When they stopped, the snow ended abruptly. They looked into a black void without horizon or sky. From somewhere far below, they heard a swishing, slapping sound, as if someone were emptying pails of water at regular intervals. Leo whispered: "Keep quiet."

He was leading her down a narrow, slippery path, in someone's footprints. She distinguished a vague shape floating on the void, a mast, a tiny spark, like a dying match.

There were no lights on the ship. She did not notice the husky figure in their path until the ray of a flashlight struck Leo's face, licked his shoulder, stopped on hers, and was gone. She saw a black beard and a hand holding a gun. But the gun was lowered.

Leo's hand crinkled in his pocket and slipped something to the man. "Another fare," Leo whispered. "This girl goes with me."

"We have no cabins left."

"That's all right. Mine's enough."

They stepped onto boards that rocked softly. Another figure rustled up from nowhere and led them to a door. Leo helped Kira down the companionway. There was a light below deck and furtive shadows; a man with a trim beard and the Cross of St. George on his breast looked at them silently; in a doorway, a woman wrapped in a coat of tarnished brocade watched them fearfully, clutching a little wooden box in her hands, the hands trembling.

Their guide opened a door and pointed inside with a jerk of his head.

Their cabin was only a bed and a narrow strip of space between cracked, unpainted walls. A board cut a corner off as a table. A smoked lantern hung over the table, and a yellow, shivering spot of light. The floor rose and fell softly, as if breathing. A shutter was locked over the porthole.

Leo closed the door and said: "Take your coat off."

She obeyed. He took his coat off and threw his cap down on the table. He wore a heavy black sweater, tight around his arms and shoulders. It was the first time that they had seen each other without overcoats. She felt undressed. She moved away a little.

The cabin was so small that even the air enveloping her seemed a part of him. She backed slowly to the table in the corner.

He looked down at her heavy felt boots, too heavy for her slim figure. She followed his glance. She took her boots off and threw them across the cabin.

He sat down on the bed. She sat at the table, hiding her legs with their tight black cotton stockings under the bench, her arms pressed closely to her sides, her shoulders hunched, her body gathered tightly, as if cringing from the cold, the white triangle of her open collar luminous in the semi-darkness.

Leo said: "My aunt in Berlin hates me. But she loved my father. My father . . . is dead."

"Shake the snow off your shoes, Leo. It's melting on the floor."

"If it weren't for you, I'd have taken a boat three days ago. But I could not go away without seeing you. So I waited for this one. The other boat disappeared. Shipwrecked or caught— no one knows. They didn't reach Germany. So you've saved my life—perhaps."

When they heard a low rumble and the boards creaked louder and the flame in the lantern fluttered against the smoked glass, Leo sprang up, blew out the light and opened the shutter over the porthole. Their faces close together in the little circle, they watched the red glow of the city moving away. The red glow died; then there were only a few lights left between earth and sky; and the lights did not move, but shrank slowly into stars, then into sparks, then into nothing. She looked at Leo; his eyes were wide with an emotion she had never seen in them before. He asked slowly, triumphantly:

"Do you know what we're leaving?"

Then his hands closed over her shoulders and his lips forced hers apart, and she felt as if she were leaning back against the air, her muscles feeling the weight of his. Her arms moved slowly over his sweater, as if she wanted to feel his body with the skin of her arms.

Then he released her, closed the shutter and lighted the lantern. The match spluttered with a blue flame. He lighted a cigarette and stood by the door, without looking at her, smoking.

She sat down by the table, obediently, without a word or a question, her eyes not leaving him.

Then he crushed the cigarette against the wall and approached her, and stood silently, his hands in his pockets, his mouth a scornful arc, his face expressionless.

She rose slowly, obediently, looking up at him. She stood still as if his eyes were holding her on a leash.

He said: "Take your clothes off."

She said nothing, and did not move her glance away from his, and obeyed.

He stood watching her. She did not think of the code of her parents' world. But that code came back once, for an instant, when she saw her skirt on the floor; then, in defiance, she regretted that her underwear was not silk, but only heavy cotton.

She unfastened the strap of her slip and let it fall under her breast. She was about to unfasten the other strap, but he tore her off the ground, and then she was arched limply in space, her hair hanging over his arm, her breast at his mouth.

Then they were on the bed, her whole weight on his hand spread wide between her naked shoulder blades. Then he blew out the lantern. She heard his sweater falling to the floor.

Then she felt his legs like a warm liquid against hers. Her hair fell over the edge of the bed. Her lips parted as in a snarl.

X

When Kira awakened, Leo's head was resting on her one breast; a sailor was looking at the other.

She jerked the blanket up to her chin and Leo awakened. They stared up together.

It was morning. The door was open. The sailor stood on the threshold; his shoulders were too wide for the door and his fist was closed over a gun at his belt; his leather jacket was open over a striped sweater and his mouth was open in a wide grin over two resplendent white stripes of teeth; he stooped a little, for his blue cap touched the top of the doorway; the cap bore a red five-pointed Soviet star.

He chuckled: "Sorry to disturb you, citizens."

Kira, her eyes glued to the red star, the star that filled her eyes, but could not reach her brain, muttered foolishly, softly, as a child: "Please go away. This is our first . . ." Her voice choked, as the red star reached her brain.

The sailor chuckled: "Well, you couldn't have selected a worse time, citizen. You couldn't have."

Leo said: "Get out of here and let us dress."

His voice was not arrogant, nor pleading; it was such an implacable command that the sailor obeyed as if at the order of a superior officer. He closed the door behind him.

Leo said: "Lie still till I gather your things. It's cold."

He got out of bed and bent for her clothes, naked as a statue and as unconcerned. A gray light came through a crack of the closed shutter.

They dressed silently. The ceiling trembled under hurrying steps above. Somewhere a woman's voice was howling in sobs, like a demented animal. When they were dressed, Leo said: "It's all right, Kira. Don't be afraid."

He was so calm that for an instant she welcomed the disaster that let her see it. Their eyes met for a second; it was a silent sanction of what they both remembered.

He flung the door open. The sailor was waiting outside. Leo said evenly: "Any confessions you want. I'll sign anything you write—if you let her go." Kira opened her mouth; Leo's hand closed it brutally. He continued: "She had nothing to do with it. I've kidnapped her. I'll stand trial for it, if you wish."

Kira screamed: "He's lying!"

Leo said: "Shut up."

The sailor said: "Shut up, both of you."

They followed him. The woman's howls were deafening. They saw her crawling on her knees after two sailors who held her little wooden box; the box was open; the jewels sparkled through the sailors' fingers; the woman's hair hung over her eyes and she howled into space.

At an open cabin door, Leo suddenly jerked Kira forward so that she passed without seeing it. Inside the cabin, men were bending over a motionless body on the floor; the body's hand was clutching the handle of a dagger in the heart, under the Cross of St. George.

On deck, the gray sky descended to the tip of the mast and steam breathed with commands from the lips of men who had taken control of the boat, men from the coast guard ship that rose and fell as a huge shadow in the fog, a red flag stirring feebly on its mast.

Two sailors held the arms of the black-bearded smugglers' captain. The captain was staring at his shoes.

The sailors looked up at the giant in the leather jacket, waiting for orders. The giant took a list out of his pocket and held it under the captain's beard; he pointed with his thumb, behind his shoulder, at Leo, and asked: "Which one is him?"

The captain's nose pointed to a name. Kira saw the giant's eyes widen in a strange expression she could not understand.

"Who's the girl?" he asked.

"Don't know," the captain answered. "She's not on our passenger list. She came at the last minute—with him."

"Seventeen of them counter-revolutionary rats that tried to sneak out of the country, Comrade Timoshenko," said a sailor.

Comrade Timoshenko chuckled, and his fist struck the muscles under his striped sweater. "Thought you could get away, eh?—from Stepan Timoshenko of the Red Baltfleet?"

The captain stared at his shoes.

"Keep your eyes and your guns ready," said Comrade Timoshenko. "Any funny business—shoot their guts out."

He grinned up at the fog, his teeth gleaming, his tanned neck open to the cold, and walked away, whistling.

When the two ships began to move, Comrade Timoshenko came back. He passed by Leo and Kira in the crowd of prisoners on the wet, glistening deck, and stopped, looking at them for a second, an inexplicable expression in his dark, round eyes. He passed and came back and said aloud to no one in particular, his thumb pointing at Kira: "The girl's all right. He kidnapped her."

"But I'm telling you . . ." Kira began.

"Make your little whore keep quiet," Timoshenko said slowly; and there was something like understanding in the glance he exchanged with Leo.

They saw the skyline of Petrograd rise like a long, low string of houses stretched in a single row at the edge of an immense, frozen sky. The dome of St. Isaac's Cathedral, a pale gold ball sliced in half, looked like a weary moon setting in the smoke of chimneys.

Leo and Kira sat on a coil of ropes. Behind them, a pock-marked sailor smoked a cigarette, his hand on his gun.

They did not hear the sailor move away. Stepan Timoshenko approached them. He looked at Kira and whispered:

"When we land—there'll be a truck waiting. The boys will be busy. I just have a hunch they'll have their backs turned. When they do—you start going—and keep going."

"No," said Kira, "I'll stay with him."

"Kira! You . . ."

"Don't be a damn little fool. You can't help him."

"You won't get any confessions from him—for my sake."

Timoshenko chuckled: "He has no confessions to make. And I don't want children mixed in with something they don't understand a damn about. See that she's gone when we reach the truck, citizen."

Kira looked into the dark, round eyes; they leaned close to her and words hissed, in a whisper, through the white teeth: "It's easier to get one—than two—out of the G.P.U. I'll be there around four this afternoon. Come and ask for Stepan Timoshenko. Maybe I'll have news for you. No one'll hurt you. Gorokhovaia 2."

He did not wait for an answer. He walked away and slapped the pock-marked sailor in the jaw for leaving the prisoners alone.

Leo whispered: "Do you want to make it harder for me? You'll go. Also—you'll stay away from Gorokhovaia 2."

When houses rose close over the mast, he kissed her. It was hard to tear her lips off his, as hard as off frozen glass.

"Kira, what's your name?" he whispered.

"Kira Argounova. And yours?"

"Leo Kovalensky."

*

"At Irina's. We talked and didn't notice the time and it was too late to come home."

Galina Petrovna sighed indifferently, her nightgown trembling on her shoulders in the cold anteroom. "And why this homecoming at seven in the morning? I suppose you awakened your Aunt Marussia and poor Marussia with her cough. . . ."

"I couldn't sleep. Aunt Marussia didn't hear me."

Galina Petrovna yawned and shuffled back to her bedroom. Kira had stayed overnight at her cousin's several times; Galina Petrovna had not been worried.

Kira sat down and her hands fell limply. There were so many hours to wait till four in the afternoon. She should be terrified, she thought, and she was; but under the terror there was something without name or words, a hymn without sound, something that laughed, even though Leo was locked in a cell on Gorokhovaia 2. Her body still felt as if it were holding him close to her.

*

House number 2 on Gorokhovaia Street was a pale green, the color of pea soup. Its paint and plaster were peeling. Its windows had no curtains and no iron bars. The windows looked quietly upon a quiet side street. It was the Petrograd Headquarters of the G.P.U.

There were words that people did not like to mention; they felt a superstitious fear in uttering their sounds, as when they spoke of a desolate cemetery, a haunted house, the Spanish Inquisition, Gorokhovaia 2. Many nights had passed over Petrograd; in the nights there had been many steps, many ringing door bells, many people gone never to be seen again; the flow of a silent terror swelled over the city, hushing voices to whispers; the flow had a heart, from which it came, to which it returned; that heart was Gorokhovaia 2.

It was a building like any of its neighbors; across the street, behind similar windows, families were cooking millet and playing the gramophone; at its corner, a woman was selling cakes; the woman had pink cheeks and blue eyes; the cakes had a golden crust and smelt of warm grease; a poster on a lamp post advertised the new cigarette of the Tobacco Trust. But as Kira walked toward that building, she saw people passing by its green walls without looking up, with tensely casual expressions, their steps hurrying involuntarily, as if afraid of their presence, of their eyes, of their thoughts. Behind the green walls was that which no one wanted to know.

The door was open. Kira walked in, her hands in her pockets, slouching deliberately, indifferently. There was a wide stairway inside, and corridors, and offices. There were many people, hurrying and waiting, as in all Soviet government buildings; there were many feet shuffling down bare floors, but not many voices. On the faces—there were no tears. Many doors were closed; the faces were set and closed like the doors.

Kira found Stepan Timoshenko sitting on a desk in an office and he grinned at her.

"It's just as I thought," he said. "They have nothing on him. It's just his father. Well, that's past. Had they got him two months ago—it would've been the firing squad and not many questions asked. But now—well, we'll see."

"What has he done?"

"Him? Nothing. It's his father. Heard of the conspiracy of Professor Gorsky, two months ago? The old fool wasn't in it—how could he, being blind?—but he hid Gorsky in his house. Well, he paid for it."

"Who was Leo's father?"

"Old Admiral Kovalensky."

"The one who . . ." Kira gasped and stopped.

"Yeah. The one who was blinded in the war—and was shot."

"Oh!"

"Well, I wouldn't have done it—not that time. But I'm not

the only one to have the say. Well, you don't make a revolution with white gloves on."

"But if Leo had nothing to do with it, why . . ."

"At that time—they'd have shot anyone that knew anyone in the conspiracy. Now—they've cooled off. It's past. He's lucky that way. . . . Don't stare like a little fool. If you'd worked here, you'd know what difference time, and days, and hours can make here. Well, that's the way we work. Well, what damn fool thinks that a revolution is all perfumed with cologne?"

"Then—you can let him . . ."

"I don't know. I'll try. We'll investigate. Then there's the business of trying to leave the country illegally. But that—I think I can. . . . We don't fight children. Especially fool children who find time for love right on a spewing volcano."

Kira looked into the round eyes; they had no expression; but the big mouth was grinning; he had a short nose that turned up, and wide, insolent nostrils.

"You're very kind," she said.

"Who's kind?" he laughed. "Stepan Timoshenko of the Red Baltfleet? Do you remember the October days of 1917? Ever heard of what went on in the Baltic fleet? Don't shudder like a cat. Stepan Timoshenko was a Bolshevik before a lot of these new punks had time to dry the milk behind their ears."

"Can I see him?"

"No. Not a chance. No visitors allowed to that bunch."

"But then . . ."

"But then you go home and stay there. And don't worry. That's all I wanted to tell you."

"I have a friend who has connections, I think, who could . . ."

"You keep your mouth shut and don't drag no connections into this. Sit still for two or three days."

"That long!"

"Well, that's not as long as never seeing him again. And don't worry, we'll keep him locked up for you—with no women around."

He got off the desk, and grinned. Then his lips fell into a straight line; he towered over Kira, looking straight into her eyes, and his eyes were not gay. He said: "When you get him back, keep your claws on him. If you haven't any—grow some. He's not an easy stud. And don't try to leave the country. You're in this Soviet Russia; you may hate it, and you may choke, but in Soviet Russia you'll stay. I think you have the claws for him. Watch him. His father loved him."

Kira extended her hand. It disappeared in Stepan Timoshenko's tanned fist.

At the door she turned and asked softly: "Why are you doing this?"

He was not looking at her; he was looking out the window. He answered: "I've gone through the war in the Baltic Fleet. Admiral Kovalensky was blinded in service in the Baltic Fleet. He was not the worst commander we had. . . . Get out of here!"

*

Lydia said: "She twists on her mattress all night long. You'd think we had mice in the house. I can't sleep."

Galina Petrovna said: "I believe you're a student, Kira Alexandrovna? Or am I mistaken? You haven't been at the Institute for three days. Victor said so. Would you condescend to inform us what kind of new foolishness is this that's come over you?"

Alexander Dimitrievitch said nothing. He awakened with a start, for he had dozed off, a half-filled saccharine tube in his hand.

Kira said nothing.

Galina Petrovna said: "Look at those circles under her eyes. No respectable girl looks like that."

"I knew it!" Lydia yelled. "I knew it! She's put eight saccharine crystals into that tube again!"

*

On the evening of the fourth day, the door bell rang.

Kira did not raise her eyes from the saccharine tube. Lydia, curious about every ringing bell, went to open the door.

Kira heard a voice asking: "Is Kira at home?"

Then the saccharine tube clattered to the floor, breaking into splinters, and Kira was at the anteroom doorway, her hand at her throat.

He smiled, the corners of his lips drooping arrogantly. "Good evening, Kira," he said calmly.

"Good evening, Leo."

Lydia stared at them.

Kira stood at the door, her eyes holding his, her lips paralyzed. Galina Petrovna and Alexander Dimitrievitch stopped counting the saccharine.

Leo said: "Get your coat, Kira, and come on."

She said: "Yes, Leo," and took her coat off the hanger on the wall, moving like a somnambulist.

Lydia coughed discreetly. Leo looked at her. His glance brought a warm, wistful smile to Lydia's lips; it always did that to women; yet there was nothing in his eyes except that when he glanced at a woman his eyes told her that he was a man and she was a woman and he remembered it.

Lydia gathered courage to disregard the lack of an introduction; but she did not know how to start and she gazed helplessly at the handsomest male ever to appear in their anteroom, and she threw bluntly the question that was on her mind: "Where do you come from?"

"From jail," Leo answered with a courteous smile.

Kira had buttoned her coat. Her eyes were fixed on him, as if she did not know that others were present. He took her arm with the gesture of an owner, and they were gone.

"Well, of all the unmannered . . ." Galina Petrovna gasped, jumping up. But the door was closed.

*

To the sleigh driver outside, Leo gave an address.

"Where is that?" he repeated her question, his lips in her fur collar, as the sleigh jerked forward. "That's my home. . . . Yes, I got it back. They had it sealed since my father's arrest."

"When did you . . ."

"This afternoon. Went to the Institute to get your address; then—home and made a fire in the fireplace. It was like a grave, hadn't been heated for two months. It will be warm for us by now."

The door they entered bore the red seal of the G.P.U. The seal had been broken; two red scabs of wax remained, parting to let them enter.

They walked through a dark drawing room. The fireplace blazed, throwing a red glow on their feet and over their reflection in the mirror of a parquet floor. The apartment had been searched. There were papers strewn over the parquet, and overturned chairs. There were crystal vases on malachite stands; one vase was broken; the splinters sparkled on the floor in the darkness, little red flames dancing and winking through them, as if live coals had rolled out of the fireplace.

In Leo's bedroom, a light was burning, a single lamp with a silver shade, over a black onyx fireplace. A last blue flame quivered on dying coals and made a purple glow on the silver bedspread.

Leo threw his coat in a corner. He unbuttoned her coat and took it off; without a word, he unbuttoned her dress; she stood still and let him undress her.

He whispered into the little warm hollow under her chin: "It was torture. Waiting. Three days—and three nights."

He threw her across the bed. The purple glow quivered over her body. He did not undress. He did not turn out the light.

*

Kira looked at the ceiling; it was a silvery white far away. Light was coming in through the gray satin curtains. She sat up in bed, her breasts stiff in the cold. She said: "I think it's already tomorrow."

Leo was asleep, his head thrown back, one arm hanging over the edge of the bed. Her stockings were on the floor, her dress—on a bed post. Leo's eyelashes moved slowly; he looked up and said: "Good morning, Kira."

She stretched her arms and crossed them behind her head, and threw her head back, shaking the hair off her face, and said: "I don't think my family will like it. I think they'll throw me out."

"You're staying here."

"I'll go to say good-bye."

"Why go back at all?"

"I suppose I must tell them something."

"Well, go. But don't take long. I want you here."

*

They stood like three pillars, towering and silent, at the dining-room table. They had the red, puffed eyes of a sleepless night. Kira stood facing them, leaning against the door, indifferent and patient.

"Well?" said Galina Petrovna.

"Well what?" said Kira.

"You won't tell us again that you were at Irina's."

"No."

Galina Petrovna straightened her shoulders and her faded flannel bathrobe. "I don't know how far your foolish innocence can go. But do you realize that people might think that . . ."

"Certainly, I've slept with him."

The cry came from Lydia.

Galina Petrovna opened her mouth and closed it.

Alexander Dimitrievitch opened his mouth and it remained open.

Galina Petrovna's arm pointed at the door. "You'll leave my house," she said. "And you'll never come back."

"All right," said Kira.

"How could you? A daughter of mine! How can you stand there and stare at us? Have you no conception of the shame, the disgrace, the depraved . . ."

"We won't discuss that," said Kira.

"Did you stop to think it was a mortal sin? . . . Eighteen years old and a man from jail! . . . And the Church . . . for centuries . . . for your fathers and grandfathers . . . all our Saints have told us that no sin is lower! You hear about those things, but God, my own daughter! . . . The Saints who, for our sins . . ."

"May I take my things," Kira asked, "or do you want to keep them?"

"I don't want one single thing of yours left here! I don't want your breath in this room! I don't want your name mentioned in this house!"

Lydia was sobbing hysterically, her head in her arms on the table. "Tell her to go, Mother!" she cried through sobs like hiccoughs. "I can't stand it! Such women should not be allowed to live!"

"Get your things and hurry!" Galina Petrovna hissed. "We have but one daughter left! You little tramp! You filthy little street . . ."

Lydia was staring, with incredulous awe, at Kira's legs.

*

Leo opened the door and took the bundle she had wrapped in an old bed sheet.

"There are three rooms," he said. "You can rearrange things any way you want. Is it cold outside? Your cheeks are frozen."

"It's a little cold."

"I have some hot tea for you—in the drawing room."

He had set a table by the fireplace. Little red tongues flickered in the old silver. A crystal chandelier hung against the gray sky of a huge window. Across the street, a line stood at the door of a co-operative, heads bent; it was snowing.

Kira held her hands against the hot silver teapot and

rubbed them across her cheeks. She said: "I'll have to gather that glass. And sweep the floor. And . . ."

She stopped. She stood in the middle of the huge room. She spread her arms out, and threw her head back, and laughed. She laughed defiantly, rapturously, triumphantly. She cried: "Leo! . . ."

He held her. She looked up into his face and felt as if she were a priestess, her soul lost in the corners of a god's arrogant mouth; as if she were a priestess and a sacrificial offering, both and beyond both, shameless in her laughter, choking, something rising within her, too hard to bear.

Then his eyes looked at her, wide and dark, and he answered a thought they had not spoken: "Kira, think what we have against us."

She bent her head a little to one shoulder, her eyes round, her lips soft, her face serene and confident as a child's; she looked at the window where, in the slanting mist of snow, men stood in line, motionless, hopeless, broken. She shook her head.

"We'll fight it, Leo. Together. We'll fight all of it. The country. The century. The millions. We can stand it. We can do it."

He said without hope: "We'll try."

XI

The Revolution had come to a country that had lived three years of war. Three years and the Revolution had broken railroad tracks, and scorched fields, and blown smokestacks into showers of bricks, and sent men to stand in line with their old baskets, waiting at the little trickle of life still dripping from provision centers. Forests stood in a silence of snow, but in the cities wood was a luxury; kerosene was the only fuel to burn; there was only one device to burn kerosene. The gifts of the Revolution were to come. But one—and the first—had been granted; that which in countless cities countless stomachs had learned to beg for the fire of their sustenance to keep the fire of their souls, the first badge of a new life, the first ruler of a free country: the PRIMUS.

Kira knelt by the table and pumped the handle of the little brass burner that bore the words: "Genuine Primus. Made in Sweden." She watched the thin jet of kerosene filling a cup; then she struck a match and set fire to the kerosene in the cup, and pumped, and pumped, her eyes very attentive, the fire licking the black tubes with a tongue of soot, sending the odor of kerosene into her nostrils, until something hissed in the tubes and a wreath of blue flames sprang up, tense and hissing like a blow-torch. She set a pot of millet over the blue flames.

Then, kneeling by the fireplace, she gathered tiny logs, damp and slippery in her fingers, with an acrid odor of swamp and mildew; she opened the little door of the "Bourgeoise" and stacked the logs inside, and stuffed crumpled newspapers over them, and struck a match, blowing hard, bending low to the floor, her hair hanging over her eyes, whirls of smoke blowing back at her, rising high to the white ceiling, the crystals of the chandelier sparkling through gray fumes, gray ashes fluttering into her nostrils, catching on her eyelashes.

The "Bourgeoise" was a square iron box with long pipes that rose to the ceiling and turned at a straight angle into a hole cut over the fireplace. They had had to install a "Bourgeoise" in the drawing room, because they could not afford wood for the fireplace. The logs hissed in the box and, through the cracks in the corners, red flames danced and little whiffs of smoke fluttered once in a while, and the iron walls blazed a dull, overheated red, smelling of burned paint. The new little stoves were called "Bourgeoise," for they had been born in the homes of those who could not afford full-sized logs to heat the full-sized stoves in their once luxurious homes.

Admiral Kovalensky's apartment had seven rooms, but four of them had had to be rented long ago. Admiral Kovalensky had had a partition built across a hall, which cut them off from the tenants. Now Leo owned three rooms, the bathroom and the front door; the tenants owned four rooms, the back door and the kitchen. Kira cooked on the Primus and washed dishes in the bathroom. At times, she heard steps and voices behind the partition, and a cat meowing; three families lived there, but she never had to meet them.

When Leo got up in the morning, he found a table set in the dining room, with a snow-white cloth and hot tea steaming, and Kira flitting about the table, her cheeks glowing, her eyes laughing, light and unconcerned, as if these things had happened all by themselves. From their first day together in her new home, she had stated her ultimatum: "When I cook—you're not to see me. When you see me—you're not to know that I've been cooking."

She had always known that she was alive; she had never given much thought to the necessity of keeping alive. She found suddenly that that mere fact of keeping alive had grown into a complicated problem which required many hours of effort, the simple keeping alive which she had always haughtily, contemptuously taken for granted. She found that she could fight it only by keeping, fiercer than ever, that very contempt; the contempt which, once dropped, would bring all of life down to the little blue flame of the Primus slowly cooking millet for dinner. She found she could sacrifice all the hours the struggle required, if only it would never rise between Leo and her, if only life itself, the life that was Leo, were kept intact and untouched. Those wasted hours did not count; she would keep silent about them. She kept silent, a hidden spark in her eyes twinkling with the exhilaration of battle. It was a battle, the first blows of a vague, immense battle she could not name, but felt, the battle of the two of them, alone, against something huge and nameless, something rising, like a tide, around the walls of their house, something in those countless, weary steps on the pavements outside, in those lines at the doors of co-operatives, the something that invaded their home with the Primus and the "Bourgeoise," that held millet and damp logs and the hunger of millions of strange, distorted stomachs against two lives fighting for their right to their future.

After breakfast Leo buttoned his overcoat and asked: "Going to the Institute today?"

"Yes."

"Need change?"

"A little."

"Back for dinner?"

"Yes."

"I'll be back at six."

He went to the University, she went to the Institute. She ran, sliding along the frozen sidewalks, laughing at strangers, blowing at a red finger in the hole of her glove, jumping on tramways at full speed, disarming with a smile the husky conductoresses who growled: "You oughta be fined, citizen. You'll get your legs cut off some day."

She fidgeted at the lectures, and glanced at her neighbor's wristwatch, when she could find a neighbor with a wristwatch.

She was impatient to return home, as she had been when, a child in school, on her birthdays, she had known that presents awaited her at home. Nothing awaited her there now, but the Primus, and millet, and cabbage to chop for soup, and, when Leo returned, a voice that said behind the closed door: "I'm home," and she answered indifferently: "I'm busy," and laughed soundlessly, rapturously, in the soup steam.

After dinner he brought his books to the "Bourgeoise" and she brought hers. He was studying history and philosophy at the Petrograd State University. He also had a job. When, after two months, he returned to pick up the life his father's execution had broken, he found the job still awaiting him. He was valuable to the "Gossizdat"—the State Publishing House. In the evenings, over a fire crackling in the "Bourgeoise," he translated books from the English, German and French. He did not like the books. They were novels by foreign authors, in which a poor, honest worker was always sent to jail for stealing a loaf of bread to feed the starving mother of his pretty, young wife who had been raped by a capitalist and committed suicide thereafter, for which the all-powerful capitalist fired her husband from the factory, so that their child had to beg on the streets and was run over by the capitalist's limousine with sparkling fenders and a chauffeur in uniform.

But Leo could do the work at home, and it paid well, although when he received his money at the Gossizdat, it was accompanied by the remark: "We have deducted two and a half per cent as your contribution to the new Red Chemical Society of Proletarian Defense. This is in addition to the five per cent deduction for the Red Air Fleet, and three per cent for the Liquidation of Illiteracy, and five per cent for your Social Insurance, and . . ."

When Leo worked, Kira moved soundlessly through the room, or sat silently over her drafts and charts and blueprints, and never interrupted him.

Sometimes they were interrupted by the Upravdom. He came in, his hat on the back of his head, and demanded their share of the house collections for frozen pipes, stuffed chimneys, electric bulbs for the stairs—"and someone's swiped 'em again"—leaking roof, broken cellar steps, and the house's voluntary subscription to the Red Air Fleet.

When Kira and Leo spoke to each other, their words were brief, impersonal, their indifference exaggerated, their expressionless faces guarding a secret they both remembered.

But when they were alone in the gray and silver bedroom,

they laughed together; their eyes, and their lips, and their bodies met hungrily. She did not know how many times they awakened in the night; nor where she felt his lips, nor whether his lips hurt her. She heard nothing in the silence but the sound of his breath. She crushed her body against his; then she laughed lazily and hid her face in the curve of her arm, and listened to his breath on her neck, on the lashes of her closed eyes. Then she lay still, her teeth in a muscle of his arm, drunk on the smell of his skin.

*

Leo had no relatives in Petrograd.

His mother had died before the revolution. He was an only son. His father had stood over vast wheat fields under a blue sky dropping into dark forests far away, and thought that some day these fields and the forests would be laid at the feet of a dark-haired, dark-eyed boy, and in his heart there was a glow brighter than the sun in the ripe wheat.

Admiral Kovalensky seldom appeared at Court functions; the deck of a ship felt steadier under his feet than the parquet of the royal palace. But when he appeared, the eyes of stunned, eager, envious faces followed the woman who moved slowly on his arm. His wife, born a countess of an ancient name, had the beauty of centuries gathered, line by line, in her perfect body. When she died, Admiral Kovalensky noticed the first gray on his temples; but deep in his heart, in words he dared not utter, he thanked God that death had chosen to take his wife rather than his son.

Admiral Kovalensky had but one voice with which he issued commands to his sailors and spoke to his son. Some said he was too kind with his sailors, and some said he was too stern with his son. But he worshipped the boy whose name foreign tutors had changed to "Leo" from the Russian "Lev"; and he was helpless before the slightest flicker of a wish in the boy's dark, haughty eyes.

The tutors, and the servants, and the guests looked at Leo as they looked at the statue of Apollo in the Admiral's study, with the same reverent hopelessness they felt for the white marble of a distant age. Leo smiled; it was the only order he had to give, the only excuse for any of his orders.

When his young friends related, in whispers, the latest French stories, Leo quoted Spinoza and Nietzsche; he quoted Oscar Wilde at the prim gatherings of his stern aunt's Ladies' Charity Club; he described the superiority of Western culture over that of Russia to the austere, gray-haired diplomats, friends of his father, rabid Slavophiles, and he greeted them with an impudent foreign "Allo"; once, when sent to confession, he made the old priest blush by revelations, at eighteen, which that venerable dignitary had not learned in his seventy years.

Resenting the portrait of the Czar in his father's study and the Admiral's unflinching, unreasoning loyalty, Leo attended a secret meeting of young revolutionists. But when an unshaved young man made a speech about men's brotherhood and called him "comrade," Leo whistled "God Save the Czar," and went home.

He spent his first night in a woman's bed at the age of sixteen. When he met her in sparkling drawing rooms, his face remained courteously expressionless while he bent to kiss her hand; and her stately, gray-haired husband did not suspect what lessons the cold, disdainful beauty he owned was giving to that slender, dark-haired boy.

Many others followed. The Admiral had to interfere once, to remind Leo that his own career could be compromised if his son were seen again leaving, at dawn, the palace of a famous ballerina whose royal patron's name was mentioned in whispers.

The revolution found Admiral Kovalensky with black glasses over his unseeing eyes and St. George's ribbon in his lapel; it found Leo Kovalensky with a slow, contemptuous smile, and a swift gait, and in his hand a lost whip he had been born to carry.

*

For two weeks Kira had no visitors and paid no visits. Then she called on Irina.

Maria Petrovna opened the door and muttered a greeting, confused, frightened, stepping back uncertainly.

The family was gathered in the dining room around a newly installed "Bourgeoise." Irina jumped up with a glowing smile and kissed her cousin, which she had never done before.

"Kira, I'm so glad to see you! I thought you didn't want to see any of us any more."

Kira looked at a tall figure that had risen suddenly in a corner of the room. "How are you, Uncle Vasili?" she smiled.

Vasili Ivanovitch did not answer; he did not look at her; he turned and left the room.

A dark red flushed Irina's cheeks and she bit her lips. Maria

Petrovna twisted a handkerchief. Little Acia stared at Kira from behind a chair. Kira stood looking at the closed door.

"Those are nice felt boots you're wearing, Kira," Maria Petrovna muttered, although she had seen them many times. "Nice for cold weather. Such weather we're having!"

"Yes," said Kira, "it's snowing outside."

Victor came in, shuffling lazily in bedroom slippers, with a bathrobe thrown open over his pajamas; it was late afternoon, but his uncombed hair hung over red eyelids swollen by an interrupted sleep.

"Kira! What a pleasant surprise!" He bowed effusively, with outstretched hand. He held her hand and looked into her eyes with a bold, mocking stare as if the two of them shared a secret. "We didn't expect you, Kira. But then, so *many* unexpected things happen, these days." He did not apologize for his appearance; his careless swagger seemed to say that such an appearance could not be shocking to her. "Well, Kira, it isn't Comrade Taganov, after all? Oh, don't look surprised. One hears things at the Institute. However, Comrade Taganov is a useful friend to have. He has such an influential position. It's handy, in case you have any friends—in jail."

"Victor," said Irina, "you look like a swine and talk it. Go wash your face."

"When I'll take orders from you, my dear sister, you may tell the news to the papers."

"Children, children," Maria Petrovna sighed helplessly.

"I have to go," said Kira, "I just dropped in on my way to the Institute."

"Oh, Kira!" Irina begged. "Please don't go."

"I have to. I have a lecture to attend."

"Oh, hell!" said Irina. "They're all afraid to ask you, but I'll ask it before you go; what's *his* name?"

"Leo Kovalensky."

"Not the son of . . ." gasped Maria Petrovna.

"Yes," said Kira.

When the door closed after Kira, Vasili Ivanovitch came back. Maria Petrovna fumbled nervously for her nail buffer and busied herself with her manicure, avoiding his eyes. He added a log to the fire in the "Bourgeoise." He said nothing.

"Father, what has Kira . . ." Irina began.

"Irina, the subject is not open to argument."

"The world's all upside down," said Maria Petrovna and coughed.

Victor looked at his father with a bright glance of mutual

understanding. But Vasili Ivanovitch did not respond; he turned away deliberately; he had been avoiding Victor for many weeks.

Acia crouched in a corner behind the buffet, sniveling softly, hopelessly.

"Acia, come here," Vasili Ivanovitch ordered.

She waddled toward him slowly, cringing, looking down at the tip of her nose, wiping her nose with her collar.

"Acia, why are your school reports as bad as ever?" Vasili Ivanovitch asked.

Acia did not answer and sniffled.

"What is it that's happened to you again in arithmetic?"

"It's the tractors."

"The what?"

"The tractors. I didn't know."

"What didn't you know?"

"The Selskosoyuz had twelve tractors and they divided them among six poor villages and how many did each village get?"

"Acia, how much is twelve divided by six?"

Acia stared at her nose and sniffled.

"At your age, Irina was always first in her class," said Vasili Ivanovitch bitterly and turned away.

Acia ran to hide behind Maria Petrovna's chair.

Vasili Ivanovitch left the room. Victor followed him to the kitchen. If Vasili Ivanovitch heard his steps following, he paid no attention. It was dark in the kitchen; the window pane was broken and the window had been covered with boards. Three narrow slits of light added three bright stripes to the long cracks of the floor. Vasili Ivanovitch's shirts were piled under the sink. He bent slowly, and stuffed the shirts into a brass pan, and filled the pan with cold water. His big fist closed over a cake of bluish soap. Slowly, awkwardly, he rubbed the collar of a shirt. They had had to let the servant go; and Maria Petrovna was too weak to work.

"What's the matter, Father?" Victor asked.

Vasili Ivanovitch answered without turning: "You know it."

Victor protested too eagerly: "Why, Father, I haven't the slightest idea! Have I done anything wrong lately?"

"Did you see that girl?"

"Kira? Yes. Why?"

"I thought I could trust in her as in my own soul. But it got her. The revolution got her. And—you're next."

"But, Father . . ."

"In my days, a woman's virtue wasn't dragged in the gutter for every passerby."

"But Kira . . ."

"I suppose I'm old-fashioned. I was born that way and that's the way I'll die. But all of you young people are rotted before you're ripe. Socialism, Communism, Marxism, and to hell with decency!"

"But I, Father . . ."

"You. . . . It will get you in another way. I've been watching. Your friends for the last few weeks have been. . . . You came from a party this morning."

"But surely you don't object to a little party?"

"Who were the guests?"

"Some charming girls."

"To be sure. Who else?"

Victor flicked a speck of dust off his sleeve and said: "A Communist or two."

Vasili Ivanovitch said nothing.

"Father, let us be broad-minded. A little vodka with them can't hurt me. But it can *help* me—a lot."

Vasili Ivanovitch's voice was stern as a prophet's; bubbles gurgled in the cold water under his hands: "There are things with which one does not compromise."

Victor laughed cheerfully and slipped his arm around the powerful, stooped shoulders: "Come on, old man, you and I can understand things together. You wouldn't want me to sit down and fold my hands and surrender—because *they* hold the power, would you? Beat them at their own game—that's what I'm going to do. Diplomacy—that's the best philosophy of our days. It's the century of diplomacy. You can't object to that, can you? But you know me. It can't touch me. It won't get me. I'm still too much of a gentleman."

Vasili Ivanovitch turned to him. A crack of light from the boarded window fell across his face. The face was not that of a prophet; the eyes under the heavy white brows were weary, helpless; the smile was timid. The smile was an effort; so were the words: "I know it, son. I trust you. I suppose—well, you know best. But these are strange days. And you—well, Irina and you are all I have left."

*

Irina was the first visitor from Kira's old world to her new home. Leo bowed gracefully, diffidently, but Irina looked straight at him, grinned and said openly:

"Well, I like you. But then, I expected to like you. And I hope you like me, because I'm the only one of your in-laws that you'll see—for a long time. But they'll all question me about you, you can be sure."

They sat in the shadows of the large drawing room and talked about Rembrandt, whom Irina was studying; and about the new perfume Vava Milovskaia had received from a smuggler—real French perfume. Coty's and fifty million rubles a bottle—and Irina had stolen a drop of it on her handkerchief —and Maria Petrovna had cried, smelling it; and about the American movie Irina had seen, in which women wore spangled gowns without sleeves—and there had been a shot of New York at night—real skyscrapers, floors and floors of lighted windows on the black sky—and she had stayed through two shows to see that shot, but it had been so brief—just a flash—she would like to draw New York.

She had picked up a book from the table and was sketching busily on the back of its white paper cover, her pencil flashing. When she finished, she threw the book to Kira across the room. Kira looked at the drawing: it was a sketch of Leo— standing erect, full figure, naked.

"Irina!"

"You may show it to him."

Leo smiled, his lips drooping, looking at Irina inquisitively.

"That's the state that fits you best," she explained. "And don't tell me that my imagination has flattered you—because it hasn't. Clothes hide nothing from a—well, yes, an artist. Any objections?"

"Yes," said Leo, "this book belongs to the Gossizdat."

"Oh, well," she tore the cover off swiftly, "tell them you've used the cover for a revolutionary poster."

Alone with Kira for a moment, before leaving, Irina looked at her earnestly, curiously, almost timidly, and whispered: "Are you . . . happy?"

Kira said indifferently: "I'm happy."

*

Kira seldom spoke of what she thought; and more seldom— of what she felt. There was a man, however, for whom she made an exception, both exceptions. She made other exceptions for him as well, and wondered dimly why she made them. Communists awakened fear in her, a fear of her own degradation if she associated, talked or even looked at them; a fear not of their guns, their jails, their secret, watchful eyes

—but of something behind their furrowed foreheads, something they had—or, perhaps, it was something they didn't have, which made her feel as if she were alone in the presence of a beast, its jaws gaping, whom she could never force to understand. But she smiled confidently up at Andrei Taganov; and pressed tightly against the wall of an empty auditorium at the Institute, her eyes radiant, her smile timid and trusting, like a child appealing to a guiding hand, she said: "I'm happy, Andrei."

He had not seen her for many weeks. He smiled warmly, quietly, looking down into her eager eyes. "I've missed you, Kira."

"I've missed you, Andrei. I . . . I've been busy."

"I didn't want to call on you. I thought you would prefer it if I never called at your house."

"You see . . ." Then she stopped. She could not tell him. She could not bring him to her new home—to Leo's home. Andrei could be dangerous; he was a member of the G.P.U.; he had a duty to fulfill; it was best not to tempt that duty. So she said only: "Yes, Andrei, I'd rather you would never call . . . at my house."

"I won't. But will you be more regular about your lectures? So that I can see you once in a while—and hear you say that you're happy? I like to hear that."

"Andrei, have you ever been happy?"

"I've never been unhappy."

"Is that enough?"

"Well, I always know what I want. And when you know what you want—you go toward it. Sometimes you go very fast, and sometimes only an inch a year. Perhaps you feel happier when you go fast. I don't know. I've forgotten the difference long ago, because it really doesn't matter, so long as you move."

"And if you want something toward which you can't move?"

"I never did."

"And if—on your way—you find a barrier that you don't want to break?"

"I never have."

She remembered suddenly: "Andrei, you haven't even asked me why I'm happy."

"Does it make any difference—so long as you are?"

He held her two hands, thin and trusting, in his five strong fingers.

*

The first signs of spring in Petrograd were tears and smiles: the men smiled, the houses dropped the tears. High on the roofs, the snow was melting, gray with city dust like dirty cotton, brittle and shining like wet sugar, and twinkling drops dripped slowly, trickled in little gurgling brooks from the mouths of drain pipes, and across the sidewalks, and into the gutters, rocking gently cigarette stubs and sunflower-seed shells. Men walked out of the houses and breathed deeply, and smiled, and did not know why they smiled, until they looked up and saw that above the roofs the sky was a feeble, hesitant, incredulous blue, a very pale blue, as if a painter had washed the color off his brush in a huge tub of water, and the water held only a drop and a promise.

Icy mush crunched under galoshes and the sun made white sparks in the black rubber toes; sleigh-runners grunted, cutting brown ridges; a voice yelled: "Saccharine, citizens!"; drops tapped the sidewalks steadily, persistently, like a soft, distant machine gun; a voice yelled: "Violets, citizens!"

Pavel Syerov bought a pair of new boots. He blinked in the sun down at Comrade Sonia and bought her a hot, shiny cabbage cake from a woman on a corner. She chewed it, smiling. She said: "At three o'clock—giving lecture at the Komsomol on 'Our drive on the NEP front.' At five o'clock—giving talk at the Club of the Rabfac, on 'Proletarian Women and Illiteracy.' At seven—discussion at the Party Club on 'Spirit of the Collective.' Why don't you drop in at nine? Seems I never see you."

He said: "Sonia, old pal, can't take up your valuable time. People like you and me have no private life but that of our class duty."

Lines stood at the doors of shoe stores; the trade unions were giving out cards for the purchase of galoshes.

Maria Petrovna stayed in bed most of the day and watched the sun on the glass of a closed window, and hid her handkerchiefs from the sight of all.

Comrade Lenin had had a second stroke and had lost his power of speech. *Pravda* said: ". . . no higher sacrifice to the cause of the Proletariat than a leader burning out his will, health and body in the superhuman effort of the responsibility placed upon his shoulders by the Workers and Peasants."

Victor invited three Communist students to his room and they discussed the future of Proletarian Electrification. He let them out through the back door to avoid Vasili Ivanovitch.

England had treacherous designs on the Republic of Workers and Peasants. Teaching of English was prohibited in schools.

Acia had to study German, sniveling over the difference of "der," "die," "das," trying to remember what it was that our German class brothers had done at Rapallo.

The boss at the Gossizdat said: "The city proletariat is marching tomorrow in a demonstration of protest against France's policy in the Ruhr. I expect all our employees to take part, Comrade Kovalensky."

Leo said: "I'll stay in bed. I'm having a headache—tomorrow."

Vasili Ivanovitch sold the shade off the lamp in the drawing room; he kept the lamp because it was the last one.

In the dark, warm evenings, churches overflowed with bowed heads, incense and candle light. Lydia prayed for Holy Russia and for the dull fear in her heart.

Andrei took Kira to the Marinsky Theater and they saw Tchaikovsky's "Sleeping Beauty" ballet. He left her at the house on Moika and she took a tramway to her other home. A light snow melted on her face, like rain.

Leo asked: "How's your Communist boy friend?"

She asked: "Have you been lonely?"

He brushed the hair off her forehead and looked at her lips, in the deliberate tension of refusing himself a kiss. He answered: "I would like to say no. But you know it's yes."

His warm lips gathered the cold spring rain off hers.

The year 1923, like any other, had a spring.

XII

Kira had waited in line for three hours to get the bread at the Institute Co-operative. It was dark when she stepped down from the tramway, her loaf pressed tightly under her arm. At distant corners, lanterns made snakes of light wiggle in black puddles. She walked straight ahead, her shoes splashing through the water, kicking little icicles that clinked like glass. When she turned the corner of her street, a hurrying shadow whistled to her in the darkness.

"Allo!" called Irina's voice. "And whom do I remind you of when I say that?"

"Irina! What are you doing here at this hour?"

"Just left your house. Waited for you for an hour. Had given up hope."

"Well, come on back."

"No," said Irina, "maybe it's better if I tell you here. I . . . well, I came to tell you something. And . . . well, maybe Leo won't like it, and he's home, and . . ." Irina hesitated, which was unusual for her.

"What is it?"

"Kira, how's . . . how're your finances?"

"Why, splendid. Why do you ask that?"

"It's just . . . you see . . . well, if I'm too presumptuous, tell me to shut up. . . . Don't be angry. . . . You know I've never mentioned them before . . . but it's your family."

Kira peered in the darkness at Irina's worried face. "What about them?"

"They're desperate, Kira. Just desperate. I know Aunt Galina'd kill me if she knew I told you, but. . . . You see, the saccharine man got arrested as a speculator. They sent him to jail for six years. And your folks . . . well, what is there left to do? You know. Last week father brought them a pound of millet. If we only could. . . . But you know how things are with us. Mother so sick. And nothing much left for the Alexandrovsky market but the wallpaper. I don't think they have a thing in the house—your folks. I thought maybe you . . . maybe you would like to know."

"Here," said Kira, "take this bread. We don't need it. We'll buy some from a private store. Tell them you've found, borrowed or stolen it, or anything. But don't tell them it's from me."

*

On the following day, Galina Petrovna rang the door bell. Kira was not at home. Leo opened the door and bowed graciously.

"I believe it is my . . . mother-in-law?" he asked.

"That's what it would like to be," Galina Petrovna stated. His smile disarmed her; it was infectious; she smiled.

When Kira came in, there were tears. Galina Petrovna crushed her in her arms, before a word was said, and sobbed: "Kira, my child! . . . . My dear child! . . . God forgive us our sins! . . . These are hard days. . . . These are very hard days. . . . After all, who are we to judge? . . . Everything's gone to pieces. . . . What difference does it all make? If we can just forget, and pull the pieces together, and . . . God show us the way. We've lost it. . . ."

When she released Kira, and powdered her nose from a little envelope full of potato flour, she muttered: "About that bread, Kira. We didn't use it all. I hid it. I was afraid—maybe you need it yourself. I'll bring it back if you do. We took only a small slice; your father was so hungry."

"Irina talks too much," said Kira. "We don't need the bread, Mother. Don't worry. Keep it."

"You must come and see us," said Galina Petrovna. "Both of you. Let by-gones be by-gones. Of course, I don't see why you two don't get . . . Oh, well, it's your business. Things aren't what they were ten years ago. . . . You must visit us, Leo—I may call you Leo, may I not? Lydia is so anxious to meet you."

*

One could buy bread in the private stores. But the price made Kira hesitate. "Let's go to a railroad station," she said to Leo.

Railroad terminals were the cheapest and most dangerous markets of the city. There were strict rules against private "speculators" who smuggled food from the villages. But the speculators in ragged overcoats dared long rides on roofs and buffers, miles on foot down slimy mud roads, lice and typhus on trains, and—on return—the vigilance of government agents. Food slinked into the city in dusty boots, in the linings of vermin-infested coats, in bundles of soiled underwear. The starved city awaited every train. After its arrival, in the dark side streets around the depot, crystal goblets and lace chemisettes were exchanged furtively for hunks of lard and mouldy sacks of flour.

Arm in arm, Kira and Leo walked to the Nikolaevsky station. Drops tapped the sidewalk. The sun dripped to the sidewalk with every drop. Leo bought a bunch of violets on a corner. He pinned it to Kira's shoulder, a purple tuft, young and fragrant on her old black coat. She smiled happily and kicked an icicle in a puddle, splashing water at the passersby, laughing.

The train had arrived. They made their way through an eager crowd that pushed them aside and drove them forward, and stuck elbows into their stomachs, and heels on their toes.

Soldiers watched the descending passengers, silent, alert, suspicious.

A man stepped down from the train. He had a peculiar nose; it was so short and turned up so sharply that his two wide, slanting nostrils were almost vertical; under the nostrils there was a wide space and a heavy mouth. His stomach shivered like gelatin as he stepped down. His coat seemed too ragged, his boots too dirty.

Soldiers seized his arms. They were going to search him. He whined softly: "Comrades, brothers! So help me God, you're wrong. I'm nothing but a poor peasant, brothers, nothing but the poorest peasant. Never heard of speculating. But I'm a responsible citizen, too. I'll tell you something. If you let me go, I'll tell you something."

"What can you tell, you son of a bitch?"

"See that woman there? She's a speculator. I know. I'll tell you where she's hiding food. I seen her."

Strong hands seized the woman. Her arms were like a skeleton's in the soldiers' fists; gray hair hung over her eyes from under an old hat with a black feather; the shawl held on her sunken chest by an ancient mosaic pin shook silently, convulsively, a thin, nervous shudder, like that of a window at the distant sound of an explosion. She moaned, showing three yellow teeth in a dark mouth: "Comrades. . . . It's my grandson. . . . I wasn't going to sell. . . . It's for my grandson. . . . Please, let me go, comrades . . . my grandson—he's got the scurvy. . . . Has to eat. . . . Please, comrades. . . . The scurvy. . . . Please. . . ."

The soldiers dragged her away. Her hat was knocked off. They did not stop to pick it up. Someone stepped on the black feather.

The man with the vertical nostrils watched them go. His wide red lips grinned.

Then he turned and saw Kira looking at him. He winked mysteriously, in understanding, and pointed with a jerk of his head to the exit. He went out; Kira and Leo followed him, puzzled.

In a dark alley by the station, he looked around cautiously, winked again and opened his coat. The ragged coat had a smooth lining of heavy, expensive fur, with the suffocating odor of carnation oil used by all travelers of means as protection against lice on trains. He unfastened some unseen hooks in the depth of the fur. His arm disappeared in the lining and returned with a loaf of bread and a smoked ham.

He smiled. His lips and the lower part of his face smiled; the upper part—the short nose, the light, narrow eyes—remained strangely immobile, as if paralyzed.

"Here you are, citizens," he said boastfully. "Bread, ham, anything you wish. No trouble. We know our business."

The next moment, Kira was running down the street, fleeing wildly, senselessly from a feeling she could not explain.

*

"Just a little party, Kira darling," said Vava Milovskaia over the telephone. "Saturday night. . . . Shall we say about ten o'clock? . . . And you'll bring Leo Kovalensky, of course? I'm simply dying to meet him. . . . Oh, just fifteen or twenty people. . . . And Kira, here's something a little difficult: I'm inviting Lydia, and . . . could you bring a boy for her? You see, I have just so many boys and girls on my list, and they're all in couples, and—well, boys are so hard to get nowadays . . . and . . . well, you know how it is, and I thought maybe you knew someone—anyone. . . ."

"Anyone? Do you care if he's a Communist?"

"A Communist? How thrilling! Is he good-looking? . . . Certainly, bring him. . . . We're going to dance. . . . And we're going to have refreshments. Yes, food. Oh, yes. . . . And, oh, Kira, I'm asking every guest to bring one log of wood. One apiece. . . . To heat the drawing room. It's so large we couldn't affo . . . You don't mind? . . . So sweet of you. See you Saturday night."

Parties were rare in Petrograd in 1923. It was Kira's first. She decided to invite Andrei. She was a little tired of the deception, a little bewildered that it had gone so far. Leo knew all about Andrei; Andrei knew nothing about Leo. She had told Leo of her friendship; he had not objected; he smiled disdainfully when she spoke of Andrei, and inquired about her "Communist boy friend." Andrei knew no one in Kira's circle and no gossip had reached him. He never asked questions. He kept his promise and never called on her. They met at the Institute. They talked of mankind, and its future, and its leaders; they talked of ballet, tramways and atheism. By a silent agreement, they never spoke of Soviet Russia. It was as if an abyss separated them, but their hands and their spirits were strong enough to clasp over the abyss.

The grim lines of his tanned face were like the effigy of a medieval saint; from the age of the Crusades he had inherited the ruthlessness, the devotion, and also the austere chastity. She could not speak of love to him; she could not think of love in his presence; not because she feared a stern condemnation; but because she feared his sublime indifference.

She did not want to conceal it forever. The two men had to meet. She feared that meeting, a little. She remembered that one of them was the son of an executed father; the other one—a member of the G.P.U. Vava's party was a convenient occasion: the two would meet; she would watch their reactions; then, perhaps, she could bring Andrei to her house; and if, at the party, he heard the truth about her—well, she thought, so much the better.

Meeting him in the library of the Institute, she asked: "Andrei, would a bourgeois party frighten you?"

"Not if you'll be there to protect me—if that's an invitation."

"I'll be there. And it is an invitation. Saturday night. Lydia and I are going. And two men. You're one of them."

"Fine—if Lydia is not too afraid of me."

"The other one—is Leo Kovalensky."

"Oh."

"I *didn't* know his address *then,* Andrei."

"I *didn't* ask you, Kira. And it does not matter."

"Call for us at nine-thirty, at the house on Moika."

"I remember your address."

"My . . . oh, yes, of course."

*

Vava Milovskaia met her guests in the anteroom.

Her smile was radiant; her black eyes and black curls sparkled like the patent leather of the narrow belt around her slim waistline; and the delicate patent leather flowers on her shoulder—the latest Soviet fashion—sparkled like her eyes.

The guests entered, logs of wood under their arms. A tall, stern maid in black, with stiff white apron and cap, silently received the logs.

"Kira! Lydia! Darlings! So glad! How are you?" Vava fluttered.

"I've heard so much about you, Leo, that I'm really frightened," she acknowledged the introduction, her hand in Leo's; even Lydia understood Leo's answering glance; as to Vava, she caught her breath and stepped back a little, and looked at Kira. But Kira paid no attention.

To Andrei, Vava said: "So you're a Communist? I think that's charming. I've always said that Communists were just like other people."

The large drawing room had not been heated all winter. The fire had just been lit. A fretful smoke struggled up the chimney, escaping back into the room once in a while. A gray fog hung over the neatly polished mirrors, the freshly dusted tables proudly displaying careful rows of worthless knick-knacks; a damp odor of mildewed wood rose to destroy the painful dignity of a room too obviously prepared for guests.

The guests sat huddled in corners, shivering under old shawls and sweaters, tense and self-conscious and too carelessly non-chalant in their old best clothes. They kept their arms pressed to their sides to hide the holes in their armpits; elbows motionless on their knees—to hide rubbed patches; feet deep under chairs —to hide worn felt boots. They smiled vacantly without purpose, laughed too loudly at nothing in particular, timid and uncomfortable and guiltily conscious of a forbidden purpose, the forgotten purpose of gaiety. They eyed the fireplace wistfully, longing and reluctant to seize upon the best seats by the fire. Everybody was cold and everybody wanted desperately to be gay.

The only one whose bright, loud gaiety seemed effortless was Victor. His wide stride bounced from group to group, offering the tonic of a ringing voice and a resplendent smile: "This way, ladies and gentlemen. . . . Move over to this lovely fire. We'll be warm in an instant. . . . Ah! my charming cousins, Kira and Lydia! . . . Delighted, Comrade Taganov, delighted! . . . Here's a lovely armchair, Lydia darling, I saved it specially for you. . . . Rita dear, you remind me of the heroine in the new Smirnov novel. Read it? Magnificent! Literature emancipated from outworn conceptions of form. A new woman—the free woman of the future. . . . Comrade Taganov, that project for the electrification of the entire R.S.F.S.R. is the most stupendous undertaking in the history of mankind. When we consider the amount of electrical power per citizen to be found in our natural resources. . . . Vava, these patent leather flowers are the latest word in feminine elegance. I understand that the most famous couturier of Paris has . . . I quite agree with you, Boris. Schopenhauer's pessimism is entirely outmoded in the face of the healthy, practical philosophical conceptions of the rising proletariat and, no matter what our personal political convictions may be, we must all be objective enough to agree that the proletariat *is* the ruling class of the future. . . ."

With perfect assurance, Victor assumed the role of host. Vava's dark eyes, that rested on him every time she flitted through the room, sanctioned his right by a long, proud, adoring glance. She flew into the anteroom at every sound of the door bell, returning with a couple that smiled shyly, rubbing their cold hands, hiding the worn seams of their clothes. The solemn maid followed silently, carrying the logs as if she were serving a dish, and piled them neatly by the fireplace.

Kolya Smiatkin, a blond, chubby young man with a pleasant smile, who was filing clerk in the Tobacco Trust, said timidly: "They say . . . er . . . I heard . . . I'm afraid there's going to be a reduction of staffs in our office—next month. Everybody's whispering about it. Maybe I'll get fired this time. Maybe not. Makes you feel sort of uncomfortable."

A tall gentleman with a gold pince-nez and the intense eyes of an undernourished philosopher said lugubriously: "I have an excellent job in the archives. Bread almost every week. Only I'm afraid there's a woman after the job—a Communist's mistress—and . . ."

Someone nudged him and pointed at Andrei, who stood by the fireplace, smoking. The tall gentleman coughed and looked uncomfortable.

Rita Eksler was the only woman in the room who smoked. She lay stretched on a davenport, her legs high on its arm, her skirt high above her knees, red bangs low over pale green eyes, painted lips puckered insolently around a cigarette. Many things were whispered about her. Her parents had been killed in the revolution. She had married a commander of the Red Army and divorced him two months later. She was homely and used her homeliness with such skillful, audacious emphasis that the most beautiful girls feared her competition.

She stretched lazily and said, her voice slow, husky: "I've heard something amusing. A boy friend of mine wrote from Berlin . . ." All eyes turned to her, eagerly, reverently. ". . . and he tells me they have cafés in Berlin that are open all night—*all night*, elegant, eh?—they call them 'Nacht Local.' And in a famous, very naughty 'Nacht Local,' a famous dancer —Rikki Rey—danced with sixteen girls and with nothing on. I mean, positively nothing. So she got arrested. And the next night, she and her girls appeared in a military number, and they wore little chiffon trunks, two gold strings crossed over their breasts, and huge fur hats. And they were considered dressed. Elegant, eh?"

She laughed huskily at the awed crowd, but her eyes were on Leo; they had been on Leo ever since he had entered the room. Leo's answer was a straight, mocking glance of understanding that insulted and encouraged Rita at the same time.

An anemic girl who sat sulkily in a corner, miserably hiding her feet and heavy felt boots, said with a dull stare, incredulous of her own words: "Abroad . . . I heard . . . they say they don't have provision cards, or co-operatives, or anything, you just go into a store just when you feel like it and just buy bread or potatoes or anything, even sugar. Me, I don't believe it myself."

"And they say you buy your clothes without a trade-union order—abroad."

"We have no future," said the philosopher with the gold pince-nez. "We have lost it in materialistic pursuits. Russia's destiny has ever been of the spirit. Holy Russia has lost her God and her Soul."

"Did you hear about poor Mitya Vessiolkin? He tried to jump off a moving tramway, and he fell under, but he was lucky: just one hand cut off."

"The West," said Victor, "has no inner significance. The old civilization is doomed. It is filling new forms with a worn-out content that can no longer satisfy anyone. We may suffer hardships, but we are building something new. On our side—we have the future."

"I have a cold," said the anemic girl. "Mother got a union order for galoshes and there were none my size and we lost our turn and we have to wait three months and I got a cold."

"Vera Borodina had her Primus explode on her. And she's blind. And her face—you'd think she'd been in the war."

"I bought myself a pair of galoshes in a private store," Kolya Smiatkin said with a touch of pride. "And now I'm afraid but what I was too hasty. What with the reductions of staffs and. . . ."

"Vava, may I add wood to the fire? It's still rather . . . cold."

"The trouble with these days," said Lydia, "is that there's no spiritual enlightenment. People have forgotten the simple faith."

"We had a reduction of staffs last month, but they didn't touch me. I'm socially active. I'm teaching a class of illiterates —free—an hour every evening—as club duty—and they know I'm a conscientious citizen."

"I'm vice-secretary of our club library," said Kolya Smiatkin. "Takes three evenings a week—and no pay—but that kept me through the last reduction. But this time, I'm afraid it's me or another guy—and the other guy, he's vice-secretary of two libraries."

"When we have a reduction of staffs," said the anemic girl, "I'm afraid they're going to throw out all the wives or husbands whose mates have employment. And Misha has such a fine job with the Food Trust. So we're thinking . . . I'm afraid we'll have to get divorced. Oh, that's nothing. We can still go on living together. It's being done."

"My career is my duty to society," said Victor. "I have selected engineering as the profession most needed by our great republic."

He threw a glance at the fireplace to make sure that Andrei had heard.

"I'm studying philosophy," said Leo, "because it's a science that the proletariat of the R.S.F.S.R. does not need at all."

"Some philosophers," said Andrei slowly, in the midst of a sudden, stunned silence, "may need the proletariat of the R.S.F.S.R."

"Maybe," said Leo. "And maybe I'll escape abroad, and sell my services to the biggest exploiter of a millionaire—and have an affair with his beautiful wife."

"Without a doubt," said Victor, "you'll succeed in *that.*"

"Really," Vava said hastily, "I think it's still cold and we had better dance. Lydia darling?"

She threw a cajoling glance of inquiry at Lydia. Lydia sighed with resignation, rose and took the seat at the upright piano. She was the only accomplished musician in the crowd. She had a suspicion about the reason of her popularity at all the rare parties that were still being given. She rubbed her cold fingers and struck the piano keys with ferocious determination. She played "John Gray."

Historians will write of the "Internationale" as the great anthem of the revolution. But the cities of the revolution had their own hymn. In days to come, the men of Petrograd will remember those years of hunger and struggle and hope—to the convulsive rhythm of "John Gray."

It was called a fox-trot. It had a tune and a rhythm such as those of the new dances far across the border, abroad. It had very foreign lyrics about a very foreign John Gray whose sweetheart Kitty spurned his love for fear of having children, as she told him plainly. Petrograd had known sweeping epidemics of cholera; it had known epidemics of typhus, which were worse; the worst of its epidemics was that of "John Gray."

Men stood in line at the co-operatives—and whistled "John Gray." At the recreation hour in schools, young couples danced in the big hall, and an obliging pupil played "John Gray." Men hung on the steps of speeding tramways, humming desperately "John Gray." Workers' clubs listened attentively to a lecture on Marxism, then relaxed while a comrade showed his skill on a piano out of tune, playing "John Gray."

Its gaiety was sad; its abrupt rhythm was hysterical; its frivolity was a plea, a moan for that which existed somewhere, forever out of reach. Through winter nights red flags whistled in the snowdrifts and the city prayed hopelessly with the short, sharp notes of "John Gray."

Lydia played fiercely. Couples shuffled slowly across the drawing room in an old-fashioned two-step. Irina, who had no voice, sang the words, half singing, half coughing them out, in a husky moan, as she had heard a German singer do in vaudeville:

> *"John Gray*
> *Was brave and daring,*
> *Kitty*
> *Was very pretty.*
> *Wildly*
> *John fell in love with*
> *Kitty.*
> *Passion's*
> *Hard to restrain—*
> *He made*
> *His feelings plain,*
> *But Kat*
> *Said 'No' to that!"*

Kira danced in Leo's arms. He whispered, looking down at her: "We would dance—like this—in a place of champagne glasses—and spangled gowns—and bare arms—a place called 'Nacht Local.' "

She closed her eyes, and the strong body that led her expertly, imperiously, seemed to carry her to that other world she had seen, long ago, by a dark river that murmured the "Song of Broken Glass."

Vava undertook to teach Andrei to dance and dragged him out into the crowd. He followed obediently, smiling, like a tiger that could not hurt a kitten. He was not a bad pupil, she thought. She felt very brave, very daring at the thought that she was actually corrupting a stern Communist. She regretted that the corruption could go no further. It was annoying to meet a man in whom her beauty awakened no response, who looked at her with calm, steady eyes, as he looked at Lydia, as he looked at the anemic girl in the felt boots.

Lydia played "Destiny Waltz." Andrei asked Kira to dance. Leo glanced at him with his cold smile, but said nothing and walked away from them.

"Vava's a good teacher," Kira whispered, as Andrei whirled her into the crowd, "but hold me tighter. Oh, yes, much tighter."

"Destiny Waltz" was slow and soft; it stopped for a breathless second once in a while and swung into rhythm again, slowly, rocking a little, as if expecting soft, billowing satin skirts to murmur gently in answer, in a ball-room such as did not exist any longer.

Kira looked up into a grave face that was smiling half ironically, half shyly. She pressed her head to his breast; her eyes flashed up at him one swift glance, like a spark; then she jerked her head back; her tousled hair caught on a button of his coat and a few strands remained entwined around the button.

Andrei felt a very soft silk in his arms and, under the silk, a very slender body. He looked down at her open collar and saw a faint shadow parting the flesh. He did not look down again.

Leo danced with Rita, their eyes meeting in a silent understanding, her body pressed to his expertly, professionally. Vava whirled, smiling proudly at every couple she passed, her hand resting triumphantly, possessively on Victor's shoulder. Kolya Smiatkin watched Vava timidly, wistfully; he was afraid to ask her for a dance: he was shorter than Vava. He knew that everybody knew of his hopeless, doggish devotion to her and that they laughed at him; he could not help it. The anemic girl's felt boots made the chandelier tremble, its fringe of glass beads ringing softly; once she stepped on Vava's sparkling patent leather pump. A thoughtful guest added a log to the fire; it hissed and smoked; someone had not been conscientious and had brought a damp log.

At two A.M. Vava's mother stuck a timid, pallid face through the crack of a half-opened door and asked the guests if they would "like to have some refreshments." The eager rush to the dining room cut a waltz short in the middle.

In the dining room, a long table stood frozen in a solemn

splendor of white and silver, crystal sparkling in a blinding light, delicate forks laid out with formal precision. Costly dishes of milky-white porcelain offered slices of black bread with a suspicion of butter, slices of dried fish, potato-skin cookies, sauerkraut and tea with sticky brown candy instead of sugar.

Vava's mother smiled hospitably: "Please take one of everything. Don't be afraid. There's enough. I've counted them."

Vava's father sat, beaming broadly, at the head of the table. He was a doctor who specialized in gynecology. He had not been successful before the revolution; after the revolution, two facts had helped his rise: the fact that, as a doctor, he belonged to the "Free Professions" and was not considered an exploiter, and the fact that he performed certain not strictly legal operations. Within a couple of years he had found himself suddenly the most prosperous member of his former circle and of many circles above.

He sat, his two fists holding his lapels, leaning back comfortably, his round stomach bulging under a heavy gold chain, costly watch-charms tinkling and shuddering with the muscles of his stomach. His narrow eyes disappeared in the thick folds of a white flesh. He smiled warmly at his guests; he was very proud of the rare, enviable position of host, a host who could afford to offer food; he relished the feeling of a patron and benefactor to the children of those before whom he had bowed in the old days, the children of the industrial magnate Argounov, of Admiral Kovalensky. He made a mental note to donate some more to the Red Air Fleet in the morning.

His smile widened when the maid entered sullenly, carrying a silver tray with six bottles of rare old wine—a token of gratitude from one of his influential patients. He poured, filling crystal glasses, chuckling amiably: "Good old stuff. Real pre-war stuff. Bet you kids never tasted anything like it." The glasses were passed down the long table, from hand to hand.

Kira sat between Leo and Andrei. Andrei raised his glass gravely, steadily, like a warrior. "Your health, Kira," he said.

Leo raised his glass lightly, gracefully, like a diplomat at a foreign bar. "Since you're toasted by my class superior, Kira," he said, "I'll drink to our charming hostess."

Vava answered with a warm, grateful smile. Leo raised his glass to her and drank looking at Rita.

When they returned to the drawing room, the dying fire had to be revived. Lydia played again. A few couples danced lazily. Vava sang a song about a dead lady whose fingers smelt of

incense. Kolya Smiatkin gave an impersonation of a drunk.
Victor told anecdotes. Others followed his example; some of
the anecdotes were political; cautious glances were thrown at
Andrei; words stopped halfway and the teller stammered,
blushing.

At five A.M. everyone was exhausted; but no one could go
home before daylight; it was too dangerous. The city militia
was helpless against burglars and holdup men. No citizen dared
to cross a street after midnight.

Doctor Milovsky and his wife retired, leaving the young
guests to await the dawn. The stern, starched maid dragged
into the drawing room mattresses borrowed from all the neighbors. The mattresses were lined up against the wall. The maid
left. Vava turned out the light.

The guests settled down comfortably, in couples. Nothing
pierced the darkness but a last glow in the fireplace, a few red
dots of cigarettes, a few whispers, a few suspicious sounds that
were not whispers. The unwritten law of parties dictated that
no one should be too curious in these last, weary and most ex-
citing hours of a party.

Kira felt Andrei's hand on her arm. "I think they have a
balcony," he whispered. "Let's go out."

Following him, Kira heard a sigh and something that sounded like a very passionate kiss from the corner where Vava
nestled in Victor's arms.

It was cold on the balcony. The street lay silent like a tunnel
under a vault slowly turning gray. Frozen puddles looked like
splinters of glass panes on the pavement. Windows looked like
puddles frozen on the walls. A militia-man leaned against a
lamp post. A flag bent over the street. The flag did not move;
neither did the man.

"It's funny," said Andrei, "I never thought I would, but I
do like dancing."

"Andrei, I'm angry at you."

"Why?"

"This is the second time that you haven't noticed my best
dress."

"It's beautiful."

The door behind them squealed on its rusty hinges. Leo
stepped out on the balcony, a cigarette hanging in the corner
of his mouth. He asked: "Is Kira nationalized state property,
too?"

Andrei answered slowly: "Sometimes I think it would be
better for her if she were."

"Well, until the Party passes the proper resolution," said Leo, "she isn't."

They returned into the warm darkness of the drawing room. Leo drew Kira down on the mattress by his side; he said nothing; she drowsed, her head on his shoulder. Rita moved away with a little shrug. Andrei stood by the balcony door, smoking.

At eight A.M. the window curtains were pulled aside. A dull white sky spread over the roofs, like soapy water. Vava muttered good-byes to her guests at the door; she swayed a little, weary circles under her eyes, one dark lock hanging to the tip of her nose, her lipstick smeared over her chin. The guests divided into groups, to walk together in clusters as long as possible.

In the cold dawn, ice breaking under their feet, Andrei took Kira aside for a moment. He pointed at Leo, who was helping Lydia over a puddle a few steps ahead of them. "Do you see him often?" he asked.

The question told her that he had not learned the truth; the tone of the question—that she would not tell him.

Lights burned in the windows of barred, padlocked shops. Many doors carried a notice:

"Comrade burglars, please don't bother. There's nothing inside."

XIII

In the summer, Petrograd was a furnace.

The wooden bricks of the pavements cracked into black gashes, dry as an empty river bed. The walls seemed to breathe of fever and the roofs smelt of burned paint. Through eyes hazy in a white glare, men looked hopelessly for a tree in the city of stone. When they found a tree, they turned away: its motionless leaves were gray with parched dust. Hair stuck to foreheads. Horses shook flies off their foaming nostrils. The Neva lay still; little drops of fire played lazily on the water, like clusters of spangles, and made the men on the bridges feel hotter.

Whenever they could, Kira and Leo went away for a day in the country.

They walked hand in hand in the stripes of sun and pine shadows. Like columns of dark brick, like sinewy bodies sunburnt to bronze and peeling in strips of light bark, the pines guarded the road and dropped, jealously, through a heavy tangle of malachite, a few rays, a few strips of soft blue. On the green slopes of ditches, little purple dots of violets bent to a patch of yellow sand; and only the crystal luster of the sand showed water over it. Kira took off her shoes and stockings. Soft dust and pine needles between her toes, she kicked the little black balls of fallen pine cones. Leo swung her slippers at the end of a dry branch, his white shirt unbuttoned, his sleeves rolled above his elbows. Her bare feet pattered over the boards of an old bridge. Through the wide cracks, she saw sparks swimming like fish scales down the stream and polliwogs wiggling in swarms of little black commas.

They sat alone in a meadow. Tall grass rose like a wall around them, over their heads; a hot blue sky descended to the sharp, green tips; the sky seemed to smell of clover. A cricket droned like an electric engine. She sat on the ground; Leo lay stretched, his head on her lap. He chewed the end of a long grass stem; the movement of his hand, holding it, had the perfection of a foreign cigarette ad. Once in a while, she bent down to kiss him.

They sat on a huge tree root over a river. The spreading stars of ferns on the slope below looked like a jungle of dwarf palms. The white trunk of a birch tree sparkled in the sun, its leaves like a waterfall that streamed down, green drops remaining suspended in the air, trembling, turning silver and white and green again, dropping once in a while to be swept away by the current. Kira leaped over the rocks, roots and ferns as swift, agile and joyous as an animal. Leo watched her. Her movements were sharp, angular, inexpressibly graceful in that contradiction of all grace, not the soft, fluent movements of a woman, but the broken, jerking, precise, geometrical movements of a futuristic dancer. He watched her perched on a dead tree trunk, looking down into the water, her hands at straight angles to her arms, her elbows at straight angles to her body, her body at a straight angle to her legs, a wild, broken little figure, tense, living, like a lightning in shape. Then he sprang up, and ran after her, and held her, breaking the straight angles into a straight line crushed against him. The dead trunk hanging over the stream creaked perilously. She laughed, that strange laughter of hers which was too joyous to be gay, a laughter that held a challenge, and triumph, and ecstasy. Her lips were moist, glistening.

*

When they returned to the city, the stifling dusk met them with posters, and banners, and headlines, four letters flaming over the streets:

U.S.S.R.

The country had a new name and a new constitution. The All-Union Congress of Soviets had just decided so. Banners said:

THE UNION OF SOCIALIST SOVIET REPUBLICS IS THE KERNEL FOR THE FUTURE GROWTH OF A WORLD STATE

Demonstrations marched through the hot, dusty streets, red kerchiefs mopping sweating foreheads.

OUR POWER IS IN THE TIGHT WELDING OF THE COLLECTIVE!

A column of children, drums beating, marched into the sunset: a layer of bare legs, and a layer of blue trunks, and a layer of white shirts, and a layer of red ties; the kindergarten of the Party, the "Pioneers." Their high, young voices sang:

> *"To the greedy bourgeois' sorrow*
> *We shall light our fire tomorrow,*
> *Our world fire of blood. . . ."*

*

Once, Kira and Leo attempted to spend a night in the country.

"Certainly," said the landlady. "Certainly, citizens, I can let you have a room for the night. But first you must get a certificate from your Upravdom as to where you live in the city, and a permit from your militia department, and then you must bring me your labor books, and I must register them with our Soviet here, and our militia department, and get a permit for you as transient guests, and there's a tax to pay, and then you can have the room."

They stayed in the city.

*

Galina Petrovna had made a bold decision and taken a job. She taught sewing in a school for workers' children. She rocked through dusty miles in a tramway across the city to the factory district; she watched little grimy hands fashioning shirts and aprons and, sometimes, letters on a red banner; she talked of the importance of needlework and of the Soviet government's constructive policy in the field of education.

Alexander Dimitrievitch slept most of the day. When he was awake, he played solitaire on the ironing board in the kitchen—and mixed painstakingly an imitation milk of water, starch and saccharine for Plutarch, the cat he had found in a gutter.

When Kira and Leo came to visit them, there was nothing to talk about. Galina Petrovna spoke too shrilly and too fast —about the education of the masses and the sacred calling of the intelligentsia in serving their less enlightened brothers. Lydia talked about the things of the spirit. Alexander Dimitrievitch said nothing. Galina Petrovna had long since dropped all hints related to the institution of marriage. Only Lydia was flustered when Leo spoke to her; she blushed, embarrassed and thrilled.

Kira visited them because Alexander Dimitrievitch watched her silently when she came, with a feeble shadow of a smile as if, had it not been for a dull haze suddenly grown between him and the life around him, he would have been glad to see her.

*

Kira sat on a window sill and watched the first autumn rain on the sidewalk. Glass bubbles sprang up in an ink puddle, a ring around each bubble, and floated for a brief second, and burst helplessly like little volcanoes. Rain drummed dully against all the pavements of the city; it sounded like the distant purring of a slow engine with just one thin trickle of water through the rumble, like a faucet leaking somewhere close by.

One single figure walked in the street below. An old collar raised between hunched shoulders, hands in pockets, arms pressed tightly to his sides, he walked away—a lonely shadow, swaying a little—into the city of glistening roofs under a fog of thin, slanting rain.

Kira did not turn on the light. Leo found her in the darkness by the window. He pressed his cheek to hers and asked: "What's the matter?"

She said softly: "Nothing. Just winter coming. A new year starting."

"You're not afraid, are you, Kira? We've stood it so far."

"No," said Kira. "I'm not afraid."

*

The new year was started by the Upravdom.

"It's like this, Citizen Kovalensky," he said, shifting from foot to foot, crumpling his cap in both hands and avoiding Leo's eyes. "It's on account of the Domicile Norm. There's a law about as how it's illegal for two citizens to have three rooms, on account of overcrowding conditions seeing as there are too many people in the city, and there are overcrowding conditions and no place to live. The Gilotdel sent me a tenant with an order for a room, and he's a good proletarian, and I got to give him one of your rooms. He can take the dining room and you can keep the other two. Also, this ain't the time when people could live in seven rooms as some people used to."

The new tenant was a meek, elderly little man who stammered, wore glasses and worked as bookkeeper for the shoe factory "Red Skorohod." He left early in the morning and came home late at night. He cooked on his own Primus and never had any visitors.

"I won't be in the way, Citizen Argounova," he had said. "I won't be in the way at all. It's just only as regards the bathroom. If you'll let me take a bath once a month—I'll be most grateful. As to the other necessities, there's a privy in the back yard, if you'll excuse the mention. I won't mind. I won't annoy a lady."

They moved their furniture out of the dining room into their remaining quarters and nailed the connecting door. When Kira cooked, in the drawing room, she asked Leo to remain in the bedroom.

"Self-preservation," she told him, "for both of us."

*

Andrei had spent the summer on a Party mission in the villages of the Volga.

He met Kira again at the Institute on the first day of the new semester. His suntan was a little deeper; the lines at the corners of his mouth were not a wound nor a scar, but looked like both.

"Kira, I knew I'd be glad to see you again. But I didn't know that I'd be so . . . happy."

"You've had a hard summer, haven't you, Andrei?"

"Thank you for your letters. They've kept me cheerful."

She looked at the grimness of his lips. "What have they done to you, Andrei?"

"Who?" But he knew that she knew. He did not look at her, but he answered: "Well, I guess everybody knows it. The villages—that's the dark spot on our future. They're not conquered. They're not with us. They have a red flag over the local Soviet and a knife behind their backs. They bow, and they nod, and they snicker in their beards. They stick pictures of Lenin over the barns where they hide their grain from us. You've read in the papers about the Clubhouse they burned and the three Communists they burned in it—alive. I was there the next day."

"Andrei! I hope you got them!"

He could not restrain a smile: "Why, Kira! Are you saying that about men who fight Communism?"

"But . . . but they could have done it to *you*."

"Well, nothing happened to me, as you see. Don't look at that scar on my neck. Just grazed. The fool wasn't used to firearms. His aim wasn't very good."

*

The boss of the Gossizdat had five pictures on the walls of his office: one of Karl Marx, one of Trotzky, one of Zinoviev and two of Lenin. On his desk stood two small plaster busts: of Lenin and Karl Marx. He wore a high-collared peasant blouse of expensive black satin.

He looked at his manicured fingernails; then he looked at Leo. "I feel certain, Comrade Kovalensky, that you will welcome this opportunity to do your duty in our great cultural drive, as we all do."

Leo asked: "What do you want?"

"This organization has taken the honorary post of *'Cultchef'* to a division of the Baltfleet. You understand what I mean, of course? In line with the new—and brilliant—move of the Party toward a wider spread of education and Proletarian Culture, we have accepted the position of 'Cultural Chief' to a less enlightened unit, as all institutions of note have done. We are thus responsible for the cultural advancement of our brave brothers of the Baltic Fleet. Such is our modest contribution to the gigantic rise of the new civilization of the new ruling class."

"Fine," said Leo. "What do you want me to do about it?"

"I think it is obvious, Comrade Kovalensky. We are organizing a free night school for our protégés. With your knowledge of foreign languages—I had a class of German in mind, twice a week—Germany is the cornerstone of our future diplomacy and the next step of the world revolution—and a class of English, once a week. Of course, you are not to expect any financial remuneration for this work, your services are to be donated, inasmuch as this is not an undertaking of the government, but our strictly voluntary gift to the State."

"Since the beginning of the revolution," said Leo, "I haven't been buying gifts for anyone, neither for my friends —nor otherwise. I can't afford them."

"Comrade Kovalensky, did it ever occur to you to consider what we think of men who merely work for their pay and take no part in social activity in their spare time?"

"Did it ever occur to you that I have a life to live—in my spare time?"

The man at the desk looked at the five pictures on his walls. "The Soviet State recognizes no life but that of a social class."

"I don't think we shall go into a discussion of the subject."

"In other words, you refuse to do your share?"

"I do."

"Very well. This service is not compulsory. Oh, not in the least. Its meaning and novelty is the free will of those participating. I was merely thinking of your own good when I made the offer. I thought, in view of certain events in your past, that you'd be only too glad to. . . . Never mind. However, I must call to your attention the fact that Comrade Zoubikov of the Communist Cell has been rather unpleasant about a man of your social past on our pay roll. And when he hears about this. . . ."

"When he does," said Leo. "tell him to come to me. I'll give *him* a free lesson—if he cares for the subject."

*

Leo came home earlier than usual.

The blue flame of the Primus hissed in the gathering dusk. Kira's white apron was a white spot bending over the Primus.

Leo threw his cap and brief case on the table. "That's that," he said. "I'm out."

Kira stood holding a spoon. She asked: "You mean . . . the Gossizdat?"

"Yes. Fired. Reduction of staffs. Getting rid of the undesirable element. Told me I had a bourgeois attitude. I'm not social-minded."

"Well . . . well, it's all right. We'll get along."

"Of course, it's all right. Think I care about their damn job? This affects me no more than a change in weather."

"Certainly. Now take your coat off and wash your hands, and we'll have dinner."

"Dinner? What do you have there?"

"Beet soup. You like it."

"When did I say I liked it? I don't want any dinner. I'm not hungry. I'm going to the bedroom to study. Please don't disturb me."

"I won't."

Left alone, Kira took a towel and lifted the cover of the pan and stirred the soup, slowly, deliberately, longer than it required. Then she took a plate from the shelf. As she was carrying it to the table, she saw that the plate was trembling. She stopped and, in the dusk, whispered, addressing herself for the first time in her life, as if speaking to a person she had never met before: "Now, Kira, you don't. You don't. You don't."

She stood and held the plate over the table and stared down, all her will in her eyes, as if a great issue depended on the plate. Presently the plate stopped trembling.

*

When he had stood in line for an hour, he smoked a cigarette.

When he had stood for two hours, he began to feel that his legs were numb.

When he had stood for three hours, he felt that the numbness had risen to his throat, and he had to lean against a wall.

When his turn came, the editor looked at Leo and said: "I don't see how we can use you, citizen. Of course, our publication is strictly artistic. But—Proletarian Art, I may remind you. Strictly class viewpoint. You do not belong to the Party —nor is your social standing suitable, you must agree. I have ten experienced reporters—Party members—on my waiting list."

*

She really didn't have to fry fish in lard, Kira decided. She could use sunflower-seed oil. If she bought good oil it would leave no odor and it was cheaper. She counted the money out carefully over the co-operative counter and walked home, cautiously watching the heavy yellow liquid in a greasy bottle.

*

The secretary said to Leo: "Sorry you had to wait so long, citizen, but the comrade editor is a very busy man. You can go in now."

The comrade editor leaned back in his chair; he held a bronze paper knife; the knife tapped the edge of a desk calendar bearing a picture of Lunacharsky, People's Commissar of Education and Art; the editor's voice sounded like a knife cutting paper:

"No. No opening. None expected. Plenty of proletarians starving and you bourgeois asking for a job. I'm a proletarian myself. Straight from the work-bench. I've been jobless—in the old days. But your bourgeois class brothers had no pity. It'll do you good to learn how it feels on your own hide."

*

"It's a misunderstanding, citizens. Help interview hours are from nine to eleven, Thursday only. . . . An hour and a half? Well, how did I know what you were sitting here for? Nobody asked you to sit."

*

When he came home in the evenings, he was silent.

Kira served dinner and he sat down at the table and ate. She had given great care to the dinner. He said nothing. He did not look into the steady gray eyes across the table, nor at the lips that smiled gently. He offered no complaint and no consolation.

Sometimes, for many long moments, he stood before the crystal vase on the malachite stand, the one that had not been broken, and looked at it, his eyes expressionless, his hands in his pockets, a cigarette hanging in the corner of his mouth; he stood without moving, without blinking, the smoke alone stirring slowly, swaying. Then he smiled and the cigarette fell to the floor, and burned, smoking, a dark ring widening on the parquet; but he did not notice it; and Kira did not notice it, for her eyes were fixed, wide and frightened, on Leo's icy, sardonic smile.

*

"Any past experience, citizen?"

"No."

"Party member?"

"No."

"Sorry. No opening. Next."

*

It was Monday and the job had been promised to him for Monday. Leo stood before the little wizened office manager and knew that he should smile gratefully. But Leo never smiled when he knew he should. And perhaps it would have been useless. The office manager met him with a worried, apologetic look and avoided his eyes.

"So sorry, citizen. Yes, I promised you this job, but—you see, the big boss' cousin came from Moscow and she's unemployed, and. . . . Unforeseen circumstances, citizen. You know—man proposes and God disposes. . . . Come again, citizen."

*

Kira went to the Institute less frequently.

But when she sat in a long, cold room and listened to lectures about steel, and bolts, and kilowatts, she straightened her shoulders as if a wrench had tightened the wires of her nerves. She looked at the man who sat beside her; at times she wondered whether those words about steel beams and girders were not about his bones and muscles, a man for whom steel had been created, or, perhaps, it was he that had been created for steel, and concrete, and white heat; she had long since forgotten where Andrei Taganov's life ended and that of engines began.

When he questioned her solicitously, she answered: "Andrei, any circles under my eyes are nothing but your own imagination. And you've never been in the habit of thinking about my eyes."

*

When Leo sat down at the table, Kira's smile was a little forced.

"You see, there's no dinner tonight," she explained softly. "That is, no real dinner. Just this bread. The co-operative ran out of millet before my turn came. But I got the bread. That's your portion. And I've fried some onions in sunflower-seed oil. They're very good on the bread."

"Where's your portion?"

"I've . . . eaten it already. before you came."

"How much did you get this week?"

"Oh . . . well . . . they gave us a whole pound, imagine? Instead of the usual half. Nice, isn't it?"

"Yes. Very. Only I'm not hungry. I'm going to bed."

*

The little man next to Leo in line had an uncomfortable laugh, a servile, hissing sound at his palate, that did not reach his throat, as if he repeated mirthlessly the printed letters: "h-ee-h-ee."

"I see you're looking at the red handkerchief in my breast pocket, citizen, hee-hee," he whispered confidentially into Leo's ear. "I'll let you in on a secret. It's no handkerchief at all. See? Just a little silk rag. When you go in, they think at first glance that it's a Party badge or something, hee-hee. Then they see it ain't, but still there's the psychological effect, hee-hee. Helps—if they have an opening for a job. . . . Go on. Your turn. Lord Jesus Christ! It's dark outside already. How time flies in lines, citizen. Hee-hee."

*

At the University co-operative, the student in line ahead of Leo said aloud to a companion, both wearing Party badges: "Funny, isn't it? the way some citizens neglect their lectures, but you're sure to find them in line for food rations."

Leo said to the clerk behind the counter, trying to make his voice pleading and making it only wooden, expressionless: "Comrade clerk, would you mind if I tear next week's coupon off, too? I'll keep it and present it to you for my bread next week. You see, I have . . . there's someone at home and I want to tell her that I got a two weeks' ration and ate my half on the way home, so that she'll eat all of this piece. . . . Thank you, comrade."

*

The burly office manager led Leo down a narrow corridor into an empty office with Lenin's picture on the wall, and closed the door carefully. He had a friendly smile and heavy cheeks.

"More privacy here, citizen. It's like this, citizen. A job's a rare thing, nowadays. A very rare thing. Now, a comrade that's got a responsible position and has jobs to hand out—he's got something valuable to hand out, hasn't he? Now then, a comrade that's got a responsible position isn't making much of a salary these days. And things are expensive. One's got to live. A fellow that gets a job has something to be grateful for, hasn't he? . . . Near broke, you say? Well, what do you want here, you bum? Expecting us proletarians to give jobs to every stray bourgeois?"

*

"English, German and French? Valuable, very valuable, citizen. We do need teachers for classes of languages. Are you a Union member? . . . Not any Trade Union? . . . Sorry, citizen, we employ only Union members."

*

"So you want to join the Union of Pedagogues? Very well, citizen. Where are you working?"

"I'm not working."

"You cannot join the Union if you're not working."

"I can't get a job if I'm not a Union member."

"If you have no job, you can't become a Union member. Next!"

*

"Half a pound of linseed oil, please. The one that's not too rancid, please, if you can. . . . No, I can't take sunflower-seed oil, it's too expensive."

*

"Kira! What are you doing here in your nightgown?"

He raised his head from the book. A single bulb over the table left shadows in the corners of the drawing room and in the circles under Leo's eyes. Kira's white nightgown trembled in the darkness.

"It's after three . . ." she whispered.

"I know it. But I have to study. There's a draft here. Please go back to bed. You're trembling."

"Leo, you'll wear yourself out."

"Well, and if I do? That'll be the end of it, so much the quicker."

He guessed the look of the eyes he could not see in the darkness. He got up and gathered the trembling white shadow in his arms.

"Kira, of course I don't mean it. . . . Just one kiss, if you go back to bed. . . . Even your lips are cold. . . . If you don't go, I'll carry you back."

He lifted her in two arms, still strong and firm and warm through her nightgown. He carried her back into the bedroom, his head pressed close to hers, whispering: "Just a few more pages and I'll be with you. Go to sleep. Good night. Don't worry."

*

"In my duty of Upravdom, Citizen Argounova, I gotta tell you. Laws is laws. The rent's raised on account of neither of you citizens being a Soviet employee. That puts you in the category of persons living off an income. . . . How do I know what income? Laws is laws."

*

Behind him, men stood in line; men cringing, shrinking, crouching; hollow chests and hunched shoulders; yellow hands clasped and trembling; a few last convulsions in the depths of extinguished souls; eyes staring with a forlorn hopelessness, a dull horror, a crushed plea; a line like that at a stock yard. He stood among them, tall, straight, young, a god's form with lips that were still proud.

A streetwalker passed by and stopped; and looked, startled, at that man among the others; and winked an invitation. He did not move, only turned his head away.

XIV

A house collapsed, early one afternoon. The front wall crashed, with a shower of bricks, in a white cloud of limey dust. Coming back from work, the inhabitants saw their bedrooms exposed to the cold light of the street, like tiers of stage settings; an upright piano, caught by a naked beam, hung precariously high over the pavement. There were a few weary moans, but no astonishment: houses, long since in need of repair, collapsed without warning all over the city. Old bricks were piled high over the tramway rails and stopped traffic. Leo got a job for two days, clearing the street. He worked, bending and rising, bending and rising, through many hours, a numb ache in his spine, red dust on bleeding fingers stiff and raw in the cold.

The Museum of the Revolution had an exhibition in honor of the visiting delegates of a Swedish Trade Union. Kira got a job lettering cardboard inscriptions. She bent through four long evenings, eyes dull, hands trembling over a ruler, painfully tracing even black letters that said: "WORKERS STARVING IN THE TENEMENTS OF THE CAPITALISTIC EXPLOITERS OF 1910," "WORKERS EXILED TO SIBERIA BY THE CZARIST GENDARMES OF 1905."

Snow grew in white drifts in the gutters, under basement windows. Leo shovelled snow for three nights, his breath fluttering in spurts of white vapor, icicles sparkling on the old scarf wound tightly around his neck.

A citizen of no visible means of support, who owned an automobile and a five-room apartment, and who held long, whispered conversations with officials of the Food Trust, decided that his children had to speak French. Kira gave lessons twice a week, dully explaining the "passé imparfait" to two haggard brats who wiped their noses with their fingers, her voice hoarse, her head swimming, her eyes avoiding the buffet where glossy white muffins sparkled with brown, well-buttered crusts.

Leo helped a proletarian student who had an examination to pass. He explained slowly the laws of capital and interest to a sleepy fellow who scratched his knuckles, for he had the itch.

Kira washed dishes two hours a day, bending over a greasy tub that smelt of old fish, in a private restaurant—until it failed.

They disappeared for hours every day and when they came home they never asked each other in what lines they had stood, what streets they had trudged wearily to what doors closed brusquely before them. At night, Kira lighted the "Bourgeoise" and they sat silently, bent over their books. They still had things to study and one goal to remember, if all the others had to be forgotten: to graduate. "It doesn't matter," Kira had said. "Nothing matters. We mustn't think. We mustn't think at all. We must remember only that we have to be ready and then . . . maybe . . . maybe we'll find a way to go abro. . . ." She had not finished. She could not pronounce the word. That word was like a silent, secret wound deep in both of them.

Sometimes they read the newspapers. Comrade Zinoviev, president of the Petrograd Soviet, said: "The world revolution is not a matter of years, comrades, not a matter of months, but a matter of days now. The flame of a Proletarian Uprising' will sweep the Earth, wiping out forever the Curse of World Capitalism."

There was also an interview with Comrade Biriuchin, third stoker on a Red battleship. Comrade Biriuchin said: "Well, and then we gotta keep the machines oiled, and again we gotta look out for rust, seeing as how it's up to us to watch over the people's engines, and we being conscientious proletarians, we do our share, on account of we don't care for no nonsense outside of good, practical work, and again, there's the foreign bourgeois watching us, and . . ."

Sometimes they read the magazines.

". . . Masha looked at him coldly.

" 'I fear that our ideologies are too far apart. We are born into different social classes. The bourgeois prejudices are too deep-rooted in your consciousness. I am a daughter of the toiling masses. Individual love is a bourgeois prejudice.

" 'Is this the end, Masha?' he asked hoarsely, a deathly pallor spreading on his handsome, but bourgeois face.

" 'Yes, Ivan,' said she, 'it is the end. I am the new woman of a new day.' "

There was also poetry to read:

> *". . . My heart is a tractor raking the soil,*
> *My soul is smoke from the factory oil. . . ."*

Once they went to a motion picture.

It was an American film. In the bright glare of showcases, clusters of shadows stood gazing wistfully at the breath-taking, incredible, *foreign* stills; big snowflakes crashed into the glass; the eager faces smiled faintly, as if with the same thought, the thought that glass—and more than glass—protected this distant, miraculous world from the hopeless Russian winter.

Kira and Leo waited, jammed in the crowd of the foyer. When a show ended and the doors were opened, the crowd tore forward, knocking aside those who tried to come out, squeezing in through the two narrow doors, painfully, furiously, with a brutal despair, like meat ground through a tight grinder.

The title of the picture shivered in huge white letters:

"THE GOLDEN OCTOPUS"
DIRECTED BY REGINALD MOORE
CENSORED BY COMRADE M. ZAVADKOV

The picture was puzzling. It trembled and flickered, showing a hazy office where blurred shadows of people jerked convulsively. An English sign on the office wall was misspelled. The office was that of an American Trade Union where a stern comrade entrusted the hero—a blondish, dark-eyed young man—with the recovery of documents of vast importance to the Union, stolen by a capitalist.

"Hell!" whispered Leo. "Do they also make pictures like that in America?"

Suddenly, as if a fog had lifted, the photography cleared. They could see the soft line of lipstick and every hair of the long lashes of a beautiful, smiling leading lady. Men and women in magnificently foreign clothes moved gracefully through a story that made no sense. The subtitles did not match the action. The subtitles clamored in glaring white letters about the suffering of "our American brothers under the capitalistic yoke." On the screen, gay people laughed happily, danced in sparkling halls, ran down sandy beaches, their hair in the wind, the muscles of their young arms taut, glistening, monstrously healthy. A woman left her room wearing a white dress and emerged on the street in a black suit. The hero had suddenly grown taller, thinner, very blond and blue-eyed. His trim full-dress suit was surprising on a toiling Trade Union member; and the papers he was seeking through the incoherent jumble of events seemed suspiciously close to something like a will for his uncle's inheritance.

A subtitle said: "I hate you. You are a blood-sucking capitalistic exploiter. Get out of my room!"

On the screen, a man was bending over the hand of a delicate lady, pressing it slowly to his lips, while she looked at him sadly, and gently stroked his hair.

The end of the picture was not shown. It finished abruptly, as if torn off. A subtitle concluded: "Six months later the bloodthirsty capitalist met his death at the hands of striking workers. Our hero renounced the joys of a selfish love into which the bourgeois siren had tried to lure him, and he dedicated his life to the cause of the World Revolution."

"I know," said Kira, when they were leaving the theater. "I know what they've done! They've shot that beginning here, themselves. They've cut the picture to pieces!"

An usher who heard her, chuckled.

*

Sometimes the door bell rang and the Upravdom came in to remind them of the house meeting of all tenants on an urgent matter. He said: "No exceptions, citizens. Social duty comes above all. Every tenant gotta attend the meeting."

Then Kira and Leo filed into the largest room of the house, a long, bare room with one electric bulb in the ceiling, in the apartment of a street-car conductor who had offered it graciously for the social duty. Tenants came bringing their own chairs and sat chewing sunflower seeds. Those who brought no chairs sat on the floor and chewed sunflower seeds.

"Seeing as how I'm the Upravdom," said the Upravdom, "I declare this meeting of the tenants of the house Number —on Sergievskaia Street open. On the order of the day is the question as regards the chimneys. Now, comrade citizens, seeing as how we are all responsible citizens and conscious of the proper class consciousness, we gotta understand that this ain't the old days when we had landlords and didn't care what happened to the house we lived in. Now this is different, comrades. Owing to the new régime and the dictatorship of the proletariat, and seeing as how the chimneys are clogged, we gotta do something about it, seeing as how we're the owners of the house. Now if the chimneys are clogged, we'll have the house full of smoke, and if we have the house full of smoke, it's sloppy, and if we're sloppy, that's not true proletarian discipline. And so, comrade citizens. . . ."

Housewives fidgeted nervously, sniffing the odor of burning food. A fat man in a red shirt was twiddling his thumbs. A young man with a mouth hanging open, was scratching his head.

". . . and the special assessment will be divided in proportion to the. . . . Is that you, Comrade Kira Argounova, trying to sneak out? Well, you better don't. You know what we think of people that sabotage their social duties. . . . And the special assessment will be divided in proportion to the social standing of the tenants. The workers pay three per cent and the Free Professions ten, and the Private Traders and unemployed—the rest. Who's for—raise your hands. . . . Comrade secretary, count the citizens' hands. . . . Who's against —raise your hands. . . . Comrade Michliuk, you can't raise your hand for and against on the one and same proposition. . . ."

*

Victor's visit was unexpected and inexplicable.

He stretched his hands to the "Bourgeoise," rubbed them energetically, smiled cheerfully at Kira and Leo.

"Just passing by and thought I'd drop in. . . . It's a charming place you have here. Irina's been telling me about it. . . . She's fine, thank you. . . . No, mother's not so well. The doctor said there's nothing he can do if we don't send her south. And who can think of affording a trip these days? . . . Been busy at the Institute. Re-elected to Students' Council. . . . Do you read poetry? Just read some verses by a woman. Exquisite delicacy of feeling. . . . Yes, it's a lovely place you have here. Pre-revolutionary luxury. . . . You two are quite the bourgeois, aren't you? Two huge rooms like these. No trouble with the Domicile Norm? We've had two tenants forced upon us last week. One's a Communist. Father's just gritting his teeth. Irina has to share her room with Acia, and they fight like dogs. . . . What can one do? People have to have a roof over their heads. . . . Yes, Petrograd is an overcrowded city, Petrograd certainly is."

*

She came in, a red bandana on her hair, streaks of powder on her nose, a bundle tied in a white sheet in her hand, one black stocking hanging out of the bundle. She asked: "Where's that drawing room?"

Kira asked, startled: "What do you want, citizen?"

The girl did not answer. She opened the first door she saw, which led to the tenant's room. She slammed it shut. She opened the other door and walked into the drawing room.

"That's it," she said. "You can get your 'Bourgeoise' out— and your dishes and other trash. I have my own."

"What do you want, citizen?" Kira repeated.

"Oh, yes," said the girl. "Here."

She handed to Kira a crumpled scrap of paper with a big official stamp. It was an order from the Gilotdel, giving Citizen Marina Lavrova the right to occupy the room known as "drawing room" in apartment Number 22, house Number—

on Sergievskaia Street; it requested the present occupants to vacate the room immediately, removing only "personal effects of immediate necessity."

"Why, it's impossible!" Kira gasped.

The girl laughed. "Get going, citizen, get going."

"Listen, you. Get out of here peacefully. You won't get this room."

"No? Who's going to stop me? You?"

She walked to a chair, saw Kira's apron on it, threw it to the floor and put her bundle on the chair.

Slamming the door behind her, Kira raced up the stairs, three floors up, to the Upravdom's apartment, and stood panting, knocking at the door ferociously.

The Upravdom opened the door and listened to her story, frowning.

"Order from the Gilotdel?" he said. "That's funny they didn't notify me. That's irregular. I'll put the citizen in her proper place."

"Comrade Upravdom, you know very well it's against the law. Citizen Kovalensky and I are not married. We're entitled to separate rooms."

"You sure are."

Kira had been paid for a month of lessons the day before. She took the little roll of bills from her pocket and, without looking at it, without counting, thrust it all into the Upravdom's hand.

"Comrade Upravdom, I'm not in the habit of begging for help, but please, oh! please, get her out. It would . . . it would simply mean the end for us."

The Upravdom slipped the bills into his pocket furtively, then looked straight at Kira, openly and innocently, as if nothing had happened. "Don't you worry, Citizen Argounova. We know our duty. We'll fix the lady. We'll throw her out on her behind in the gutter where she belongs."

He slammed his hat over one ear and followed Kira downstairs.

"Look here, citizen, what's all this about?" the Upravdom asked sternly.

Citizen Marina Lavrova had taken her coat off and opened her bundle. She wore a tailored white shirt, an old skirt, a necklace of imitation pearls, and slippers with very high heels. She had piled underwear, books and a teapot in a jumble on the table.

"How do you do, Comrade Upravdom?" she smiled pleasantly. "We might as well get acquainted."

She took a little wallet from her pocket and handed it to him, open, showing a little card. It was a membership card of the Communist Union of Youth—the Komsomol.

"Oh," said the Upravdom. "Oh." He turned to Kira: "What do you want, citizen? You have two rooms and you want a toiling girl to be thrown out on the streets? The time is past for bourgeois privileges, citizen. People like you had better watch their step."

＊

Kira and Leo appealed the case in the People's Court.

They sat in a bare room that smelt of sweat and of an unswept floor. Lenin and Karl Marx, without frames, bigger than life-size, looked at them from the wall. A cotton strip said: "Proletarians of the wo . . ." The rest was not to be seen, for the end of the strip had become untacked and swayed, curled like a snake, in a draft.

The presiding magistrate yawned and asked Kira: "What's your social position, citizen?"

"Student."

"Employed?"

"No."

"Member of a Trade Union?"

"No."

The Upravdom testified that although Citizen Argounova and Citizen Kovalensky were not in the state of legal matrimony, their relations were those of "sexual intimacy," there being only one bed in their rooms, of which, he, the Upravdom, had made certain, and which made them for all purposes "same as married," and the Domicile Norm allowed but one room to a married couple, as the Comrade Judge well knew; furthermore, "the room known as drawing room" together with their bedroom gave the citizens in question three square feet of living space over the prescribed norm; furthermore, the citizens in question had been, of late, quite irregular about their rent.

"Who was your father, Citizen Argounova?"

"Alexander Argounov."

"The former textile manufacturer and factory owner?"

"Yes."

"I see. Who was your father, Citizen Kovalensky?"

"Admiral Kovalensky."

"Executed for counter-revolutionary activities?"

"Executed—yes."

"Who was your father, Citizen Lavrova?"

"Factory worker, Comrade Judge. Exiled to Siberia by the Czar in 1913. My mother's a peasant, from the plow."

"It is the verdict of the People's Court that the room in question rightfully belongs to Citizen Lavrova."

"Is this a court of justice or a musical comedy?" Leo asked.

The presiding magistrate turned to him solemnly: "So-called impartial justice, citizen, is a bourgeois prejudice. This is a court of class justice. It is our official attitude and platform. Next case!"

"Comrade Judge!" Kira appealed. "How about the furniture —our furniture?"

"You can't put all that furniture into one room."

"No, but we could sell it. We're . . . we're quite hard up."

"So? You would sell it for profit and a proletarian girl, who didn't happen to accumulate any furniture, would have to sleep on the floor? . . . Next case!"

*

"Tell me one thing," Kira asked Citizen Lavrova. "How did you happen to get an order for that particular room of ours? Who told you about it?"

Citizen Lavrova gave an abrupt giggle with a vague stare. "One has friends," was all she answered.

She had a pale face with a short nose and small, pouting lips that looked chronically discontented. She had light, bluish eyes, cold and suspicious. Her hair curled in vague ringlets on her forehead and she always wore tiny earrings, a brass circle close around the lobe of her ear, with a tiny imitation turquoise. She was not sociable and talked little. But the door bell rang continuously in the hands of visitors to Comrade Lavrova. Her friends called her Marisha.

In Leo's gray and silver bedroom, a hole was pierced over the black onyx fireplace—for the pipe of the "Bourgeoise." Two shelves of his wardrobe were emptied for dishes, silverware and food. Bread crumbs rolled down into their underwear and the bed sheets smelt of linseed oil. Leo's books were stacked on the dresser; Kira's—under the bed. Leo whistled a fox-trot, arranging his books. Kira did not look at him.

After some hesitation, Marisha surrendered the painting of Leo's mother, which hung in the drawing room. But she kept the frame; she put a picture of Lenin in it. She also had pictures of Trotzky, Marx, Engels and Rosa Luxemburg; also —a poster representing the Spirit of the Red Air Fleet. She had a gramophone. Late into the night, she played old records, of which her favorite was a song about Napoleon's defeat in Russia—"It roared, it flamed, the fire of Moscow." When she was tired of the gramophone, she played the "Dog's Waltz" on the grand piano.

The bathroom had to be reached through the bedroom. Marisha kept shuffling in and out, wearing a faded, unfastened bathrobe.

"When you have to go through, I wish you'd knock," Kira told her.

"What for? It's not your bathroom."

*

Marisha was a student of the University Rabfac.

The Rabfacs were special workers' faculties with an academic program a little less exacting than that of the University, with a program of revolutionary sciences a great deal more exacting, and with an admission on the strictest proletarian basis.

Marisha disliked Kira, but spoke to Leo at times. She flung the door open so that her posters rustled on the walls, and yelled imperiously: "Citizen Kovalensky, can you help me with this damn French history? What century did they burn Martin Luther in? Or was that Germany? Or did they burn him?"

At other times she flung the door open and announced to no one in particular: "I'm going to the Komsomol Club meeting. If Comrade Rilenko comes, tell him he'll find me at the Club. But if that louse Mishka Gvozdev comes, tell him I've gone to America. You know who he is—the little one with the wart on his nose."

She came in, a cup in her hand: "Citizen Argounova, can I borrow some lard? Didn't know I was all out of it. . . . Nothing but linseed oil? How can you eat that stinking stuff? Well, gimme half a cup."

Going out at seven in the morning, passing through her room, Leo found Marisha asleep, her head on a table littered with books. Marisha jerked, awakening with a start at the sound of his steps.

"Oh, damnation!" she yawned, stretching. "It's this paper I have to read at the Marxist Circle tonight, for our less enlightened comrades—on the 'Social Significance of Electricity as a Historical Factor.' Citizen Kovalensky, who the hell is Edison?"

Late at night they could hear her coming home. She slammed the door and threw her books on a chair, and they could hear the books scattering over the floor, and her voice intermingled with the deep, adolescent basso of Comrade Rilenko: "Aleshka, pal, be an angel. Light that damn Primus. I'm starving."

Aleshka's steps shuffled across the room, and the Primus hissed.

"You're an angel, Aleshka. Always said you were an angel. I'm tired like a dray-horse. The Rabfac this morning; the Komsomol Club at noon; a committee on day-nurseries in factories at one-thirty; the Marxist Circle at two; demonstration against Illiteracy at three—and do my feet sweat!—lecture on Electrification at four; at seven—editors' board of the Wall Newspaper—I'm gonna be editor; meeting of the women houseworkers at seven-thirty or something; conference on our comrades in Hungary at. . . . You can't say your girl friend ain't class-minded and socially active, Aleshka, you really can't say it."

Aleshka sat at the piano and played "John Gray."

Once, in the middle of the night, Kira was awakened by someone slinking furtively into the bathroom. She caught a glimpse of an undressed boy with blond hair. There was no light in Marisha's room.

*

One evening, Kira heard a familiar voice behind the door. A man was saying: "Of course, we're friends. You know we are. Perhaps—perhaps there's more—on my part—but I do not dare to hope. I've proven my devotion to you. You know the favor I've done you. Now, do one for me. I want to meet that Party friend of yours."

Passing through Marisha's room, on her way out, Kira stopped short. She saw Victor sitting on the davenport, holding Marisha's hand. He jumped up, his temples reddened.

"Victor! Were you coming to see me or . . ." Her voice broke off; she understood.

"Kira, I don't want you to think that I . . ." Victor was saying.

Kira was running out of the room, out of the lobby, down the stairs.

When she told Leo about it, he threatened to break every

bone in Victor's body. She begged him to keep quiet. "If you raise this issue, his father will know. It will break Uncle Vasili and he's so unhappy as it is. What's the use? We won't get the room back."

*

In the Institute co-operative, Kira met Comrade Sonia and Pavel Syerov. Comrade Sonia was chewing a crust of bread broken off the loaf she had received. Pavel Syerov looked as trim as a military fashion plate. He smiled effusively: "How are you, Comrade Argounova? We don't see you so often at the Institute these days."

"I've been busy."

"We don't see you with Comrade Taganov any more. You two haven't quarreled, have you?"

"Why does that interest you?"

"Oh, it's of no particular interest to me personally."

"But it does interest us as a Party duty," Comrade Sonia remarked sternly. "Comrade Taganov is a valuable Party worker. Naturally, we are concerned, for his friendship with a woman of your social origin might hurt his Party standing."

"Nonsense, Sonia, nonsense," Pavel Syerov protested with sudden eagerness. "Andrei's Party standing is too high. Nothing can hurt it. Comrade Argounova doesn't have to worry and break off a lovely friendship."

Kira looked at him fixedly and asked: "But his Party standing does worry you because it's so high, doesn't it?"

"Why, Comrade Taganov is a very good friend of mine and . . ."

"Are *you* a very good friend of his?"

"A peculiar question, Comrade Argounova."

"One does hear peculiar things nowadays, doesn't one? Good day, Comrade Syerov."

*

Marisha came in when Kira was alone. Her little pouting mouth was swollen; her eyes were red, swollen with tears. She asked sullenly: "Citizen Argounova, what do you use to keep from having children?"

Kira looked at her, startled.

"I'm afraid I'm in trouble," Marisha wailed. "It's that damn louse Aleshka Rilenko. Said I'd be bourgeois if I didn't let him. . . . Said he'd be careful. What am I gonna do? What am I gonna do?"

Kira said she didn't know.

*

For three weeks, Kira worked secretly on a new dress. It was only her old dress, but slowly, painfully, awkwardly, she managed to turn it inside out. The blue wool was smooth and silky on the inside; it looked almost fresh. It was to be a surprise for Leo; she worked on it at night when he had gone to bed. She put a candle on the floor and opened the big mirror door of the wardrobe and used it as a screen, crouching on the floor behind it, by the candle. She had never learned how to sew. Her fingers moved slowly, helplessly. She wiped drops of blood on her petticoat, when she pricked her finger with the needle. Her eyes felt as if tiny needles pricked them continuously from behind the lids; and her lids felt so heavy that when she blinked they stayed closed and it took an effort to pull them open to the huge yellow glare of the candle. Somewhere in the darkness, behind the yellow glare, Leo breathed heavily in his sleep.

The dress was ready on the day when she met Vava in the street. Vava was smiling happily, mysteriously once in a while, for no apparent reason, smiling at a secret thought of her own. They walked home together, and Vava could not resist it any longer: "Won't you come in, Kira?" she begged. "For just a second? I have something to show you. Something—from *abroad*."

Vava's room smelt of perfume and clean linen. A big teddy-bear with a pink bow sat on the white lace cover of her bed.

Vava opened a parcel carefully wrapped in tissue paper. She handled the objects inside with a frightened reverence, with delicate, trembling fingers. The parcel contained two pairs of silk stockings and a black celluloid bracelet.

Kira gasped. She extended her hand. She hesitated. She touched a stocking with her finger tips, caressing it timidly, like the fur of a priceless animal.

"It's smuggled," Vava whispered. "A lady—father's patient —her husband's in the business—they smuggled it from Riga. And the bracelet—that's their latest fashion abroad. Imagine? Fake jewelry. Isn't it fascinating?"

Kira held the bracelet reverently on the palm of her hand; she did not dare to slip it on.

Vava asked suddenly, timidly, without smiling: "Kira, how's Victor?"

"He's fine."

"I . . . I haven't seen him for some time. Well, I know, he's so busy. I've given up all my dates, waiting for him to. . . . Oh, well, he's such an active person. . . . I'm so happy over these stockings. I'll wear them when . . . when he comes. I just had to throw out my last silk pair this morning."

"You . . . threw them out?"

"Why, yes. I think they're still in the waste basket. They're ruined. One has a big run in the back."

"Vava . . . could I have them?"

"What? The torn ones? But they're no good."

"It's just . . . just for a joke."

Kira went home, clutching a soft little ball in her pocket. She kept her hand in her pocket. She could not let it go.

When Leo came in, that evening, his hand opened the door and flung his brief case into the room. The brief case opened, spilling the books over the floor. Then he came in.

He did not take his coat off; he walked straight to the "Bourgeoise" and stood, his blue hands extended to the fire, rubbing them furiously. Then he took his coat off and threw it across the room at a chair; it missed the chair and fell to the floor; he didn't pick it up. Then he asked: "Anything to eat?"

Kira stood facing him, silent, motionless in the splendor of her new dress and carefully mended real silk stockings. She said softly: "Yes. Sit down. Everything's ready."

He sat down. He had looked at her several times. He had not noticed. It was the same old blue dress; but she had trimmed it carefully with bands and buttons of black oilcloth which looked almost like patent leather. When she served the millet and he dipped his spoon hungrily into the steaming yellow mush, she stood by the table and, raising her skirt a little, swung her leg forward into the circle of light, watching happily the shimmering, tight silk. She said timidly: "Leo, look."

He looked and asked curtly: "Where did you get them?"

"I . . . Vava gave them to me. They . . . they were torn."

"I wouldn't wear other people's discarded junk."

He did not mention the new dress. She did not call it to his attention. They ate silently.

Marisha had had an abortion. She moaned, behind the closed door. She shuffled heavily across the room, cursing aloud the midwife who did not know her business.

*

"Citizen Lavrova, will you please clean the bathroom? There's blood all over the floor."

"Leave me alone. I'm sick. Clean it yourself, if you're so damn bourgeois about your bathroom."

Marisha slammed the door, then opened it again, cautiously: "Citizen Argounova, you won't tell your cousin on me, will you? He doesn't know about . . . my trouble. He's —a gentleman."

*

Leo came home at dawn. He had worked all night. He had worked in caissons for a bridge under construction, deep on the bottom of a river on the point of freezing.

Kira had waited for him. She had kept a fire in the "Bourgeoise."

He came in, oil and mud on his coat, oil and sweat on his face, oil and blood on his hands. He swayed a little and held onto the door. A strand of hair was glued across his forehead.

He went into the bathroom. He came out, asking: "Kira, do I have any clean underwear?"

He was naked. His hands were swollen. His head drooped to one shoulder. His eyelids were blue.

His body was white as marble and as hard and straight; the body of a god, she thought, that should climb a mountainside at dawn, young grass under his feet, a morning mist on his muscles in a breath of homage.

The "Bourgeoise" was smoking. An acrid fog hung under the electric bulb. The gray rug under his feet smelt of kerosene. Black drops of soot fell slowly, with a soft thud, from a joint of the stove pipes to the gray rug.

Kira stood before him. She could say nothing. She took his hand and raised it to her lips.

He swayed a little. He threw his head back and coughed.

*

Leo was late. He had been detained at a University lecture. Kira waited, the Primus hissing feebly, keeping his dinner hot.

The telephone rang. She heard a child's voice, trembling, panicky, gulping tears between words: "Is that you, Kira? . . . It's Acia. . . . Kira, please come over immediately, right away. . . . I'm scared. . . . There's something wrong. . . . I think it's mother. . . . There's no one home but father —and he won't call, and he won't speak, and I'm scared. . . . There's nothing to eat in the house. . . . Please, Kira,

I'm so scared. . . . Please come over. Please, Kira. . . ."

With all the money she had, Kira bought a bottle of milk and two pounds of bread in a private store, on her way over.

Acia opened the door. Her eyes were slits in a purple, swollen face. She grabbed Kira's skirt and sobbed dully, convulsively, her shoulders shaking, her nose buried in Kira's hem.

"Acia! What happened? Where's Irina? Where's Victor?"

"Victor's not home. Irina's gone for the doctor. I called a tenant and he said to get the hell out. I'm scared. . . ."

Vasili Ivanovitch sat by his wife's bed. His hands hung limply between his knees and he did not move. Maria Petrovna's hair was spilled over the white pillow. She breathed, hissing, the white coverlet rising and falling jerkily. On the white coverlet there was a wide, dark stain.

Kira stood helplessly, clutching the milk bottle in one hand, the bread in the other. Vasili Ivanovitch raised his head slowly and looked at her.

"Kira . . ." he said indifferently. ". . . Milk. . . . Would you mind heating it? . . . It might help. . . ."

Kira found the Primus. She heated the milk. She held a cup to the trembling blue lips. Maria Petrovna swallowed twice and pushed the cup away.

"Hemorrhage . . ." said Vasili Ivanovitch. "Irina's gone for the doctor. He has no phone. No other doctor will come. I have no money. The hospital won't send anyone—we're not Trade Union members."

A candle burned on the table. Through a sickly, yellow haze, a dusty fog more than a light, three tall, bare, curtainless windows stared like black gashes. A white pitcher lay upturned on a table, slowly dripping a few last drops into a dark puddle on the floor. A yellow circle shivered on the ceiling, over the candle, and a yellow glow shivered on Maria Petrovna's hands, as if her skin were trembling.

Maria Petrovna whined softly: "I'm all right . . . I'm all right . . . I know I'm all right. . . . Vasili just wants to frighten me. . . . No one can say I'm not all right. . . . I want to live . . . I'll live. . . . Who said I won't live?"

"Of course, you will, Aunt Marussia. You're all right. Just lie still. Relax."

"Kira, where's my nail buffer? Find my nail buffer. Irina's lost it again. I told her not to touch it. Where's my nail buffer?"

Kira opened a drawer in search of the buffer. A sound

stopped her. It was like pebbles rolling on a hard floor, like water gurgling through a clogged pipe and like an animal howling. Maria Petrovna was coughing. A dark froth ran down her white chin.

"Ice, Kira!" Vasili Ivanovitch cried. "Have we any ice?"

She ran, stumbling, down a dark corridor, to the kitchen. A thick coating of ice was frozen over the edge of the sink. She broke some off with the sharp, rusty blade of an old knife, cutting her hands. She came back, running, water dripping from the ice between her fingers.

Maria Petrovna howled, coughing: "Help me! Help me! Help me!"

They rolled the ice into a towel and put it on her chest. Red stains spread on her nightgown.

Suddenly she jerked herself up. The ice rolled, clattering, to the floor. A long pink strand of froth hung on her lower lip. Her eyes were wide with a horror beyond all human dignity. She was staring at Kira. She screamed:

"Kira! I want to live! I want to live!"

She fell back. Her hair jerked like snakes on the pillow and lay still. Her arm fell over the edge of the bed and lay still. A red bubble grew over her open mouth and burst in a spurt of something black and heavy, gurgling like the last drop through the clogged pipe. She did not move. Nothing moved on the bed but the black that slithered slowly down the skin of her throat.

Kira stood still.

Someone seized her hand. Vasili Ivanovitch buried his face in her hip and sobbed. He sobbed without a sound. She saw the gray hair shaking on his neck.

Behind a chair in a corner, Acia crouched on the floor and whined softly, monotonously.

Kira did not cry.

When she came home, Leo was sitting by the Primus, heating her dinner. He was coughing.

*

They sat at a small table in a dark corner of the restaurant. Kira had met Andrei at the Institute and he had invited her for a cup of tea with "real French pastry." The restaurant was almost empty. From the sidewalk outside, a few faces stared through the window, dull, incredulous faces watching those who could afford to sit in a restaurant. At a table in the center, a man in a huge fur coat was holding a dish of pastry for a smiling woman who hesitated in her choice, her fingers fluttering over the glistening chocolate frostings, a diamond glistening on her finger. The restaurant smelt of old rubber and stale fish. A long, sticky paper tube dangled from the central chandelier, brown with glue, black-dotted with dead flies. The tube swayed every time the kitchen door was opened. Over the kitchen door hung a picture of Lenin trimmed with bows of red crêpe paper.

"Kira, I almost broke my word. I was going to call on you. I was worried. I still am. You look so . . . pale. Anything wrong, Kira?"

"Some . . . trouble . . . at home."

"I had tickets for the ballet—'Swans' Lake.' I waited for you, but you missed all your lectures."

"I'm sorry. Was it beautiful?"

"I didn't go."

"Andrei, I think Pavel Syerov is trying to make trouble for you in the Party."

"He probably is. I don't like Pavel Syerov. While the Party is fighting speculators, he patronizes them. He's been known to buy a foreign sweater from a smuggler."

"Andrei, why doesn't your Party believe in the right to live while one is not killed?"

"Do you mean Syerov or—yourself?"

"Myself."

"In our fight, Kira, there is no neutrality."

"You may claim the right to kill, as all fighters do. But no one before you has ever thought of forbidding life to those still living."

She looked at the pitiless face before her; she saw two dark triangles in the sunken cheeks; the muscles of his face were taut. He was saying: "When one can stand any suffering, one can also see others suffer. This is martial law. Our time is dawn. There is a new sun rising, such as the world has never seen before. We are in the path of its first rays. Every pain, every cry of ours will be carried by these rays, as on a gigantic radius, down the centuries; every little figure will grow into an enormous shadow that will wipe out decades of future sorrow for every minute of ours."

The waiter brought the tea and pastry.

There was a convulsive little jerk in Kira's fingers as she raised a piece of pastry to her mouth, an involuntary, frightened hurry which was not mere greed for a rare delicacy.

"Kira!" Andrei gasped and dropped his fork. "Kira!"

She stared at him, frightened.

"Kira! Why didn't you tell me?"

"Andrei . . . I don't know what you're talking ab . . ." she tried to say, but knew what he had guessed.

"Wait! Don't eat that. Waiter! A bowl of hot soup right away. Then—dinner. Everything you have. Hurry! . . . Kira, I didn't know . . . I didn't know it was that bad."

She smiled feebly, helplessly: "I tried to find work. . . ."

"Why didn't you tell me?"

"I know you don't believe in using Party influence to help friends."

"Oh, but this . . . Kira . . . this!" It was the first time she had ever seen him frightened. He jumped up: "Excuse me a moment."

He strode across the room to a telephone. She could hear splinters of conversation: "Comrade Voronov. Urgent. . . . Andrei Taganov. . . . Conference? Interrupt it! . . . Comrade Voronov? . . . who has to be . . . immediately. . . . Yes . . . I don't care. Make one. . . . Yes. . . . No . . . No! . . . . Tomorrow morning. . . . Yes. . . . . Thank you, comrade. Good-bye."

Andrei came back to the table. He smiled down at her startled, incredulous face. "Well, you go to work tomorrow. In the office of the 'House of the Peasant.' It's not very much of a job, but it's one I could get for you right away—and it won't be hard. Be there at nine. Ask for Comrade Voronov. He'll know who you are. And—here." He opened his wallet and, emptying it, pressed a roll of bills into her hand.

"Oh, Andrei! I can't!"

"Well, maybe you can't—for yourself. But you can—for someone else. Isn't there someone at home who needs it—your family?"

She thought of someone at home who needed it. She took the money.

XV

When Kira slept, her head fell back on the pillow, so that the faint starlight outside made a white triangle under her chin. Her lashes lay still on pale, calm cheeks. Her lips breathed softly, half open, like a child's, with the hint of a smile in the corners, trusting and expectant, timid and radiantly young.

The alarm clock rang at six-thirty A.M. It had been ringing at six-thirty A.M. for the last two months.

Her first movement of the day was a convulsive leap into an icy precipice. She seized the alarm clock after its first hysterical shriek and turned it off—to let Leo sleep; then stood swaying, shivering, the sound of the alarm still ringing in her ears like an insult, a dark hatred in her body, a cry rising in every muscle like the pain of a great illness, calling her back into bed, her head too heavy for her body, the cold floor like fire under her bare feet.

Then she staggered blindly, groping in the darkness, into the bathroom. Her eyes wouldn't open. She reached for the bathtub faucet; it had been running slowly, gurgling in the darkness, all night; it had to be left running or the pipes would freeze. Eyes closed, she slapped cold water over her face with one hand; with the other, she leaned unsteadily on the edge of the bathtub, to keep from falling forward head first.

Then her eyes opened and she pulled her nightgown off, steam rising from her wet arms in the frozen air, while she tried to smile, her teeth chattering, telling herself that she was awake now and the worst was over.

She dressed and slipped back into the bedroom. She did not turn on the light. She could see the black silhouette of the Primus on the table against the dark blue of the window. She struck a match, her body shielding the bed from the little flare of light. She pumped the handle nervously. The Primus wouldn't light. The clock ticked in the darkness, the precious fleeting seconds hurrying her on. She pumped furiously, biting her lips. The blue flame sprang up at last. She put a pan of water over the flame.

She drank tea with saccharine and chewed slowly a piece of dry bread. The window before her was frozen into a solid pattern of white ferns that sparkled softly; beyond the window it was still night. She sat huddled by the table, afraid to move, trying to chew without a sound. Leo slept restlessly. He turned uneasily; he coughed, a dry, choking cough smothered by the pillow; he sighed once in a while in his sleep, a raucous sigh that was almost a moan.

She pulled on her felt boots, her winter coat, wound an old scarf around her throat. She tiptoed to the door, threw a last glance at the pale blur in the darkness that was Leo's face, and brushed her lips with her finger tips in a soundless kiss. Then she opened the door very slowly and as slowly closed it again behind her.

The snow was still blue outside. Above the roofs, the blue darkness receded in circles, so that far away down the sky one could guess a paler blue if one looked hard. Somewhere beyond the houses, a tramway shrieked like an early bird of prey.

Kira bent forward, gathered her hands into her armpits, in a tight, shivering huddle against the wind. The cold caught her breath with a sharp pain in her nostrils. She ran, slipping on the frozen sidewalks, toward the distant tramway.

A line waited for the tramway. She stood, bent to the wind and silent as the others. When the tramway came, yellow squares of light in space, shaking toward them through the darkness, the line broke. There was a swift whirlpool at the narrow door, a rustle of crushed bodies; the yellow squares of lighted windows filled speedily with shadows pressed tightly together, and Kira was left outside as the bell rang and the tramway tore forward. There was half an hour to wait for the next one; she would be late; if she were late, she would be fired; she ran after the tramway, leaped, caught a brass handle; but there was no room on the steps; her feet were dragged down the frozen ground as the tramway gained speed; someone's strong arm seized her shoulder blade and pulled her up; her one foot found space on the steps; a hoarse voice roared into her ear: "You—insane, citizen? That's how so many get killed!"

She hung in a cluster of men on the tramway steps, holding on with one hand and one foot, watching the streaked snow speed by on the ground, pressing herself with all her strength into the cluster of bodies, when a passing truck came too close and threatened to grind her off the tramway steps.

The "House of the Peasant" occupied someone's former mansion. It had a stairway of pale pink marble with a bronze balustrade, lighted by a huge stained-glass window where purple grapes and pink peaches rolled out of golden cornucopias. A sign was posted over the stairs: COMRADES! DO NOT SPIT ON THE FLOOR.

There were other signs: a huge sickle and hammer of gilded papier-mâché, a poster with a peasant woman and a sheaf of wheat, more posters of sheafs, golden sheafs, green sheafs, red sheafs, a picture of Lenin, a peasant grinding under foot a spider with the head of a priest, a picture of Trotzky, a peasant and a red tractor, a picture of Karl Marx, "Proletarians of the World, Unite!" "Who does not toil, shall not eat!"

"Long live the reign of workers and poor peasants!" "Comrade peasants, crush the hoarders in your midst!"

A new movement had been started in a blare of newspapers and posters for "a closer understanding between workers and peasants, a wider spread of city ideas through the country," a movement called "The Clamping of City and Village." The "House of the Peasant" was dedicated to such clamping. There were posters of workers and peasants shaking hands, of a worker and a peasant woman, also of a peasant and a working woman, of work bench and plow, of smokestacks and wheat fields, "Our future lies in the Clamping of City and Village!," "Comrades, strengthen the Clamping!," "Comrades, do your share for the Clamping!," "Comrades, what have *you* done for the Clamping?"

The posters rose like foam from the entrance door, up the stairway, to the office. In the office there were carved marble columns and partitions of unpainted wood; also—desks, files, pictures of proletarian leaders and a typewriter; also—Comrade Bitiuk, the office manager, and five office workers, among them Kira Argounova.

Comrade Bitiuk was a tall woman, thin, gray-haired, military and in strict sympathy with the Soviet Government; her chief aim in life was to give constant evidence of how strict that sympathy was, even though she had graduated from a women's college and wore on her breast an old-fashioned watch on a bow of burnished silver.

Her four office workers were: a tall girl with a long nose and a leather jacket, who was a Party member and could make Comrade Bitiuk shudder at her slightest whim, and knew it; a young man with a bad complexion, who was not a Party member yet, but had made an application and was a candidate, and never missed a chance to mention it; and two young girls who worked merely because they needed the wages: Nina and Tina. Nina wore earrings and answered the telephone; Tina powdered her nose and ran the typewriter. A habit which had sprung from nowhere and spread over the country, which even Party members could not check or resist, for which no one was responsible nor could be punished, referred to all products of local inefficiency as "Soviet"; there were "Soviet matches" that did not light, "Soviet kerchiefs" that tore the first time worn, "Soviet shoes" with cardboard soles. Young women like Nina and Tina were called "Soviet girls."

There were many floors and many offices in the "House of the Peasant." Many feet hurried up and down its many corridors in a steady drone of activity. Kira never learned just what that activity was, nor who worked in the building, besides those in her office and the imposing Comrade Voronov whom she had seen once on her first day in the "House of the Peasant."

As Comrade Bitiuk reminded them constantly, the "House of the Peasant" was "the heart of a gigantic net whose veins poured the beneficial light of the new Proletarian Culture into the darkest corners of our farthest villages." It represented the hospitable arms of the city open wide in welcome to all peasant delegations, all comrades from the villages who came to the city. It stood there as their guide and teacher, as the devoted servant of their cultural and spiritual needs.

From her desk, Kira watched Comrade Bitiuk gushing into the telephone: "Yes, yes, comrade, it's all arranged. At one o'clock the comrade peasants of the Siberian delegation go to the Museum of the Revolution—the history of our Revolutionary movement from its first days—an easy, visualized course in Proletarian history—within two hours—very valuable—and we have made arrangements for a special guide. At three o'clock the comrade peasants go to our Marxist Club where we have arranged a special lecture on the 'Problems of the Soviet City and Village.' At five o'clock the comrade peasants are expected at a club of the Pioneers where the children have called a special meeting in their honor—there will be a display of physical culture drills by the dear little tots. At seven o'clock the comrade peasants go to the opera—we have reserved two boxes at the Marinsky Theater—where they will hear 'Aïda.' "

When Comrade Bitiuk hung up the receiver, she whirled around in her chair, snapping a military command: "Comrade Argounova! Do you have the requisition for the special lecturer?"

"No, Comrade Bitiuk."

"Comrade Ivanova! Have you typed that requisition?"

"What requisition, Comrade Bit . . . ?"

"The requisition for the special lecturer for the delegation of the comrade peasants from Siberia!"

"But you didn't tell me to type any requisitions, Comrade Bitiu . . ."

"I wrote it myself and put it on your desk."

"Oh, yes, sure, oh, that's what it was for? Oh, well, I saw it, but I didn't know I was to type it, Comrade Bitiuk. And my typewriter ribbon is torn."

"Comrade Argounova, do you have the approved requisition for a new typewriter ribbon for Comrade Ivanova's typewriter?"

"No, Comrade Bitiuk."

"Where is it?"

"In Comrade Voronov's office."

"What is it doing there?"

"Comrade Voronov hasn't signed it yet."

"Have the others signed?"

"Yes, Comrade Bitiuk. Comrade Semenov has signed it, and Comrade Vlassova, and Comrade Pereverstov. But Comrade Voronov has not returned it yet."

"Some people do not realize the tremendous cultural importance of the work we're doing!" Comrade Bitiuk raged, but noticing the cold, suspicious stare of the girl in the leather jacket, who heard this criticism of a higher official, she hastened to correct herself. "I meant you, Comrade Argounova. You do not show sufficient interest in your work nor any proletarian consciousness. It's up to you to see that this requisition is signed."

"Yes, Comrade Bitiuk."

Through the hours, thin and pale in her faded dress, Kira filed documents, typewritten documents, certificates, reports, accounts, requisitions that had to be filed where no one ever looked at them again; she counted books, columns of books, mountains of books, fresh from the printers, ink staining her fingers, books in red and white paper covers to be sent to Peasant Clubs all over the country: "What you can do for the Clamping," "The Red Peasant," "The work-bench and the plow," "The ABC of Communism," "Comrade Lenin and Comrade Marx." There were many telephone calls; there were many people coming in and going out, to be called "comrades" and "citizens"; there were many times to repeat mechanically, like a well-wound gramophone, imitating Comrade Bitiuk's enthusiastic inflations: "Thus, comrade, you will be doing your share for the Clamping," and "The cultural progress of the Proletariat, comrade, requires that . . ."

Sometimes a comrade peasant came into the office in person. He stood behind the low, unpainted partition, timidly crumpling his fur cap in one hand, scratching his head with the other. He nodded slowly, his bewildered eyes staring at Kira without comprehension, as she told him: ". . . and we have arranged an excursion for the comrades of your delegation through the Winter Palace where you can see how the

Czar lived—an easy, visualized lesson in class tyranny—and then . . ."

The peasant mumbled in his blond beard: "Now, about that grain shortage matter, comrade. . . ."

"Then, after the excursion, we have a special lecture arranged for you on 'The Doom of Capitalism.'"

When the comrade peasant left, Nina or Tina snooped cautiously around the place where he had stood, inspecting the wooden railing. Once, Kira saw Nina cracking something on her thumb nail.

This morning, on her way up to the office, Kira stopped on the stair landing and looked at the Wall Newspaper. The "House of the Peasant," like all institutions, had a Wall Newspaper written by the employees, edited by the local Communist Cell, pasted in a prominent spot for all comrades to read; the Wall Newspapers were to "stimulate the social spirit and the consciousness of collective activity"; they were devoted to "local news of social importance and constructive proletarian criticism."

The Wall Newspaper of the "House of the Peasant" was a square meter of typewritten strips pasted on a blackboard with headlines in red and blue pencil. There was a prominent editorial on "What each one of us comrades here does for the Clamping," there was a humorous article on "How we'll puncture the foreign Imperialist's belly," there was a poem by a local poet about "The Rhythm of Toil," there was a cartoon by a local artist, representing a fat man in a high silk hat sitting on a toilet. There were many items of constructive proletarian criticism:

"Comrade Nadia Chernova is wearing silk stockings. Time to be reminded that such flaunting of luxury is un-proletarian, Comrade Chernova."

"A certain comrade in a high position has lately allowed his position to go to his head. He has been known to be curt and rude to young members of the Komsomol. This is a warning, comrade * * * Many a better head has been known to fall when the time came for a reduction of staffs."

"Comrade E. Ovsov indulges in too much talk when asked about business. This leads to a waste of valuable time and is not at all in the spirit of proletarian efficiency."

"A certain comrade whom many will recognize, neglects to turn off the light when leaving the rest-room. Electricity costs money to the Soviet State, comrade."

"We hear that Comrade Kira Argounova is lacking in social

spirit. The time is past, Comrade Argounova, for arrogant bourgeois attitudes."

She stood very still and heard her heart beating. No one dared to ignore the mighty pointing finger of the Wall Newspaper. All watched it carefully and a little nervously, all bowed reverently to its verdict, from Nina and Tina up to Comrade Voronov himself. The Wall Newspaper was the voice of Social Activity. No one could save those branded as "anti-social element," not even Andrei Taganov. There had been talk of a reduction of staffs. Kira felt cold. She thought that Leo had had nothing but millet for dinner the night before. She thought of Leo's cough.

At her desk, she watched the others in the room, wondering who had reported her to the Wall Newspaper, who and why. She had been so very careful. She had never uttered a word of criticism against the Soviets. She had been as loyally enthusiastic in her work as Comrade Bitiuk herself, or as nearly as she could imitate her. She had been careful never to argue, nor to answer sharply, nor to make an enemy of anyone. Her fingers counting rapidly volumes of the works of Karl Marx, she asked herself helplessly, desperately: "Am I still different? Am I different from them? How do they know I'm different? What have I done? What is it I haven't done?"

When Comrade Bitiuk left the office, which happened frequently, work stopped. The staff congregated around Tina's typewriter. There were eager whispered conferences about the co-operative that gave the loveliest printed calico that made the loveliest blouses, about the Nepman's stand in the market that sold cotton stockings "so thin it's just like silk," and about lovers, particularly Tina's lovers. Tina was considered the prettiest in the office, and the most successful with men. No one had ever seen her little nose without its whitish coat of powder; there was a strong suspicion in the office that she blackened her eyelashes; and several different masculine figures had been seen waiting to take her home after work. The girl with the leather jacket, being a Party member, was the undisputed leader and final authority in all their discussions; but in matters of romance, she conceded first rank to Tina. She listened with a superior, condescending smile that did not hide her eager curiosity, while Tina whispered breathlessly:

". . . And Mishka rang the bell and here was Ivashka in his underdrawers and I hear Elena Maximovna—that's the tenant in the next room—I hear Elena Maximovna say: 'A guest for you, Tina,' and before I know it, here's Mishka walking right in and Ivashka in his underdrawers—and you should've seen Mishka's face, honest, it was better than a comedy show —and I think quick and I say: 'Mishka dear, this is Ivan, the neighbor, he lives with Elena Maximovna and he wasn't feeling well, so he came in for an aspirin tablet,' and you should've seen Ivashka's face, and Elena Maximovna she says: 'Sure, he lives with me. Come on back to my room, darling.' And do you think that louse Ivashka refused?"

The young man who was a Party candidate did not join these conversations, but stayed modestly at his desk, listening intently and remarking once in a while: "You comrades women! I bet you say things that a serious citizen who is a Party candidate shouldn't even hear."

They giggled, flattered, and rewarded him with friendly glances.

Kira stayed at her desk and went on with her work, and did not listen. She never talked to anyone outside of business matters. If any glances were thrown at her occasionally, they were not friendly.

She wondered with a cold feeling of panic whether that was what they resented, whether that was her arrogant bourgeois attitude. She needed this job. Leo needed this job. She had made up her mind to keep it. She would keep it.

She rose and walked casually to Tina's desk. The little group noticed her presence by a few cold, astonished glances and went on with their whispers.

She waited for a pause and said suddenly, irrelevantly, forcing all of the artificial enthusiasm she had learned into her flat, unsteady voice: "Funny thing happened last night. My boy friend—he quarreled with me because . . . because he had seen me coming home with another man . . . and he . . . he bawled me out terribly . . . and I told him it was an old-fashioned bourgeois attitude of proprietorship, but he . . . well . . . he quarreled with me. . . ."

She felt her blouse sticking to the cold spot between her shoulder blades. She tried to make her voice as gaily flippant as Tina's. She tried to believe the story she was inventing; it was strange to think of the fantastic boy friend offered to those prying, hostile eyes, and of the Leo whom Irina had drawn naked as a god.

". . . and he bawled me out terribly. . . ."

"Uh-huh," said Nina.

The girl in the leather jacket said nothing.

"In the Kouznetzky market," said Tina, "I've seen them selling lipstick, the new Soviet lipstick of the Cosmetic Trust. Cheap, too. Only they say it's dangerous to use it. It's made from horse fat and the horses died of glanders."

*

At twelve-thirty the office closed for lunch. At twelve-twenty-five, Comrade Bitiuk said: "I shall remind you once more, comrades, that at one-thirty, instead of reporting back to the office, you are to report at the Smolny Institute to take part in the demonstration of all the workers of Petrograd in honor of the delegation of the British Trade Unions. The office will be closed this afternoon."

Kira spent her lunch hour standing in line at the co-operative to get bread on her employee's ration card. She stood motionless, in a blank stupor; a movement or a thought seemed too far away, far in a world where she did not belong any longer. The locks of hair under her old hat were white with frost. She thought that somewhere beyond all these many things which did not count, was her life and Leo. She closed her eyes for one swift second of rest with nothing but his name. Then she opened her eyes and watched dully, through lids heavy with white-frosted lashes, puffy sparrows picking horse dung in the snow.

She had brought her lunch with her—a piece of dried fish wrapped in paper. She ate it, because she knew she had to eat. When she got the bread—a two-pound brown square that was still fresh—she smelled its comforting, warm odor and chewed slowly a piece of crust; the rest, tucked firmly under her arm, was for Leo.

She ran after a tramway and leaped on just in time for the long ride to the Smolny Institute at the other end of the city, for the demonstration of all the workers of Petrograd in honor of the delegation of the British Trade Unions.

*

Nevsky looked as if it were a solid spread of heads motionless on a huge belt that rolled slowly, carrying them forward. It looked as if red banners, swollen like sails between two poles, were swimming slowly over motionless heads, the same heads of khaki caps, fur caps, red kerchiefs, hats, khaki caps, red kerchiefs. A dull beating filled the street from wall to wall, up to the roofs, the crunching, creaking, drumming roll of many feet against frozen cobblestones.

Tramways stopped and trucks waited on corners to let the

demonstration pass. A few heads appeared at windows, stared indifferently at the heads below and disappeared again: Petrograd was used to demonstrations.

WE, TOILERS OF PETROGRAD, GREET OUR BRITISH CLASS BROTH-ERS! WELCOME TO THE LAND OF THE SOVIETS WHERE LABOR IS FREE!
THE WOMEN OF THE STATE TEXTILE PLANT NUMBER 2 PLEDGE THEIR SUPPORT TO ENGLAND'S PROLETARIAT IN ITS STRUGGLE WITH IMPERIALISTS

Kira marched between Nina and Comrade Bitiuk. Comrade Bitiuk had changed her hat to a red kerchief for the occasion. Kira marched steadily, shoulders thrown back, head high. She had to march here to keep her job; she had to keep her job for Leo; she was not a traitor, she was marching for Leo— even though the banner above her, carried by Tina and the Party candidates, said:

WE, SOVIET PEASANTS, STAND AS ONE FOR OUR BRITISH CLASS BROTHERS!

Kira could not feel her feet any longer; but she knew that she was walking, for she was moving ahead like the others. Her hands felt as if her mittens were filled with boiling water. She had to walk. She was walking.

Somewhere in the long snake that uncoiled slowly down Nevsky, someone's hoarse, loud voice began to sing the "Internationale." Others joined. It rolled in raucous, discordant waves down the long column of weary throats choked by frost.

On the Palace Square, now called Square of Uritzki, a wooden amphitheater had been erected. Against the red walls and mirror-like windows of the Winter Palace, on the wooden stand draped in red bunting, stood the delegation of the British Trade Unions. The workers of Petrograd slowly marched past. The British class brothers stood, a little stiff, a little embarrassed, a little bewildered.

Kira's eyes saw but one person: the woman delegate of the British Trade Unions. She was tall, thin, not young, with the worried face of a school teacher. But she wore a tan sports coat and that coat yelled louder than the hurrahs of the crowd, louder than the "Internationale," that it was *foreign*. With firm, pressed folds of rich material, trim, well-fitted, serene, that coat did not moan, like all those others around Kira, of the misery of the muscles underneath. The British comrade wore silk stockings; a rich, brownish sheen, tight on feet in trim, new, well-polished brown shoes.

And suddenly Kira wanted to scream and to hurl herself at the stand, and to grab these thin, glittering legs and hang on with her teeth as to an anchor, and be carried away with them into their world which was possible somewhere, which was now here, close, within hearing of a cry for help.

But she only swayed a little and closed her eyes.

The demonstration stopped. It stood, knocking heels together to keep warm, listening to speeches. There were many speeches. The comrade woman of the British Trade Unions spoke. A hoarse interpreter bellowed her words into the Square red and khaki with heads packed tightly together.

"This is a thrilling sight. We were sent here by England's workers to see for ourselves and to tell the world the truth about the great experiment you are conducting. We shall tell them that we saw the great masses of Russian toilers in a free and magnificent expression of loyalty to the Soviet Government."

For one insane second, Kira wondered if she could tear through the crowd, rush up to that woman and yell to her, to England's workers, to the world, the truth they were seeking. But she thought of Leo at home, marble pale, coughing. It was Leo against the truth to a world which would not listen. Leo won.

*

At five P.M. a glittering limousine whisked the delegates away and the demonstration broke up. It was growing dark. Kira had time for a lecture at the Institute.

The cold, badly lighted auditoriums were a tonic to her, with the charts, drafts and prints on the walls, showing beams and girders and cross sections that looked precise, impersonal and unsullied. For a short hour, even though her stomach throbbed with hunger, she could remember that she was to be a builder who would build aluminum bridges and towers of steel and glass; and that there was a future.

After the lecture, hurrying out through dim corridors, she met Comrade Sonia.

"Ah, Comrade Argounova," said Comrade Sonia. "We haven't seen you for a long time. Not so active in your studies any more, are you? And as to social activity—why, you're the most privately individualistic student we've got."

"I . . ." Kira began.

"None of my business, Comrade Argounova, I know, none of my business. I was just thinking of things one hears nowadays about things the Party may do about students who are not social-minded. Don't give it a thought."

"I . . . you see . . ." Kira knew it wiser to explain. "I'm working and I'm very active socially in our Marxist Club."

"So? You are, are you? We know you bourgeois. All you're active for is to keep your measly jobs. You're not fooling anyone."

*

When Kira entered the room, Marisha jumped up like a spring unwinding: "Citizen Argounova! You keep your damn cat in your own room or I'll wring her neck!"

"My cat? What cat? I have no cat."

"Well, who's done this? Your boy friend?" Marisha was pointing at a puddle in the middle of her room. "And what's that? An elephant?" She raged as a meow and a pair of gray, furry ears emerged from under a chair.

"It's not my cat," said Kira.

"Where's she come from, then?"

"How do I know?"

"You never know anything!"

Kira did not answer and went to her room. She heard Marisha in the little hall off the lobby, pounding at the partition that separated them from the other tenants. She heard her yelling: "Hey, you there! Your God-damn cat's torn a board loose and here she is, crapping all over the place! You take her away or I'll gut her alive and report you to the Upravdom!"

Leo was not at home. The room was dark, cold as a cellar. Kira switched on the light. The bed was not made; the blanket was on the floor. She lighted the "Bourgeoise," blowing at the damp logs, her eyes swelling. The pipes were leaking. She hung a tin can on a wire to catch the dripping soot.

She pumped the Primus. It would not light; its tubes were clogged again. She searched all over the room for the special wire cleaner. She could not find it. She knocked at the door.

"Citizen Lavrova, have you taken my Primus cleaner again?" There was no answer. She flung the door open. "Citizen Lavrova, have you taken my Primus cleaner?"

"Aw, hell," said Marisha. "Stingy, aren't you, of a little Primus cleaner? Here it is."

"How many times do I have to ask you, Citizen Lavrova, not to touch any of my things in my absence?"

"What are you gonna do about it? Report me?"

Kira took the Primus cleaner and slammed the door.

She was peeling potatoes when Leo came in.

"Oh," he said, "you're home?"

"Yes. Where have you been, Leo?"

"Any of your business?"

She did not answer. His shoulders were drooping and his lips were blue. She knew where he had been; and that he had not succeeded.

She went on peeling the potatoes. He stood with his hands extended to the "Bourgeoise," his lips twisted with pain. He coughed. Then he turned abruptly and said: "Same thing. You know. Since eight this morning. No opening. No job. No work."

"It's all right, Leo. We don't have to worry."

"No? We don't, do we? You're enjoying it, aren't you, to see me living off you? You're glad to remind me that I don't have to worry while you're working yourself into a scarecrow of a martyr?"

"Leo!"

"Well, I don't want to see you work! I don't want to see you cook! I don't . . . Oh, Kira!" He seized her and put his head on her shoulder, and buried his face in her neck, over the blue flame of the Primus. "Kira, you forgive me, don't you?"

She patted his hair with her cheek, for her hands were sticky with potato peelings. "Of course. . . . Dearest. . . . Why don't you lie down and rest? Dinner will be ready in just a little while."

"Why don't you let me help you?"

"Now there's an argument that we've closed long ago."

He bent down to her, lifting her chin. She whispered, shuddering a little: "Don't, Leo. Don't kiss me—here." She held out her dirty hands over the Primus.

He did not kiss her. A bitter little smile of understanding jerked one corner of his mouth. He walked to the bed and fell down.

He lay so still, his head thrown back, one arm hanging to the floor, that she felt uncomfortable. Once in a while, she called softly: "Leo," just to see him open his eyes. Then she wished she hadn't called: she did not want his eyes to stay open, watching her fixedly. She—who had so carefully closed the door between them so that he might not see her as she did not want to be seen—she stood before him now, bent over a Primus, in an aura of kerosene and onion smell, her hands slimy with raw mud, her hair hanging down in sticky strands over a nose shiny without powder, her eyes and nostrils red on a white face, her body sagging limply under a filthy apron she had no time to wash, her movements heavy and slurred, not the sharp play of muscles, but the slothful fall of limbs pushed by a weariness beyond control.

And when dinner was ready and they sat facing each other across the table, she thought with a pain which would not become a habit, that he—whom she wanted to face, looking young, erect, vibrant with all of her worship—he now looked into eyes swollen with smoke and at a pale mouth that smiled an effort she could not hide.

They had millet, potatoes, and onions fried in linseed oil. She was so hungry that her arms were limp. But she could not touch the millet. She felt suddenly an uncontrollable revulsion, a hatred that could let her starve rather than swallow one more spoonful of the bitter stuff she had eaten, it seemed, all her life. She wondered dully whether there was a place on earth where one could eat without being sick of every mouthful; a place where eggs and butter and sugar were not a sublime ideal longed for agonizingly, never attained.

She washed the dishes in cold water, grease floating over the pan. Then she pulled on her felt boots. "I have to go out, Leo," she said with resignation. "It's the Marxist Club night. Social activity, you know."

He did not answer; he did not look at her as she went out.

*

The Marxist Club held its sessions in the library of the "House of the Peasant." The library was like all the other rooms in the building except that it had more posters and fewer books; and the books were lined on shelves, instead of being stacked in tall columns ready for shipping.

The girl in the leather jacket was chairman of the Club; the employees of the "House of the Peasant" were members. The Club was dedicated to "political self-education" and the study of "historical revolutionary philosophy"; it met twice a week; one member read a thesis he had prepared, the others discussed it.

It was Kira's turn. She read her thesis on "Marxism and Leninism."

"Leninism is Marxism adapted to Russian reality. Karl Marx, the great founder of Communism, believed that Socialism was to be the logical outcome of Capitalism in a country of highly developed Industrialism and with a proletariat attuned to a high degree of class-consciousness. But our great leader, Comrade Lenin, proved that . . ."

She had copied her thesis, barely changing the words, from the "ABC of Communism," a book whose study was compulsory in every school in the country. She knew that all her listeners had read it, that they had also read her thesis, time and time again, in every editorial of every newspaper for the last six years. They sat around her, hunched, legs stretched out limply, shivering in their overcoats. They knew she was there for the same reason they were. The girl in the leather jacket presided, yawning once in a while.

When Kira finished, a few hands clapped drowsily.

"Who desires to make comments, comrades?" the chairman inquired.

A young girl with a very round face and forlorn eyes, said lisping, showing eagerly her active interest: "I think it was a very nice thesis, and very valuable and instructive, because it was very nice and clear and explained a valuable new theory."

A consumptive and intellectual young man with blue eyelids and a pince-nez, said in the professional manner of a scientist: "I would make the following criticism, Comrade Argounova: when you speak of the fact that Comrade Lenin allowed a place for the peasant beside the industrial worker in the scheme of Communism, you should specify that it is a *poor* peasant, not just any kind of a peasant, because it is well known that there are rich peasants in the villages, who are hostile to Leninism."

Kira knew that she had to argue and defend her thesis; she knew that the consumptive young man had to argue to show his activity; she knew that he was no more interested in the discussion than she was, that his blue eyelids were weary with sleeplessness, that he clasped his thin hands nervously, not daring to glance at his wristwatch, not daring to let his thoughts wander to the home and its cares that awaited him somewhere.

She said dully: "When I mention the peasant beside the

worker in Comrade Lenin's theory, it is to be taken for granted that I mean the poor peasant, as no other has a place in Communism."

The young man said drowsily: "Yes, but I think we should be scientifically methodical and say: *poor* peasant."

The chairman said: "I agree with the last speaker. The thesis should be corrected to read: *poor* peasant. Any other comments, comrades?"

There were none.

"We shall thank Comrade Argounova for her valuable work," said the chairman. "Our next meeting will be devoted to a thesis by Comrade Leskov on 'Marxism and Collectivism.' I now declare this meeting closed."

With a convulsive jerk and a clatter of chairs, they rushed out of the library, down the dark stairs, into the dark streets. They had done their duty. The evening—or what was left of it—belonged to them now.

Kira walked fast and listened to her own footsteps, listened blankly, without thought; she could think now, but after so many hours of such a tremendous effort not to think, not to think, to remember only not to think, thoughts seemed slow to return; she knew only that her steps were beating, fast, firm, precise, until their strength and their hope rose to her body, to her heart, to the throbbing haze in her temples. She threw her head back, as if she were resting, swimming on her back, close under a clear black sky, with stars at the tip of her nose, and roof tops with snow clean in the frozen starlight like white virgin mountain peaks.

Then she swung forward with the sharp, light movements of Kira Argounova's body and she whispered to herself, as she had talked to herself often in the last two months: "Well, it's war. It's war. You don't give up, do you, Kira? It's not dangerous so long as you don't give up. You're a soldier, Kira, and you don't give up. And the harder it gets the happier you should be that you can stand it. That's it. The harder—the happier. It's war. You're a good soldier, Kira Argounova."

*

When Leo put his arms around her and whispered into her hair: "Oh, yes, yes, Kira. Tonight. Please!" she knew that she could not refuse any longer. Her body, suddenly limp again, cried for nothing but sleep, an endless sleep. It horrified her, that reluctant surrender, numb, lifeless, without response.

He held her body close to his, and his skin was warm under

the cold blanket. His skin was warm, and soothing, and she closed her eyes.

"What's the matter, Kira?"

She smiled and forced all of her last strength into her lips in the hollow of his collar bone, into her arms locked around his body. Her arms relaxed and one hand slipped, soft and weak, over the edge of the bed. She jerked her eyes open, she loved him, she wanted him, she wanted to want him—she screamed to herself almost aloud. He was kissing her body, but she was thinking of what they thought of her thesis, of Tina and the girl in the leather jacket, of the probable reduction of staffs—and suddenly she was seized with revulsion for his soft, hungry lips, because something in her, or of her, or around her was too unworthy of him. But she could keep awake a little while longer and she stiffened her body as for an ordeal, all her thoughts of love reduced to a tortured hurry to get it over with.

*

It was past midnight and she did not know whether she had been asleep or not. Leo breathed painfully on the pillow beside her, his forehead clammy with cold perspiration. In the haze of her mind, one thought stood out clearly: the apron. That apron of hers was filthy; it was loathsome; she could not let Leo see her wearing it another day; not another day.

She crawled out of bed and slipped her coat over her night-gown; it was too cold and she was too tired to dress. She put the pan of cold water on the bathroom floor, and fell down by its side and crammed the apron, the soap and her hands into a liquid that felt like acid.

She did not know whether she was quite awake and she did not care. She knew only that the big yellow grease spot wouldn't come off, and she rubbed, and she rubbed, and she rubbed, with the dry, acrid, yellow soap, with her nails, with her knuckles, soap suds on the fur cuffs of her coat, huddled on the floor, her breasts panting against the tin edge of the pan, her hair falling down, down into the suds, beyond the narrow crack of the bathroom door a tall blue window sparkling with frost, her knuckles raw, the skin rubbed off, beyond the bedroom door someone in Marisha's room playing "John Gray" on a piano with a missing key, the pain growing in her knuckles, in her eyes, in her knees, across her back, the soap suds brown and greasy over purple hands.

*

They saved the money for many months and on a Sunday evening they bought two tickets to see "Bajadere," advertised as the "latest sensation of Vienna, Berlin and Paris."

They sat, solemn, erect, reverent as at a church service, Kira a little paler than usual in her gray silk dress, Leo trying not to cough, and they listened to the wantonest operetta from over there, from *abroad*.

It was very gay nonsense. It was like a glance straight through the snow and the flags, through the border, into the heart of that other world. There were colored lights, and spangles, and crystal goblets, and a real foreign bar with a dull glass archway where a green light moved slowly upward, preceding every entrance—a real foreign elevator. There were women in shimmering satin from a place where fashions existed, and people dancing a funny foreign dance called "Shimmy," and a woman who did not sing, but barked words out, spitting them contemptuously at the audience, in a flat, hoarse voice that trailed suddenly into a husky moan—and a music that laughed defiantly, panting, gasping, hitting one's ears and throat and breath, an impudent, drunken music, like the challenge of a triumphant gaiety, like the "Song of Broken Glass," a promise that existed somewhere, that was, that could be.

The public laughed, and applauded, and laughed. When the lights went on after the final curtain, in the procession of cheerful grins down the aisles many noticed with astonishment a girl in a gray silk dress, who sat in an emptying row, bent over, her face in her hands, sobbing.

XVI

At first there were whispers.

Students gathered in groups in dark corners and jerked their heads nervously at every approaching newcomer, and in their whispers one heard the words: "The Purge."

In lines at co-operatives and in tramways people asked: "Have you heard about the Purge?"

In the columns of *Pravda* there appeared many mentions

of the deplorable state of Red colleges and of the coming Purge.

And then, at the end of the winter semester, in the Technological Institute, in the University and in all the institutions of higher education, there appeared a large notice with huge letters in red pencil:

THE PURGE

The notice directed all students to call at the office, receive questionnaires, fill them out promptly, have their Upravdom certify to the truth of the answers and return them to the Purging Committee. The schools of the Union of Socialist Soviet Republics were to be cleaned of all socially undesirable persons. Those found socially undesirable were to be expelled, never to be admitted to any college again.

Newspapers roared over the country like trumpets: "Science is a weapon of the class struggle! Proletarian schools are for the Proletariat! We shall not educate our class enemies!"

There were those who were careful not to let these trumpets be heard too loudly across the border.

Kira received her questionnaire at the Institute, and Leo—his at the University. They sat silently at their dinner table, filling out the answers. They did not eat much dinner that night. When they signed the questionnaires, they knew they had signed the death warrant of their future; but they did not say it aloud and they did not look at each other.

The main questions were:

> Who were your parents?
> What was your father's occupation prior to the year 1917?
> What was your father's occupation from the year 1917 to the year 1921?
> What is your father's occupation now?
> What is your mother's occupation?
> What did you do during the civil war?
> What did your father do during the civil war?
> Are you a Trade Union member?
> Are you a member of the All-Union Communist Party?

Any attempt to give a false answer was futile; the answers were to be investigated by the Purging Committee and the

G.P.U. A false answer was to be punished by arrest, imprisonment or any penalty up to the supreme one.

Kira's hand trembled a little when she handed to the Purge Committee the questionnaire that bore the answer:

What was your father's occupation prior to the year 1917?
Owner of the Argounov Textile Factory.

What awaited those who were to be expelled, no one dared to think; no one mentioned it; the questionnaires were turned in and the students waited for a call from the committee, waited silently, nerves tense as wires. In the long corridors of the colleges, where the troubled stream of students clotted into restless clusters, they whispered that one's "social origin" was most important—that if you were of "bourgeois descent," you didn't have a chance—that if your parents had been wealthy, you were still a "class enemy," even though you were starving—and that you must try, if you could, at the price of your immortal soul, if you had one, to prove your "origin from the work-bench or the plough." There were more leather jackets, and red kerchiefs, and sunflower-seed shells in the college corridors, and jokes about: "My parents? Why, they were a peasant woman and two workers."

It was spring again, and melting snow drilled the sidewalks, and blue hyacinths were sold on street corners. But those who were young had no thought left for spring and those who still thought were not young any longer.

Kira Argounova, head high, stood before the Purge Committee of the Technological Institute. At the table, among the men of the committee whom she did not know, sat three persons she knew: Comrade Sonia, Pavel Syerov, Andrei Taganov.

It was Pavel Syerov who did most of the questioning. Her questionnaire lay on the table before him. "So, Citizen Argounova, your father was a factory owner?"

"Yes."

"I see. And your mother? Did she work before the revolution?"

"No."

"I see. Did you employ servants in your home?"

"Yes."

"I see."

Comrade Sonia asked: "And you've never joined a Trade Union, Citizen Argounova? Didn't find it desirable?"

"I have never had the opportunity."

"I see."

Andrei Taganov listened. His face did not move. His eyes were cold, steady, impersonal, as if he had never seen Kira before. And suddenly she felt an inexplicable pity for him, for that immobility and what it hid, although he showed not the slightest sign of what it hid.

But when he asked her a question suddenly, even though his voice was hard and his eyes empty, the question was a plea: "But you've always been in strict sympathy with the Soviet Government, Citizen Argounova, haven't you?"

She answered very softly: "Yes."

*

Somewhere, around a lamp, late in the night, amid rustling papers, reports and documents, a committee was holding a conference.

"Factory owners were the chief exploiters of the Proletariat."

"Worse than landowners."

"Most dangerous of class enemies."

"We are performing a great service to the cause of the Revolution and no personal feelings are to interfere with our duty."

"Order from Moscow—children of former factory owners are in the first category to be expelled."

A voice asked, weighing every word: "Any exceptions to that rule, Comrade Taganov?"

He stood by a window, his hands clasped behind his back. He answered: "None."

*

The names of those expelled were typewritten on a long sheet of paper and posted on a blackboard in the office of the Technological Institute.

Kira had expected it. But when she saw the name on the list: *"Argounova, Kira,"* she closed her eyes and looked again and read the long list carefully, to make sure.

Then she noticed that her brief case was open; she clasped the catch carefully; she looked at the hole in her glove and stuck her finger out, trying to see how far it would go, and twisted an unraveled thread into a little snake and watched it uncoil.

Then she felt that someone was watching her. She turned. Andrei stood alone in a window niche. He was looking at her, but he did not move forward, he did not say a word, he did not incline his head in greeting. She knew what he feared, what he hoped, what he was waiting for. She walked to him, and looked up at him, and extended her hand with the same trusting smile he had known on the same young lips, only the lips trembled a little.

"It's all right, Andrei. I know you couldn't help it."

She had not expected the gratitude, a gratitude like pain, in his low voice when he answered: "I'd give you my place—if I could."

"Oh, it's all right. . . . Well . . . I guess I won't be a builder after all. . . . I guess I won't build any aluminum bridges." She tried to laugh. "It's all right, because everybody always told me one can't build a bridge of aluminum anyway." She noticed that it was harder for him to smile than for her. "And, Andrei," she said softly, knowing that he did not dare to ask it, "this doesn't mean that we won't see each other any more, does it?"

He took her hand in both of his. "It doesn't, Kira, if . . ."

"Well, then, it doesn't. Give me your phone number and address, so I can call you, because we . . . we won't meet here . . . any more. We're such good friends that—isn't it funny?—I've never even known your address. All's for the best. Maybe . . . maybe we'll be better friends now."

*

When she came home, Leo was sprawled across the bed, and he didn't get up. He looked at her and laughed. He laughed dryly, monotonously, senselessly.

She stood still, looking at him.

"Thrown out?" he asked, rising on a wavering elbow, his hair falling over his face. "Don't have to tell me. I know. You're kicked out. Like a dog. So am I. Like two dogs. Congratulations, Kira Alexandrovna. Hearty proletarian congratulations!"

"Leo, you've . . . you've been drinking!"

"Sure. To celebrate. All of us did. Dozens and dozens of us at the University. A toast to the Dictatorship of the Proletariat. . . . Many toasts to the Dictatorship of the Proletariat. . . . Don't stare at me like that. . . . It's a good old custom to drink at births, and weddings, and funerals. . . . Well, we weren't born together, Comrade Argounova. . . . And we've never had a wedding, Comrade Argounova. . . . But we might yet see the other. . . . We might . . . yet . . . the other . . . Kira. . . ."

She was on her knees by the bed, gathering to her breast a pale face with a contorted wound of a mouth, she was brushing damp hair off his forehead, she was whispering: "Leo . . . dearest . . . you shouldn't do that. . . . Now's the time you shouldn't. . . . We have to think clearly now. . . ." She was whispering without conviction. "It's not dangerous so long as we don't give up. . . . You must take care of yourself, Leo. . . . You must spare yourself. . . ."

His mouth spat out: "For what?"

*

Kira met Vasili Ivanovitch in the street.

It took an effort not to let her face show the change of his. She had seen him but once since Maria Petrovna's death, and he had not looked like that. He walked like an old man. His clear, proud eyes darted at every face, a bitter look of suspicion, and hatred, and shame. His wrinkled, sinewy hands tottered uncertainly in useless movements, like an old woman's. Two lines were slashed from the corners of his lips to his chin, lines of such suffering that one felt guilty of intrusion for having seen and guessed.

"Kira, glad to see you again, glad to see you," he muttered, his voice, his words clinging to her helplessly. "Why don't you come over any more? It's sort of lonesome, at home. Or . . . or maybe you've heard . . . and don't want to come?"

She had not heard. But something in his voice told her not to ask him what it was that she could have heard. She said with her warmest smile: "Why, no, Uncle Vasili, I'll be glad to come. It's just that I've been working so hard. But I'll be over tonight, may I?"

She did not ask about Irina and Victor, and whether they, too, had been expelled. As after an earthquake, all were looking around cautiously, counting the victims, afraid to ask questions.

That night, after dinner, she called on the Dunaevs. She had persuaded Leo to go to bed; he had a fever; his cheekbones flamed with bright red spots; she had left a jug of cold tea by the bed and told him that she would be back early.

At a bare table without table cloth, under a lamp without

a shade, Vasili Ivanovitch sat reading an old volume of Chekhov. Irina her hair uncombed, sat drawing senseless figures on a huge sheet of paper. Acia slept, full dressed, curled in an armchair in a dark corner. A rusty "Bourgeoise" smoked.

"Allo," said Irina, her lips twisting. Kira had never seen her smile like that.

"Would you like some tea, Kira? Hot tea? Only . . . only we have no saccharine left."

"No, thank you, Uncle Vasili, I've just had dinner."

"Well?" said Irina. "Why don't you say it? Expelled?"

Kira nodded.

"And Leo, too?"

Kira nodded.

"Well? Why don't you ask? Oh, I'll tell you myself: sure, I'm out. What could you expect? Daughter of the wealthy Court Furrier!"

"And—Victor?"

Irina and Vasili Ivanovitch exchanged a glance, a strange glance. "No," Irina answered slowly, "Victor is not expelled."

"I'm glad, Uncle Vasili. That's good news, isn't it?" She knew the best way to cheer her uncle: "Victor's such a talented young man, I'm glad they've spared his future."

"Yes," Vasili Ivanovitch said slowly, bitterly. "Victor is such a talented young man."

"She had a white lace gown," Irina said hysterically, "and, really, she has a gorgeous voice—oh—I mean—I'm speaking of the new production of 'La Traviata' at the Mikhailovsky Theater—and you've seen it, of course? Oh, well, you must see it. Old classics are . . . old classics are . . ."

"Yes," said Vasili Ivanovitch, "old classics are still the best. In those days, they had culture, and moral values, and . . . and integrity. . . ."

"Really," said Kira, nervous and bewildered, "I'll have to see 'La Traviata.' "

"In the last act," said Irina, "in the last act, she. . . . Oh, hell!" She threw her drawing board down with a crash that awakened Acia, who sat up staring, blinking. "You'll hear it sooner or later: Victor has joined the Party!"

Kira was holding the book of Chekhov and it clattered down to the floor. "He . . . what?"

"He joined the Party. The All-Union Communist Party. With a red star, a Party ticket, a bread card, and his hand in all the blood spilled, in all the blood to come!"

"Irina! How . . . how could he get admitted?"

She was afraid to look at Vasili Ivanovitch. She knew she should not ask questions, questions that were like knives turned in a wound; but she could not resist it.

"Oh, it seems he had it planned for a long time. He's been making friends—carefully and judiciously. He's been a candidate for months—and we never knew it. Then—he got admitted. Oh, they accepted him all right—with the kind of sponsors he had selected to vouch for his proletarian spirit, even though his father did sell furs to the Czar!"

"Did he know this—the purge, I mean—was coming?"

"Oh, don't be silly. It isn't that. Of course, he didn't know that in advance. He's aiming higher than merely to keep his place at the Institute. Oh, my brother Victor is a brilliant young man. When he wants to climb—he knows the stepping stones."

"Well," Kira tried to smile, to say for Vasili Ivanovitch's sake, without looking at him, "it's Victor's business. He knows what he wants. Is he . . . is he still here?"

"If it were up to me, he . . ." Irina checked herself abruptly. "Yes. The swine's still here."

"Irina," Vasili Ivanovitch said wearily, "he's your brother."

Kira changed the subject; but it was not easy to keep up a conversation. Half an hour later, Victor came in. The dignity of his expression and the red star in his lapel were very much in evidence.

"Victor," Kira said. "I hear you're a good Communist, now."

"I have had the honor of joining the All-Union Communist Party," Victor answered, "and I'll have it understood that the Party is not to be referred to lightly."

"Oh," said Kira. "I see."

But it happened that she did not see Victor's extended hand when she was leaving.

At the door, in the lobby, Irina whispered to her: "At first, I thought father would throw him out. But . . . with mother gone . . . and all . . . and you know how he's always been crazy about Victor . . . well, he thinks he'll try to be broadminded. I think it will break him. . . . For God's sake, Kira, come often. He likes you."

*

Because there was no future, they hung on to the present. There were days when Leo sat for hours reading a book, and hardly spoke to Kira, and when he spoke his smile held a bitter, endless contempt for himself, for the world, for eternity.

Once, she found him drunk, leaning against the table, staring intently at a broken glass on the floor.

"Leo! Where did you get it?"

"Borrowed it. Borrowed it from our dear neighbor Comrade Marisha. She always has plenty."

"Leo, why do you?"

"Why shouldn't I? Why shouldn't I? Who in this whole damn world can tell me why I shouldn't?"

But there were days when a new calm suddenly cleared his eyes and his smile. He waited for Kira to come home from work and when she entered he drew her hastily into his arms. They could sit through an evening without a word, their presence, a glance, the pressure of a hand drugging them into security, making them forget the coming morning, all the coming mornings.

Arm in arm, they walked through silent, luminous streets in the white nights of spring. The sky was like dull glass glowing with a sunless radiance from somewhere beyond. They could look at each other, at the still, sleepless city, in the strange, milky light. He pressed her arm close to his, and when they were alone on a long street dawn-bright and empty, he bent to kiss her.

Kira's steps were steady. There were too many questions ahead; but here, beside her, were the things that gave her certainty: his straight, tense body, his long, thin hands, his haughty mouth with the arrogant smile that answered all questions. And, sometimes, she felt pity for those countless nameless ones somewhere around them who, in a feverish quest, were searching for some answer, and in their search crushed others, perhaps even her; but she could not be crushed, for she had the answer. She did not wonder about the future. The future was Leo.

*

Leo was too pale and he was silent too often. The blue on his temples looked like veins in marble. He coughed, choking. He took cough medicine, which did not help, and refused to see a doctor.

Kira saw Andrei frequently. She had asked Leo if he minded it. "Not at all," he had answered, "if he's your friend. Only— would you mind?—don't bring him here. I'm not sure I can be polite to . . . to one of them."

She did not bring Andrei to the house. She telephoned him on Sundays and smiled cheerfully into the receiver: "Feel like seeing me, Andrei? Two o'clock—Summer Garden—the quay entrance."

They sat on a bench, with the oak leaves fighting the glare of the sun above their heads, and they talked of philosophy. She smiled sometimes when she realized that Andrei was the only one with whom she could think and talk about thoughts.

They had no reason for meeting each other. Yet they met, and made dates to meet again, and she felt strangely comfortable, and he laughed at her short summer dresses, and his laughter was strangely happy.

Once, he invited her to spend a Sunday in the country. She had stayed in the city all summer; she could not refuse. Leo had found a job for Sunday: breaking the wooden bricks of pavements, with a gang repairing the streets. He did not object to her excursion.

In the country, she found a smooth sea sparkling in the sun; and a golden sand wind-pleated into faint, even waves; and the tall red candles of pines, their convulsed roots naked to the sand and wind, pine cones rolling to meet the sea shells.

Kira and Andrei had a swimming race, which she won. But when they raced down the beach in their bathing suits, sand flying from under their heels, spurting sand and water at the peaceful Sunday tourists, Andrei won. He caught her and they rolled down together, a whirl of legs, arms and mud, into the lunch basket of a matron who shrieked with terror. They disentangled themselves from each other and sat there screaming with laughter. And when the matron struggled to her feet, gathered her lunch and waddled away, grumbling something about "this vulgar modern youth that can't keep their love-affairs to themselves," they laughed louder.

They had dinner in a dirty little country restaurant, and Kira spoke English to the waiter who could not understand a word, but bowed low and stuttered and spilled water all over the table in his eagerness to serve the first comrade foreigner in their forgotten corner. When they were leaving, Andrei gave him twice the price of their dinner. The waiter bowed to the ground, convinced that he was dealing with genuine foreigners. Kira could not help looking a little startled. Andrei laughed when they went out: "Why not? Might as well make a waiter happy. I make more money than I can spend on myself anyway."

In the train, as it clattered into the evening and the smoke of the city, Andrei asked: "Kira, when will I see you again?"

"I'll call you."

"No. I want to know now."

"In a few days."

"No. I want a definite day."

"Well, then, Wednesday night?"

"All right."

"After work, at five-thirty, at the Summer Garden."

"All right."

When she came home, she found Leo asleep in a chair, his hands dust-streaked, smears of dust on his damp, flushed face, his dark lashes blond with dust, his body limp with exhaustion.

She washed his face and helped him to undress. He coughed.

The two evenings that followed were long, furious arguments, but Leo surrendered: he promised to visit a doctor on Wednesday.

*

Vava Milovskaia had a date with Victor for Wednesday night. Wednesday afternoon, Victor telephoned her, his voice impatiently apologetic: he was detained on urgent business at the Institute and would not be able to see her. Urgent business had detained him the last three times he had promised to come. Vava had heard rumors; she had heard a name; she knew what to suspect.

In the evening, she dressed carefully; she pulled a wide black patent leather belt tight around the slim waist of her best new white coat; she touched her lips faintly, cautiously with her new foreign lipstick; she slipped on her foreign celluloid bracelet. She tilted her white hat recklessly over her black curls and told her mother that she was going out to call on Kira Argounova.

She hesitated on the stair landing before Kira's apartment, and her hand trembled a little when she pressed the bell.

The tenant opened the door. "To see Citizen Argounova? This way, comrade," he told her. "You have to pass through Citizen Lavrova's room. This door here."

Resolutely, Vava jerked the door open without knocking.

They were there—together—Marisha and Victor—bending over the gramophone that played "The Fire of Moscow."

Victor's face was cold, silent fury. But Vava did not look at him. She tossed her head up and said to Marisha, as proudly, as dramatically as she could, in a shaking voice, swallowing tears: "I beg your pardon, citizen, I'm just calling on Citizen Argounova."

Surprised and suspecting nothing, Marisha pointed to Kira's door with her thumb. Head high, Vava walked across the room. Marisha could not understand why Victor left in such a hurry.

Kira was not at home, but Leo was.

*

Kira had had a restless day. Leo had promised to telephone her at the office and tell her the doctor's diagnosis. He had not called. She telephoned him three times. There was no answer. On her way home, she remembered that it was Wednesday night and that she had a date with Andrei.

She could not keep him waiting indefinitely at a public park gate. She would drop by the Summer Garden and tell him that she couldn't stay. She reached the Garden on time.

Andrei was not there.

She looked up and down the darkening quay. She peered into the trees and shadows of the garden. She waited. Twice, she asked a militia-man what time it was. She waited. She could not understand it.

He did not come.

When she finally went home, she had waited for an hour.

She clutched her hands angrily in her pockets. She could not worry about Andrei when she thought of Leo, and the doctor, and of what she still had to hear. She hurried up the stairs. She darted through Marisha's room and flung the door open. On the davenport, her white coat trailing to the floor, Vava was clasped in Leo's arms, their lips locked together.

Kira stood looking at them calmly, an amazed question in her lifted eyebrows.

They jumped up. Leo was not very steady. He had been drinking again. He stood swaying, with his bitter, contemptuous smile.

Vava's face went a dark, purplish red. She opened her mouth, choking, without a sound. And as no one said a word, she screamed suddenly into the silence: "You think it's terrible, don't you? Well, I think so too! It's terrible, it's vile! Only I don't care! I don't care what I do! I don't care any more! I'm rotten? Well, I'm not the only one! Only I don't care! I don't care! I don't care!"

She burst into hysterical sobs and rushed out, slamming the door. The two others did not move.

He sneered: "Well, say it."

She answered slowly: "I have nothing to say."

"Listen, you might as well get used to it. You might as well get used to it that you can't have me. Because you can't have me. You won't have me. You won't have me long."

"Leo, what did the doctor say?"

He laughed: "Plenty."

"What is it you have?"

"Nothing. Not a thing."

"Leo!"

"Not a thing—yet. But I'm going to have it. Just a few weeks longer. I'm going to have it."

"What, Leo?"

He swayed with a grand gesture: "Nothing much. Just—tuberculosis."

*

The doctor asked: "Are you his wife?"

Kira hesitated, then answered: "No."

The doctor said: "I see." Then, he added: "Well, I suppose you have a right to know it. Citizen Kovalensky is in a very bad condition. We call it incipient tuberculosis. It can still be stopped—now. In a few weeks—it will be too late."

"In a few weeks—he'll have—tuberculosis?"

"Tuberculosis is a serious disease, citizen. In Soviet Russia —it is a fatal disease. It is strongly advisable to prevent it. If you let it start—you will not be likely to stop it."

"What . . . does he need?"

"Rest. Plenty of it. Sunshine. Fresh air. Food. Human food. He needs a sanatorium for this coming winter. One more winter in Petrograd would be as certain as a firing squad. You'll have to send him south."

She did not answer; but the doctor smiled ironically, for he heard the answer without words and he looked at the patches on her shoes.

"If that young man is dear to you," he said, "send him south. If you have a human possibility—or an inhuman one— send him south."

*

Kira was very calm when she walked home.

When she came in, Leo was standing by the window. He turned slowly. His face was so profoundly, serenely tranquil that he looked younger; he looked as if he had had his first night of rest; he asked quietly: "Where have you been, Kira?"

"At the doctor's."

"Oh, I'm sorry. I didn't want you to know all that."

"He told me."

"Kira, I'm sorry about last night. About that little fool. I hope you didn't think that I . . ."

"Of course, I didn't. I understand."

"I think it's because I was frightened. But I'm not—now. Everything seems so much simpler—when there's a limit set. . . . The thing to do now, Kira, is not to talk about it. Don't let's think about it. There's nothing we can do—as the doctor probably told you. We can still be together—for a while. When it becomes contagious—well . . ."

She was watching him. Such was his manner of accepting his death sentence.

She said, and her voice was hard: "Nonsense, Leo. You're going south."

*

In the first State hospital she visited, the official in charge told her: "A place in a sanatorium in the Crimea? He's not a member of the Party? And he's not a member of a Trade Union? And he's not a State employee? You're joking, citizen."

In the second hospital, the official said: "We have hundreds on our waiting list, citizen. Trade Union members. Advanced cases. . . . No, we cannot even register him."

In the third hospital, the official refused to see her.

There were lines to wait in, ghastly lines of deformed creatures, of scars, and slings, and crutches, and open sores, and green, mucous patches of eyes, and grunts, and groans, and—over a line of the living—the smell of the morgue.

There were State Medical headquarters to visit, long hours of waiting in dim, damp corridors that smelt of carbolic acid and soiled linen. There were secretaries who forgot appointments, and assistants who said: "So sorry, citizen. Next, please"; there were young executives who were in a hurry, and attendants who groaned: "I tell you he's gone, it's after office hours, we gotta close, you can't sit here all night."

At the end of the first two weeks she learned, as firmly as if it were some mystic absolute, that if one had consumption one had to be a member of a Trade Union and get a Trade Union despatchment to a Trade Union Sanatorium.

There were officials to be seen, names mentioned, letters of recommendation offered, begging for an exception. There were

Trade Union heads to visit, who listened to her plea with startled, ironic glances. Some laughed; some shrugged; some called their secretaries to escort the visitor out; one said he could and he would, but he named a sum she could not earn in a year.

She was firm, erect, and her voice did not tremble, and she was not afraid to beg. It was her mission, her quest, her crusade.

She wondered sometimes why the words: "But he's going to *die*," meant so little to them, and the words: "But he's not a registered worker," meant so little to her, and why it seemed so hard to explain.

She made Leo do his share of inquiries. He obeyed without arguing, without complaining, without hope.

She tried everything she could. She asked Victor for help. Victor said with dignity: "My dear cousin, I want you to realize that my Party membership is a sacred trust not to be used for purposes of personal advantage."

She asked Marisha. Marisha laughed. "With all our sanatoriums stuffed like herring-barrels, and waiting lists till the next generation, and comrade workers rotting alive waiting—and here he's not even sick yet! You don't realize reality, Citizen Argounova."

She could not call on Andrei. Andrei had failed her.

For several days after the date he had missed, she called on Lydia with the same question: "Has Andrei Taganov been here? Have you had any letters for me?"

The first day, Lydia said: "No." The second day, she giggled and wanted to know what was this, a romance? and she'd tell Leo, and with Leo so handsome! and Kira interrupted patiently: "Oh, stop this rubbish, Lydia! It's important. Let me know the minute you hear from him, will you?"

Lydia did not hear from him.

One evening, at the Dunaevs', Kira asked Victor casually if he had seen Andrei Taganov at the Institute. "Sure," said Victor, "he's there every day."

She was hurt. She was angry. She was bewildered. What had she done? For the first time, she questioned her own behavior. Had she acted foolishly that Sunday in the country? She tried to remember every word, every gesture. She could find no fault. He had seemed happier than ever before. After a while, she decided that she must trust their friendship and give him a chance to explain.

She telephoned him. She heard the old landlady's voice

yelling into the house: "Comrade Taganov!" with a positive inflection that implied his presence; there was a long pause; the landlady returned and asked: "Who's calling him?" and before she had pronounced the last syllable of her name, Kira heard the landlady barking: "He ain't home!" and slamming her receiver.

Kira slammed hers, too. She decided to forget Andrei Taganov.

*

It took a month, but at the end of a month, she was convinced that the door of the State sanatoriums was locked to Leo and that she could not unlock it.

There were private sanatoriums in the Crimea. Private sanatoriums cost money. She would get the money.

She made an appointment to see Comrade Voronov and asked for an advance on her salary, an advance of six months —just enough to start him off. Comrade Voronov smiled faintly and asked her how she could be certain that she would be working there another month, let alone six.

She called on Doctor Milovsky, Vava's father, her wealthiest acquaintance, whose bank account had been celebrated by many envious whispers. Doctor Milovsky's face got very red and his short, pudgy hands waved at Kira hysterically, as if shooing off a ghost: "My dear little girl, why, my dear little girl, what on earth made you think that I was rich or something? Heh-heh. Very funny indeed. A capitalist or something —heh-heh. Why, we're just existing, from hand to mouth, living by my own toil like proletarians one would say, barely existing, as one would say—that's it—from hand to mouth."

She knew her parents had nothing. She asked if they could try to help. Galina Petrovna cried.

She asked Vasili Ivanovitch. He offered her his last possession—Maria Petrovna's old fur jacket. The price of the jacket would not buy a ticket to the Crimea. She did not take it.

She knew Leo would resent it, but she wrote to his aunt in Berlin. She said in her letter: "I am writing, because I love him so much—to you, because I think you must love him a little." No answer came.

Through mysterious, stealthy whispers, more mysterious and stealthy than the G.P.U. who watched them sharply, she learned that there was private money to be lent, secretly and on a high percentage, but there was. She learned a name and an address. She went to the booth of a private trader in a market, where a fat man bent down to her nervously across a counter loaded with red kerchiefs and cotton stockings She whispered a name. She named a sum.

"Business?" he breathed. "Speculation?"

She knew it best to say yes. Well, he told her, it could be arranged. The rates were twenty-five per cent a month. She nodded eagerly. What security did the citizen have to offer? Security? Surely she knew they didn't lend it on her good looks? Furs or diamonds would do; good furs and any kind of diamonds. She had nothing to offer. The man turned away as if he had never spoken to her in his life.

On her way back to the tramway, through the narrow, muddy passages between the market stalls, she stopped, startled; in a little prosperous-looking booth, behind a counter heavy with fresh bread loaves, smoked hams, yellow circles of butter, she saw a familiar face: a heavy red mouth under a short nose with wide, vertical nostrils. She remembered the train speculator of the Nikolaevsky station, with the fur-lined coat and the smell of carnation oil. He had progressed in life. He was smiling at the customers, from under a fringe of salami.

On her way home, she remembered someone who had said: "I make more money than I can spend on myself." Did anything really matter now? She would go to the Institute and try to see Andrei.

She changed tramways for the Institute. She saw Andrei. She saw him coming down the corridor and he was looking straight at her, so that her lips moved in a smile of greeting; but he turned abruptly and slammed the door of an auditorium behind him.

She stood frozen to the spot for a long time.

When she came home, Leo was standing in the middle of the room, a crumpled paper in his hand, his face distorted by anger.

"So you would?" he cried. "So you're meddling in my affairs now? So you're writing letters? Who asked you to write?"

On the table, she saw an envelope with a German stamp. It was addressed to Leo. "What does she say, Leo?"

"You want to know? You really want to know?"

He threw the letter at her face.

She remembered only the sentence: "There is no reason why you should expect any help from us; the less reason since you are living with a brazen harlot who has the impudence to write to respectable people."

*

On the first rainy day of autumn, a delegation from a Club of Textile Women Workers visited the "House of the Peasant." Comrade Sonia was an honorary member of the delegation. When she saw Kira at the filing cabinet in Comrade Bitiuk's office, Comrade Sonia roared with laughter: "Well, well, well! A loyal citizen like Comrade Argounova in the Red 'House of the Peasant'!"

"What's the matter, comrade?" Comrade Bitiuk inquired nervously, obsequiously. "What's the matter?"

"A joke," roared Comrade Sonia, "a good joke!"

Kira shrugged with resignation; she knew what to expect.

When a reduction of staffs came to the "House of the Peasant" and she saw her name among those dismissed as "anti-social element," she was not surprised. It made no difference now. She spent most of her last salary to buy eggs and milk for Leo, which he would not touch.

*

In the daytime, Kira was calm, with the calm of an empty face, an empty heart, a mind empty of all thoughts but one. She was not afraid: because she knew that Leo had to go south, and he would go, and she could not doubt it, and so she had nothing to fear.

But there was the night.

She felt his body, icy and moist, close to hers. She heard him coughing. Sometimes, in his sleep, his head fell on her shoulder, and he lay there, trusting and helpless as a child, and his breathing was like a moan.

She saw the red bubble on Maria Petrovna's dying lips, and she heard her screaming: "Kira! I want to live! I want to live!"

She could feel Leo's breath in hot, panting gasps on her neck.

Then, she was not sure whether it was Maria Petrovna or Leo screaming when it was too late: "Kira! I want to live! I want to live!"

Was she going insane? It was so simple. She just needed money; a life, *his* life—and money.

"I make more money than I can spend on myself."

"Kira! I want to live! I want to live!"

*

She made one last attempt to get money.

She was walking down a street slippery with autumn rain, yellow lights melting on black sidewalks. The doctor had said every week counted; every day counted now. She saw a resplendent limousine stopping in the orange cube of light at a theater entrance. A man stepped out; his fur coat glistened like his automobile fenders. She stood in his path. Her voice was firm and clear:

"Please! I want to speak to you. I need money. I don't know you. I have nothing to offer you. I know it isn't being done like this. But you'll understand, because it's so important. It's to save a life."

The man stopped. He had never heard a plea that was a command. He asked, squinting one eye appraisingly: "How much do you need?"

She told him.

"What?" he gasped. "For one night? Why, your sisters don't make that in a whole career!"

He could not understand why the strange girl whirled around and ran across the street, straight through the puddles, as if he were going to run after her.

*

She made one last plea to the State.

It took many weeks of calls, letters, introductions, secretaries and assistants, but she got an appointment with one of Petrograd's most powerful officials. She was to see him in person, face to face. He could do it. Between him and the power he could use stood only her ability to convince him.

The official sat at his desk. A tall window rose behind him, admitting a narrow shaft of light, creating the atmosphere of a cathedral. Kira stood before him. She looked straight at him; her eyes were not hostile, nor pleading; they were clear, trusting, serene; her voice was very calm, very simple, very young.

"Comrade Commissar, you see, I love him. And he is sick. You know what sickness is? It's something strange that happens in your body and then you can't stop it. And then he dies. And now his life—it depends on some words and a piece of paper—and it's so simple when you just look at it as it is—it's only something made by us, ourselves, and perhaps we're right, and perhaps we're wrong, but the chance we're taking on it is frightful, isn't it? They won't send him to a sanatorium because they didn't write his name on a piece of paper with many other names and call it a membership in a Trade Union. It's only ink, you know, and paper, and something we think. You can write it and tear it up, and write it again. But the other—that which happens in one's body—you can't stop that. You don't ask questions about that. Comrade Commissar, I know they are important, those things, money, and the Unions, and those papers, and all. And if one has to sacrifice and suffer for them, I don't mind. I don't mind if I have to work every hour of the day. I don't mind if my dress is old—like this—don't look at my dress, Comrade Commissar, I know it's ugly, but I don't mind. Perhaps, I haven't always understood you, and all those things, but I can be obedient and learn. Only—only when it comes to life itself, Comrade Commissar, then we have to be serious, don't we? We can't let those things take life. One signature of your hand—and he can go to a sanatorium, and he doesn't have to die. Comrade Commissar, if we just think of things, calmly and simply—as they are—do you know what death is? Do you know that death is—nothing at all, not at all, never again, never, no matter what we do? Don't you see why he can't die? I love him. We all have to suffer. We all have things we want, which are taken away from us. It's all right. But—because we are living beings—there's something in each of us, something like the very heart of life condensed—and *that* should not be touched. You understand, don't you? Well, he is that to me, and you can't take him from me, because you can't let me stand here, and look at you, and talk, and breathe, and move, and then tell me you'll take him—we're not insane, both of us, are we, Comrade Commissar?"

The Comrade Commissar said: "One hundred thousand workers died in the civil war. Why—in the face of the Union of Socialist Soviet Republics—can't one aristocrat die?"

Kira walked home very slowly and looked at the dark city; she looked at the glistening pavements built for many thousands of old shoes; at the tramways for men to ride in; at the stone cubes into which men crawled at night; at the posters that cried of what men dreamed and of what men ate; and she wondered whether any of those thousands of eyes around her saw what she saw, and why it had been given her to see.

*

Because:

In a kitchen on the fifth floor, a woman bent over a smoking stove and stirred cabbage in a kettle, and the cabbage smelt, and the woman blinked, and groaned with the pain in her back, and scratched her head with the spoon,

Because:

In a corner saloon, a man leaned against the bar and raised a foaming glass of beer, and the foam spilled over the floor and over his trousers, and he belched and sang a gay song,

Because:

In a white bed, on white sheets stained with yellow, a child slept and sniveled in its sleep, its nose wet,

Because:

On a sack of flour in the basement, a man tore a woman's pants off, and bit into her throat, and they rolled, moaning, over the sacks of flour and potatoes,

Because:

In the silence of stone walls slowly dripping frozen dampness, a figure knelt before a gilded cross, and raised trembling arms in exaltation, and knocked a pale forehead against a cold stone floor,

Because:

In the roar of machines whirling lightnings of steel and drops of burning grease, men swung vigorous arms, and panted, heaving chests of muscles glistening with sweat, and made soap,

Because:

In a public bath, steam rose from brass pans, and red, gelatinous bodies shook scrubbing themselves with the soap, sighing and grunting, trying to scratch steaming backs, and murky water and soap suds ran down the floor into the drain—

—Leo Kovalensky was sentenced to die.

XVII

It was her last chance and she had to take it.

A modest house stood before her, on a modest street that lay deserted in the darkness. An old landlady opened the door and looked at Kira suspiciously: Comrade Taganov did not receive women visitors. But she said nothing and shuffled, leading Kira down a corridor, then stopped, pointed at a door and shuffled away.

Kira knocked.

His voice said: "Come in."

She entered.

He was sitting at his desk and he was about to rise, but he didn't. He sat looking at her, and then rose very slowly, so slowly that she wondered how long she stood there, at the door, while he was rising, his eyes never leaving her.

Then, he said: "Good evening, Kira."

"Good evening, Andrei."

"Take your coat off."

She was suddenly frightened, uncomfortable, uncertain; she lost all the bitter, hostile assurance that had brought her here; obediently, she took off her coat and threw her hat on the bed. It was a large, bare room with whitewashed walls, a narrow iron bed, one desk, one chair, one chest of drawers, no pictures, no posters, but books, an ocean of books and papers and newspapers, running over the desk, over the chest, over the floor.

He said: "It's cold tonight, isn't it?"

"It's cold."

"Sit down."

She sat by the desk. He sat on the bed, his hands clasping his knees. She wished he would not look at her like that, every second of every long minute. But he said calmly: "How have you been, Kira? You look tired."

"I am a little tired."

"How is your job?"

"It isn't."

"What?"

"Reduction of staffs."

"Oh, Kira, I'm sorry. I'll get you another one."

"Thanks. But I don't know whether I need one. How is your job?"

"The G.P.U.? I've been working hard. Searches, arrests. You still aren't afraid of me, are you?"

"No."

"I don't like searches."

"Do you like arrests?"

"I don't mind—when it's necessary."

They were silent, and then she said: "Andrei, if I make you uncomfortable—I'll go."

"No! Don't go. Please don't go." He tried to laugh. "Make me uncomfortable? What makes you say that? I'm just . . . just a little embarrassed . . . this room of mine . . . it's in no condition to receive such a guest."

"Oh, it's a nice room. Big. Light."

"You see, I'm home so seldom, and when I am, I just have time to fall in bed, without noticing what's around me."

"Oh."

They were silent.

"How is your family, Kira?"

"They are fine, thank you."

"I often see your cousin, Victor Dunaev, at the Institute. Do you like him?"

"No."

"Neither do I."

They were silent.

"Victor has joined the Party," said Kira.

"I voted against him. But most of them were eager to admit him."

"I'm glad you voted against him. He's the kind of Party man I despise."

"What kind of Party man don't you despise, Kira?"

"Your kind, Andrei."

"Kira . . ." It began as a sentence, but stopped on the first word.

She said resolutely: "Andrei, what have I done?"

He looked at her, and frowned, and looked aside, shaking his head slowly: "Nothing." Then he asked suddenly: "Why did you come here?"

"It's been such a long time since I saw you last."

"Two months, day after tomorrow."

"Unless you saw me at the Institute three weeks ago."

"I saw you."

She waited, but he did not explain, and she tried to ignore it, her words almost a plea: "I came because I thought . . . because I thought maybe you wanted to see me."

"I didn't want to see you."

She rose to her feet.

"Don't go, Kira!"

"Andrei, I don't understand!"

He stood facing her. His voice was flat, harsh as an insult: "I didn't want you to understand. I didn't want you to know. But if you want to hear it—you'll hear it. I never wanted to see you again. Because . . ." His voice was like a dull whip. "Because I love you."

Her hands fell limply against the wall behind her. He went on: "Don't say it. I know what you're going to say. I've said it to myself again and again and again. I know every word. But it's useless. I know I should be ashamed, and I am, but it's useless. I know that you liked me, and trusted me, because we were friends. It was beautiful and rare, and you have every right to despise me."

She stood pressed to the wall, not moving.

"When you came in, I thought 'Send her away.' But I knew that if you went away, I'd run after you. I thought 'I won't say a word.' But I knew that you'd know it before you left. I love you. I know you'd think kindlier of me if I said that I hate you."

She said nothing; she cringed against the wall, her eyes wide, her glance holding no pity for him, but a plea for his pity.

"You're frightened? Do you see why I couldn't face you? I knew what you felt for me and what you could never feel. I knew what you'd say, how your eyes would look at me. When did it start? I don't know. I knew only that it must end —because I couldn't stand it. To see you, and laugh with you, and talk of the future of humanity—and think only of when your hand would touch mine, of your feet in the sand, the little shadow on your throat, your skirt blowing in the wind. To discuss the meaning of life—and wonder if I could see the line of your breast in your open collar!"

She whispered: "Andrei . . . don't. . . ."

It was not an admission of love, it was the confession of a crime: "Why am I telling you all this? I don't know. I'm not sure I'm really saying it to you. I've been crying it to myself so often, for such a long time! You shouldn't have come here. I'm not your friend. I don't care if I hurt you. All you are to me is only this: I want you."

She whispered: "Andrei . . . I didn't know. . . ."

"I didn't want you to know. I tried to stay away from you, to break it. You don't know what it's done to me. There was one search. There was a woman. We arrested her. She rolled on the floor, in her nightgown, at my feet, crying for mercy. I thought of you. I thought of you there, on the floor, in your nightgown, crying for pity as I have been crying to you so many months. I'd take you—and I wouldn't care if it were the floor, and if those men stood looking. Afterward, perhaps I'd shoot you, and shoot myself—but I wouldn't care—because it would be afterward. I thought I could arrest you— in the middle of the night—and carry you wherever I wanted —and have you. I could do it, you know. I laughed at the woman and kicked her. My men stared at me—they had never seen me do that. They took the woman to jail—and I found an excuse to run away, to walk home alone—thinking of you. . . . Don't look at me like that. You don't have to be afraid that I'd do it. . . . I have nothing to offer you. I cannot offer you my life. My life is twenty-eight years of that for which you feel contempt. And you—you're everything I've always expected to hate. But I want you. I'd give everything I have—everything I could ever have—Kira—for something you can't give me!"

He saw her eyes open wide at a thought he could not guess. She breathed: "What did you say, Andrei?"

"I said, everything I have for something you can't. . . ."

It was terror in her eyes, a terror of the thought she had seen for a second so very clearly. She whispered, trembling: "Andrei . . . I'd better go. . . . I'd better go now."

But he was looking at her fixedly, approaching her, asking in a voice suddenly very soft and low: "Or is it something you . . . can . . . Kira?"

She was not thinking of him; she was not thinking of Leo; she was thinking of Maria Petrovna and of the red bubble on dying lips. She was pressed to the wall, cornered, her ten fingers spread apart on the white plaster. His voice, his hope were driving her on. Her body rose slowly against the wall, to her full height, higher, on tiptoe, her head thrown back, so that her throat was level with his mouth when she threw at him:

"I can! I love you."

She wondered how strange it was to feel a man's lips that were not Leo's.

She was saying: "Yes . . . for a long time . . . but I didn't know that you, too . . ." and she felt his hands and his mouth, and she wondered whether this was joy or torture to him and how strong his arms were. She hoped it would be quick.

*

The street light beyond the window made a white square and a black cross on the wall above the bed. Against the white square, she could see his face on the pillow; he did not move. Her arm, stretched limply against his naked body, felt no movement but the beating of his heart.

She threw the blanket off, and sat up, crossing her arms over her breasts, her hands clutching her bare shoulders.

"Andrei, I'm going home."

"Kira! Not now. Not tonight."

"I have to go."

"I want you here. Till morning."

"I have to go. There's . . . there's my family. . . . Andrei, we'll have to keep this very secret."

"Kira, will you marry me?"

She did not answer. He felt her trembling. He pulled her down and tucked the blanket under her chin.

"Kira, why does that frighten you?"

"Andrei . . . Andrei . . . I can't. . . ."

"I love you."

"Andrei . . . there's my family. You're a Communist. You know what they are. You must understand. They've suffered so much. If I marry you—it would be too much for them. Or if they learn—about this. We can spare them. Does it . . . does it make any difference to us?"

"No. Not if you want it that way."

"Andrei!"

"Yes, Kira?"

"You'll do anything I want?"

"Anything."

"I want only one thing: secrecy. Complete secrecy. You promise?"

"Yes."

"You see . . . with me—there's my family. With you— there's the Party. I'm not . . . I'm not the kind of a . . . mistress your Party would approve. So it's better . . . You see, it's a dangerous thing we're doing. A very dangerous thing. I want to try not to let it . . . not to let it break our lives."

"Break our lives? Kira!" He was laughing happily, pressing her hand to his lips.

"It's better if no one—not a soul anywhere—knows this, but you and I."

"No, Kira, I promise, no one will know but you and I."

"And now I'll go."

"No. Please don't go tonight. Just tonight. You can explain to them somehow—make up a reason. But stay. I can't let you go. . . . Please, Kira. . . . Just to see you here when I awaken. . . . Good night . . . Kira. . . ."

*

She lay very still for a very long time, until he was asleep. Then she slipped noiselessly out of bed and, holding her breath, her bare feet soundless on the cold floor, she dressed hurriedly. He did not hear her open the door and slip out.

There was a wind whistling down the long, empty streets and a sky like pencil lead. She walked very fast. She knew there was something she had to escape and she tried to hurry.

The dead, dark glass panes were watching her, following her, rows and rows of them, on guard along her way. She walked faster. Her steps beat too loudly and the houses of the whole city threw echoes back at her, echoes screaming something. She walked faster. The wind whirled her coat, raising it high over her knees, hurling it between her legs. She walked faster. She passed the poster of a worker with a red banner; the worker was laughing.

Suddenly she was running, like a shivering streak between dark shop windows and lamp posts, her coat whistling, her steps beating like a machine gun, her legs flashing and blending, like the spokes of a wheel, into one circle of motion carrying her forward. She was running or flying or being rocketed through space by something outside her body, and she knew it was all right, everything was all right if only she could run faster and faster and faster.

She came panting up the stairs. At the door, she stopped. She stopped and stood looking at the door knob, panting. And suddenly she knew that she could not go in; that she could not take her body into Leo's room, into his bed, close to his body. She ran her finger tips over the door, feeling it, caressing it uncertainly, for she could come no closer to him.

She sat down on the steps. She felt as if she could hear him —somewhere behind that door—sleeping, breathing with effort. She sat there for a long time, her eyes empty.

When she turned her head and saw that the square of the window on the landing was a dark, bright blue which was not night any longer, she got up, took her key and went in. Leo was asleep. She sat by the window, gathered into a tight huddle. He would not know what time she had come home.

*

Leo was leaving for the south.

His bag was packed. His ticket was bought. His place was reserved in a private sanatorium in Yalta and a month paid for in advance.

She had explained about the money: "You see, when I wrote to your aunt in Berlin, I also wrote to my uncle in Budapest. Oh, yes, I have an uncle in Budapest. You've never heard him mentioned because . . . you see . . . there's a family quarrel behind it—and he left Russia before the war, and my father forbade us ever to mention his name. But he's not a bad fellow, and he always liked me, so I wrote him, and that's what he sent, and he said he'd help me as long as I need it.

But please don't ever mention it to my family, because father would—you understand."

She wondered dimly how simple and easy it was to lie.

To Andrei, she had mentioned her starving family. She did not have to ask: he gave her his whole monthly salary and told her to leave him only what she could spare. She had expected it, but it was not an easy moment when she saw the bills in her hand; then, she remembered the comrade commissar and why one aristocrat could die in the face of the Union of Socialist Soviet Republics—and she kept most of the money, with a hard, bright smile.

It had not been easy to convince Leo to go. He said he would not let her—or her uncle—keep him. He said it tenderly and he said it furiously. It took many hours and many evenings. "Leo—your money or my money or anyone's money—does it really matter? Who made it matter? But you want to live. I want you to live. So much is still possible to us. You love me. Don't you love me enough to live for me? I know it will be hard. Six months. All winter. I'll miss you. But we can do it. . . . Leo, I love you. I love you. I love you. So much is still possible!"

She won.

His train was to leave at eight-fifteen in the evening. At nine, she would meet Andrei; she had asked him to take her to the opening of a new cabaret.

Leo was silent when they left their room, and in the cab on the way to the station. She went into the car with him to see the wooden bench on which he was to sleep for many nights; she had brought a pillow for him and a warm plaid blanket. Then, they stepped out again and waited on the platform by the car. They had nothing to say.

When the first bell rang, Leo said: "Please, Kira, don't let's have any nonsense when the train starts. I won't look out of the window. No waving, or running after the train, or anything like that."

"No, Leo."

She looked at a poster on a steel pillar; it promised a huge orchestra, foreign fox-trots and delicious food at the grand opening of the new cabaret, at nine o'clock tonight. She said, wondering, bewildered, a little frightened, as if realizing it for the first time: "Leo . . . at nine o'clock tonight . . . you won't be here any more."

"No. I won't."

The third bell rang.

He seized her roughly and held her lips in a long, choking kiss, as long as the train whistle that wailed shrilly. He whispered: "Kira . . . my own only one. . . . I love you. . . . I love you so much. . . ."

He leaped to the steps of the car as it started moving, and disappeared inside. He did not come to the window.

She stood and heard iron chains stretching, wheels grinding rails, the engine panting far ahead, white steam spreading slowly under the steel vaults. The yellow squares of windows were suddenly pulled past her. The station smelt of carbolic acid. A faded red banner hung on a steel girder. The windows were streaming faster and faster, melting into a yellow line. There was nothing ahead but steel, steam, smoke and, under an arch very far away, a piece of sky black as a hole.

And suddenly she understood that it was a train, and that Leo was on the train, and that the train was leaving her. And something beyond terror, immense and unnamable, something which was not a human feeling, seized her. She ran after the train. She grasped an iron handle. She wanted to stop it. She knew that there was something huge and implacable moving over her, which she had to stop, which she was alone to stop, and couldn't. She was jerked forward, falling, she was whirled along down the wooden planks of the platform, and then a husky soldier in a peaked khaki cap with a red star grabbed her by the shoulders, and tore her off the handle, and threw her aside, pushing her away from the train with his elbow in her breast.

He roared:

"What do you think you're doing, citizen?"

❧ *Part Two* ❧

I

It was St. Petersburg; the war made it Petrograd; the revolution made it Leningrad.

It is a city of stone, and those living in it think not of stone brought upon a green earth and piled block on block to raise a city, but of one huge rock carved into streets, bridges, houses, and earth brought in handfuls, scattered, ground into the stone to remind them of that which lies beyond the city.

Its trees are rare strangers, sickly foreigners in a climate of granite, forlorn and superfluous. Its parks are reluctant concessions. In spring, a rare dandelion sticks a bright yellow head through the stones of its embankments, and men smile at it incredulously and condescendingly as at an impudent child. Its spring does not rise from the soil; its first violets, and very red tulips, and very blue hyacinths come in the hands of men, on street corners.

Petrograd was not born; it was created. The will of a man raised it where men did not choose to settle. An implacable emperor commanded into being the city and the ground under the city. Men brought earth to fill a swamp where no living thing existed but mosquitoes. And like mosquitoes, men died and fell into the grunting mire. No willing hands came to build the new capital. It rose by the labor of soldiers, thousands of soldiers, regiments who took orders and could not refuse to face a deadly foe, a gun or a swamp. They fell, and the earth they brought and their bones made the ground for the city. "Petrograd," its residents say, "stands on skeletons."

Petrograd is not in a hurry; it is not lazy; it is gracious and

226

leisurely, as befits the freedom of its vast streets. It is a city that threw itself down amid the marshes and pine forests, luxuriously, both arms outflung. Its squares are paved fields; its streets are as broad as tributaries to the Neva, the widest river to cross a great city.

On Nevsky, the capital of the capital's streets, the houses were built by generations past for generations to come. They are set and unchangeable like fortresses; their walls are thick and their windows are tiers of deep niches, rising over wide sidewalks of reddish-brown granite. From the statue of Alexander III, a huge gray man on a huge gray horse, silver rails stretch tense and straight to the Admiralty building far away, its white colonnade and thin golden spire raised like the crown, the symbol, the trade mark of Nevsky, over the broken skyline where every turret and balcony and gargoyle bending over the street are ageless features of a frozen stone face.

A golden cross on a small golden cupola rises to the clouds halfway down Nevsky, over the Anichkovsky palace, a bare red cube slashed by bare gray windows. And further, beyond the palace, a chariot raises to the clouds the black heads of its rearing horses, their hoofs hanging high over the street, over the stately columns of the Alexandrinsky theater. The palace looks like a barracks; the theater looks like a palace.

At the foot of the palace, Nevsky is cut by a stream, and a bridge arches over its swirling, muddy water. Four black statues stand at the four corners of the bridge. They may be only an accident and an ornament; they may be the very spirit of Petrograd, the city raised by man against the will of nature. Each statue is of a man and a horse. In the first one, the furious hoofs of a rearing beast are swung high in the air, ready to crush the naked, kneeling man, his arm stretched in a first effort toward the bridle of the monster. In the second, the man is up on one knee, his torso leaning back, the muscles of his legs, of his arms, of his body ready to burst through his skin, as he pulls at the bridle, in the supreme moment of the struggle. In the third, they are face to face, the man up on his feet, his head at the nostrils of a beast bewildered by a first recognition of its master. In the fourth, the beast is tamed; it steps obediently, led by the hand of the man who is tall, erect, calm in his victory, stepping forward with serene assurance, his head held straight, his eyes looking steadily into an unfathomable future.

On winter nights, strings of large white globes flare up over Nevsky—and snow sparkles over the white lights like salt crystals—and the colored lanterns of tramways, red, green, yellow, wink far away, swimming over a soft darkness—and through lashes moist with frost the white globes look like crosses of long white searchlights on a black sky.

Nevsky starts on the shore of the Neva, at a quay as trim and perfect as a drawing room, with a red-granite parapet and a row of palaces, of straight angles, tall windows, chaste columns and balustrades, severe, harmonious and luxuriously stern in their masculine grace.

Divided by the river, Petrograd's greatest mansion, the Winter Palace, faces Petrograd's greatest prison, the Peter-Paul Fortress. The Czars lived in the Winter Palace; when they died, they crossed the Neva: in the cathedral of the Fortress, white slabs rose over the graves of the Czars. The prison stood behind the cathedral. The walls of the Fortress guarded the dead Czars and the Czar's living enemies. In the long, silent halls of the palace, tall mirrors reflected the ramparts behind which men were forgotten, alive for decades in lonely stone graves.

Bridges rise over the river, as long humps of steel, with tramways crawling slowly up to the middle and rolling swiftly, clattering, down to the other shore. The right bank, beyond the Fortress, is a gradual surrender of the city to that earth, that countryside it has driven out; the Kamenostrovsky, a broad, quiet, endless avenue, is like a stream full of the fragrance of a future sea, a street where each step is a forecast of the country to come. The avenue and the city and the river end at the Islands, where the Neva breaks among bits of land held together by delicate bridges, where heavy white cones rise in tiers edged with dark green, over a deep silence of snow, and fir branches and bird footprints alone break the white desolation, and beyond the last island, the sky and sea are an unfinished water color of pale gray with a faint greenish band smeared across to mark a future horizon.

But Petrograd also has side streets. Petrograd's side streets are of colorless stone rain-washed into the gray of the clouds above and of the mud below. They are bare as jail corridors; they cut each other in naked corners of square buildings that look like prisons. Old gateways are locked at night over mud-swollen ruts. Little shops frown with faded signs over turbid windows. Little parks choke with consumptive grass into which mud and dust and mud again have been ground for a century. Iron parapets guard canals of refuse-thickened water.

On dark corners, rusty ikons of the Madonna are nailed over forgotten tin boxes, begging coppers for orphanages.

And farther up the Neva, rise forests of red-brick chimneys, spewing a black cloud that hangs over old, stooping, wooden houses, over an embankment of rotting logs at the placid, indifferent river. Rain falls slowly through the smoke; rain, smoke and stone are the theme-song of the city.

Petrograd's residents wonder, sometimes, at the strange bonds that hold them. After the long winter, they curse the mud and the stone, and cry for pine forests; they flee from the city as from a hated stepmother; they flee to green grass and sand and to the sparkling capitals of Europe. And, as to an unconquerable mistress, they return in the fall, hungry for the wide streets, the shrieking tramways and the cobblestones, serene and relieved, as if life were beginning again. "Petrograd," they say, "is the only *City*."

Cities grow like forests, like weeds. Petrograd did not grow. It was born finished and complete. Petrograd is not acquainted with nature. It was the work of man.

Nature makes mistakes and takes chances; it mixes its colors and knows little of straight lines. But Petrograd is the work of man who knows what he wants.

Petrograd's grandeur is unmarred, its squalor unrelieved. Its facets are cut clearly, sharply; they are deliberate, perfect with the straight-forward perfection of man's work.

Cities grow with a people, and fight for the place at the head of cities, and rise slowly up the steps of years. Petrograd did not rise. It came to be at the height. It was commanded to command. It was a capital before its first stone was laid. It was a monument to the spirit of man.

Peoples know nothing of the spirit of man, for peoples are only nature, and man is a word that has no plural. Petrograd is not of the people. It has no legend, no folklore; it is not glorified in nameless songs down nameless roads. It is a stranger, aloof, incomprehensible, forbidding. No pilgrims ever traveled to its granite gates. The gates had never been opened in warm compassion to the meek, the hurt and the maimed, like the doors of the kindly Moscow. Petrograd does not need a soul; it has a mind.

And perhaps it is only a coincidence that in the language of the Russians, Moscow is "she," while Petrograd has ever been "he."

And perhaps it is only a coincidence that those who seized

the power in the name of the people, transferred their capital to the meek Moscow from the haughty aristocrat of cities.

In 1924, a man named Lenin died and the city was ordered to be called Leningrad. The revolution also brought posters to the city's walls, and red banners to its houses, and sunflower-seed shells to its cobblestones. It cut a proletarian poem into the pedestal of the statue of Alexander III, and put a red rag on a stick into the hand of Catherine II in a small garden off Nevsky. It called Nevsky "Prospect of October 25th" and Sadovaia, a cross street—"Street of July 3rd," in honor of dates it wanted remembered; and at the intersection, hefty conductoresses yell in the crowded tramways: "Corner of October twenty-fifth and July third! Terminal for yellow tickets. New fare, citizens!'

In the early summer of 1925 the State Textile Trust put out new cotton prints. And women smiled in the streets of Petrograd, women wearing dresses made of new materials for the first time in many years.

But there were only half-a-dozen patterns of prints in the city. Women in black and white checks passed women in black and white checks; women in red-dotted white met women in green-dotted white; women with spirals of blue on a gray dress met women with the same spirals of brown on a tan dress. They passed by like inmates of a huge orphanage, frowning, sullen, uncomfortable, losing all joy in their new garments.

In a store on Nevsky, the State Porcelain Trust displayed a glistening window of priceless china, a white tea service with odd, fuzzy, modern flowers engraved in thin black by the hand of a famous new artist. The service had stood there for months; no one could afford to buy it.

Windows sparkled with foreign imitation jewelry—strings of flowered wax beads, earrings of bright celluloid circles, the latest fashion, protected by a stupendous price from the wistful women who stopped to admire them.

In a street off Nevsky, a foreign book store had been opened; a window two floors high flaunted the glossy, radiant, incredible covers of volumes that had come from across the border.

Bright awnings spread over Nevsky's wide, dry sidewalks, and barometers sparkled in the sun with the clear, piercing fire of clean glass.

A huge cotton billboard stood leaning against a building, presenting the tense face, enormous eyes and long, thin hands of a famous actor painted in bold brush strokes under the name of a German film.

Pictures of Lenin looked down at the passersby, a suspicious face with a short beard and narrow Oriental eyes, draped in red bunting and mourning crêpe.

On street corners, in the sun, ragged men sold saccharine and plaster busts of Lenin. Sparrows chirped on telephone wires. Lines stood at the doors of co-operatives; women took off their jackets and, in short-sleeved, wrinkled blouses, offered flabby white arms to the first heat of the summer sun.

A poster hung high on a wall. On the poster, a huge worker swung a hammer toward the sky, and the shadow of the hammer fell like a huge black cross over the little buildings of the city under his boots.

Kira Argounova stopped by the poster to light a cigarette.

She took a paper box from the pocket of her old coat and, with two straight fingers, swiftly, without looking, swung a cigarette into her mouth. Then she opened her old handbag of imitation leather and took out an expensive foreign lighter engraved with her initials. She flicked a brief little flame, hurled a jet of smoke from the corner of her mouth and slammed the bag shut over the lighter. She jerked the frayed cuff of her coat sleeve and glanced at a sparkling watch on a narrow gold band. She swung forward; the high heels of her slippers rang hurriedly, resonantly down the granite sidewalk. Her slippers were patched; her legs displayed the tight, sheer luster of foreign silk stockings.

She walked toward an old palace that bore a red, five-pointed star over the entrance and an inscription in gold letters:

DISTRICT CLUB OF THE ALL-UNION COMMUNIST PARTY

Its glass door was severely, immaculately polished, but the latch on its garden gate was broken. Weeds grew over what had been gravelled walks, and cigarette stubs rocked softly in an abandoned fountain, around a dejected marble cupid with a greenish patch of rust across its stomach, at the dry mouth of an urn.

Kira hurried down deserted walks, through a thick, neglected green tangle that drowned the clatter of tramways outside; blue pigeons fluttered lazily into the branches at the sound of her steps, and a bee rocked on a heavy purple tuft of clover. A giant regiment of oaks stood with arms outstretched, hiding the palace from the eyes of the street.

In the depths of the garden stood a small two-storied wing

linked to the palace by the bridge of a short gallery. The windows of the first floor were broken and a sparrow sat on a sharp glass edge, jerking its head sidewise to look into the mouldy, deserted rooms. But on a window sill of the second floor lay a pile of books.

The heavy, hand-carved door was not locked. Kira went in and swung impatiently up the long stairway. It was a very long stairway. It rose to the second floor in a straight line, an endless flight of bare stone steps, cracked and crumbling in little trails of gravel. The stairway had had a magnificent white balustrade; but the balustrade was broken; empty holes gaped over the jagged stumps of marble columns and their white bodies still lay at the foot of the stairs. Hollow echoes rolled against the walls, against the murals of graceful white swans on blue lakes, of rose garlands, of sensual nymphs fleeing from grinning satyrs; the murals were faded and cut by gashes of peeling plaster.

Kira knocked at the door on the top of the stairs.

Andrei Taganov opened it and stepped back, astonished; his eyes widened in the slow, incredulous glance of a man looking at a miracle that could not become habitual; he forgot to move, he stood before her, the collar of a white shirt thrown open at his sunburnt throat.

"Kira!"

She laughed, a clear, metallic laughter: "How are you, Andrei?"

His hands closed slowly, softly over her shoulders, so softly that she could not feel his hands, only their strength, their will holding her, bending her backward; but his lips on hers were brutal, uncontrollable. His eyes were closed; hers were open, looking indifferently up at the ceiling.

"Kira, I didn't expect you till tonight."

"I know. But you won't throw me out, will you?"

She stepped aside, preceding him through the dim little lobby into his room, throwing her bag on a chair, her hat on a table, with imperious familiarity.

She alone knew why Andrei Taganov had had to economize, that winter; why he had given up his room and moved into an abandoned wing of the palace, which the Party Club could not use and had given to him free of rent.

It had been the secret love nest of a prince. Many years ago, a forgotten sovereign had waited there for the light, stealthy footsteps and the rustle of a silk skirt up the long marble stairway. His magnificent furniture was gone; but the walls, the fireplace and the ceiling remained.

The walls were covered with a white brocade hand-embroidered in delicate little wreaths of blue and silver leaves. A marble row of cupids with garlands and cornucopias spouting frozen white flowers encircled the cornice. A marble Leda reclined voluptuously in the embrace of white wings over the fireplace. And from the soft blue of a sky painted on the ceiling, among pale, downy clouds, white doves—that had watched long nights of luxurious orgies—now looked at an iron bed, broken-down chairs, a long unpainted table loaded with books in bright red covers, wooden boxes piled as a dresser, posters of Red Army soldiers hiding the splits in the white brocade, and a leather jacket hanging on a nail in a corner.

Kira said peremptorily: "I came now to tell you that I can't come tonight."

"Oh! . . . You can't, Kira?"

"No. I can't. Now don't look tragic. Here, I brought you something to cheer you up."

She took a small toy from her pocket, a glass tube that ended in a bulb filled with a red liquid in which a little black figure floated, trembling.

"What's that?"

She held the bulb in her closed fist, but the little figure did not move. "I can't do it. You try. Hold it this way."

She closed his fingers over the bulb. No expression, no movement of his told it to her, but she knew that he was not indifferent to the touch of her fingers on his, that all of the past winter had not made him accustomed and indifferent. The red liquid in the sealed tube spurted up suddenly in furious, boiling bubbles; the little black, horned figure jumped ecstatically up and down through the storm.

"See? They call it American Resident. I bought it on a street corner. Cute, isn't it?"

He smiled and watched the imp dancing. "Very cute. . . . Kira, why can't you come tonight?"

"It's . . . some business that I have to attend. Nothing important. Do you mind?"

"No. Not if it's inconvenient for you. Can you stay now?"

"Only for a little while." She tore her coat off and threw it on the bed.

"Oh, Kira!"

"Like it? It's your own fault. You insisted on a new dress."

The dress was red, very plain, very short, trimmed in black patent leather: a belt, four buttons, a flat round collar and a huge bow. She stood, leaning against the door, slouching a little, suddenly very fragile and young, a child's dress clinging to a body that looked as helpless and innocent as a child's, her tangled hair thrown back, her skirt high over slender legs pressed closely together, her eyes round and candid, but her smile mocking and confident, her lips moist, wide. He stood looking at her, frightened by a woman who looked more dangerous, more desirable than he had ever known.

She jerked her head impatiently: "Well? You don't like it?"

"Kira, you are . . . the dress is . . . so lovely. I've never seen a woman's dress like that."

"What do you know about women's dresses?"

"I looked through a whole magazine of Paris fashions at the Censorship bureau yesterday."

"*You* looking through a fashion magazine?"

"I was thinking of you. I wanted to know what women liked."

"And what did you learn?"

"Things I'd like you to have. Funny little hats. And slippers like sandals—with nothing but straps. And jewelry. Diamonds."

"Andrei! You didn't tell that to your comrades at the Censorship bureau, did you?"

He laughed, still looking at her intently, incredulously: "No. I didn't."

"Stop staring at me like that. What's the matter? Are you afraid to come near me?"

His fingers touched the red dress. Then his lips sank suddenly into the hollow of her naked elbow.

He sat in the deep niche of the window sill and she stood beside him, in the tight circle of his arms. His face was expressionless, and only his eyes laughed soundlessly, cried to her soundlessly what he could not say.

Then he was talking, his face buried in the red dress: "You know, I'm glad you came now, instead of tonight. There were still so many hours to wait. . . . I've never seen you like this. . . . I've tried to read and I couldn't. . . . Will you wear this dress next time? Was that your own idea, this leather bow? . . . Why do you look so . . . so much more grownup in a childish dress like this? . . . I like that bow. . . . Kira, you know, I've missed you so terribly. . . . Even when I'm working I . . ."

Her eyes were soft, pleading, a little frightened: "Andrei, you shouldn't think of me when you're working."

He said slowly, without smiling: "Sometimes, it's only thoughts of you that help me—through my work."

"Andrei! What's the matter?"

But he was smiling again: "Why don't you want me to think of you? Remember, last time you were here, you told me about that book you read with a hero called Andrei and you said you thought of me? I've been repeating it to myself ever since, and I bought the book. I know it isn't much, Kira, but . . . well . . . you don't say them often, things like that."

She leaned back, her hands crossed behind her head, mocking and irresistible: "Oh, I think of you so seldom I've forgotten your last name. Hope I read it in a book. Why, I've even forgotten that scar, right there, over your eye." Her finger was following the line of the scar, sliding down his forehead, erasing his frown; she was laughing, ignoring the plea she had understood.

"Kira, would it cost so very much to install a telephone in your house?"

"But they . . . we . . . have no electrical connections in the apartment. It's really impossible."

"I've wished so often that you had a phone. Then I could call you . . . once in a while. Sometimes, it's so hard to wait, just wait for you."

"Don't I come here as often as you wish, Andrei?"

"It isn't that. Sometimes . . . you see . . . I want just a look at you . . . the same day you've been here . . . sometimes even a minute after you've left. It's that feeling that you're gone and I have no way of calling, of finding you, no right to approach the house where you live, as if you had left the city. Sometimes, I look at all the people in the streets—and it frightens me—that feeling that you're lost somewhere among them—and I can't get to you, I can't scream to you over all those heads."

She said, implacably: "Andrei, you've promised never to call at my house."

"But wouldn't you allow me to telephone, if we could arrange it?"

"No. My parents might guess. And . . . oh, Andrei, we have to be careful. We have to be so careful—particularly now."

"Why particularly now?"

"Oh, no more than usual. It isn't so hard, is it, that one condition, just to be careful—for my sake?"

"No, dear."

"I'll come often. I'll still be here when you'll become tired of me."

"Kira, why do you say that?"

"Well, you'll be tired of me, some day, won't you?"

"You don't think that, do you?"

She said hastily: "No, of course not. . . . Well, of course, I love you. You know it. But I don't want you to feel . . . to feel that you're tied to me . . . that your life . . ."

"Kira, why don't you want me to say that my life. . ."

"This is why I don't want you to say anything."

She bent and closed his mouth with a kiss that hurt it.

Beyond the window, some club member in the palace was practising the "Internationale," slowly, with one hand, on a sonorous concert piano.

Andrei's lips moved hungrily over her throat, her hands, her shoulders. He tore himself away with an effort. He made himself say lightly, gaily, as an escape, rising: "I have something for you, Kira. It was for tonight. But then . . ."

He took a tiny box from a drawer of his desk, and pressed it into her hand. She protested helplessly: "Oh, Andrei, you shouldn't. I've asked you not to. With all you've done for me and . . ."

"I've done nothing for you. I think you're too unselfish. It has always been your family. I've had to fight to have you get this dress."

"And the stockings, and the lighter, and . . . Oh, Andrei, I'm so grateful to you, but . . ."

"But don't be afraid to open it."

It was a small, flat bottle of real French perfume. She gasped. She wanted to protest. But she looked at his smile and she could only laugh happily: "Oh, Andrei!"

His hand moved slowly in the air, without touching her, following the line of her neck, her breast, her body, cautiously, attentively, as if modeling a statue.

"What are you doing, Andrei?"

"Trying to remember."

"What?"

"Your body. As you stand—just now. Sometimes when I'm alone, I try to draw you in the air—like this—to feel as if you were standing before me."

She pressed herself closer to him. Her eyes were growing

darker; her smile seemed slow and heavy. She said, extending the perfume bottle: "You must open it. I want you to give me the first drop—yourself." She drew him down to her side, on the bed. She asked: "Where will you put it?"

His finger tips moist with the bewildering fragrance from another world, he pressed them timidly into her hair.

She laughed defiantly: "Where else?"

His finger tips brushed her lips.

"Where else?"

His hand drew a soft line down her throat, stopping abruptly at the black patent leather collar.

Her eyes holding his, she jerked her collar, tearing the snaps of her dress open. "Where else?"

He was whispering, his lips on her breast: "Oh, Kira, Kira, I wanted you—here—tonight. . . ."

She leaned back, her face dark, challenging, pitiless, her voice low: "I'm here—now."

"But . . ."

"Why not?"

"If you don't . . ."

"I do. That's why I came."

And as he tried to rise, her arms pulled him down imperiously. She whispered: "Don't bother to undress. I haven't the time."

*

He could forgive her the words, for he had forgotten them, when he saw her exhausted, breathing jerkily, her eyes closed, her head limp in the curve of his arm. He was grateful to her for the pleasure he had given her.

He could forgive anything, when she turned to him suddenly at the door, gathering her coat over the wrinkled red dress, when she whispered, her voice pleading, wistful and tender: "You won't miss me too much till next time, will you? . . . I . . . I've made you happy, haven't I?"

*

She ran swiftly up the stairs to her apartment, the home that had been Admiral Kovalensky's. She unlocked the door, looking impatiently at her wristwatch.

In the former drawing room, Marisha Lavrova was busy, standing over a Primus, stirring a kettle of soup with one hand, holding a book in the other, memorizing aloud: "The relationships of social classes can be studied on the basis of the distribution of the economic means of production at any given historical . . ."

Kira stopped beside her. "How's the Marxist theory, Marisha?" she interrupted loudly, tearing her hat off, shaking her hair. "Do you have a cigarette? Smoked my last one on the way home."

Marisha nodded with her chin toward the dresser. "In the drawer," she answered. "Light one for me, too, will you? How's things?"

"Fine. Wonderful weather outside. Real summer. Busy?"

"Uh-uh. Have to give a lecture at the Club tomorrow—on Historical Materialism."

Kira lighted two cigarettes and stuck one into Marisha's mouth.

"Thanks," Marisha acknowledged, swirling the spoon in the thick mixture. "Historical Materialism and noodle soup. That's for a guest," she winked slyly. "Guess you know him. Name's Victor Dunaev."

"I wish you luck. You and Victor both."

"Thanks. How's everything with you? Heard from the boy friend lately?"

Kira answered reluctantly: "Yes. I received a letter. . . . And a telegram."

"How's he getting along? When's he coming back?"

It was as if Kira's face had frozen suddenly into a stern, reverent calm, as if Marisha were looking again at the austere Kira of eight months ago. She answered:

"Tonight."

II

A telegram lay on the table before Kira. It contained four words:

"Arriving June fifth. Leo."

She had read it often; but two hours remained till the arrival of the Crimean train and she could still re-read it many times. She spread it out on the gray, faded satin cover of the bed and knelt by its side, carefully smoothing every wrinkle of the paper. It had four words: a word for every two months past; she wondered how many days she had paid for every letter, she did not try to think of how many hours and of what the hours had been.

But she remembered how many times she had cried to herself: "It doesn't matter. He'll come back—saved." It had become so simple and so easy: if one could reduce one's life to but one desire—life could be cold, clear and bearable. Perhaps others still knew that there were people, streets, and feelings; she didn't; she knew only that he would come back saved. It had been a drug and a disinfectant; it had burned everything out and left her icy, limpid, smiling.

There had been her room—suddenly grown so empty that she wondered, bewildered, how four walls could hold such an enormous void. There had been mornings when she awakened to stare at a day as dim and hopeless as the gray square of snow clouds in the window, and it took her a tortured effort to rise; days when each step across the room was a conquest of will, when all the objects around her, the Primus, the cupboard, the table, were enemies screaming to her of what they had shared with her, of what they had lost.

But Leo was in the Crimea where every minute was a ray of sunlight, and every ray of sunlight—a new drop of life.

There had been days when she fled from her room to people and voices, and fled from the people, for she found herself suddenly still lonelier, and she fled to wander through the streets, her hands in her pockets, her shoulders hunched, watching the sleigh runners, the sparrows, the snow around the lights, begging of them something she could not name. Then she returned home, and lighted the "Bourgeoise," and ate a half-cooked dinner on a bare table, lost in a dim room, crushed under the huge sound of the logs crackling, the clock ticking on a shelf, hoofs crunching snow beyond the window.

But Leo drank milk and ate fruit with skins bursting into fresh, sparkling juice.

There had been nights when she buried her head under the blanket and her face in the pillow, as if trying to escape from her own body, a body burning with the touch of a stranger's hands—in the bed that had been Leo's.

But Leo was lying on a beach by the sea and his body was growing suntanned.

There had been moments when she saw, in sudden astonishment, as if she had not grasped it before, just what she was doing to her own body; then she closed her eyes, for behind that thought was another one, more frightening, forbidden: of what she was doing to another man's soul.

But Leo had gained five pounds and the doctors were pleased.

There had been moments when she felt as if she were actually seeing the downward movement of a smiling mouth, the swift, peremptory wave of a long, thin hand, seeing them for a second briefer than lightning, and then her every muscle screamed with pain, so that she thought that she was not alone to hear it.

But Leo wrote to her.

She read his letters, trying to remember the inflection of his voice as it would pronounce each word. She spread the letters around her and sat in the room as with a living presence.

He was coming back, cured, strong, saved. She had lived eight months for one telegram. She had never looked beyond it. Beyond the telegram, there was no future.

*

The train from the Crimea was late.

Kira stood on the platform, motionless, looking at the empty track, two long bands of steel that turned to brass far away, in the clear, summer sunset beyond the terminal vaults. She was afraid to look at the clock and learn that which she had feared: that the train was hopelessly, indefinitely late. The platform trembled under the grating wheels of a heavy baggage truck. Somewhere in the long steel tunnel, a voice cried mournfully at regular intervals, the same words that blended into one, like the call of a bird in the dusk: "Grishka shove it over." Boots shuffled lazily, aimlessly past her. Across the tracks a woman sat on a bundle, her head drooping. The glass panes above were turning a desolate orange. The voice called plaintively: "Grishka shove it over. . . ."

When Kira went to the office of the station commandant, the executive answered briskly that the train would be quite late; unavoidable delay; a misunderstanding at a junction; the train was not expected till tomorrow morning.

She stood on the platform for a little while longer, aimlessly, reluctant to leave the place where she had almost felt his presence. Then she walked out slowly, walked down the stairs, her arms limp, her feet lingering unsteadily on every step she descended.

Far down at the end of the street, the sky was a flat band of bright, pure, motionless yellow, like the spilled yoke of an egg, and the street looked brown and wide in a warm twilight. She walked away slowly.

She saw a familiar corner, passed it, then came back and swerved into another direction, toward the house of the Dunaevs. She had an evening that had to be filled.

Irina opened the door. Her hair was wild, uncombed, but she wore a new dress of black and white striped batiste, and her tired face was powdered neatly.

"Well, Kira! Of all people! What a rare surprise! Come in. Take your coat off. I have something—someone—to show you. And how do you like my new dress?"

Kira was laughing suddenly. She took off her coat: she wore a new dress of black and white striped batiste. Irina gasped: "Oh . . . oh, hell! When did you get it?"

"About a week ago."

"I thought that if I got the plain stripes, I wouldn't see so many of them around, but the first time I wore it, I met three ladies in the same dress, within fifteen minutes. . . . Oh, what's the use? . . . Oh, well, come on!"

In the dining room the windows were open, and the room felt spacious, fresh with the soft clatter of the street. Vasili Ivanovitch got up hastily, smiling, dropping tools and a piece of wood on the table. Victor rose gracefully, bowing. A tall, blond, husky young man jumped up and stood stiffly, while Irina announced: "Two little twins from the Soviet reformatory! . . . Kira, may I present Sasha Chernov? Sasha—my cousin, Kira Argounova."

Sasha's hand was big and firm, and his handshake too strong. He grinned shyly, a timid, candid, disarming grin.

"Sasha, this is a rare treat for you," said Irina. "A rare guest. The recluse of Petrograd."

"Of Leningrad," Victor corrected.

"Of Petrograd," Irina repeated. "How are you, Kira? I hate to admit how glad I am to see you."

"I'm delighted to meet you," Sasha muttered. "I've heard so much about you."

"Without a doubt," said Victor, "Kira is the most talked about woman in the city—and even in Party circles." Kira glanced at him sharply; but he was smiling pleasantly: "Glamorous women have always been an irresistible theme for admiring whispers. Like Madame de Pompadour, for instance. Charm refutes the Marxist theory: it knows no class distinctions."

"Shut up," said Irina. "I don't know what you're talking about, but I'm sure it's something rotten."

"Not at all," said Kira quietly, holding Victor's eyes, "Victor is very complimentary, even though he does exaggerate."

Awkwardly, diffidently, Sasha moved a chair for Kira, offering it to her silently with a wave of his hand and a helpless grin.

"Sasha is studying history," said Irina, "that is, he was. He's been thrown out of the University for trying to think in a country of free thought."

"I will have you understand, Irina," said Victor, "that I won't tolerate such remarks in my presence. I expect the Party to be respected."

"Oh, stop acting!" Irina snapped. "The Party Collective won't hear you."

Kira noticed Sasha's long, silent glance at Victor; Sasha's steely blue eyes were neither bashful nor friendly.

"I'm sorry about the University, Sasha," said Kira, feeling suddenly that she liked him.

"I did not mind it," Sasha drawled in a quiet, measured tone of conviction. "It, really, was not essential. There are some outward circumstances which an autocratic power can control. There are some values it can never reach nor subjugate."

"You will discover, Kira," Victor smiled coldly, "that you and Sasha have much in common. You are both inclined to disregard the rudiments of caution."

"Victor, will you . . ." Vasili Ivanovitch began.

"Father, I have a right to expect, as long as I'm feeding this family, that my views . . ."

"You're feeding whom?" a shrill voice asked from the next room. Acia appeared on the threshold, her stockings loose around her ankles, the shreds of a torn magazine in one hand and a pair of scissors in the other. "I wish someone'd feed someone. I'm still hungry and Irina wouldn't give me a second helping of soup."

"Father, I expect something to be done about this child," said Victor. "She's growing up like a bum. If she were to join a children's organization, such as the Pioneers . . ."

"Victor, we won't discuss that again," Vasili Ivanovitch interrupted firmly, quietly.

"Who wants to be a stinking Pioneer?" asked Acia.

"Acia, you go back to your room," Irina ordered, "or I'll put you to bed."

"You and who else?" stated Acia, disappearing behind a slammed door.

"Really," Victor observed, "if I'm able to study as I do and work besides and provide for this household, I don't see why Irina can't take proper care of one brat."

No one answered.

Vasili Ivanovitch bent over the piece of wood he had been carving. Irina drew pictures with a spoon handle on the old table cloth. Victor rose to his feet: "Sorry, Kira, to desert such a rare guest, but I have to go. I have a dinner engagement."

"Sure," said Irina. "See that the hostess doesn't borrow any silverware from Kira's room."

Victor left. Kira noticed that the tools were trembling in Vasili Ivanovitch's wrinkled fingers.

"What are you doing, Uncle Vasili?"

"Making a frame," Vasili Ivanovitch raised his head, showing his work proudly, "for one of Irina's pictures. They're good pictures. It's a shame to let them get crumpled and ruined in a drawer."

"It's beautiful, Uncle Vasili. I didn't know you could do that."

"Oh, I used to be good at it. I haven't done it for years. But I used to be good in the . . . in the old days, when I was a young man, in Siberia."

"How's your job, Uncle Vasili?"

"No more," said Irina. "How long do you think one can keep a job in a private store?"

"What happened?"

"Haven't you heard? They closed the store for back taxes. And the boss, himself, is now more broke than we are. . . . Would you like some tea, Kira? I'll fix it. The tenants stole our Primus, but Sasha will help me to light the samovar in the kitchen. Come on!" she threw at him imperiously, and Sasha rose obediently. "I don't know why I ask him to help," she winked at Kira, "he's the most helpless, useless, awkward thing born." But her eyes were sparkling happily. She took his arm and wheeled him out of the room.

It was growing dark, and the open window was a sharp, bright blue. Vasili Ivanovitch did not light a lamp. He bent lower over his carving.

"Sasha is a nice boy," he said suddenly, "and I'm worried."

"Why?" asked Kira.

He whispered: "Politics. Secret societies. Poor doomed little fool."

"And Victor suspects?"

"I think so."

It was Irina who switched on the light, returning with a sparkling tray of cups, preceding Sasha with a steaming samovar.

"Here's the tea. And some cookies. I made them. See how you like them, Kira, for an artist's cooking."

"How's the art, Irina?"

"The job, you mean? Oh, I still have it. But I'm afraid I'm not too good at drawing posters. I've been reprimanded twice in the Wall Newspaper. They said my peasant women looked like cabaret dancers and my workers were too graceful. My bourgeois ideology, you know. Well, what do they want? It's not my specialty. I could scream, sometimes, I can't get any ideas at all for one more of those damn posters."

"And now they have that competition," Vasili Ivanovitch said mournfully.

"What competition?"

Irina spilled tea on the table cloth. "An inter-club competition. Who'll make the most, the best and the reddest posters. Have to work two hours extra every day—free—for the glory of the Club."

"Under the Soviets," drawled Sasha, "there is no exploitation."

"I thought," said Irina, "that I had a good idea for a winner: a real proletarian wedding—a worker and a peasant woman on a tractor, God damn them! But I heard that the Club of Red Printers is making a symbolic one—the union of an airplane and a tractor—sort of the spirit of Electrification and Proletarian State Construction."

"And the wages," sighed Vasili Ivanovitch. "She spent all of her last month's salary on shoes for Acia."

"Well," said Irina, "she couldn't go barefooted."

"Irina, you work too hard," Sasha remarked, "and you take the work too seriously. Why waste your nerves? It's all temporary."

"It is," said Vasili Ivanovitch.

"I hope it is," said Kira.

"Sasha's my life-saver," Irina's weary mouth smiled tremulously and sarcastically at once, as if trying to deny the involuntary tenderness in her voice. "He took me to the theater last week. And week before last, we went to the Museum of Alexander III, and we wandered there for hours, looking at the paintings."

"Leo's coming back tomorrow," Kira said suddenly, irrelevantly, as if she could not keep it any longer.

"Oh!" Irina's spoon clattered down. "You never told us. I'm so glad! And he's quite well?"

"Yes. He was to return tonight, but the train is late."

"How is his aunt in Berlin?" asked Vasili Ivanovitch. "Still helping you? There's an example of family loyalty. I have the greatest admiration for that lady, even though I've never seen her. Anyone who's safe, away, free and can still understand us, buried alive in this Soviet graveyard, must be a wonderful person. She's saved Leo's life."

"Uncle Vasili," said Kira, "when you see Leo, will you remember never to mention it? His aunt's help, I mean. You remember I explained to you how sensitive he is about being under obligation to her, and so we'll all be careful not to remind him of it, will we?"

"Certainly, I understand, child. Don't worry. . . . But that's Europe for you. That's abroad. That's what a human life does to a human being. I think it's hard for us to understand kindness and what used to be called ethics. We're all turning into beasts in a beastly struggle. But we'll be saved. We'll be saved before it gets us all."

"We don't have long to wait," said Sasha.

Kira noticed a frightened, pleading look in Irina's eyes.

It was late when Kira and Sasha rose to go. He lived far on the other side of the city, but he offered to escort her home, for the streets were dark. He wore an old coat and he walked fast, slouching. They hurried together through a soft, transparent twilight, through the city full of the fragrance of a warm earth somewhere far under the pavements and cobblestones.

"Irina isn't happy," he said suddenly.

"No," said Kira, "she isn't. No one is."

"We're living in difficult times. But things will change. Things are changing. There still are men to whom freedom is more than a word on posters."

"Do you think they have a chance, Sasha?"

His voice was low, tense with a passionate conviction, a quiet strength that made her wonder why she had ever thought him bashful: "Do you think the Russian worker is a beast that licks its yoke while his mind is being battered out of him? Do you think he's fooled by the clatter of a very noisy gang of tyrants? Do you know what he reads? Do you know the books that are hidden in the factories? The papers that pass secretly through many hands? Do you know that the people is awakening and . . ."

"Sasha," she interrupted, "aren't you playing a very dangerous game?"

He did not answer. He looked at the old roofs of the city against a milky, bluish sky.

"The people," she said, "has claimed too many victims already—of your kind."

"Russia has a long revolutionary history," he said. "*They* know it. They're even teaching it in their schools, but they think it's ended. It isn't. It's just beginning. And it has never lacked men who did not think of the danger. In the Czar's days—or at any other time."

She stopped and looked at him in the dusk, and said desperately, forgetting that she had met him for the first time but a few hours ago: "Oh, Sasha, is it worth the chance you're taking?"

He towered over her, strands of blond hair sticking out from under his old cap, his mouth grinning slowly over the raised collar of his coat. "You mustn't worry, Kira. And Irina mustn't worry. I'm not in danger. They won't get me. They won't have the time."

*

In the morning, Kira had to go to work.

She had insisted on working; Andrei had found a job for her—the job of lecturer and excursion guide in the Museum of the Revolution. The job consisted of sitting at home and waiting for a call from the Excursion Center. When they called, she hurried to the Museum and led a group of bewildered people through the halls of what had been the Winter Palace. She received a few rubles for each excursion; she was listed as a Soviet employee by the Upravdòm of her house; it saved her from an exorbitant rent and from the suspicion of being bourgeois.

In the morning, she had telephoned the Nikolaevsky station; the train from the Crimea was not expected until early in the afternoon. Then the Excursion Center called her; she had to go.

The halls of the Winter Palace displayed faded photographs of revolutionary leaders, yellowed proclamations, maps, diagrams, models of Czarist prisons, rusty guns, splinters of leg irons. Thirty workers were waiting in the Palace lobby for the "comrade guide." They were on vacation, but their Educational Club had arranged the excursion and they could not ignore its command. They removed their caps respectfully, and shuffled timidly, obediently after Kira, and listened attentively, scratching their heads.

". . . and this photograph, comrades, was taken just before his execution. He was hanged for the assassination of a tyrant, one of the Czar's henchmen. Such was the end of another glorious victim on the tortuous path of the Worker-Peasant Revolution."

". . . and this diagram, comrades, gives us a clear, visual illustration of the strike movement in Czarist Russia. You will note that the red line drops sharply after the year 1905. . . ."

Kira recited her lecture evenly, mechanically; she was no longer conscious of words; it was nothing but a succession of memorized sounds, each dragging the next one automatically, without any assistance of will; she did not know what she was going to say; she knew that her hand would rise at a given word and point at the right picture; she knew at which word the gray, impersonal blot that was her audience would laugh and at which word it would gasp and grunt with social indignation. She knew that her listeners wanted her to hurry and that the Excursion Center wanted the lecture to be long and detailed.

". . . and this, comrades, is the genuine carriage in which Alexander II was riding on the day of his assassination. This shattered back was torn by the bomb in the hands of . . ."

But she was thinking of the train from the Crimea; perhaps it had arrived; perhaps the lonely room she hated had now become a temple.

"Comrade guide, can you tell me if Alexander II was paid by International Imperialists?"

*

The room was empty when she came home.

"No," said Marisha, "he hasn't arrived."

"No," said the gruff voice over the telephone, "the train isn't in. Is that you again, citizen? What's the matter with you? Trains aren't run for your personal convenience. It's not expected until tonight."

She took off her coat. She raised her hand and glanced at her wristwatch; her hand froze in midair; she remembered whose gift it was; she took the watch off and threw it into a drawer.

She curled in an armchair by the window and tried to read a newspaper; the newspaper slipped to the floor; she sat still, her head on her arm.

It was an hour later that she heard steps behind the door, and the door was thrown open without a knock. The first thing she saw was a dusty suitcase. Then she saw the smile, the drooping lips arched over very white teeth in a tanned face. Then she stood with the back of her hand at her mouth and could not move.

He said: "Allo, Kira."

She did not kiss him. Her hands fell on his shoulders and moved down his arms, all her weight in her fingers, for she was sagging suddenly and her face was sliding slowly down his chest, down the cloth of his coat; and as he tried to lift her head, she pressed her mouth to his hand and held it; her shoulders jerked; she was sobbing.

"Kira, you little fool!"

He was laughing softly; his fingers caressed her hair; the fingers were trembling. He lifted her in his arms and carried her to the armchair, and sat down, holding her on his lap, forcing her lips to meet his.

"And that's the strong Kira who never cries. You shouldn't be so glad to see me, Kira. . . . Stop it, Kira. . . . You little fool. . . . My dearest, dearest . . ."

She tried to get up: "Leo. . . . You must take your coat off and . . ."

"Stay still."

He held her, and she leaned back, and she felt suddenly that she had no strength to lift her arms, that she had no strength ever to move again; and the Kira who despised femininity, smiled a tender, radiant, trusting smile, weaker than a woman's, the smile of a lost, bewildered child, her lashes heavy and sparkling with tears.

He looked at her, his eyes half-closed, and his glance was insulting in its open, mocking understanding of his power, a glance more voluptuous than a lover's caress.

Then he turned away and asked: "Was it terribly hard for you—this winter?"

"A little. But we don't have to talk about it. It's past. Do you cough any more, Leo?"

"No."

"And you're well? Quite, quite, completely well? Free to live again?"

"I am well—yes. As to living again. . . ."

He shrugged. His face was tanned, his arms were strong, his cheeks were not hollow any longer; but she noticed something in his eyes that had not been cured; something that, perhaps, had grown beyond cure.

She said: "Leo, isn't the worst of it over? Aren't we ready now to begin. . . ."

"Begin with what? I have nothing to bring back to you—but a healthy body."

"What else can I want?"

"Nothing else—from a gigolo."

"Leo!"

"Well, am I not one?"

"Leo, don't you love me?"

"I love you. I love you too much. I wish I didn't. It would all be so simple if I didn't. But to love a woman and to see her dragging herself through this hell they call life here, and not to help her, but to let her drag you instead . . . Did you really think I'd bless this health you gave back to me? I hate it because *you* gave it back to me. And because I love you."

She laughed softly: "Would you rather hate me, too?"

"Yes. I'd rather. You are that which I've lost long ago. But I love you so much that I'm trying to hold on to it, to that which you think I am, which I know I was, even though I can't hold on much longer. And that's all I have to offer you, Kira."

She looked up at him quietly, and her eyes were dry, and her smile was not a child's and stronger than a woman's. She said: "There is only one thing that matters and that that we'll remember. The rest doesn't matter. I don't care what life is to be nor what it does to us. But it won't break us. Neither you nor me. That's our only weapon. That's the only banner we can hold against all those others around us. That's all we have to know about the future."

He said more tenderly, more earnestly than she had ever heard him say: "Kira, I wish you weren't what you are."

Then she buried her face on his shoulder and whispered: "And we won't ever talk about it again. And now we don't have to talk at all, do we? I have to get up and powder my nose, and you have to take that coat off, and take a bath, and I'll fix you some lunch. . . . But first let me sit with you, for just a few moments, just sit still . . . don't move . . . Leo. . . ."

Her head slid slowly to his breast, to his knees, to his feet.

III

In the afternoon, three days later, the door bell rang and Kira went to answer it.

She threw the door half-open, protected by a chain. On the stair-landing stood a heavy woman in a smart, expensive overcoat. Her face, slanting back from a prominent, pointed chin, was raised with a studied movement of graceful inquiry, revealing a stout, white neck; her full lips, smeared with a violent magenta, were half-open, revealing strong white teeth. Her hand poised on a broad expanse of green silk scarf, she drawled in a self-consciously gracious voice: "Does Leo Kovalensky live here?"

Kira looked incredulously at the diamond rings sparkling on the short, white fingers. She answered: "Why . . . yes."

She did not remove the chain; she stood staring at the woman. The woman said with a little accent of gentle firmness: "I want to see him."

Kira let her enter. The woman looked at Kira curiously, inquisitively, narrowing her eyes.

Leo rose with a surprised frown when they entered the room. The woman extended both hands to him in a dramatic greeting. "Leo! So delightful to see you again! I've remembered my threat to find you. I really intend to be a nuisance!"

Leo did not smile in answer to her expectant giggle; he bowed graciously; he said: "Kira, this is Antonina Pavlovna Platoshkina—Kira Alexandrovna Argounova."

"Oh! . . . *Argounova?* . . . Oh . . ." said Antonina Pavlovna, as if noting the fact that Kira's name was not Leo's; she sounded almost relieved. She extended her arm, in a straight line, her fingers drooping, as if she were giving her hand to a man and expecting him to kiss it.

"Antonina Pavlovna and I were neighbors in the sanatorium," Leo explained.

"And he was a perfectly ungracious neighbor, I must complain," Antonina Pavlovna laughed huskily. "He wouldn't wait for me—and I wanted so much to leave on the same train. And, Leo, you didn't give me your apartment number and I had a perfectly terrible time trying to get it out of the Upravdom. Upravdoms are one of the unavoidable nuisances of our era, and all we of the intelligentsia can do is bear with it with a sense of humor."

She took off her coat. She wore a plain black dress of new, expensive silk in the latest fashion, and foreign earrings of green celluloid circles. Her hair was combed back severely off her forehead and two trim, sleek coils were flattened against her cheeks smeared with a very white powder. Her hair was an incredible orange, the color of a magnificent string of amber that swung like a pendulum, striking her stomach, when she moved. Her dress fitted tightly, slanting sharply from very wide hips down to heavy legs with very thin ankles and very small feet that seemed crushed under their disproportionate burden. She sat down and her stomach settled in a wide fold over her lap.

"When did you return, Tonia?" Leo asked.

"Yesterday. And oh, what a trip!" she sighed. "These Soviet trains! Really, I believe I lost everything I accomplished in the sanatorium. I was taking a rest cure for my nerves," she explained, pointing her chin at Kira. "And what sensitive person isn't a nervous wreck these days? But the Crimea! That place saved my life."

"It was beautiful," Leo agreed.

"But, really, it lost all its charm after you left, Leo. You know, he was the most charming patient in that dull sanatorium and everybody admired him so much—oh, purely platonically, my dear, if you're worried," she winked at Kira.

"I'm not," said Kira.

"Leo was so kind as to help me with my French lessons. I was learning . . . that is, brushing up on my French. It is such a relief, in these drab days, to stumble upon a person like Leo. You must forgive me, Leo. I realize that I may be an unwelcome guest, but it would be too much to expect of a woman if you asked her to give up a beautiful friendship in this revolting city where real people are so rare!"

"Why, no, Tonia, I'm glad you took the trouble to find me."

"Ah, these people here! I know so many of them. We meet, we talk, we shake hands. What does it mean? Nothing. Nothing but an empty physical gesture. Who among them knows the deeper significance of the spirit or the real meaning of our lives?"

Leo's slow, faint smile was not one of understanding; but he said: "One could forget one's troubles in some engrossing activity—if it were permitted these days."

"How profoundly true! Of course, the modern woman of culture is organically incapable of remaining inactive. I have a tremendous program outlined for myself for this coming winter. I'm going to study. I propose to master ancient Egypt."

"What?" asked Kira.

"Ancient Egypt," said Antonina Pavlovna. "I want to recapture its spirit in all its entirety. There is a profound significance in these far-away cultures, a mysterious bond with the present, which we moderns do not appreciate fully. I am certain that in a former incarnation . . . You are not interested in theosophy, are you, Leo?"

"No."

"I can appreciate your viewpoint, of course, but I have given it a thorough study and a great deal of thought. There is a transcendental truth in it, an explanation for so many of the baffling phenomena of our existence. Of course, I have one of those natures that long for the mystical. However, you must not think me old-fashioned. You mustn't be surprised if I tell you that I'm studying political economy."

"You are, Tonia? Why?"

"One cannot be out of tune with one's time, you know. To criticize, we must understand. I find it surprisingly thrilling. There is a certain peculiar romance in labor and markets and machines. Apropos, have you read the latest volume of verse by Valentina Sirkina?"

"No, I haven't."

"Thoroughly delightful. Such depth of emotion, and yet— completely modern, so esentially modern! There is a verse about—how does it go?—about my heart is asbestos that remains cool over the blast-furnace of my emotions—or something like that—it is really superb."

"I must admit I don't read modern poets."

"I'll bring you that book, Leo. I know you'll understand and appreciate it. And I'm sure Kira Alexandrovna will enjoy it."

"Thank you," said Kira, "but I never read poetry."

"Indeed? How peculiar! I'm sure you care for music?"

"Fox-trots," said Kira.

"Really?" Antonina Pavlovna smiled condescendingly. When she smiled, her chin pointed further forward and her forehead slanted back; her lips opened slowly, uncomfortably, as if slithering apart. "Speaking of music," she turned to Leo, "it is another essential item on my winter's program. I've made Koko promise me a box for every concert at the State Philharmony. Poor Koko! He's really very artistic at heart, if one knows how to approach him, but I'm afraid that his unfortunate early upbringing has not trained him for an appreciation of symphonic music. I shall, probably, have to be alone in my box. Oh—here's a happy thought!—you may share it with me, Leo. . . . And Kira Alexandrovna, of course," she nodded to Kira and turned to Leo again.

"Thank you, Tonia," he answered, "but I'm afraid we won't have much time for that, this winter."

"Leo, my dear!" she spread her arms in a wide gesture of sympathy, "don't you think I understand? Your financial position is. . . . Ah, these are not times for men like you. However, do not lose courage. With my connections . . . Koko cannot refuse me anything. He hated to see me leave for the Crimea. He missed me so much—you wouldn't believe how glad he was to see me back. He could not be more devoted if he were my husband. In fact, he couldn't be as devoted as he is. Marriage is an outmoded prejudice—as you know." She smiled at Kira.

"I'm sure the Crimea has helped your health," Leo said hastily, coldly.

"Ah, there's no other place like it! It is a bit of paradise. The dark, velvet sky, the diamond stars, the sea, and that divine moonlight! You know, I've wondered why you remained so indifferent to its magic spell. I thought you were essentially unromantic. Of course, I can understand the reason—now."

She threw a swift glance at Kira. The glance froze, as if seized and held by Kira's fixed eyes. Then Antonina Pavlovna's lips slithered into a cold smile and she turned away, sighing: "You men are strange creatures. To understand you is a whole science in itself and the first duty of every real woman. I've mastered it thoroughly in the bitter classroom of experience!" She sighed wearily, with a deprecatory shrug. "I've known heroic officers of the White Army. I've known brutal, iron commissars." She laughed shrilly. "I confess it openly. Why not? We are all moderns here. . . . I've known many people who misunderstood me. But I do not mind. I can forgive them. You know—*noblesse oblige.*"

Kira sat on the arm of a chair, watching the toes of her old slippers, studying her fingernails, while they talked. It was dark beyond the window, when Antonina Pavlovna glanced at a diamond-studded wristwatch.

"Oh, how late it is! It's been so delightful that I haven't noticed the time at all. I must hurry home. Koko is probably getting melancholy without me, the poor child."

She opened her bag, took out a little mirror and, holding it delicately in two straight fingers, inspected her face carefully through narrowed eyes. She took out a little scarlet bottle with a tiny brush and smeared a purplish blot over her lips.

"Delightful stuff," she explained, showing the bottle to Kira, "infinitely better than lipstick. I notice you don't use much lipstick, Kira Alexandrovna. I would recommend it strongly. As woman to woman, one should never neglect one's appearance, you know. Particularly," she laughed, a friendly, intimate laughter, "particularly when one has such valuable property to guard."

At the door in the lobby, Antonina Pavlovna turned to Leo: "Don't worry about this coming winter, Leo. With my connections . . . Koko, of course, knows the highest . . . why, I'd be afraid to whisper some of the names he knows and . . . of course, Koko is putty in my hands. You must meet him, Leo. We can do a lot for you. I shall see to it that a magnificent young man like you is not lost in this Soviet swamp."

"Thank you, Tonia. I appreciate your offer. But I hope that I'm not quite lost—yet."

"Just what is his position?" Kira asked suddenly.

"Koko? He's assistant manager of the Food Trust—*officially*," Antonina Pavlovna winked mysteriously with a brief chuckle, lowering her voice; then, waving a hand with a diamond that flashed a swift spark in the light of an electric bulb, she drawled: "*Au revoir, mes amis*. I shall see you soon."

Slamming the chain over the door, Kira gasped: "Leo, I'm surprised!"

"By what?"

"That you can be acquainted with such an unspeakable . . ."

"I do not presume to criticize your friends."

They were passing through Marisha's room. In a corner by the window, Marisha raised her head from her book and looked at Leo curiously, startled by the tone of his voice. They crossed the room and Leo slammed the door behind them.

"You could have been civil, at least," he stated.

"What do you mean?"

"You could have said a couple of words—every other hour."

"She didn't come to hear me talk."

"I didn't invite her. And she's not a friend of mine. You didn't have to be so tragic about it."

"But, Leo, where did you pick that up?"

"*That* was in the same sanatorium and it happened to have foreign books, which is a rare treat when you have to spend your days reading Soviet trash. That's how we got acquainted. What's wrong with that?"

"But, Leo, don't you see what she's after?"

"Of course I do. Are you really afraid she'll get it?"

"Leo!"

"Well, then, why can't I speak to her? She's a harmless fool who's trying to amount to something. And she really does have connections."

"But to associate with that type of person. . . ."

"She's no worse than the Red trash one has to associate with, these days. And, at least, she's not Red."

"Well, as you wish."

"Oh, forget it, Kira. She'll never come again."

He was smiling at her, suddenly, warmly, his eyes bright, as if nothing had happened, and she surrendered, her hands on his shoulders, whispering: "Leo, don't you see? Nothing of that type should even dare to look at you."

He laughed, patting her cheek: "Let her look. It won't hurt me."

*

Leo had said: "Write to your uncle in Budapest at once. Thank him and tell him not to send us money any longer. I'm well. We'll struggle on our own. I have written down the exact sum of everything you sent me. Have you kept track of what you spent here, as I asked? We'll have to start repaying him—if he's patient, for the devil alone knows how long it will take."

She had whispered: "Yes, Leo," without looking at him.

He had noticed her gold wristwatch and frowned: "Where did that come from?"

She had said: "It's a present. From . . . Andrei Taganov."

"Oh, really? So you're accepting presents from him?"

"Leo!" She had whirled upon him defiantly, then she had pleaded: "Why not, Leo? It was my birthday and I couldn't hurt his feelings."

He had shrugged contemptuously: "Oh, I don't mind. It's your own business. Personally, I wouldn't feel comfortable wearing something paid for with G.P.U. money."

She had hidden the cigarette lighter, and the silk stockings, and the perfume. She had told Leo that the red dress had been made for his return. He wondered why she did not like to wear it.

She spent most of her days in the halls of the Winter Palace, saying to the gaping excursionists: ". . . and it is the duty of every conscientious citizen to be acquainted with the history of our revolutionary movement in order to become a trained, enlightened fighter in the ranks of the World Revolution—our highest goal."

In the evenings, she tried to tell Leo: "I have to go out tonight. I've promised Irina . . ." or: "I really must go out tonight. It's a meeting of Excursion Workers." But he made her stay at home.

She looked into the mirror, sometimes, and wondered about the eyes people had told her were so clear, so honest.

She did not go out at night. She could not tear herself away. She could not satisfy the hunger of looking at him, of sitting silently, huddled in an armchair, watching him move across the room. She would watch the lines of his body as he stood at a window, turned away from her, his hands spread on his waistline, holding his back, his body leaning lightly backward against his hands, one tense, sunburned muscle of his neck showing under dark, dishevelled hair, thrilling as a suggestion, a promise of his face which she could not see. Then she would rise and walk hesitantly toward him and let her hand run slowly down the hard tendon of his neck, without a word, without a kiss.

Then she could think, with a cold wonder, of another man who was waiting for her somewhere.

But she knew that she had to see Andrei. One evening, she put on the red dress and told Leo that she had promised to call on her family.

"May I go with you?" he asked. "I haven't seen them since my return and I owe them a visit."

"No, not this time, Leo," she answered calmly. "I'd rather you wouldn't. Mother is . . . she's so changed . . . I know you won't get along with her."

"Do you have to go tonight, Kira? I hate to let you go and to stay here alone. I've been without you for such a long time."

"I've promised them I'd come tonight. I won't stay late. I'll be back soon."

She was putting on her coat when the door bell rang.

It was Marisha who went to open the door and they heard Galina Petrovna's voice sweeping through the room, approaching: "Well, I'm glad they're home. Well, if I thought they were visiting others and neglecting their old parents and . . ."

Galina Petrovna entered first; Lydia followed; Alexander Dimitrievitch shuffled in behind them.

"Leo, my dear child!" Galina Petrovna swept toward him and kissed him on both cheeks. "I'm so glad to see you! Welcome back to Leningrad."

Lydia shook hands limply; she removed her old hat, sat down heavily, as if collapsing, and fumbled with her hairpins: a long strand of hair was falling loosely out of the careless roll at the back of her neck. She was very pale and used no powder; her nose was shiny; she stared mournfully at the floor.

Alexander Dimitrievitch muttered: "I'm glad you're well, my boy," and patted Leo's shoulder uncertainly, with the timid, frightened look of an animal expecting to be hurt.

Kira faced them calmly and said with cold assurance: "Why did you come? I was just starting for your house, as I promised."

"As you . . ." Galina Petrovna began, but Kira interrupted: "Well, since you're here, take your coats off."

"I'm so happy you're well again, Leo," said Galina Petrovna. "I feel as if you were my son. You really are my son. Everything else is just bourgeois prejudices."

"Mother!" Lydia remonstrated feebly, hopelessly.

Galina Petrovna settled down in a comfortable armchair. Alexander Dimitrievitch sat apologetically on the edge of a chair by the door.

"Thank you for coming," Leo smiled graciously. "My only excuse for neglecting to call, as I should have, is . . ."

"Kira," Galina Petrovna finished for him. "Do you know that we haven't seen her more than three times while you were away?"

"I have a letter for you, Kira," Lydia said suddenly.

"A letter?" Kira's voice jerked slightly.

"Yes. It came today."

There was no return address on the envelope; but Kira knew the handwriting. She threw the letter indifferently down on the table.

"Don't you want to open it?" Leo asked.

"No hurry," she said evenly. "Nothing important."

"Well, Leo?" Galina Petrovna's voice boomed; her voice had become louder, clearer. "What are your plans for the winter? This is such an interesting year we're entering. So many opportunities, particularly for the young."

"So many . . . what?" Leo asked.

"Such a wide field of activity! It's not like in the dying, decadent cities of Europe where people slave all their lives for measly wages and a pitiful little existence. Here—each one of us has an opportunity to be a useful, creative member of a stupendous whole. Here—one's work is not merely a wasted effort to satisfy one's petty hunger, but a contribution to the gigantic building of humanity's future."

"Mother," Kira asked, "who wrote all that down for you?"

"Really, Kira," Galina Petrovna drew her shoulders up, "you're not only impertinent to your mother, but I think you're also a bad influence on Leo's future."

"I wouldn't worry about that, Galina Petrovna," said Leo.

"And of course, Leo, I hope that you're modern enough to outlive the prejudices we've all shared. We must admit that the Soviet Government is the only progressive government in the world. It utilizes all its human resources. Even an old person like me, who has been useless all her life, can find an opportunity for creative toil. And as for young people like you . . ."

"Where are you working, Galina Petrovna?" Leo asked.

"Oh, don't you know? I'm teaching in a Labor School—they used to be called High Schools, you know. Sewing and fancy needlework. We all realize that a practical subject like sewing is much more important to our little future citizens than the dead, useless things, such as Latin, which were taught in the old bourgeois days. And our methods? We're centuries ahead of Europe. For instance, take the complex method that we're . . ."

"Mother," Lydia said wearily, "Leo may not be interested."

"Nonsense! Leo is a modern young man. Now, this method we're using at present. . . . For instance, what did they do in the old days? The children had to memorize mechanically so many dry, disjoined subjects—history, physics, arithmetic—with no connection between them at all. What do we do now? We have the complex method. Take last week, for instance. Our subject was Factory. So every teacher had to build his course around that central subject. In the history class they taught the growth and development of factories; in the physics class they taught all about machinery; the arithmetic teacher gave them problems about production and consumption; in the art class they drew factory interiors. And in my class—we made overalls and blouses. Don't you see the advantage of the method? The indelible impression it will leave in the children's minds? Overalls and blouses—practical, concrete, instead of teaching them a lot of dry, theoretical seams and stitches."

Lydia's head drooped listlessly; she had heard it all many times.

"I'm glad you're enjoying your work, Galina Petrovna," said Leo.

"I'm glad you get your rations," said Kira.

"I do, indeed," Galina Petrovna stated proudly. "Of course, our distribution of commodities has not as yet reached a level of perfection and, really, the sunflower-seed oil I got last week was so rancid we couldn't use it . . . but then, this is a transitional period of . . ."

". . . State Construction!" Alexander Dimitrievitch yelled suddenly, hastily, as a well-memorized lesson.

"And what are you doing, Alexander Dimitrievitch?" Leo asked.

"Oh, I'm working!" Alexander Dimitrievitch jerked as if ready to jump forward, as if defending himself hastily against a dangerous accusation. "Yes, I'm working. I'm a Soviet employee. I am."

"Of course," Galina Petrovna drawled, "Alexander's position is not as responsible as mine. He's a bookkeeper in a district office somewhere way on the Vasilievsky Island—such a long trip every day!—and just what kind of an office is it, Alexander? But, anyway, he does have a bread card—though he doesn't get enough even for himself alone."

"But I'm working," Alexander Dimitrievitch said meekly.

"Of course," said Galina Petrovna, "I get better ration cards because I'm in a preferred class of pedagogues. I'm very active socially. Why, do you know, Leo, that I've been elected assistant secretary of the Teachers' Council? It is gratifying to know that the present regime appreciates qualities of leadership. I even gave a speech on the methodology of modern education at an inter-club meeting where Lydia played the 'Internationale' so beautifully."

"Sure," Lydia said mournfully, "The 'Internationale.' I'm working, too. Musical director and accompanist in a Workers' Club. A pound of bread a week and carfare and, sometimes, money, what's left after the contributions each month."

"Lydia is not pliable," sighed Galina Petrovna.

"But I play the 'Internationale,'" said Lydia, "and the Red funeral march—'You fell as a victim'—and the Club songs. I even got applauded when I played the 'Internationale' at the meeting where mother made the speech."

Kira rose wearily to make tea. She pumped the Primus and put the kettle on, and watched it thoughtfully—and through the hissing of the flame, Galina Petrovna's voice boomed loudly, rhythmically, as if addressing a class: ". . . yes, twice, imagine? Two honorable mentions in our students' Wall Newspaper, as one of the three most modern and conscientious pedagogues. . . . Yes, I do have some influence. When that insolent young teacher tried to run the school, she was dismissed fast enough. And you can be sure I had something to say about that. . . ."

Kira did not hear the rest. She was watching the letter on the table, wondering. When she heard a voice again, it was Lydia's and it was saying shrilly: ". . . spiritual consolation. I know. It has been revealed to me. There are secrets beyond our mortal minds. Holy Russia's salvation will come from faith. It has been predicted. Through patience and long suffering shall we redeem our sins. . . ."

Behind the door, Marisha wound her gramophone and played "John Gray." It was a new record and the swift little notes jerked gaily, clicking in sharp, short knocks.

> *"John Gray*
> *Was brave and daring,*
> *Kitty*
> *Was very pretty . . ."*

Kira sat, her chin in her hands, the glow of the Primus flame flickering under her nostrils, and she smiled suddenly, very softly, and said: "I like that song."

"That awful, vulgar thing, so overplayed that I'm sick of it?" Lydia gasped.

"Yes. . . . Even if it is overplayed. . . . It has such a nice rhythm . . . clicking . . . like rivets driven into steel. . . ." She was speaking softly, simply, a little helplessly, as she seldom spoke to her family. She raised her head and looked at them, and—they had never seen it before—her eyes were pleading and hurt.

"Still thinking of your engineering, aren't you?" asked Lydia.

"Sometimes . . ." Kira whispered.

"I can't understand what's wrong with you, Kira," Galina Petrovna boomed. "You're never satisfied. You have a perfectly good job, easy and well-paid, and you mope over some childish idea of yours. Excursion guides, like pedagogues, are considered no less important than engineers, these days. It is quite an honorary and responsible position, and contributes a great deal to social construction—and isn't it more fascinating to build with living minds and ideologies rather than with bricks and steel?"

"It's your own fault, Kira," said Lydia. "You'll always be unhappy since you refuse the consolation of faith."

"What's the use, Kira?" sighed Alexander Dimitrievitch.

"Who said anything about being unhappy?" Kira asked loudly, sharply, jerking her shoulders; she got up, took a cigarette and lighted it, bending, from the Primus flame.

"Kira has always been unmanageable," said Galina Petrovna, "but one would think that these are times to make one come down to earth."

"What are your plans for the winter, Leo?" Alexander Dimitrievitch asked, suddenly, indifferently, as if he expected no answer.

"None," said Leo. "Nor for any winter to come."

"I had a dream," said Lydia, "about a crow and a hare. The hare crossed the road—and that's an unlucky omen. But the crow sat on a tree that looked like a huge white chalice."

"You take my nephew Victor, for instance," said Galina Petrovna. "There's a smart, modern young man. He's graduating from the Institute this fall and he has an excellent job already. Supporting his whole family. Now there's nothing sentimental about him. He has his eyes open to modern reality. He'll go far, that boy."

"But Vasili isn't working," Alexander Dimitrievitch remarked with a dull, quiet wonder.

"Vasili has never been practical," stated Galina Petrovna. Alexander Dimitrievitch said suddenly, irrelevantly: "It's a pretty red dress you have, Kira."

She smiled wearily: "Thank you, Father."

"You don't look so well, child. Tired?"

"No. Not particularly. I'm fine."

Then Galina Petrovna's voice drowned out the roar of the Primus: ". . . and, you know, it's only the best teachers who are praised in the Wall Newspaper. Our students are very severe and . . ."

Late at night, when the guests had gone, Kira took the letter into the bathroom and opened it. It contained two lines:

Kira dearest,
    Please forgive me for writing. But won't you telephone me?

                                                    Andrei

                            *

She led two excursions on the following day. Coming home, she told Leo that she would be dismissed if she did not attend a guides' meeting that evening. She put on her red dress. On the stair-landing, she kissed Leo lightly, as he stood watching her go; she waved to him, vaulting down the stairs, with a cold, gay chuckle. On a street corner, she opened her purse, took out the little French bottle and pressed a few drops of perfume into her hair. She leaped into a tramway at full speed and stood hanging onto a leather strap, watching the lights swim past. When she got off, she walked, lightly, swiftly, with a cold, precise determination, toward the palace that was a Party Club.

She ran soundlessly up the crumbling marble stairway of the pavilion. She knocked sharply at the door.

When Andrei opened the door, she laughed, kissing him: "I know, I know, I know. . . . Don't say it . . . I want to be forgiven first, and then I'll explain."

He whispered happily: "You're forgiven. You don't have to explain."

She did not explain. She did not let him utter a complaint. She whirled around the room, and he tried to catch her, and the cloth of her coat felt cold in his hands, cold and fragrant of summer night air. He could whisper only: "Do you know that it's been two weeks since . . ." But he did not finish the sentence.

Then she noticed that he was dressed for the street. "Were you going out, Andrei?"

"Oh . . . yes, I was, but it's not important."

"Where were you going?"

"Just to a Party Cell meeting."

"A Party Cell meeting? And you say it's not important? But you can't miss that."

"Yes, I can. I'm not going."

"Andrei, I'd rather come tomorrow and let you . . ."

"No."

"Well, then, let's go out together. Take me to the European roof."

"Tonight?"

"Yes. Now."

He did not want to refuse. She did not want to notice the look in his eyes.

They sat at a white table in the roof garden on top of the European Hotel. They sat in a dim corner, and they could see nothing of the long room but the naked white back of a woman a few tables away, with a little strand of golden hair curling at the nape of her neck, escaping from the trim, lustrous waves of her coiffure, with a little golden shadow between her shoulder blades, her long fingers holding a glass with a liquid the color of her hair, swaying slowly; and beyond the woman, beyond a haze of yellow lights and bluish, rippling smoke, an orchestra played fox-trots from "Bajadere," and the violinists swayed to the rhythm of the golden glass.

Andrei said: "It's been two weeks, Kira, and . . . and you probably need it." He slipped a roll of bills into her hand, his monthly salary.

She whispered, pushing it back, closing his fingers over the bills: "No, Andrei. . . . Thank you. . . . But I don't need it. And . . . and I don't think I'll need it again. . . ."

"But . . ."

"You see, I get so many excursions to lead, and mother got more classes at the school, and we all have clothes and everything we need, so that . . ."

"But, Kira, I want you to . . ."

"Please, Andrei! Don't let's argue. Not about that. . . . Please. . . . Keep it. . . . If . . . if I need it, I'll tell you."

"Promise?"

"Yes."

The violins rumbled dully, heavily, and suddenly the music burst out like a firecracker, so that the swift, laughing notes could almost be seen as sparks shooting to the ceiling.

"You know," said Kira, "I shouldn't ask you to bring me here. It's not a place for you. But I like it. It's only a caricature and a very poor little one at that, but still it's a caricature of what Europe is. Do you know that music they're playing? It's from 'Bajadere.' I saw it. They're playing it in Europe, too. Like here . . . almost like here."

"Kira," Andrei asked, "that Leo Kovalensky, is he in love with you or something?"

She looked at him, and the reflection of an electric light stood still as two sparks in her eyes and as a bright little oval on her patent leather collar. "Why do you ask that?"

"I saw your cousin, Victor Dunaev, at a club meeting and

he told me that Leo Kovalensky was back, and he smiled as if the news should mean something to me. I didn't even know that Kovalensky had been away."

"Yes, he's back. He's been away somewhere in the Crimea, for his health, I think. I don't know whether he's in love with me, but Victor was in love with me once, and he's never forgiven me for that."

"I see. I don't like that man."

"Victor?"

"Yes. And Leo Kovalensky, too. I hope you don't see him often. I don't trust that type of man."

"Oh, I see him occasionally."

The orchestra had stopped playing.

"Andrei, ask them to play something for me. Something I like. It's called the 'Song of Broken Glass.' "

He watched her as the music burst out again, splattering sparks of sound. It was the gayest music he had ever heard; and he had never seen her look sad; but she sat, motionless, staring helplessly, her eyes forlorn, bewildered.

"It's very beautiful, this music, Kira," he whispered, "why do you look like that?"

"It's something I liked . . . long ago . . . when I was a child. . . . Andrei, did you ever feel as if something had been promised to you in your childhood, and you look at yourself and you think 'I didn't know, then, that this is what would happen to me'—and it's strange, and funny, and a little sad?"

"No, I was never promised anything. There were so many things that I didn't know, then, and it's so strange to be learning them now. . . . You know, the first time I brought you here, I was ashamed to enter. I thought it was no place for a Party man. I thought . . ." he laughed softly, apologetically, "I thought I was making a sacrifice for you. And now I like it."

"Why?"

"Because I like to sit in a place where I have no reason to be, no reason but to sit and look at you across the table. Because I like those lights on your collar. Because you have a very stern mouth—and I like that—but when you listen to that music, your mouth is gay, as if it were listening, too. And all those things, they have no meaning for anyone on earth but me, and when I've lived a life where every hour had to have a purpose, and suddenly I discover what it's like to feel things that have no purpose but myself, and I see suddenly how sacred a purpose that can be, so that I can't even argue, I can't doubt, I can't fight it, and I know, then, that a life is possible whose only justification is my own joy—then everything, everything else suddenly seems very different to me."

She whispered: "Andrei, you shouldn't talk like that. I feel as if I were taking you away from your own life, from everything that has been your life."

"Don't you want to feel it?"

"But doesn't it frighten you? Don't you think sometimes that it may bring you to a choice you have no right to make?"

He answered with so quiet a conviction that the word sounded light, unconcerned, with a calm beyond earnestness: "No." He leaned toward her across the table, his eyes serene, his voice soft and steady: "Kira, you look frightened. And, really, you know, it's not a serious question. I've never had many questions to face in my life. People create their own questions, because they're afraid to look straight. All you have to do is look straight and see the road, and when you see it, don't sit looking at it—walk. I joined the Party because I knew I was right. I love you because I know I'm right. In a way, you and my work are the same. Things are really very simple."

"Not always, Andrei. You know your road. I don't belong on it."

"That's not in the spirit of what you taught me."

She whispered helplessly: "What did I teach you?"

The orchestra was playing the "Song of Broken Glass." No one sang it. Andrei's voice sounded like the words of that music. He was saying: "You remember, you said once that we had the same root somewhere in both of us, because we both believed in life? It's a rare capacity and it can't be taught. And it can't be explained to those in whom that word—life—doesn't awaken the kind of feeling that a temple does, or a military march, or the statue of a perfect body. It is for that feeling that I joined a Party which, at the time, could lead me only to Siberia. It is for that feeling that I wanted to fight against the most senseless and useless of monsters standing in the way of human life—and that's something we call now humanity's politics. And so my own existence was only the fight and the future. You taught me the present."

She made a desperate attempt. She said slowly, watching him: "Andrei, when you told me you loved me, for the first time, you were hungry. I wanted to satisfy that hunger."

"And that's all?"

"That's all."

He laughed quietly, so quietly that she had to give up. "You don't know what you're saying, Kira. Women like you don't love *only* like that."

"What are women like me?"

"What temples are, and military marches, and . . ."

"Let's have a drink, Andrei."

"*You* want a drink?"

"Yes. Now."

"All right."

He ordered the drinks. He watched the glow of the glass at her lips, a long, thin, shivering line of liquid light between fingers that looked golden in its reflection. He said: "Let's drink a toast to something I could never offer but in a place like this: to my life."

"Your new life?"

"My only one."

"Andrei, what if you lose it?"

"I can't lose it."

"But so many things can happen. I don't want to hold your life in my hands."

"But you're holding it."

"Andrei, you must think . . . once in a while . . . that it's possible that . . . What if anything should happen to me?"

"Why think about it?"

"But it's possible."

She felt suddenly as if the words of his answer were the links of a chain she would never be able to break: "It's also possible for every one of us to have to face a death sentence some day. Does it mean that we have to prepare for it?"

IV

They left the roof garden early, and Kira asked Andrei to take her home; she was tired; she did not look at him.

He said: "Certainly, dearest," and called a cab, and let her sit silently, her head on his shoulder, while he held her hand and kept silent, not to disturb her.

He left her at her parents' house. She waited on a dark stair-landing and heard his cab driving away; she waited longer; for ten minutes, she stood in the darkness, leaning against a cold glass pane; beyond the pane there was a narrow airshaft and a bare brick wall with one window; in the window, a yellow candle shivered convulsively and the huge shadow of a woman's arm kept rising and falling, senselessly, monotonously.

After ten minutes, Kira walked downstairs and hurried to a tramway.

Passing through Marisha's room, she heard a stranger's voice behind the door of her own room, a slow, deep, drawling voice that paused carefully, meticulously on every letter "o" and then rolled on as if on buttered hinges. She threw the door open.

The first person she saw was Antonina Pavlovna in a green brocaded turban, pointing her chin forward inquisitively; then she saw Leo; then she saw the man with the drawling voice —and her eyes froze, while he lumbered up, throwing at her a swift glance of appraisal and suspicion.

"Well, Kira, I thought you were spending the night with the excursion guides. And you said you'd be back early," Leo greeted her sharply, while Antonina Pavlovna drawled:

"Good evening, Kira Alexandrovna."

"I'm sorry. I got away as soon as I could," Kira answered, her eyes staring at the stranger's face.

"Kira, may I present? Karp Karpovitch Morozov—Kira Alexandrovna Argounova."

She did not notice that Karp Karpovitch's big fist was shaking her hand. She was looking at his face. His face had large blond freckles, light, narrow eyes, a heavy red mouth and a short nose with wide, vertical nostrils. She had seen it twice before; she remembered the speculator of the Nikolaevsky station, the food trader of the market.

She stood without removing her coat, without saying a word, cold with a feeling of sudden, inexplicable panic.

"What's the matter, Kira?" Leo asked.

"Leo, haven't we met Citizen Morozov before?"

"I don't believe so."

"Never had the pleasure, Kira Alexandrovna," Morozov drawled, his eyes at once shrewd and naïve and complacently friendly.

While Kira was removing her coat slowly, he turned to Leo: "And the store, Lev Sergeievitch, we'll have it in the neighborhood of the Kouznetzky market. Best neighborhood. I have my eyes on a vacant store—just what we need. One

window, narrow room—not many square meters to pay for—
and I slipped a couple of tens to the Upravdom, and he'll
let us have a good, big basement thrown in—just what we
need. I can take you there tomorrow, you'll be most pleased."

Kira's coat dropped to the floor. A lamp stood on the table;
in its glow, she could see Morozov's face leaning toward Leo's,
his slow words muffled on his heavy lips to a sly, guilty whisper. She stared at Leo. He was not looking at her; his eyes
were cold, widened slightly by a strange eagerness. She stood
in the semi-darkness, beyond the circle of lamp light. The
men paid no attention to her. Antonina Pavlovna threw a slow,
expressionless glance at her and turned to the table, flicking
ashes off her cigarette.

"How's the Upravdom?" Leo asked.

"Couldn't be better," Morozov chuckled. "A friendly fellow, easy-going and . . . practical. A few ten-ruble bills and
some vodka once in a while—with careful handling, he won't
cost us much. I told him to have the store cleaned for you.
And we'll order new signs—'Lev Kovalensky. Food Products.' "

"What are you talking about?" Kira threw the words at
Morozov with the violence of a slap in the face. She stood
over him, the lamp light scattering broken shadows across her
face. Morozov leaned away from her, closer to the table,
startled.

"It's a little business deal we're discussing, Kira Alexandrovna," he explained in a soft. conciliating drawl.

"I've promised you that Koko would do a great deal for
Leo," Antonina Pavlovna smiled.

"Kira, I'll explain later," Leo said slowly. The words were
a command.

Silently, she pulled a chair to the table and sat facing
Morozov, leaning forward on her crossed elbows. Morozov
continued, trying not to look at her fixed eyes that seemed
to register his every word: "You understand the advantage of
the arrangement, Lev Sergeievitch. A private trader is no easy
title to bear these days. Consider the rent on your living quarters, for instance. That alone could swallow all the profits.
Now if we say you're the sole owner—well, the rent won't
be so much since you have just this one room here to pay
for. Now me, for instance, we have three large rooms, Tonia
and me, and if they brand me a private trader—Good Lord
Almighty!—the rent on that will wreck the whole business."

"That's all right," said Leo. "I'll carry it. I don't mind if

I'm called private trader or Nicholas II or Mephistopheles."

"That's it," Morozov chuckled too loudly, his chin and stomach shaking. "That's it. And, Lev Sergeievitch, sir, you won't regret it. The profits—Lord bless us!—the profits will make the old what-they-called-bourgeois look like beggars. With our little scheme, we'll sweep in the rubles, easy as picking 'em off the street. A year or two and we're our own masters. A few hundreds slipped where necessary and we can fly abroad—to Paris, or Nice or Monte Carlo, or any of the foreign places that are pleasant and artistic."

"Yes," said Leo wearily. "Abroad." Then he shook his head, as if breaking off an unbearable thought, and turned imperiously, throwing orders to the man who was hiring him: "But that friend of yours—the Communist—that's the danger point of the whole scheme. Are you sure of him?"

Morozov spread his fat arms wide, shaking his head gently, reproachfully, his smile as soothing as Vaseline: "Lev Sergeievitch, soul of mine, you don't think I'm a helpless babe making my first steps in business, do you? I'm as sure of him as of the eternal salvation of our souls, that's how sure I am. He's as smart a young man as ever you could hope to find. Quick and reasonable. And not one of those windbags that like to hear themselves talk. He's not aiming to get nothing but big words and dried herring out of his life, no, sir. He knows when he has bread and butter in his hands—and he won't let it slip through. And then again, he's the one who takes the big chance. One of us common folks, if caught, might wiggle out with ten years in Siberia, but for one of them Party men—it's the firing squad and no time to say good-bye."

"You don't have to worry, Leo," Antonina Pavlovna smiled, "I've met the young man. We entertained him at a little tea —champagne and caviar, to be exact. He is smart and thoroughly dependable. You can have absolute faith in Koko's business judgment."

"And it's not so difficult for him, either," Morozov lowered his voice to a barely audible whisper. "He's got one of those engineering positions with the railroad—and he's got pull in all directions, like a river with tributaries. All he has to do is see that the food shipment is damaged a bit—dropped accidentally, or dampened a little, or something—and see that it's pronounced worthless. That's all. The rest is simple. The shipment goes quietly to the basement of our little store—'Lev Kovalensky. Food Products.' Nothing suspicious in that—is there?—just supplies for the store. The State co-operatives are short a load of stuff and the good citizens get nothing on their ration cards but an excuse and a promise. We wait a couple of weeks and we break up the load and ship it to our own customers—private dealers all over three provinces, a whole net of them, reasonable and discreet—I have all the addresses. And that's all. Who has to know? If anyone comes snooping around the store—well, we'll have some punk clerk there and he'll sell them half a pound of butter if they ask for it, and that's all we're doing, for all they know—retail trade—open and legal."

"And furthermore . . ." Antonina Pavlovna whispered, "if anything should go wrong, that young Communist has . . ."

"Yes," Morozov whispered, and looked around furtively, and paused to listen for any suspicious sound from behind the door, and, reassured, murmured, his lips at Leo's ear: "He has connections in the G.P.U. A powerful friend and protector. I'd be scared to mention the name."

"Oh, we'll be safe from that quarter," Leo said contemptuously, "if we have enough money."

"Money? Why, Lev Sergeievitch, soul of mine, we'll have so much money you'll be rolling ten-ruble bills to make cigarettes. We split it three ways, you understand; me, yourself and the Communist pal. We'll have to slip a little to his friends at the railroad, and to the Upravdom, and we'll pay your rent here—that'll go under expenses. But then you must remember that on the face of it, you're the sole owner. It's your store, in your name. I have my position with the State Food Trust to think about. If I had a private store registered to my name, they'd kick me out. And I've got to keep that job. You can see how useful it will be to us."

He winked at Leo. Leo did not smile in answer, but said: "You don't have to worry. I'm not afraid."

"Then, it's settled, eh? Why, pal, in a month from now you won't believe you ever lived like this. You'll put some flesh on those sunken cheeks of yours, and some pretty clothes on Kira Alexandrovna, and a diamond bracelet or two, and then maybe a motor-car and . . ."

"Leo, are you insane?"

Kira's chair clattered against the wall, and the lamp rocked and settled, shivering with a thin, glassy tinkle. She stood, the three startled faces turned to her.

"This isn't a joke you're playing on me, is it? Or have you lost your mind entirely?"

Leo leaned back slowly, looking straight at her, and asked coldly: "When did you assume the privilege of talking to me like that?"

"Leo! If that's a new way of committing suicide, there are much simpler ones!"

"Really, Kira Alexandrovna, you are unnecessarily tragic about it," Antonina Pavlovna remarked coolly.

"Now, now, Kira Alexandrovna, soul of mine," Morozov said amicably, "sit down and calm yourself and let's talk it over quietly. There's nothing to be excited about."

She cried: "Leo, don't you see what they're doing? You're nothing but a living screen for them! They're investing money. You're investing your life!"

"I'm glad to find some use for it," Leo said evenly.

"Leo, listen, I'll be calm. Here. I'll sit down. Listen to me: you don't want to do a thing like that with your eyes closed. Look at it, think it over: you know how hard life is these days. You don't want to make it harder, do you? You know the government we're facing. It's difficult enough to keep from under its wheels. Do you want to invite it to grind you? Don't you know that it's the firing squad for anyone caught in a crooked, criminal speculation?"

"I believe Leo has made it clear that he did not need advice," said Antonina Pavlovna, holding her cigarette poised gracefully in mid-air.

"Kira Alexandrovna," Morozov protested, "why use such strong names for a simple business proposition which is perfectly permissible and almost legal and . . ."

"You keep quiet," Leo interrupted him and turned to Kira. "Listen, Kira, I know that this is as rotten and crooked a deal as could be made. And I know I'm taking a chance on my life. And I still want to do it. You understand?"

"Even if I begged you not to?"

"Nothing you can say will change things. It's a filthy, low, disgraceful business. Certainly. But who forced me into it? Do you think I'll spend the rest of my life crawling, begging for a job, starving, dying slowly? I've been back two weeks. Have I found work? Have I found a promise of work? So they shoot food speculators? Why don't they give us a chance at something else? You don't want me to risk my life. And what is my life? I have no career. I have no future. I couldn't do what Victor Dunaev is doing if I were boiled in oil for punishment! I'm not risking much when I risk my life."

"Lev Sergeievitch, soul of mine," Morozov sighed with admiration, "how you can talk!"

"You two can go now," Leo ordered. "I'll see you tomorrow, Morozov, and we'll look at the store."

"Indeed, Leo, I'm surprised," Antonina Pavlovna remarked, rising with dignity. "If you let yourself be influenced and do not seem to be gracious about appreciating an opportunity, when I thought you'd be grateful and . . ."

"Who's to be grateful?" he threw at her sharply, rudely. "You need me and I need you. It's a business deal. That's all."

"Sure, sure, that's what it is," said Morozov, "and I appreciate your help, Lev Sergeievitch. It's all right, Tonia, soul of mine, you come along now and we'll settle all the details tomorrow."

He spread his legs wide apart and got up with effort, his hands leaning on his knees. His heavy stomach shivered when he moved, making his body seem uncomfortably close and apparent under the wrinkles of his suit.

At the door, he turned to Leo: "Well, Lev Sergeievitch, shall we shake on it? We can't sign a contract, of course, you understand, but we'll depend on your word."

His mouth arched contemptuously, Leo extended his hand, as if the gesture were a victory over himself. Morozov shook it warmly, lengthily—and bowed low, in the old peasant manner, on his way out. Antonina Pavlovna followed without looking at Kira.

Leo accompanied them to the lobby. When he came back, Kira still stood as he had left her. He said before she had turned to him: "Kira, we won't argue about it."

"There's only one thing, Leo," she whispered, "and I couldn't say it in front of them. You said you had nothing left in life. I thought you had . . . me."

"I haven't forgotten it. And that's one of the reasons for what I'm doing. Listen, do you think I'm going to live off you for the rest of my days? Do you think I'm going to stand by and watch you dragging excursions and swallowing soot over the Primus? That fool Antonina doesn't have to lead excursions. She wouldn't wear your kind of dresses to scrub floors in—only she doesn't have to scrub floors. Well, you won't have to, either. You poor little fool! You don't know what life can be. You've never seen it. But you're going to see it. And I'm going to see it before they finish me. Listen, if I knew for certain that it's the firing squad in six months— I'd still do it!"

She leaned against the table, because she felt faint. She whispered: "Leo, if I begged you, for all of my love for you, for all of yours, if I told you that I'd bless every hour of every excursion, every floor I'd scrub, every demonstration I'd have to attend, and every Club, and every red flag—if only you wouldn't do this—would you still do it?"

He answered: "Yes."

*

Citizen Karp Morozov met Citizen Pavel Syerov in a restaurant. They sat at a table in a dark corner. Citizen Morozov ordered cabbage soup. Citizen Syerov ordered tea and French pastry. Then Citizen Morozov leaned forward and whispered through the soup steam: "All settled, Pavlusha. I got the man. Saw him yesterday."

Pavel Syerov held his cup at his lips, and his pale mouth barely moved, so that Morozov guessed rather than heard the question: "Who?"

"Lev Kovalensky is the name. Young. Hasn't got a brass coin in the world and doesn't give a damn. Desperate. Ready for anything."

The white lips formed without sound: "Dependable?"

"Thoroughly."

"Easy to handle?"

"Like a child."

"Will keep his mouth shut?"

"Like a tomb."

Morozov unloaded a heavy spoonful of cabbage into his mouth; one strand remained hanging out; he drew it in with a resounding smack. He leaned closer and breathed: "Besides, he's got a social past. Father executed for counter-revolution. In case of anything . . . he'll be the right person to blame. A treacherous aristocrat, you know."

Syerov whispered: "All right." His spoon cut into a chocolate éclair, and a soft, yellow custard spurted, spreading over his plate. He hissed through white lips, low, even sounds without expression: "Now listen here. I want my share in advance—on every load. I don't want any delays. I don't want to ask twice."

"So help me God, Pavlusha, you'll get it, you don't have to tell me, you . . ."

"And another thing, I want caution. Understand? Caution. From now on, you don't know me, see? If we meet by chance

—we're strangers. Antonina delivers the money to me in that whorehouse, as agreed."

"Sure. Sure. I remember everything, Pavlusha."

"Tell that Kovalensky bum to keep away. I don't want to meet him."

"Sure. You don't have to."

"Got the store?"

"Renting it today."

"All right. Now sit still. I go first. You sit here for twenty minutes. Understand?"

"Sure. The Lord bless us."

"Keep that for yourself. Good day."

*

A secretary sat at a desk in the office of the railroad terminal. She sat behind a low wooden railing and typed, concentrating intently, drawing her upper lip in and biting her lower one. In front of the railing, there was an empty stretch of unswept floor and two chairs; six visitors waited patiently, two of them sitting. A door behind the secretary was marked: "Comrade Syerov."

Comrade Syerov returned from lunch. He strode swiftly through the outer office, his tight, shiny military boots creaking. The six heads of the visitors jerked anxiously, following him with timid, pleading glances. He crossed the room as if it were empty. The secretary followed him into his inner office.

A picture of Lenin hung on the wall of the inner office, over a broad, new desk; it hung between a diagram showing the progress of the railroads, and a sign with red letters saying: COMRADES, STATE YOUR BUSINESS BRIEFLY. PROLETARIAN EFFICIENCY IS THE DISCIPLINE OF PEACE-TIME REVOLUTIONARY CONSTRUCTION.

Pavel Syerov took a flat, gold cigarette case from his pocket, lighted a cigarette, sat down at the desk and looked through a stack of papers. The secretary stood waiting diffidently.

Then he raised his head and asked: "What's doing?"

"There are those citizens outside, Comrade Syerov, waiting to see you."

"What about?"

"Mostly jobs."

"Can't see anyone today. Got to hurry to the Club meeting in half-an-hour. Have you typed my Club report on "Railroads as the blood vessels of the Proletarian State'?"

"Yes, Comrade Syerov. Here it is."

"Fine."

"Those citizens out there, Comrade Syerov, they've been waiting for three hours."

"Tell them to go to hell. They can come tomorrow. If anything important comes up, call me at the Railroad Workers' Union headquarters. I'll be there after the Club. . . . And, by the way, I'll be in late tomorrow."

"Yes, Comrade Syerov."

*

Pavel Syerov walked home from the Railroad Workers' Union headquarters, with a Party friend. Syerov was in a cheerful mood. He whistled merrily and winked at passing girls. He said: "Think I'm going to throw a party tonight. Haven't had any fun for three weeks. Feel like dissipating. What do you say?"

"Swell," said the friend.

"Just a little crowd, our own bunch. At my place?"

"Swell."

"I know a fellow who can get vodka—the real stuff. And let's go to Des Gourmets and buy up everything they have in the joint."

"I'm with you, pal."

"Let's celebrate."

"What'll we celebrate?"

"Never mind. Just celebrate. And we don't have to worry about expenses. Hell! I'm not worrying about expenses when I want a good time."

"That's right, comrade."

"Whom'll we call? Let's see: Grishka and Maxim, with their girls."

"And Lizaveta."

"Sure, I'll call your Lizaveta. And Valka Dourova—there's a girl!—she'll bring half a dozen fellows along. And, I guess, Victor Dunaev with his girl, Marisha Lavrova. Victor's a nit that's going to be a big louse some day—have to keep on the good side of him. And . . . say, pal, do you think I should invite Comrade Sonia?"

"Sure. Why not?"

"Oh, hell. That cow's after me. Has been for over a year. Trying to make me. And I'll be damned if I . . . No appetite."

"But then, Pavlusha, you've got to be careful. If you hurt her feelings, with Comrade Sonia's position . . ."

"I know. Hell! Two profunions and five women's clubs wrapped around her little finger. Oh, hell! Oh, all right. I'll call her."

∗

Pavel Syerov had pulled the curtains down over the three windows of his room. One of the girls had draped an orange scarf over the lamp, and it was almost dark. The guests' faces were whitish blots strewn over the chairs, the davenport, the floor. In the middle of the floor stood a dish with a chocolate cake from Des Gourmets; someone had stepped on the cake. A broken bottle lay on the pillow of Syerov's bed; Victor and Marisha sat on the bed. Victor's hat lay on the floor by the davenport; it was being used as an ashtray. A gramophone played "John Gray"; the record was stuck, whirling, repeating persistently the same hoarse, grating notes; no one noticed it. A young man sat on the floor, leaning against a bed post, trying to sing; he muttered a tuneless, mournful chant into his collar; once in a while, he jerked his head up and screeched a high note, so that the others shuddered and someone flung a shoe or a pillow at him, yelling: "Grishka, shut up!" Then his head drooped again. A girl lay in a corner, by the cuspidor, asleep, her hair glued in sticky strands to a glistening, flushed face.

Pavel Syerov staggered across the room, waving an empty bottle, muttering in an offended, insistent voice: "A drink. . . . Who wants a drink? . . . Doesn't anyone want a drink? . . ."

"Hell, Pavel, your bottle's empty . . ." someone called from the darkness.

He stopped, swaying, held the bottle up to the light, spat, and threw the bottle under the bed. "So you think I haven't any more?" he waved his fist menacingly at the room. "Think I'm a piker, don't you? . . . A measly piker who can't afford enough vodka? . . . A measly piker, that's what you think, don't you? . . . Well, I'll show you . . . I'll show you who can't afford things. . . . I'll show you. . . ."

He fumbled in a box under the table and rose, swaying, brandishing an unopened bottle over his head. He laughed: "I can't afford it, can I?" and reeled toward the corner from where the voice had come. He giggled at the white spots that turned to look up at him; he swung the bottle in a huge circle and brought it down to smash with a ringing blast against a book case. A girl screamed; glass splattered in a tinkling rain. A man swore violently.

"My stockings, Pavel, my stockings!" the girl sobbed, pulling her skirt high over drenched legs.

A man's arms reached for her from the darkness: "Never mind, sweetheart. Take 'em off."

Syerov giggled triumphantly: "So I can't afford it, can I? . . . Can I? . . . Pavel Syerov can afford anything now! . . . Anything on this God-damn earth! . . . He can buy you all, guts and souls!"

Someone had crawled under the table and was fumbling in the box, looking for more bottles.

A hand knocked at the door.

"Come in!" roared Syerov. No one came in. The hand knocked again. "What the hell? What do you want?" He tottered to the door and threw it open.

His next-door neighbor, a fat, pallid woman, stood in the corridor, shivering in a long, flannel nightgown, clutching an old shawl over her shoulders, brushing strands of gray hair out of her sleepy eyes.

"Citizen Syerov," she whined with indignation, "won't you please stop that noise? At such an indecent hour . . . you young people have no shame left these days . . . no fear of God . . . no . . ."

"On your way, grandma, on your way!" Syerov ordered. "You crawl under your pillow and keep your damn mouth shut. Or would you like to take a ride to the G.P.U?"

The woman wheeled about hastily and shuffled away, making the sign of the cross.

Comrade Sonia sat in a corner by the window, smoking. She wore a tailored khaki tunic with pockets on her hips and breast; it was made of expensive foreign cloth, but she kept dropping ashes on her skirt. A girl's voice pleaded in a plaintive whisper at her elbow: "Say, Sonia, why did you have Dashka fired from the office? She needed the job, she did, and honest . . ."

"I do not discuss business matters outside of office hours," Comrade Sonia answered coldly. "Besides, my actions are always motivated by the good of the collective."

"Oh, sure, I don't doubt it, but, listen, Sonia. . . ."

Comrade Sonia noticed Pavel Syerov swaying at the door. She rose and walked to him, cutting the girl off in the middle of a sentence.

"Come here, Pavel," said Comrade Sonia, her strong arm supporting him, leading him to a chair. "You'd better sit down. Here. Let me make you comfortable."

"You're a pal, Sonia," he muttered, while she stuffed a pillow between his shoulder blades, "you're a real pal. Now you wouldn't holler at me if I made a little noise, would you?"

"Of course not."

"You don't think that I can afford a little vodka, like some skunks here think, do you, Sonia?"

"Of course not, Pavel. Some people don't know how to appreciate you."

"That's it. That's just the trouble. I'm not appreciated. I'm a great man. I'm going to be a very great man. But they don't know it. No one knows it. . . . I'm going to be a very, very powerful man. I'm going to make the foreign capitalists look like mice. . . . That's what: mice. . . . I'm going to give orders to Comrade Lenin himself."

"Pavel, our great chief is dead."

"That's right. So he is. Comrade Lenin's dead. . . . Oh, what's the use? . . . I've got to have a drink, Sonia. I feel very sad. Comrade Lenin's dead."

"That's very nice of you, Pavel. But you'd better not have another drink just now."

"But I'm very sad, Sonia. No one appreciates me."

"I do, Pavel."

"You're a pal. You're a real, real pal, Sonia. . . ."

On the bed, Victor held Marisha in his arms. She giggled, counting the buttons on his tunic; she lost count after the third one and started over again. She was whispering: "You're a gentleman, Victor, that's what you are, a gentleman. . . . That's why I love you, because you're a gentleman. . . . And I'm only a gutter brat. My mother, she was a cook before . . . before. . . . Well, anyway, before. I remember, many, many years ago, she used to work in a big, big house, they had horses and carriages and a bathroom, and I used to peel vegetables for her, in their kitchen. And there was an elegant young man, their son, oh, he had such pretty uniforms and he spoke all sorts of foreign languages, he looked just like you. And I didn't even dare to look at him. And now I have a gentleman of my own," she giggled happily, "isn't it funny? I, Marishka the vegetable peeler!"

Victor said: "Oh, shut up!" and kissed her, his head drooping sleepily.

A girl giggled, standing over them in the darkness: "When are you two going to get registered at the marriage office?"

"Go 'way," Marisha waved at her. "We'll be registered. We're engaged."

Comrade Sonia had pulled a chair close to Syerov's, and he sprawled, his head on her lap, while she stroked his hair. He was muttering: "You're a rare woman, Sonia. . . . You're a wonderful woman. . . . You understand me. . . ."

"I do, Pavel. I've always said that you were the most talented, the most brilliant young man in our collective."

"You're a wonderful woman, Sonia." He was kissing her, moaning: "No one appreciates me."

He had pulled her down to the floor, leaning over her soft, heavy body, whispering: "A fellow needs a woman. . . . A smart, understanding, strong and hefty woman. . . . Who cares for those skinny scarecrows? . . . I like a woman like you, Sonia. . . ."

He did not know how he found himself suddenly in the little storage closet between his room and that of his neighbors. A cobwebbed window high under the ceiling threw a dusty ray of moonlight on a towering pile of boxes and baskets. He was leaning against Comrade Sonia's shoulder, stammering: "They think Pavel Syerov's just gonna be another stray mongrel eating outta slop pails all his life. . . . Well, I'll show 'em! Pavel Syerov'll show 'em who's got the whip. . . . I've got a secret . . . a great secret, Sonia. . . . But I can't tell you. . . . But I've always liked you, Sonia. . . . I've always needed a woman like you, Sonia . . . soft and comfortable. . . ."

When he tried to stretch himself on the flat top of a large wicker basket, the piled tower shuddered, swayed and came down with a thundering crash. The neighbors knocked furiously, protesting, against the wall.

Comrade Sonia and Pavel Syerov, on the floor, paid no attention.

V

The clerk wiped his nose with the back of his hand and wrapped a pound of butter in a newspaper. He had cut the butter from a soggy, yellow circle that stood on a wooden barrel top on the counter before him; he wiped the knife on his apron that had once been white. His pale eyes watered; his lips were a concavity on a crumpled face; his long chin hovered uncomfortably over a counter too high for the wizened skeleton under his old blue sweater. He sniffled and, showing two broken, blackened teeth, grinned at the pretty customer in the blue hat trimmed with cherries:

"Best butter in town, citizen, very best butter in town."

On the counter stood a pyramid of square bread loaves, dusty black and grayish white. Above the counter hung a fringe of salami, bagles and dried mushrooms. Flies hovered at the greasy brass bowls of old weighing scales and crawled up the dusty panes of a single, narrow window. Over the window, smeared by the first rain of September, hung a sign:

LEV KOVALENSKY. FOOD PRODUCTS

The customer threw some silver coins on the counter and took her package. She was turning to go when she stopped involuntarily, for a brief, startled moment, looking at the young man who had entered. She did not know that he was the owner of the store; but she knew that she could not have many occasions to see that kind of young man on the streets of Petrograd. Leo wore a new, foreign overcoat with a belt pulled tightly across his trim, slender waistline; he wore a gray foreign felt hat, one side of its brim turned up over an arrogant profile with a cigarette held in the corner of his mouth by two long, straight fingers in a tight, glistening, foreign leather glove. He moved with the swift, confident, unconscious grace of a body that seemed born for these clothes, like the body of an animal for its regal fur, like the body of a foreign fashion plate.

The girl looked straight at him, softly, defiantly. He answered with a glance that was an invitation, and a mocking insult, and almost a promise. Then he turned and walked to the counter, as she went out slowly.

The clerk bowed low, so that his chin touched the circle of butter: "Good day, Lev Sergeievitch, good day, sir."

Leo flicked the ashes off his cigarette into an empty can on the counter and asked: "Any cash in the register?"

"Yes, sir, can't complain, business was good today, sir, and . . ."

"Let me have it."

The man's gnarled hand fingered his chin uncertainly; he muttered: "But, sir, Karp Karpovitch said last time you . . ."

"I said let me have it."

"Yes, sir."

Leo stuffed the bills carelessly into his wallet. He asked, lowering his voice: "Did that shipment arrive last night?"

The clerk nodded, blinking confidentially, with an intimate little giggle.

"Shut up," said Leo. "And be careful."

"Why, yes, sir, yes indeed, sir, you know I'm the soul of discretion, as they say in society, if I may say so, sir. Karp Karpovitch knows that he can trust a loyal old servant who has worked for him for . . ."

"You could use some flypaper here once in a while."

"Yes, sir, I . . ."

"I won't be in again today. Keep the store open till the usual hour."

"Yes, sir. Good day, sir."

Leo walked out without answering.

On the corner, the girl in the blue hat trimmed with cherries was waiting for him. She smiled hopefully, uncertainly. He hesitated for a second; then he smiled and turned away; his smile spread a flush of red on the cheeks and nose under the blue brim. But she stood, watching him jump into a cab and drive away.

He drove to the Alexandrovsky market. He walked swiftly past the old wares spread on the sidewalk, ignoring the eager, pleading eyes of their owners. He stopped at a little booth displaying porcelain vases, marble clocks, bronze candlesticks, a priceless loot that had found its way from some demolished palace into the dusty twilight of the market.

"I want something for a gift," he threw at the clerk who bowed solicitously. "A wedding gift."

"Yes, indeed," the clerk bowed. "Ah . . . for your bride, sir?"

"Certainly not. For a friend."

He looked indifferently, contemptuously at the delicate, cracked dusty treasures that should have reposed on velvet cushions in a museum showcase.

"I want something better," he ordered.

"Yes, indeed, sir," the clerk bowed, "something beautiful for a beloved friend."

"No. For someone I hate." He pointed at a vase of blue and gold porcelain in a corner. "What's that?"

"Ah, sir, that!" The clerk reached timidly for the vase and brought it slowly, cautiously to the counter; its price had made him hesitate to show it even to a customer in a foreign overcoat. "Genuine Sèvres, sir," he whispered, brushing cobwebs out of the vase, upturning it to show the delicate mark on the bottom. "A royal object, sir," he breathed, "a truly royal object."

"I'll take it," said Leo.

The clerk swallowed and fumbled at his tie, watching the wallet in the gloved fingers of a customer who had not even asked the price.

*

"Comrades, in these days of peaceful State Construction, the workers of Proletarian culture are the shock battalion in the vanguard of the Revolution. The education of the Worker-Peasant masses is the great problem of our Red week-days. We, excursion leaders, are a part of the great peace-time army of educators, imbued with the practical methodology of historical materialism, attuned to the spirit of Soviet reality, dedicated to . . ."

Kira sat in the ninth row, on a chair that threatened to fold under her at any moment. The meeting of excursion guides was coming to an end. Around her, heads drooped wearily and eyes looked furtively, hopefully at a large clock on the wall, over the speaker's head. But Kira tried to listen; she held her eyes fixed on the speaker's mouth to catch every word; she wished the words were louder. But the words could not drown out the voices ringing in her mind: a voice over the telephone, pleading, trying not to sound pleading: "Kira, why do I see you so seldom?"; an imperious voice in the darkness of her room at night: "What are those visits of yours, Kira? You said you were at Irina's yesterday. But you weren't." How long could she keep it up? She had not seen Andrei for three weeks.

The chairs around her clattered; the meeting was over. She hurried down the stairway. She was saying to a fellow guide: ". . . yes, a splendid speech. Of course, our cultural duty to the proletariat is our primary goal . . ." It was easy to say. It was easy, after she had looked straight at Leo and laughed: "Leo, why those foolish questions? Don't you trust me?" pressing her hand to her breast to hide the mark of Andrei's teeth.

She hurried home. In Marisha's room, two trunks and a wicker basket stood in the middle of the floor; empty drawers gaped open; posters were torn off the walls and piled on the trunks. Marisha was not at home.

In Kira's room, a maid hurried from the hissing Primus by the window to take her coat.

"Leo hasn't returned yet, has he?" Kira asked.

"No, ma'am."

Kira's coat was old, with rubbed patches on the elbows. Her dress had grease stains on the collar and threads hanging out of its frayed hem. With one swift movement, Kira pulled it off over her head and threw it to the maid, shaking her dishevelled hair. Then she fell on the bed, kicking off her old shoes with run-down heels, tearing off her darned, cotton stockings. The maid knelt by the bed, pulling thin silk stockings up Kira's slender legs, slipping delicate, high-heeled pumps on her feet; then she rose to help her into a trim dark woolen dress. The maid put the old coat and shoes into a wardrobe that contained four new coats and six pairs of new shoes.

But Kira had to keep her job for the protection of the title of Soviet employee; and she had to wear her old clothes to protect her job.

An extravagant bouquet of white lilies, Leo's latest gift, stood on the table. The white petals had caught a few specks of soot from the Primus. Kira had a maid, but no kitchen. The maid came for five hours every day and cooked their meals on the Primus by the window.

Leo came home, carrying the Sèvres vase wrapped in newspapers.

"Isn't dinner ready yet?" he asked. "How many times have I told you that I hate to have that thing smoking when I come home?"

"It's ready, sir." The maid hurried to turn off the Primus, her young, round face obedient and frightened.

"Have you bought the present?" Kira asked.

"There it is. Don't unwrap it. It's fragile. Let's have dinner. We'll be late."

After dinner, the maid washed the dishes and left. Kira sat at her mirror, carefully outlining her lips with a real French lipstick.

"You're not wearing that dress, are you?" Leo asked.

"Why, yes."

"No, you're not. Put on the black velvet one."

"But I don't feel like dressing up. Not for Victor's wedding. I wouldn't go at all, if it weren't for Uncle Vasili."

"Well, since we're going, I want you to look your best."

"But, Leo, is it wise? He's going to have many of his Party friends there. Why show them that we have money?"

"Why not? Certainly, we have money. Let them see that we have money. I'm not going to act like trash for the benefit of trash."

"All right, Leo. As you wish."

He looked at her appraisingly when she stood before him, severe as a nun, graceful as a Marquise of two centuries past, her hands very white and thin on the soft black velvet. He smiled with approval and took her hand, as if she were a lady at a Court reception, and kissed her palm, as if she were a courtesan.

"Leo, what did you buy for them?" she asked.

"Oh, just a vase. You may see it, if you wish."

She unwrapped the newspapers and gasped. "Leo! But this . . . this cost a fortune!"

"Certainly. It's Sèvres."

"Leo, we can't give it to them. We can't let them see that we can afford it. Really, it's dangerous."

"Oh, nonsense."

"Leo, you're playing with fire. Why bring such a present for all the Communists to see?"

"That's exactly why."

"But they know that a regular private trader couldn't afford gifts like this."

"Oh, stop being foolish!"

"Take that thing back and exchange it."

"I won't."

"Then I'm not going to the party."

"Kira . . ."

"Leo, please!"

"Oh, very well!"

He seized the vase and flung it to the floor. It burst into glittering splinters. She gasped. He laughed: "Well, come on. You can buy them something else on our way there."

She stood looking at the splinters. She said dully: "Leo, all that money . . ."

"Will you ever forget that word? Can't we live without thinking of it all the time?"

"But you promised to save. We'll need it. Things may not last as they are."

"Oh, nonsense! We have plenty of time to start saving."

"But don't you know what they mean, all those hundreds, there, on the floor? Don't you remember it's your life that you're gambling for every one of those rubles?"

"Certainly, I remember. That's just what I do remember. How do I know I have a future? Why save? I may never need it. I've trembled over money long enough. Can't I throw it away if I want to—while I can?"

"All right, Leo. Come on. We'll be late."

"Come on. Stop frowning. You look too lovely to frown."

*

In the Dunaev dining room, a bunch of asters stood in a bowl on the table, and a bunch of daisies on the buffet, and a bunch of nasturtiums on an upright piano. The piano had been borrowed from the tenants; long streaks remained on the parquet, following its trail from the door.

Victor wore a modest dark suit and a modest expression of youthful happiness. He shook hands and smiled and bowed graciously, acknowledging congratulations. Marisha wore a purple woolen dress, and a white rose on her shoulder. She looked bewildered; she watched Victor's movements with a timid, incredulous pride; she blushed and nodded hastily to the compliments of guests, and shook hands without knowing whose hands they were, her eyes vague, roving, searching for Victor.

The guests shuffled in, and muttered best wishes, and settled down uncomfortably. The friends of the family were strained, suspicious and cautiously, elaborately polite to the Party members. The Party members were awkward, uncertain and helplessly polite to the friends of Victor's bourgeois past. The guests did not sound quite natural in their loud assurances of happiness, when they looked at the silent, stooped figure of Vasili Ivanovitch with a quiet, anguished question frozen in his eyes; at Irina in her best patched dress, with her jerky movements and her strident voice of unnatural gaiety.

Little Acia wore a pink bow on a stiff strand of hair, that kept slipping toward her nose. She giggled, once in a while, glancing up at a guest, biting her knuckles. She stared at Marisha with insolent curiosity. She snooped around the table that displayed the wedding gifts, an odd assortment of objects: a bronze clock, a China ashtray in the shape of a skull, a new Primus, a complete set of Lenin's works in red paper covers. Irina watched her closely, to drag her away in time from the buffet and the dishes of pastry.

Galina Petrovna followed Victor persistently, patting him on the shoulder, repeating: "I'm so happy, so happy, my dear boy!" The muscles of Victor's face were fixed in a wide grin, over his sparkling white teeth; he did not have to smile; he merely turned his head to her and nodded without a change of expression.

When Victor escaped from her, Galina Petrovna patted

Vasili Ivanovitch's shoulder, repeating: "I'm so happy, so happy, Vasili. You have a son to be proud of." Vasili Ivanovitch nodded as if he had not heard.

When Kira entered, the first person she saw, standing alone by a window, was Andrei.

She stopped short at the door. His eyes met hers and moved slowly to the man who held her arm. Leo smiled faintly, contemptuously.

Kira walked straight to Andrei; she looked graceful, erect, supremely confident, in her regal black gown; she extended her hand, saying aloud: "Good evening, Andrei. I'm so glad to see you."

His eyes told her silently that he understood, that he would be cautious, while he shook her hand with a friendly, impersonal smile.

Leo approached them slowly, indifferently. He bowed to Andrei and asked, his voice courteous, his smile insolent: "So you're a friend of Victor's, too?"

"As yourself," Andrei answered.

Kira walked on, without hurry, to congratulate Victor and Marisha. She nodded to acquaintances, and smiled, and talked to Irina. She knew that the eyes of the man by the window were following her; she did not turn to look at him.

She had talked to many guests before she approached Andrei again, as if by chance; Leo was busy listening to Lydia at the other end of the room.

Andrei whispered eagerly: "Victor has always been inviting me. This is the first time that I've accepted. I knew you'd be here. Kira, it has been three weeks . . ."

"I know. I'm sorry, Andrei. But I couldn't. I'll explain later. I'm glad to see you—if you're careful."

"I'll be careful. What a lovely dress, Kira. New?"

"Oh . . . yes. It's a present from mother."

"Kira, do you always go to parties with him?"

"Do you mean Leo?"

"Yes."

"I hope you don't presume to dictate the friends with whom I may . . ."

"Kira!" He was startled by the icy firmness of her voice; he was apologizing: "Kira, I'm sorry. Of course I didn't mean . . . Forgive me. I know I have no right to say . . . But you see, I've always disliked him."

She smiled gaily, as if nothing had happened, and leaning

into the shadow of the window niche, pressed his fingers swiftly.

"Don't worry," she whispered and, moving away from him, turned, shaking her hair, throwing at him through the tousled locks a glance of such warm, sparkling understanding that he caught his breath, thrilled by the secret they were guarding together, among strangers, for the first time.

Vasili Ivanovitch sat alone in a corner, under a lamp, and the light of a rose satin shade made his white hair pink. He looked at the shuffling feet, at the military boots of young Communists, at the blue fog of smoke streaks that billowed halfway up to the ceiling, in soft, round waves, like a heavy, transparent mixture boiling slowly, at a gold cross on a black velvet ribbon around Lydia's throat, a bright spark piercing the fog across the room.

Kira approached and sat down beside him. He patted her hand, and said nothing, and knew that she knew. Then he said, as if she had followed his unspoken thoughts: ". . . I wouldn't mind so much if he loved her. But he doesn't. . . . Kira, you know, when he was a little boy with such big black eyes, I used to look at my customers, those ladies that were like paintings of empresses, and I wondered which one of them was the mother of the little beauty, growing up somewhere, who, some day, would be my daughter, too. . . . Have you met Marisha's parents, Kira?"

Galina Petrovna had cornered Leo; she was saying enthusiastically: ". . . so glad you're successful, Leo. I've always said that a brillaint young man, like you, would have no trouble at all. That dress of Kira's is magnificent. I'm so happy to see what good care you take of my little girl. . . ."

Victor sat on the arm of a chair occupied by red-headed Rita Eksler. He leaned close to her, holding his cigarette to light the one at her lips. Rita had just divorced her third husband; she narrowed her eyes under the long red bangs and whispered confidential advice. They were laughing softly.

Marisha approached timidly and took Victor's hand with a clumsy movement of coquetry. He jerked his hand away; he said impatiently: "We can't neglect our guests, Marisha. Look, Comrade Sonia is alone. Go and talk to her."

Marisha obeyed humbly. Rita's glance followed her through a jet of smoke; Rita pulled her short skirt up and crossed her long, thin legs.

"Indeed," said Comrade Sonia coldly with an accent of final authority, "I cannot say that I congratulate you upon your

choice, Comrade Lavrova. A true proletarian does not marry
out of her class."

"But, Comrade Sonia," Marisha protested, stupefied, "Victor
is a Party member."

"I've always said that the rules of Party admission were
not sufficiently strict," said Comrade Sonia.

Marisha wandered dejectedly through the crowd of guests.
No one looked at her and she had nothing to say. She saw
Vasili Ivanovitch alone by the buffet, lining up bottles and
glasses. She approached him and smiled hesitantly. He looked
at her, astonished. She said with determination, very quickly,
bluntly, running her words together, blushing: "I know you
don't like me, Vasili Ivanovitch. But, you see, I . . . I love
him so much."

Vasili Ivanovitch looked at her, then said: "It's very nice,
child," his voice expressionless.

Marisha's family sat in a dark corner, solemn, morose, uncomfortable. Her father—a stooped, gray-haired man in a
worker's blouse and patched trousers—clasped long, calloused
hands over his knee; his face, with a bitter slash of a mouth,
leaned forward, his fierce, brilliant eyes studying the room
fixedly; his eyes were dark and young on a withered face. His
wife huddled timidly behind him, pallid and shapeless in a
flowered calico dress, her face like a sandy shore washed by
many rains into a dull, quiet gray. Marisha's young brother,
a lanky boy of eight, stood holding onto his mother's skirt,
throwing angry, suspicious glances at little Acia.

Victor joined Pavel Syerov and a group of three men in
leather jackets. He threw one arm around Syerov's shoulders
and the other around those of the secretary of their Party
Cell; he leaned on them both, intimately, confidentially, his
dark eyes smiling. Comrade Sonia, approaching, heard him
whisper: ". . . yes, I'm proud of my wife's family and their
revolutionary record. Her father—you know—he was exiled
to Siberia, under the Czar."

Comrade Sonia remarked: "Comrade Dunaev is a very
smart man."

Neither Victor nor Syerov liked the tone of her voice. Syerov protested: "Victor's one of our best workers, Sonia."

"I said Comrade Dunaev is very smart," she repeated, and
added: "I wouldn't doubt his class loyalty. I'm sure he has
nothing in common with patrician gentlemen such as that Citizen Kovalensky over there."

Pavel Syerov looked fixedly at Leo's tall figure bending over

Rita Eksler. He asked: "Say, Victor, that man's name—it's Lev Kovalensky, isn't it?"

"Leo Kovalensky, yes. He's a very dear friend of my cousin's. Why?"

"Oh, nothing. Nothing at all."

Leo noticed Kira and Andrei sitting side by side on a window sill. He bowed to Rita, who shrugged impatiently, and walked toward them slowly.

"Am I intruding?" he asked.

"Not at all," said Kira.

He sat down beside her. He took out his gold cigarette case and, opening it, held it out to her. She shook her head. He held it over to Andrei. Andrei took a cigarette. Leo bent forward to light it, leaning over Kira.

"Sociology being the favorite science of your Party," said Leo, "don't you find this wedding an occasion of particular interest, Comrade Taganov?"

"Why, Citizen Kovalensky?"

"As an opportunity to observe the essential immutability of human nature. A marriage for reasons of state is one of the oldest customs of mankind. It has always been advisable to marry into the ruling class."

"You must remember," said Andrei, "the social class to which the person concerned belongs."

"Oh, nonsense!" said Kira. "They're in love with each other."

"Love," said Leo, "is not part of the philosophy of Comrade Taganov's Party. Is it?"

"It is a question that has no reason to interest you," Andrei answered.

"Hasn't it?" Leo asked slowly, looking at him. "That's what I'm trying to find out."

"Is it a question that contradicts your . . . theory on the subject?" Andrei asked.

"No. I think it supports my theory. You see, my theory is that members of your Party have a tendency to place their sexual desires high above their own class." He was looking straight at Andrei, but he pointed lightly, with his cigarette, at Marisha across the room.

"If they do," Andrei answered slowly, "they're not always unsuccessful." He was looking straight at Kira, but he pointed at Victor.

"Marisha looks happy," said Kira. "Why do you resent it, Leo?"

"I resent the arrogant presumption of friends—" Leo began.

"—who do not know the limit of a friendship's rights," Andrei finished.

"Andrei," said Kira, "we're not being gallant to . . . Marisha."

"I'm sorry," he said hastily. "I'm sure Citizen Kovalensky won't misunderstand me."

"I don't," said Leo.

Irina had lined glasses on trays and Vasili Ivanovitch had filled them. She passed them to the guests, smiling vaguely at the hands that took the glasses; her smile was resigned, indifferent; she was silent, which was unusual for her.

The trays were emptied swiftly; the guests held the glasses eagerly, impatiently. Victor rose and the clatter of voices stopped short in a solemn silence.

"My dear friends," Victor's voice was clear, vibrant with his warmest persuasiveness, "I have no words to describe my deep gratitude to all of you for your kindness on this great day of my life. Let us all join in a toast to a person who is very dear to my heart, not only as a relative, but as a man who symbolizes a splendid example to us, young revolutionaries starting out on our lives of service to the cause of the Proletariat. A man who has devoted his life to that cause, who had risen bravely against the tyranny of the Czar, who has sacrificed his best years in the cold wastes of a Siberian exile, fighting for the great goal of the people's freedom. And since that goal is ever paramount for all of us, since it is higher than all thoughts of personal happiness, let us drink our first toast to one of the first fighters for the triumph of the Worker-Peasant Soviets, my beloved father-in-law, Glieb Ilyitch Lavrov!"

Hands applauded noisily; glasses rose, clinking; all eyes turned to the corner where the gaunt, stooped figure of Marisha's father got up slowly. Lavrov was holding his glass, but he did not smile; his gnarled hand motioned for silence. He said slowly, firmly, evenly:

"Listen here, you young whelps. I spent four years in Siberia. I spent them because I saw the people starved and ragged and crushed under a boot, and I asked for freedom. I still see the people starved and ragged and crushed under a boot. Only the boot is red. I didn't go to Siberia to fight for a crazed, power-drunk, bloodthirsty gang that strangles the people as they've never been strangled before, that knows less of freedom than any Czar ever did! Go ahead and drink all you want, drink till you drown the last rag of conscience in your fool brains, drink to anything you wish. But when you drink to the Soviets, don't drink to me!"

In the dead silence of the room, a man laughed suddenly, a loud, ringing, resonant laughter. It was Andrei Taganov.

Pavel Syerov jumped up and, throwing his arm around Victor's shoulders, yelled, waving his glass: "Comrades, there are traitors even in the ranks of the workers! Let's drink to those who are loyal!"

Then there was much noise, too much noise, glasses clinked, voices rose, hands slapped shoulders, everybody yelled at once. No one looked at Lavrov.

Only Vasili Ivanovitch approached him slowly and stood looking at him. Their eyes met. Vasili Ivanovitch extended his glass and said: "Let us drink to our children's happiness, even though you don't think that they will be happy, and I don't, either."

They drank.

At the other end of the room, Victor seized Marisha's wrist, dragging her aside, and whispered, his white lips at her ear: "You damn fool! Why didn't you tell me about him?"

She muttered, blinking, her eyes full of tears: "I was scared. I knew you wouldn't like it, darling. . . . Oh, darling, you shouldn't have . . . "

"Shut up!"

There were many drinks to follow. Victor had provided a good supply of bottles and Pavel Syerov helped to open them speedily. The trays of pastry were emptied. Dirty dishes were stacked on the tables. A few glasses were broken. Cigarette smoke hung as a motionless blue cloud under the ceiling.

Marisha's family had left. Galina Petrovna sat sleepily, trying to keep her head erect. Alexander Dimitrievitch snored softly, his head on the arm of his chair. Little Acia had fallen asleep on a trunk in the corridor, her face smeared with chocolate frosting. Irina sat in a corner, watching the crowd indifferently. Comrade Sonia bent under the pink lamp, reading a newspaper. Victor and Pavel Syerov were the center of a group at the buffet that clinked glasses and tried to sing revolutionary songs in muffled voices. Marisha wandered about listlessly, her nose shiny, the white rose wilted and brownish on her shoulder.

Lydia staggered to the piano and put an arm around Marisha's waist. "It's beautiful," said Lydia in a thick, sad voice, "it's beautiful."

"What's beautiful?" Marisha asked.

"Love," said Lydia. "Romance. That's it: romance. . . . Ah, love is rare in this world. They are few, the chosen few. . . . We wander through a barren existence without romance. There are no beautiful feelings left in the world. Has it ever occurred to you that there are no beautiful feelings left in the world?"

"That's too bad," said Marisha.

"It's sad," Lydia sighed. "That's what it is: sad. . . . You're a very lucky girl. . . . But it's sad. . . . Listen, I'm going to play something beautiful for you. . . . Something beautiful and sad. . . ."

She struck the keys uncertainly. She played a gypsy love song, her fingers rushing suddenly into quick, sharp trills, then lingering on long, sad chords, then slipping on the wrong notes, her head nodding.

Andrei whispered to Kira: "Let's go, Kira. Let me take you home."

"I can't, Andrei. I . . . "

"I know. You came with him. But I don't think he's in a condition to take you home."

He pointed at Leo across the room. Leo's head, thrown back, was leaning heavily against an armchair. His one arm encircled Rita's waist; the other was thrown across the shoulders of a pretty blonde who giggled softly at something he was muttering. Rita's head rested on his shoulder and her hand caressed his dishevelled hair.

Kira rose silently, leaving Andrei, and walked to Leo. She stood before him and said softly: "Leo, we had better go home."

He waved sleepily. "Leave me alone. Get out of here."

She noticed suddenly that Andrei stood behind her. He said: "You'd better be careful of what you say, Kovalensky."

Leo pushed Rita aside and the blonde slid, giggling, to the floor. He said, frowning, pointing at Kira: "And you'd better keep away from her. And you'd better stop sending her gifts and watches and such. I resent it."

"What right have you to resent it?"

Leo stood up, swaying, smiling ominously: "What right? I'll tell you what right. I'll . . ."

"Leo," Kira interrupted firmly, weighing her every word, her voice loud, her eyes holding his, "people are looking at you. Now what is it you wanted to say?"

"Nothing," said Leo.

"If you weren't drunk . . ." Andrei began.

"If I weren't drunk, you'd what? You seem sober. And yet not sober enough not to be making a fool of yourself over a woman you have no right to approach."

"Well, listen to me, you . . ."

"You'd better listen, Leo," Kira interrupted again. "Andrei finds this the proper time to tell you something."

"What is it, Comrade G.P.U.?"

"Nothing," said Andrei.

"Then you'd better leave her alone."

"Not while you seem to forget the respect that you owe to . . ."

"Are you defending *her* against *me*?" Leo burst out laughing. Leo's laughter could be more insulting than his smile, more insulting than a slap in the face.

"Come on, Kira," said Andrei, "I'll take you home."

"Yes," said Kira.

"You're not taking her anywhere!" Leo roared. You're . . ."

"Yes, he is!" Irina interrupted, stepping suddenly between them. Leo stared at her, amazed. With sudden strength, she whirled him about, pushing him into a window niche, while she nodded to Andrei, ordering him to hurry. He took Kira's arm and led her out; she followed silently, obediently.

Irina hissed into Leo's face: "Are you insane? What were you trying to do? Yell for all of them to hear that she's your mistress?"

Leo shrugged and laughed indifferently: "All right. Let her go with anyone she pleases. If she thinks I'm jealous, she's mistaken."

Kira sat silently in the cab, her head thrown back, her eyes closed.

"Kira," Andrei whispered, "that man is no friend of yours. You shouldn't be seen with him."

She did not answer.

When they were driving by the palace garden, he asked: "Kira, are you too tired to . . . stop at my house?"

She said indifferently: "No. I'm not. Let's stop."

*

When she came home, Leo was sprawled on the bed, fully dressed, asleep. He raised his head and looked at her.

"Where have you been, Kira?" he asked softly, helplessly.

"Just . . . just driving around," she answered.

"I thought you had gone. Forever. . . . What was it I said, tonight, Kira?"

"Nothing," she whispered, kneeling by his side.

"You should leave me, Kira. . . . I wish you could leave me. . . . But you won't. . . . You won't leave me, Kira . . . Kira . . . will you?"

"No," she whispered. "Leo, will you leave that business of yours?"

"No. It's too late. But before . . . before they get me . . . I still have you, Kira . . . Kira . . . Kira . . . I love you . . . I still have you. . . ."

She whispered: "Yes," pressing his face, white as marble, to the black velvet of her dress.

VI

"Comrades! The Union of Socialist Soviet Republics is surrounded by a hostile ring of enemies who watch and plot for its downfall. But no external enemy, no heinous plot of world imperialists is as dangerous to us as the internal enemy of dissension within our own ranks."

Tall windows checkered into small square panes were closed against the gray void of an autumn sky. Columns of pale golden marble rose spreading into dim vaults. Five portraits of Lenin, somber as ikons, looked down upon a motionless crowd of leather jackets and red kerchiefs. A tall lectern, like the high, thin stem of a torch, stood at the head of the hall; above the lectern, like the flame of the torch spurting high to the ceiling, hung a banner of scarlet velvet with gold letters: "The All-Union Communist Party is the leader of the world fight for Freedom!" The hall had been a palace; it looked like a temple; those in it looked like an army, stern, silent and tense, receiving its orders. It was a Party meeting.

A speaker stood at the lectern. He had a little black beard, and wore a pince-nez that sparkled in the twilight; he waved long arms with very small hands. Nothing moved in the hall before him, but drops of rain rolling slowly down the window panes.

"Comrades! A grave new danger has been growing among

us in this last year. I call it the danger of over-idealism. We've all heard the accusations of its deluded victims. They cry that Communism has failed, that we've surrendered our principles, that since the introduction of NEP—our New Economic Policy—the Communist Party has been retreating, fleeing before a new form of private profiteering which now rules our country. They claim that we are holding power for the sake of power and have forgotten our ideals. Such is the whining of weaklings and cowards who cannot face practical reality. It is true that we've had to abandon the policy of Military Communism, which had brought us to the brink of total starvation. It is true that we've had to make concessions to private traders. What of it? A retreat is not a defeat. A temporary compromise is not a surrender. We were betrayed by the spineless, weak-kneed, anemic socialists of foreign countries who sold out their working masses to their bourgeois masters. The World Revolution, which was to make a pure world Communism possible, has been delayed. We, therefore, have had to compromise, for the time being. We have had to abandon our theories of pure Communism and come down to earth, to the prosaic task of economic reconstruction. Some may think it a slow, drab, uninspiring process; but loyal Communists know the epic grandeur of our new economic front. Loyal Communists know the revolutionary value and significance of our ration cards, our Primuses, the lines at our co-operatives. Our great leader, Comrade Lenin, with his usual farsightedness, warned us several years ago against the danger of being 'over-idealistic.' That perilous fallacy has smitten some of our best heads. It has taken from us the man who had been one of our first leaders—Leon Trotzky. None of his past services to the Proletariat could redeem the treachery of his assertion that we've betrayed Communism. His followers have been thrown out of our ranks. That is why we've had Party purges. That is why these purges will continue. We must follow, with absolute discipline, the program dictated by our Party—and not the petty doubts and personal opinions of the few who still think of themselves and of their so-called conscience in terms of bourgeois individualism. We don't need those who take a selfish, old-fashioned pride in the purity of their own convictions. We need those who are not afraid of a little compromise. We don't need the obstinate, unbending Communist of iron. The new Communist is of rubber! Idealism, comrades, is a good thing in its proper amount. Too much of it is like too much of a good old wine: one's liable to lose one's head. Let this be a warning to any of Trotzky's secret sympathizers who might still remain within the Party: no past services, no past record will save them from the axe of the next Party purge. They are traitors and they will be kicked out, no matter who they are or what they've been!"

Hands applauded clamorously. Then the still, black rows of jackets broke into motion; men rose; the meeting was closed.

They gathered in groups, whispering excitedly. They giggled, muffling the sound with a hand pressed to a mouth. They pointed furtively at a few solitary figures. Behind the huge checkered windows, the lead of the sky was turning to a dark blue steel.

"Congratulations, pal," someone slapped Pavel Syerov's shoulder. "I heard you've been elected vice-president of the Railroad Workers Union's Club of Leninism."

"Yes," Syerov answered modestly.

"Good luck, Pavlusha. You're an example of activity for all of us to follow. No worries about Party purges for you."

"I've always striven to keep my Party loyalty above suspicion," Syerov answered modestly.

"Say, pal, you see, it's still two weeks till the first of the month and I've . . . well . . . I'm slightly in need of cash . . . and . . . well . . . I thought maybe. . . ."

"Sure," said Syerov, opening his wallet, "with pleasure."

"You never turn a friend down, Pavlusha. And you always seem to have enough to . . ."

"Just being economical with my salary," Syerov said modestly.

Comrade Sonia was waving her short arms, trying to plough her way through an eager group that followed her persistently. She was snapping at them: "I'm sorry, comrade, that's out of the question. . . . Yes, comrade, I'll be glad to give you an appointment. Call my secretary at the Zhenotdel. . . . You will find it wise to follow my suggestion, comrade. . . . I'd be happy to address your Circle, comrade, but unfortunately, I'm giving a lecture at a Rabfac Club at that hour. . . ."

Victor had taken the bearded speaker of the meeting aside and was whispering eagerly, persuasively: "I received my diploma at the Institute two weeks ago, comrade. . . . You understand that the job I'm holding at present is quite unsatisfactory for a full-fledged engineer and . . ."

"I know, Comrade Dunaev, I know the position you desire. Personally, I know of no better man to fill it. And I'd do anything in my power for the husband of my friend Marisha Lavrova. But . . ." He looked around cautiously, over the rim of his pince-nez, and drew closer to Victor, lowering his voice. "Just between you and me, comrade, there's a grave obstacle in your way. You understand that that hydroelectric project is the most stupendous undertaking of the republic at present, and every job connected with it is assigned with particular caution and . . ." his voice dropped to a whisper, "your Party record is magnificent, Comrade Dunaev, but you know how it is, there are always those inclined to suspicion, and . . . Frankly, I've heard it said that your social past . . . your father and family, you know . . . But don't give up hope. I'll do all I can for you."

Andrei Taganov stood alone in an emptying row of chairs. He was buttoning his leather jacket slowly. His eyes were fixed on the flaming scarlet banner above the lectern.

At the top of the stairs, on his way out, he was stopped by Comrade Sonia.

"Well, Comrade Taganov," she asked loudly, so that others turned to look at them, "what did you think of the speech?"

"It was explicit," Andrei answered slowly, all the syllables of his voice alike, as grains of lead.

"Don't you agree with the speaker?"

"I prefer not to discuss it."

"Oh, you don't have to," she smiled pleasantly. "You don't have to. I know—we know—what you think. But what I'd like you to answer is this: why do you think you are entitled to your own thoughts? Against those of the majority of your Collective? Or is the majority's will sufficient for you, Comrade Taganov? Or is Comrade Taganov becoming an individualist?"

"I'm very sorry, Comrade Sonia, but I'm in a hurry."

"It's all right with me, Comrade Taganov. I have nothing more to say. Just a little advice, from a friend: remember that the speech has made it plain what awaits those who think themselves smarter than the Party."

Andrei walked slowly down the stairs. It was dark. Far below, a bluish gleam showed a floor of polished marble. A street lamp beyond the tall window threw a blue square of light, checkered into panes, on the wall by the staircase; little shadows of raindrops rolled slowly down the wall. Andrei walked down, his body slender, erect, unhurried, steady, the kind of body that in centuries past had worn the armor of a Roman, the mail of a crusader; it wore a leather jacket now.

Its tall, black shadow moved slowly across the blue square of light and raindrops on the wall.

*

Victor came home. He flung his coat on a chair in the lobby and kicked his galoshes into a corner. The galoshes upset an umbrella stand that clattered down to the floor. Victor did not stop to pick it up.

In the dining room, Marisha sat before a pile of opened volumes, bending her head to one side, writing studiously, biting her pencil. Vasili Ivanovitch sat by a window, carving a wooden box. Acia sat on the floor, mixing sawdust, potato peelings and sunflower-seed shells in a broken bowl.

"Dinner ready?" snapped Victor.

Marisha fluttered up to throw her arms around him. "Not . . . not quite, darling," she apologized. "Irina's been busy and I have this thesis to write for tomorrow and . . ."

He threw her arms off impatiently and walked out, slamming the door. He went down a dim corridor to Irina's room. He threw the door open without knocking. Irina stood by the window, in Sasha's arms, his lips on hers. She jerked away from him; she cried: "Victor!", her voice choked with indignation. Victor wheeled about without a word and slammed the door behind him.

He returned to the dining room. He roared at Marisha: "Why the hell isn't the bed made in our room? The room's like a pigsty. What have you been doing all day?"

"But darling," she faltered, "I . . . I've been at the Rabfac, and then at the Lenin's Library meeting, and the Wall Newspaper's Editorial Board, and then there's this thesis on Electrification I have to read tomorrow at the Club, and I don't know a thing about Electrification and I've had to read so much and . . ."

"Well, go and see if you can heat something on the Primus. I expect to be fed when I come home."

"Yes, dear."

She gathered her books swiftly, nervously. She hurried, pressing the heavy pile to her breast, dropped two books by the door, bent awkwardly to pick them up, and went out.

"Father," said Victor, "why don't you get a job?"

Vasili Ivanovitch raised his head slowly and looked at him. "What's the matter, Victor?" he asked.

"Nothing. Nothing at all. Only it's rather foolish to be registered as an unemployed bourgeois and be constantly under suspicion."

"Victor, we haven't discussed our political views for a long time, you know. But if you want to hear it—I will not work for your government so long as I live."

"But surely, Father, you're not hoping still that . . ."

"What I'm hoping is not to be discussed with a Party man. And if you're tired of the expense . . ."

"Oh, no, Father, of course it isn't that."   ,

Sasha passed through the dining room on his way out. He shook hands with Vasili Ivanovitch. He patted Acia's head. He went out without a word or a glance at Victor.

"Irina, I want to speak to you," said Victor.

"What is it?" she asked.

"I want to speak to you—alone."

"Anything you have to say, father may hear it."

"Very well. It's about that man," he pointed at the door that had closed behind Sasha.

"Yes?"

"I hope you realize the infernal situation."

"No. I don't. What situation?"

"Do you know with what type of man you're carrying on an affair?"

"I'm not carrying on any affair. Sasha and I are engaged."

Victor jerked forward, opening his mouth and closing it again, then said slowly, with an effort to control himself: "Irina, that's utterly impossible."

She stood before him, her eyes steady, menacing, scornful. She asked: "Is it? Just exactly why?"

He learned toward her, his mouth twitching. "Listen," he hissed, "don't make any useless denials. I know what your Sasha Chernov is. He's up to his neck in counter-revolutionary plots. It's none of my business. I'm keeping my mouth shut. But it won't be long before others in the Party discover it. You know the end for bright lads like him. Do you expect me to stand by and watch my sister marrying a counter-revolutionary? What do you think it will do to my Party standing?"

"What it will do to your Party standing or to yourself," Irina said with meticulous precision, "concerns me less than the cat's leavings on the back stairs."

"Irina!" Vasili Ivanovitch gasped. Victor whirled upon him.

"You tell her!" Victor roared. "It's hard enough to get anywhere with the millstone of this family tied around my neck!

You can roll straight down to hell, if you all enjoy it so nobly, but I'll be damned if you're going to drag me along!"

"But, Victor," Vasili Ivanovitch said quietly, "there's nothing either you or I can do about it. Your sister loves him. She has a right to her own happiness. God knows, she's had little enough of it these last few years."

"If you're so afraid for your damn Party hide," said Irina, "I'll get out of here. I'm making enough for myself. I could starve on my own on what one of your Red clubs considers a living salary! I'd have gone long ago, if it weren't for father and Acia!"

"Irina," Vasili Ivanovitch moaned, "you won't do that!"

"In other words," Victor asked, "you refuse to give up that young fool?"

"And also," Irina answered, "I refuse to discuss him with you."

"Very well," said Victor, "I've warned you."

"Victor!" Vasili Ivanovitch cried. "You're—you're not going to harm Sasha, are you?"

"Don't worry," Irina hissed, "he won't. It would be too compromising for his Party standing!"

*

Kira met Vava Milovskaia in the street, but could hardly recognize her, and it was Vava who approached timidly, muttering: "How are you, Kira?"

Vava wore an old felt hat made over from her father's derby, with a broken brim that looked as if it had not been brushed for days. One black curl hung carelessly over her right cheek, her mouth was smeared unevenly with a faded, purplish lipstick, and her little nose was shiny, but her eyes were dull; her eyes looked swollen, aged, indifferent.

"Vava, I haven't seen you for such a long time. How are you?"

"I'm . . . I'm married, Kira."

"You . . . Why, congratulations. . . . When?"

"Thanks. Two weeks ago." Vava's eyes were looking away; she muttered, staring at the street: "I . . . we . . . we didn't have a big wedding, so we didn't invite anyone. Just the family. You see, it was a church wedding, and Kolya didn't want that known at the office where he works."

"Kolya . . . ?"

"Yes, Kolya Smiatkin, you probably don't remember him, you met him at my party, though. . . . That's what I am now: Citizen Smiatkina. . . . He works at the Tobacco Trust, and it's not a very big job, but they say he'll get a raise. . . . He's a very nice boy . . . he . . . he loves me very much. . . . Why shouldn't I have married him?"

"I didn't say you shouldn't have, Vava."

"What is there to wait for? What can one do with oneself, these days, if one isn't . . . if one isn't a. . . . What I like about you, Kira, is that you're the first person who didn't say she wished me to be happy!"

"But I do wish it, Vava."

"Well, I'm happy!" She tossed her head defiantly. "I'm perfectly happy!"

Vava's hand in a soiled glove rested on Kira's arm; she hesitated, as if she feared Kira's presence, and closed her fingers tighter over Kira's arm, as if she were afraid to let her go, as if she were hanging on desperately to something she did not want to utter. Then she whispered, looking away: "Kira . . . do you think . . . *he's* happy?"

"Victor is not a person who cares about being happy," Kira answered slowly.

"I wouldn't mind . . ." Vava whispered, "I wouldn't mind . . . if she were pretty. . . . But I saw her. . . . Oh, well, anyway, it doesn't concern me at all. Not in the least. . . I'd like you to come over and visit us, Kira, you and Leo. Only . . . only we haven't found a place to live yet. I moved into Kolya's room, because . . . because my old room . . . well, father didn't approve, you see, so I thought it would be better to move out. And Kolya's room—it's a former storage closet in a big apartment, and it's so small that we . . . But when we find a room, I'll invite you to come over and . . . Well, I have to run along. . . . Good-bye, Kira."

"Good-bye, Vava."

*

"He's not in," said the gray-haired woman.

"I'll wait," said Comrade Sonia.

The woman shuffled uncomfortably from foot to foot and chewed her lips. Then she said: "Don't see how you can wait, citizen. We've got no reception room. I'm only Citizen Syerov's neighbor and my quarters . . ."

"I'll wait in Citizen Syerov's room."

"But, citizen . . ."

"I said I'll wait in Citizen Syerov's room."

Comrade Sonia walked resolutely down the corridor. The

old neighbor followed, nodding dejectedly, watching the swift heels of Comrade Sonia's flat, masculine shoes.

Pavel Syerov jumped up when Comrade Sonia entered. He threw his arms wide in a gesture of surprise and welcome.

"Sonia, my dear!" he laughed very loudly. "It's you! My dear, I'm so sorry. I was busy and I had given orders . . . but had I known . . ."

"It's quite all right," Comrade Sonia dismissed the subject. She threw a heavy brief case on the table and unbuttoned her coat, unwinding a thick, masculine scarf from her neck. She glanced at her wristwatch. "I have half an hour to spare," she said. "I'm on my way to the Club. We're opening a Lenin's Nook today. I had to see you about something important."

Syerov offered her a chair and pulled on his coat, adjusting his tie before a mirror, smoothing his hair, smiling ingratiatingly.

"Pavel," said Comrade Sonia, "we've going to have a baby."

Syerov's hands dropped. His mouth fell open. "A . . . ?"

"A baby," Comrade Sonia said firmly.

"What the . . ."

"It's been three months, I know," said Comrade Sonia.

"Why didn't you tell me sooner?"

"I wasn't sure."

"But hell! You'll have to . . ."

"It's too late to do anything now."

"Why the devil didn't you . . ."

"I said it was too late."

Syerov fell on a chair before her and stared intently at her unruffled calm. "Are you sure it's mine?" he asked hoarsely.

"Pavel," she said without raising her voice, "you're insulting me."

He jumped up, and walked to the door, and came back, and sat down again, and jumped up. "Well, what in hell are we to do about it?"

"We're going to be married, Pavel."

He bent toward her, his closed fist on the table. "You've gone crazy," he said heavily.

She looked at him, silently, waiting.

"You're crazy, I tell you! I have no such intention."

"But you'll have to do it."

"I will, will I? You get out of here, you . . ."

"Pavel," she said softly, "don't say anything you may regret."

"Listen . . . what the . . . we're not living in a bourgeois country. Hell! There's no such thing as a betrayed virgin . . . and you were no virgin anyway . . . and. . . . Well, if you want to go to court—try and collect for its support—and the devil take you—but there's no law to make me marry you! Marry! Hell! You'd think we lived in England or something!"

"Sit down, Pavel," said Comrade Sonia, adjusting a button on her cuff, "and don't misunderstand me. My attitude on the subject is not old-fashioned in the least. I am not concerned over morals or public disgrace or any such nonsense. It is merely a matter of our duty."

"Our . . . what?"

"Our duty, Pavel. To a future citizen of our republic."

Syerov laughed; it sounded as if he were blowing his nose. "Cut that out!" he said. "You're not addressing a Club meeting."

"Indeed," said Comrade Sonia, "so loyalty to our principles is not part of your private life?"

He jumped up again. "Now, Sonia, don't misunderstand me. Of course, I am always loyal and our principles . . . of course, it is a fine sentiment and I appreciate it . . . but then, what's the difference to the . . . future citizen?"

"The future of our republic is in the coming generation. The upbringing of our youth is a vital problem. Our child shall have the advantage of a Party mother—and father—to guide its steps."

"Hell, Sonia! That's not at all up to date. There are day-nurseries and, you know, collective training, one big family, the spirit of the collective learned early in life, and . . ."

"State nurseries are to be the great accomplishment of the future. At present—they are imperfect. Our child shall be brought up as a perfect citizen of our great republic. Our child . . ."

"Our child! Oh, hell! how do I know . . ."

"Pavel, are you intimating that . . ."

"Oh, no, no, I didn't mean anything, but . . . Hell! Sonia, I was drunk. You should have known better than . . ."

"Then you regret it, Pavel?"

"Oh, no, no, of course not. You know I love you, Sonia. . . . Sonia, listen, honest, I can't get married right now. Really, I'd like nothing better and I'd be proud to marry you, but look here, I'm just starting, I've got a career to think about. I've just made such a fine beginning, and . . . and it's my duty to the Party to train and perfect myself and rise . . ."

"I could help you, Pavel, or . . ." She said it slowly, looking at him. She did not have to finish; he understood.

"But, Sonia . . ." he moaned helplessly.

"I'm as upset about it as you are," she said calmly. "It was a more painful surprise to me than it is to you. But I'm prepared to do what I consider my duty."

He fell heavily on his chair and said dully, without raising his head: "Listen, Sonia, give me two days, will you? To think it over and get sort of used to the idea and . . ."

"Certainly," she answered, rising, "think it over. My time's up anyway. Have to run. So long."

"So long," he muttered, without looking at her.

Pavel Syerov got drunk, that evening. On the following day, he called at the Railroad Workers Union's Club. The president said: "Congratulations, Comrade Syerov. I hear you're going to marry Comrade Sonia. You couldn't make a better match." At the Party Cell, the secretary said: "Well, Pavlusha, all set to go far in this world? With such a wife . . ." At the Marxist Club, an imposing official, whom he had never met before, smiled, slapping his shoulder: "Come and see me any time, Comrade Syerov. I'm always in to a friend of your future wife."

That evening, Pavel Syerov called Antonina Pavlovna and swore at Morozov and requested a larger share than he had been getting, and demanded it in advance—and, receiving it, bought drinks for a girl he met on the street.

Three days later, Pavel Syerov and Comrade Sonia were married. They stood before a clerk in the bare room of the Zags and signed a large register. Comrade Sonia signified her intention of retaining her maiden name.

That evening, Comrade Sonia moved into Syerov's room, which was larger than her own. "Oh, darling," she said, "we must think of a good revolutionary name for our child."

*

A hand knocked on Andrei's door, a weighty knock followed by a thud, as if a fist had leaned heavily against the panel.

Andrei sat on the floor, studying, with a lamp by his side, with the huge white sheets of drafts spread before him. He raised his head and asked impatiently: "Who's there?"

"It's me, Andrei," a man's voice answered heavily. "Open the door. It's me, Stepan Timoshenko."

Andrei jumped up and threw the door open. Stepan Timoshenko, who had served in the Baltic Fleet and in the Coast Guard of the G.P.U., stood on the stair-landing, swaying a little, leaning against the wall. He wore a sailor's cap, but its band bore no star, no ship's name; he wore civilian clothes, a short jacket with a mangy rabbit fur collar, with rubbed spots on the elbows of sleeves too tight for his huge arms; the fur collar was unfastened; his tanned neck with bulging cords was open to the cold. He grinned, the light glistening on his white teeth, in his dark eyes.

"Good evening, Andrei. Mind if I butt in?"

"Come in. I'm glad to see you. I thought you had forgotten your old friends."

"No," said Timoshenko. "No, I haven't." He lumbered in, and closed the door behind him, reeling a little. "No, I haven't. . . . But some of the old friends are only too damn glad to forget me. . . . I don't mean you, Andrei. No. Not you."

"Sit down," said Andrei. "Take that coat off. Aren't you cold?"

"Who, me? No. I'm never cold. And if I was, it would do me no good because this here is all I've got. . . . I'll take the damn thing off. . . . Here. . . . Sure, all right, I'll sit down. I bet you want me to sit down because you think I'm drunk."

"No," said Andrei, "but . . ."

"Well, I am drunk. But not very much. You don't mind if I'm a little drunk, do you?"

"Where have you been, Stepan? I haven't seen you for months."

"Oh, around. I was kicked out of the G.P.U., you know that, don't you?"

Andrei nodded slowly, looking down at his drafts on the floor.

"Yep," said Timoshenko, stretching his feet out comfortably, "I was kicked out. Not reliable. No. Not reliable. Not revolutionary enough. Stepan Timoshenko of the Red Baltfleet."

"I'm sorry," said Andrei.

"Shut up. Who's asking you for sympathy? That's funny, that's what it is. . . . Very, very humorous. . . ." He looked up at the cupids on the cornice. "And you've got a funny place here. It's a hell of a place for a Communist to live in."

"I don't mind," said Andrei. "I could move, but rooms are so hard to get these days."

"Sure," said Timoshenko and laughed suddenly, loudly, senselessly. "Sure. It's hard for Andrei Taganov. It wouldn't be hard for little Comrade Syerov, for instance. It wouldn't be hard for any bastard that uses a Party card as a butcher knife.

It wouldn't be hard to throw some poor devil out on the ice of the Neva."

"You're talking nonsense, Stepan. Would you . . . would you like something to eat?"

"No. Hell, no. . . . What are you driving at, you little fool? Think I'm starving?"

"Why, no, I didn't even . . ."

"Well, don't. I still have enough to eat. And to drink. Plenty to drink. . . . I just came around because I thought little Andrei needed someone to look after him. Little Andrei needs it badly. He will need it very badly."

"What are you talking about?"

"Nothing. Nothing, pal. Just talking. Can't I talk? Are you like the rest of them? Want everybody to talk, order them to talk, talk, talk, without the right to say anything?"

"Here," said Andrei, "put that pillow under your neck and take it easy. Rest. You're not feeling well."

"Who, me?" Timoshenko took the pillow and flung it at the wall and laughed. "I've never felt better in my life. I feel grand. Free and finished. No worries. No worries of any kind any more."

"Stepan, why don't you come here more often? We used to be friends. We could still help each other."

Timoshenko leaned forward, and stared at Andrei, and grinned somberly: "I can't help you, kid. I could help you only if you could take me by the scruff of my neck and kick me out and with me kick out everything that goes with me, and then go and bow very low and lick a very big boot. But you won't do it. And that's why I hate you, Andrei. And that's why I wish you were my son. Only I'll never have a son. My sons are strewn all over the whorehouses of the U.S.S.R."

He looked down at the white drafts on the floor, and kicked a book, and asked: "What are you doing here, Andrei?"

"I was studying. I haven't had much time to study. I've been busy at the G.P.U."

"Studying, eh? How many years you got left at the Institute?"

"Three years."

"Uh-huh. Think you'll need it?"

"Need what?"

"The learning."

"Why wouldn't I?"

"Say, pal, did I tell you they kicked me out of the G.P.U.?

Oh, yes, I told you. But they haven't kicked me out of the Party. Not yet. But they will. At the next purge—I go."

"I wouldn't think of that in advance. You can still . . ."

"I know what I'm talking about. And you do, too. And do you know who'll go next?"

"No," said Andrei.

"You," said Stepan Timoshenko.

Andrei rose, crossed his arms, looked at Timoshenko, and said quietly: "Maybe."

"Listen, pal," Timoshenko asked, "have you got something to drink here?"

"No," said Andrei. "And you're drinking too much, Stepan."

"Oh, am I?" Timoshenko chuckled, and his head rocked slowly, mechanically, so that its huge shadow on the wall swung like a pendulum. "Am I drinking too much? And have I no reason to drink? Say, I'll tell you," he rose, swaying, towering over Andrei, his shadow hitting the doves on the ceiling. "I'll tell you the reason and then you'll say I don't drink enough, you poor little pup in the rain, that's what you'll say!"

He pulled at his sweater, too tight under the arms, and scratched his shoulder blades, and roared suddenly: "Once upon a time, we made a revolution. We said we were tired of hunger, of sweat and of lice. So we cut throats, and broke skulls, and poured blood, our blood, their blood, to wash a clean road for freedom. Now look around you. Look around you, Comrade Taganov, Party member since 1915! Do you see where men live, men, our brothers? Do you see what they eat? Have you ever seen a woman falling on the street, vomiting blood on the cobblestones, dying of hunger? I have. Did you see the limousines speeding at night? Did you see who's in them? There's a nice little comrade we have in the Party. A smart young man with a brilliant future. Pavel Syerov's the name. Have you ever seen him open his wallet to pay for a whore's champagne? Did you ever wonder where he gets the money? Did you ever go to the European roof garden? Not often, I bet. But if you had, you'd see the respectable Citizen Morozov getting indigestion on caviar. Who is he? Just assistant manager of the Food Trust. The State Food Trust of the Union of Socialist Soviet Republics. We're the leaders of the world proletariat and we'll bring freedom to all suffering humanity! Look at our Party. Look at the loyal members with ink still wet on their Party tickets. Watch them reaping the harvest from the soil that our blood had fertilized. But we're not red enough for them. We're not revolutionaries. We're kicked out as traitors. We're kicked out for Trotzkyism. We're kicked out because we didn't lose our sight and our conscience when the Czar lost his throne, the sight and the conscience that made him lose it. We're kicked out because we yelled to them that they've lost the battle, strangled the revolution, sold out the people, and there's nothing left now but power, brute power. They don't want us. Not me nor you. There's no place for men like you, Andrei, not anywhere on this earth. Well, you don't see it. And I'm glad you don't. Only I hope I'm not there on the day when you will!"

Andrei stood, silent, his arms crossed. Timoshenko seized his jacket and pulled it on hastily, reeling.

"Where are you going?" asked Andrei.

"Going. Anywhere. I don't want to stay here."

"Stepan, don't you think that I see it, too? But screaming about it won't help. And drinking yourself to death won't help. One can still fight."

"Sure. Go on fighting. It's none of my business. I'm going to have a drink."

Andrei watched him buttoning the jacket, pulling the starless sailor cap over one ear. "Stepan, what are you going to do?"

"Now?"

"No. In the years to come."

"The years to come?" Timoshenko laughed, throwing his head back, the mangy rabbit collar shaking on his huge shoulders. "That's a cute sentence: the years to come. Why are you so sure they're coming?" He leaned toward Andrei, and winked slyly, mysteriously. "Did it ever occur to you, Comrade Taganov, what a peculiar thing it is that so many of our Party comrades are dying of overwork? You've read it in the papers, haven't you? Another glorious victim fallen on the path of the revolution, a life burned out in a ceaseless task. . . . You know what they are, don't you, those comrades dying of a ceaseless task? Suicides. That's what they are. Suicides. Only the papers will never say it. Funny how many of them are killing themselves these days. Wonder why."

"Stepan," Andrei took a huge, hot, clammy hand into his strong, cold ones, "you're not thinking of . . ."

"I'm not thinking of anything. Hell, no. All I want is a drink. And, anyway, if I do think, I'll come to say good-bye. I promise."

At the door, Andrei stopped him once again: "Stepan, why don't you stay here? For a while?"

Stepan Timoshenko waved with the majesty of sweeping a

mantle over his shoulders, and shook his head, reeling out to the landing of the long marble stairway:

"No. Not here. I don't want to see you, Andrei. I don't want to see that damn face of yours. Because . . . you see, I'm an old battleship, ready for the scrap heap, with all its guts rusted and rotted. But I don't mind that. And I'd give the last of these rotted guts to help the only man I know left in the world—and that's you. But I don't mind that. What I mind is that I know that could I take my guts out and give them for you—it still wouldn't save you!"

VII

Kira stood looking at a building under construction.

Jagged walls of red bricks, new and raw, checkered by a net of fresh, white cement, rose to a gray sky darkening slowly in an early twilight. High against the clouds, workers knelt on the walls, and iron hammers knocked, ringing sonorously over the street, and engines roared hoarsely, and steam whistled somewhere in a tangled forest of planks, beams, scaffoldings splattered with lime. She stood watching, her eyes wide, her lips smiling. A young man, with a tanned face and a pipe in the corner of his mouth, walked swiftly up the narrow planks in the perilous framework, and the movements of his hands were brusque, precise, implacable like the blows of a hammer. She did not know how long she had been standing there. She had forgotten all but the work before her. Then, suddenly, her world returning to her with a jolt, in a blinding second of clear, sharp perception—as if new eyes were taking a first glance at a new world and saw it as she had forgotten to see it—she wondered, astonished, why she was not there, on the scaffolding, giving orders like the man with the pipe, what reason could possibly keep her from her work, her life work, her only desire. It was one swift second, so swift that she felt it only after it was over; and after it was over, she saw the world again as she had grown accustomed to see it, and she remembered why she was not on the scaffolding, what reason had closed to her, forever, the only work she wanted. And in her mind, four words filled the void she felt rising from somewhere in her breast: "Perhaps . . . Some day . . . Abroad . . ."

A hand touched her shoulder: "What are you doing here, citizen?"

A militia-man was staring suspiciously down at her. He wore a peaked khaki cap, with a red star, over a low forehead. He squinted, opening soft lips that had no shape, like pillows: "You have been standing here for half an hour, citizen. What do you want?"

"Nothing," said Kira.

"Well, then, on your way, citizen."

"I was just looking," said Kira.

"You," decreed the militia-man, opening lips shapeless as pillows, "have no business looking."

She turned silently and walked away.

Against her skin, sewn on to her shirt, a little pocket was growing thicker, slowly, week by week. She kept in it the money she managed to save from Leo's reckless spending. It was a foundation rising for their future and perhaps—some day—abroad. . . .

She was returning home from a meeting of excursion guides. There had been a political examination at the Excursion Center. A man with a close-cropped head had sat at a broad desk, and trembling, white-lipped guides had stood before him, one after the other, answering questions in jerking, unnaturally bright voices. Kira had recited adequately the appropriate sounds about the importance of historical excursions for the political education and class-consciousness of the working masses; she had been able to answer the question about the state of the latest strike of textile workers in Great Britain; she had known all about the latest decree of the Commissar of People's Education in regard to the Schools for the Illiterates of the Turkestan; but she could not name the latest amount of coal produced by the mines of the Don basin.

"Don't you read the newspapers, comrade?" the examining official had asked sternly.

"Yes, comrade."

"I would suggest that you read them more thoroughly. We do not need limited specialists and old-fashioned academicians who know nothing outside their narrow professions. Our modern educators must be politically enlightened and show an active interest in our Soviet reality, in all the details of our state construction. . . . Next!"

She might be dismissed, Kira thought indifferently, walking home. She would not worry. She could not worry any longer.

She would not allow herself to reach the state of Comrade Nesterova, an elderly guide who had been a school teacher for thirty years. Comrade Nesterova, between excursions, school classes, clubs, and cooking for a paralyzed mother, spent all her time reading the newspapers, memorizing every item word for word, preparing herself for the examination. Comrade Nesterova needed her job badly. But when she had stood before the examiner, Comrade Nesterova had not been able to utter a word; she had opened her mouth senselessly, without a sound, and collapsed suddenly, shrieking, in hysterical tears; she had had to be carried out of the room and a nurse had been called. Comrade Nesterova's name had been crossed off the list of excursion guides.

Kira had forgotten the examination by the time she reached her house: she was thinking of Leo; she was wondering how she would find him that evening. The question arose, with a small twist of anxiety, every time she came home late and knew that she would find him there. He would leave in the morning, smiling and cheerful and brisk with energy; but she never knew what to expect at the end of the day. Sometimes she found him reading a foreign book, barely answering her greeting, refusing to eat, chuckling coldly once in a while at the bright lines of a world so far from their own. Sometimes she found him drunk, staggering across the room, laughing bitterly, tearing banknotes before her eyes when she spoke of the money he had spent. Sometimes she found him discussing art with Antonina Pavlovna, yawning, talking as if he did not hear his own words. Sometimes—rarely—he smiled at her, his eyes young and clear as they had been long ago, on their first meetings, and he pressed money into her hand, whispering: "Hide it from me. . . . For the escape. For Europe. . . . We'll do it . . . some day . . . if you can keep me from thinking . . . until then. . . . If we can only keep from thinking. . . ."

She had learned to keep from thinking; she remembered only that he was Leo and that she had no life beyond the sound of his voice, the movements of his hands, the lines of his body —and that she had to stand on guard between him and the something immense, unnamable which was moving slowly toward him, which had swallowed so many. She would stand on guard; nothing else mattered; she never thought of the past; the future—no one around her thought of the future.

She never thought of Andrei; she never allowed herself to wonder what the days, perhaps the years, ahead of them would have to be. She knew that she had gone too far and could not retreat. She was wise enough to know that she could not leave him; she was brave enough not to attempt it. In averting a blow he would not be able to stand, she was paying him, silently, for what she had done. Some day, she felt dimly, she would have to end the payment; the day when, perhaps, a passage abroad would open for Leo and her; then she would end it without hesitation, since Leo would need her; then Leo would be safe; nothing else mattered.

"Kira?" a gay voice called from the bathroom, when she entered their room.

Leo came out, a towel in his hand, naked from the waist up, shaking drops of water off his face, throwing tangled hair off his forehead, smiling.

"I'm glad you're back, Kira. I hate to come home and not find you here."

He looked as if he had just stepped out of a stream on a hot summer day, and one could almost see the sun sparkling in the drops of water on his shoulders. He moved as if his whole body were a living will, straight, arrogant, commanding, a will and a body that could never bend because both had been born without the capacity to conceive of bending.

She stood still, afraid to approach him, afraid to shatter one of the rare moments when he looked what he could have been, what he was intended to be.

He approached her and his hand closed over her throat and he jerked her head back to hold her lips to his. There was a contemptuous tenderness in his movement, and a command, and hunger; he was not a lover, but a slave owner. Her arms holding him, her mouth drinking the glistening drops on his skin, she knew the answer, the motive for all her days, for all she had to bear and forget in those days, the only motive she needed.

*

Irina came to visit Kira, once in a while, on the rare evenings she could spare from her work at the Club. Irina laughed sonorously, and scattered cigarette ashes all over the room, and related the latest, most dangerous political anecdotes, and drew caricatures of all their acquaintances on the white table cloth.

But on the evenings when Leo was busy at the store, when Kira and Irina sat alone at a lighted fireplace, Irina did not always laugh. Sometimes, she sat silently for long minutes and when she raised her head and looked at Kira, her eyes were bewildered, pleading for help. Then she whispered, looking into the fire:

"Kira, I . . . I'm afraid. . . . I don't know why, it's only at times, but I'm so afraid. . . . What's going to happen to all of us? That's what frightens me. Not the question itself, but that it's a question you can't ask anyone. You ask it and watch people, and you'll see their eyes, and you'll know that they feel the same thing, the same fear, and you can't question them about it, but if you did, they couldn't explain it, either. . . . You know, we're all trying so hard not to think at all, not to think beyond the next day, and sometimes even not beyond the next hour. . . . Do you know what I believe? I believe *they're* doing it deliberately. *They* don't want us to think. That's why we have to work as we do. And because there's still time left after we've worked all day and stood in a few lines, we have the social activities to attend, and then the newspapers. Do you know that I almost got fired from the Club, last week? I was asked about the new oil wells near Baku and I didn't know a damn thing about them. Why should I know about the oil wells near Baku if I want to earn my millet drawing rotten posters? Why do I have to memorize newspapers like poems? Sure, I need the kerosene for the Primus. But does it mean that in order to have kerosene in order to cook millet, I have to know the name of every stinking worker in every stinking well where the kerosene comes from? Two hours a day of reading news of state construction for fifteen minutes of cooking on the Primus? . . . Well, and there's nothing we can do about it. If we try, it's worse. Take Sasha, for instance . . . Oh, Kira! I'm . . . I'm so afraid! . . . He . . . he . . . Well, I don't have to lie to you. You know what he's doing. It's a secret organization of some kind and they think they can overthrow the government. Set the people free. His duty to the people, Sasha says. And you and I know that any one of that great people would be only too glad to betray them all to the G.P.U. for an extra pound of linseed oil. They have secret meetings and they print things and distribute them in the factories. Sasha says we can't expect help from abroad, it's up to us to fight for our own freedom. . . . Oh, what can I do? I would like to stop him and I have no right to stop him. But I know they'll get him. Remember the students they sent to Siberia last spring? Hundreds, thousands of them. You'll never hear from any of them again. He's an orphan, hasn't a soul in the world, but me. I would try to stop him, but he won't listen, and he's right, only I love him. I love him. And he'll go to Siberia some day. And what's the use? Kira! What's the use?"

*

Sasha Chernov turned the corner of his street, hurrying home. It was a dark October evening and the little hand that seized his coat belt seemed to have shot suddenly out of nowhere. Then he distinguished a shawl thrown over a little head and a pair of eyes staring up at him, huge, unblinking, terrified.

"Citizen Chernov," the girl whispered, her trembling body pressed to his legs, stopping him, "don't go home."

He recognized his neighbor's daughter. He smiled and patted her head, but, instinctively, stepped aside, into the shadow of a wall. "What's the matter, Katia?"

"Mother said . . ." the girl gulped, "mother said to tell you not to come home. . . . There are strange men there. . . . They've thrown your books all over the room. . . ."

"Thank your mother for me, kid," Sasha whispered and whirled about and disappeared behind the corner. He had had time to catch sight of a black limousine standing at the door of his house.

He raised his collar and walked swiftly. He walked into a restaurant and telephoned. A strange man's voice answered gruffly. Sasha hung up without a word; his friend had been arrested.

They had had a secret meeting, that night. They had discussed plans, agitation among the workers, a new printing press. He grinned a little at the thought of the G.P.U. agents looking at the huge pile of anti-Soviet proclamations in his room. He frowned; tomorrow the proclamations would have been distributed into countless hands in Petrograd's factories.

He jumped into a tramway and rode to another friend's house. Turning the corner, he saw a black limousine at the door. He hurried away.

He rode to a railroad terminal and telephoned again, a different number. No one answered.

He walked, shuffling through a heavy slush, to another address. He saw no light in the window of his friend's room. But he saw the janitor's wife at the back yard gate, whispering excitedly to a neighbor. He did not approach the house.

He blew at his frozen, gloveless hands. He hurried to one more address. There was a light in the window for which he was looking. But on the window sill stood a vase of peculiar shape and that had been the danger signal agreed upon.

He took another tramway. It was late and the tramway was almost empty; it was lighted too brightly. A man in a military tunic entered at the next stop. Sasha got out.

He leaned against a dark lamp post and wiped his forehead. His forehead was burning with a sweat colder than the melting snow drops.

He was hurrying down a dark street when he saw a man in an old derby hat strolling casually on the other side. Sasha turned a corner, and walked two blocks, and turned again, and walked a block, and turned once more. Then he looked cautiously over his shoulder. The man in the old derby was studying the window of an apothecary shop three houses behind him.

Sasha walked faster. A gray snow fluttered over yellow lights over closed gates. The street was deserted. He heard no sound but that of his own steps crunching mud. But through the sound, and through the distant grating of wheels, and through the muffled, rumbling, rising knocks somewhere in his chest, he heard the shuffling, soft as a breath, of steps following him.

He stopped short and looked back. The man in the derby was bending to tie a shoe lace. Sasha looked up. He was at the door of a house he knew well. It took the flash of a second. He was behind the door and, pressed to a wall in a dark lobby, without movement, without breath, he watched the square of the glass pane in the door. He saw the man in the derby pass by. He heard his steps crunching away, slowing down, stopping, hesitating, coming back. The derby swam past the glass square again. The steps creaked, louder and lower, back and forth, somewhere close by.

Sasha swung noiselessly up the stairs and knocked at a door.

Irina opened it.

He pressed a finger to his lips and whispered: "Is Victor home?"

"No," she breathed.

"Is his wife?"

"She's asleep."

"May I come in? They're after me."

She pulled him in and closed the door slowly, steadily, taking a long, patient minute. The door touched the jamb without a sound.

*

Galina Petrovna came in with a bundle under her arm.

"Good evening, Kira. . . . My Lord, Kira, what a smell in this room!"

Kira rose indifferently, dropping a book. "Good evening, Mother. It's the Lavrovs next door. They're making sauerkraut."

"My Lord! So that's what he was mixing in the big barrel. He's certainly uncivil, that old Lavrov. He didn't even greet me. And after all, we're relatives, in a way."

Behind the door, a wooden paddle grated in a barrel of cabbage. Lavrov's wife sighed monotonously: "Heavy are our sins . . . heavy are our sins. . . ." The boy was chipping wood in a corner and the crystal chandelier tinkled, shuddering, with every blow. The Lavrovs had moved into the room vacated by their daughter; they had shared a garret with two other families in a workers' tenement; they had been glad to make the change.

Galina Petrovna asked: "Isn't Leo home?"

"No," said Kira, "I'm expecting him."

"I'm on my way to evening classes," said Galina Petrovna, "and I just dropped in for a minute . . ." She hesitated. fingered her bundle, smiled apologetically, and said too casually: "I just dropped in to show you something, see if you like it . . . maybe you'll want to . . . buy it."

"To buy it?" Kira repeated, astonished. "What is it, Mother?"

Galina Petrovna had unwrapped the bundle; she was holding an old-fashioned gown of flowing white lace; its long train touched the floor; Galina Petrovna's hesitant smile was almost shy.

"Why, Mother!" Kira gasped. "Your wedding gown!"

"You see," Galina Petrovna explained very quickly, "it's the school. I got my salary yesterday and . . . and they had deducted so much for my membership in the Proletarian Society of Chemical Defense—and I didn't even know I was a member—that I haven't . . . You see, your father needs new shoes—the cobbler's refused to mend his old ones—and I was going to buy them this month . . . but with the Chemical Defense and . . . You see, you could alter it nicely—the dress, I mean—it's good material, I've only worn it . . . once. . . . And I thought, if you liked it, for an evening gown, maybe, or . . ."

"Mother," Kira said almost severely, and wondered at the

little jerking break in her voice, "you know very well that if you need anything . . ."

"I know, child, I know," Galina Petrovna interrupted, and the wrinkles on her face were suddenly flushed with pink. "You've been a wonderful daughter, but . . . with all you've given us already . . . I didn't feel I could ask . . . and I thought I'd rather . . . but then, if you don't like the dress . . ."

"Yes," Kira said resolutely, "I like it. I'll buy it, Mother."

"I really don't need it," Galina Petrovna muttered, "and I don't mind at all."

"I was going to buy an evening gown, anyway," Kira lied.

She found her pocketbook. It was stretched, stuffed full, bursting with crisp new bills. The night before, coming home late, kissing her, staggering, Leo had slipped his hand into his pocket and dropped crumpled bills all over the floor, and stuffed her pocketbook, laughing: "Go on, spend it! Plenty more coming. Just another little deal with Comrade Syerov. Brilliant Comrade Syerov. Spend it, I say!"

She emptied the pocketbook into Galina Petrovna's hand. "Why, child!" Galina Petrovna protested. "Not all that! I didn't want that much. It isn't worth that!"

"Of course, it's worth it. All that lovely lace. . . . Don't let's argue, Mother. . . . And thank you so much."

Galina Petrovna crammed the bills into her old bag, with a frightened hurry. She looked at Kira and shook her head wisely, very sadly, and muttered: "Thank you, child. . . ."

When she had gone, Kira tried on the wedding gown. It was long and plain as a medieval garment; its tight sleeves were low over the backs of her hands; its tight collar was high under her chin; it was all lace with no ornaments of any kind.

She stood before a tall mirror, her arms at her sides, palms up, her head thrown back, her hair tumbling down on her white shoulders, her body suddenly tall and too thin, fragile in the long, solemn folds of a lace delicate as a cobweb. She looked at herself as at a strange figure from somewhere many centuries away. And her eyes seemed suddenly very large, very dark, frightened.

She took the dress off and threw it into a corner of her wardrobe.

Leo came home with Antonina Pavlovna. She wore a sealskin coat and a turban of violet satin. Her heavy French perfume floated through the odor of sauerkraut from Lavrov's quarters.

"Where's the maid?" Leo asked.

"She had to go. We waited, but you're late, Leo."

"That's all right. We had dinner at a restaurant, Tonia and I. You haven't changed your mind, have you, Kira? Will you go with us to that opening?"

"I'm sorry, Leo, I can't. I have a guides' meeting tonight. . . . And, Leo, are you sure you want to go? This is the third night club opening in two weeks."

"This is different," said Antonina Pavlovna. "This is a real casino, just like abroad. Just like Monte Carlo."

"Leo," Kira sighed helplessly, "gambling again?"

He laughed: "Why not? We don't have to worry if we lose a few hundreds, do we, Tonia?"

Antonina Pavlovna smiled, pointing her chin forward: "Certainly not. We just left Koko, Kira Alexandrovna." She lowered her voice confidentially. "There's another shipment of white flour coming from Syerov day after tomorrow. How that boy can handle his business! I admire him tremendously."

"I'll jump into my dinner jacket," Leo said. "It won't take me a second. Do you mind turning to the window for a moment, Tonia?"

"Certainly," Antonina Pavlovna smiled coquettishly, "I do mind. But I promise not to peek, no matter how much I'd love to."

She stood at the window, putting a friendly hand on Kira's shoulder. "Poor Koko!" Antonina Pavlovna sighed. "He works so much. He has a meeting tonight—the Food Trust's Employees' Educational Circle. He's vice-secretary. He has to keep up his social activity, you know." She winked significantly. "He has so many meetings and sessions and things. I'd positively wilt of loneliness if our dear Leo wasn't gallant enough to take me out once in a while."

Kira looked at Leo's tall black figure in his immaculate dinner clothes, as she had looked at herself in the medieval wedding gown: as if he were a being from many centuries away, and it seemed strange to see him standing by the table with the Primus.

He took Antonina Pavlovna's arm with a gesture that belonged in a foreign film scene, and they left. When the door had closed behind them in Lavrov's room, Kira heard Lavrov's wife grunting: "And they say private traders don't make no money."

"Dictatorship of the Proletariat!" Lavrov growled and spat loudly.

Kira put on her old coat. She was not going to the excursion guides' meeting. She was going to the pavilion in a lonely palace garden.

*

A fire was burning in Andrei's fireplace. The logs creaked with sharp little explosions, long hulks broken into checks of an even, transparent, luminous red, and little orange flames swayed, fluttering, meeting, curving softly, dying suddenly, leaping up again, little blue tongues licking glowing coals; over the logs, as if suspended motionless in the air, long red flames tapered into the darkness of the chimney; yellow sparks shot upward, dying against black sooted bricks. An orange glow danced, trembling, on the white brocaded walls, on the posters of Red soldiers, smokestacks and tractors. One of Leda's feet drooped over the edge of the mantlepiece, its toes pink in the glow.

Kira sat on a box before the fireplace. Andrei sat at her feet, his face was buried in her knees; his hand caressed slowly the silken arch of her foot; his fingers dropped to the floor and came back to her tight silk stocking.

". . . and then, when you're here," he whispered, "it's worth all the torture, all the waiting. . . . And then I don't have to think any more. . . ."

He raised his head. He looked at her and pronounced words she had never heard from him before: "I'm so tired. . . ."

She held his head, her two hands spread on his temples. She asked: "What's the matter, Andrei?"

He turned away, to the fire. He said: "My Party." Then he whirled back to her. "You know it, Kira. Perhaps you knew it long ago. You were right. Perhaps you're right about many things, those things we've tried not to discuss."

She whispered: "Andrei, do you want to discuss it—with me? I don't want to hurt you."

"You can't hurt me. Don't you think I can see it all, myself? Don't you think I know what that great revolution of ours has come to? We shoot one speculator and a hundred others hire taxis on Nevsky every evening. We raze villages to the ground, we fire machine guns into rows of peasants crazed with misery, when they kill a Communist. And ten of the avenged victim's Party brothers drink champagne at the home of a man with diamond studs in his shirt. Where did he get the diamonds? Who's paying for the champagne? We don't look into that too closely."

"Andrei, did you ever think that it was you—your Party—who drove the men you call speculators into what they are doing—because you left them no choice?"

"I know it. . . . We were to raise men to our own level. But they don't rise, the men we're ruling, they don't grow, they're shrinking. They're shrinking to a level no human creatures ever reached before. And we're sliding slowly down into their ranks. We're crumbling, like a wall, one by one. Kira, I've never been afraid. I'm afraid, now. It's a strange feeling. I'm afraid to think. Because . . . because I think, at times, that perhaps our ideals have had no other result."

"That's true! The fault was not in men, but in the nature of your ideals. And I . . . No, Andrei, I won't speak about it. I wish I could help you. But of all people, I'm the one who can help you least. You know it."

He laughed softly: "But you are helping me, Kira. You're the only one in this whole world who's helping me."

She whispered: "Why?"

"Because, no matter what happens, I still have you. Because, no matter what human wreckage I see around me, I still have you. And—in you—I still know what a human being can be."

"Andrei," she whispered, "are you sure you know me?"

He whispered, his lips in her hand so that she heard the words as if she were gathering them, one by one, in the hollow of her palm: "Kira, the highest thing in a man is not his god. It's that in him which knows the reverence due a god. And you, Kira, are my highest reverence. . . ."

*

"It's me," a voice whispered behind the door, "Marisha. Let me in, Irina."

Irina unlocked the door, cautiously, uncertainly. Marisha stood on the threshold with a loaf of bread in her hand.

"Here," she whispered, "I brought you something to eat. Both of you."

"Marisha!" Irina screamed.

"Keep quiet!" Marisha whispered with a cautious glance down the corridor. "Sure, I know. But don't worry. My mouth's shut. Here, take this. It's my own bread ration. No one will notice. I know why you didn't eat any breakfast this morning. But you can't keep that up."

Irina seized her arm, jerked her into the room, closed the door and giggled hysterically: "I . . . You see . . . oh,

Marisha, I didn't expect it of you to . . ." Her hair hung over one eye; the other eye was full of tears.

Marisha whispered: "I know how it is. Hell! You love him. . . . Well, I don't know anything officially, so I don't have to tell anything, if they ask me? But for God's sake don't keep him here long. I'm not so sure about Victor."

"Do you think he . . . suspects?"

"I don't know. He's acting mighty queer. And if he knows —I'm afraid of him, Irina."

"It's just till tonight," Irina whispered, "*he's* leaving . . . tonight."

"I'll try to watch Victor for you."

"Marisha . . . I can't thank you . . . I . . ."

"Oh, hell! Nothing to cry about."

"I'm not crying . . . I . . . It's just . . . I haven't slept for two nights and . . . Marisha, you're so . . . I thank you and . . ."

"Oh, that's all right. Well, so long. I won't hang around here."

When the door closed, Irina listened cautiously till Marisha's steps died down the corridor; then she stood listening for other sounds, trembling; the house was silent. She locked the door and tiptoed across the room, and slipped noiselessly into the little storage closet that opened by her bed. Sasha sat on an old trunk in the closet, watching a sparrow behind a dusty glass pane on the sill of a tiny window high under the ceiling.

"Irina," he whispered, his eyes on the window, "I think I'd better go now."

"Why, of course not! I won't let you."

"Listen, I've been here for two days. I didn't intend to do that. I'm sorry I gave in to you. If anything happens—do you know what they'll do to you for this?"

"If anything happens to you," she whispered, slipping her arm around his big, stooped shoulders, "I don't care what they do to me."

"I was to expect it some day. But you . . . I don't want to drag you into it."

"Listen, nothing will happen. I have your ticket for Baku. And the clothes. Victor has a Party meeting tonight. We'll sneak out safely. And, anyway, you can't go now, in broad daylight. The street is watched."

"I almost wish I had let them take me without ever coming here. Irina, I'm so sorry!"

"Darling, I'm so glad!" She laughed soundlessly. "I really think I've saved you. They've arrested everyone of your group. I've pumped that out of Victor. Everyone but you."

"But if . . ."

"Oh, we're safe now. Just a few more hours to wait." She crouched on a box by his side, dropping her head on his shoulder, brushing the hair out of her feverish, sparkling eyes. "Then, when you get abroad, be sure and write to me the very first day, remember? The very first."

"Sure," he said dully.

"Then I'll manage to get out somehow. And just think of it! Abroad! We'll go to a night club and you'll look so funny in full dress clothes! Really, I think the tailors will refuse to fit you."

"Probably," he said, trying to smile.

"And then we'll see girls dancing in funny costumes, just like the ones I draw. And think! I can get a job designing fashions and costumes and stage sets. No more posters for me. Not a single poster! I won't draw another proletarian so long as I live!"

"I hope so."

"But, you know, I must warn you. I'm a very bad house-keeper. Really, I'll be impossible to live with. Your steak will be burned for dinner—oh, yes, we'll have steak every day!—and your socks won't be darned, and I won't let you complain. If you try to—I'll batter the life out of you, you poor little helpless, delicate creature!" She laughed hysterically, and buried her face on his shoulder, and bit his shirt, for her laughter was slipping into sounds that were not laughter.

He kissed her hair; he whispered bravely: "I won't complain at all if you can go ahead with your drawing. That's one more crime I'll never forgive this country. I think you could be a great artist. And listen, do you know that you've never given me a drawing, and I've asked you so often?"

"Oh, yes!" she sighed. "I've promised them to so many people, but I never concentrate long enough to finish one properly. Here's a promise, though: I'll draw two dozen pictures—there, abroad—and you can stick them all over the walls of our house. Sasha, *our house!*"

His arms closed tightly over a trembling body with a tousled head turned away from him.

*

"This mush," said Victor, "is burned."

"I'm sorry," Irina muttered, "I guess I didn't watch it closely and I . . ."

"Is there anything else for lunch?"

"No, Victor, I'm sorry. There's nothing in the house and . . ."

"There's never anything in this house! Funny, how the food seems to have disappeared—these last few days."

"No more than usual," said Marisha. "And remember, I didn't get my bread ration this week."

"Well, why didn't you?"

"I was too busy to stand in line and . . ."

"Why couldn't Irina get it?"

"Victor," said Vasili Ivanovitch, "your sister is not feeling well."

"So I notice."

"I'll eat your mush, if you don't want it," said Acia, reaching for his plate.

"You've had enough, Acia," Irina protested. "You have to hurry back to school."

"Oh, hell!" said Acia.

"Acia! Where did you learn such language?"

"I don't wanna go back," Acia whined. "We've gotta decorate Lenin's Nook this afternoon. Oh, I hate gluing pictures outta magazines on their old red blotters. I got bawled out twice, 'cause I get them on crooked."

"You hurry and get your coat. You'll be late."

Acia sighed with a resigned glance at the empty lunch dishes and shuffled out.

Victor leaned back in his chair, his hands in his pockets, and looked at Irina closely. "Not going to work today, Irina?" he asked casually.

"No. I've telephoned them. I don't feel well. I think I have a temperature."

"It's better not to take the chance of going out in this awful weather," said Marisha. "Look at it snowing."

"No," said Victor, "Irina shouldn't take chances."

"I'm not afraid," said Irina, "only I think it's safer to stay in."

"No," said Victor, "you've never been afraid of anything. A commendable trait—sometimes. And sometimes—it may go too far."

"Just what do you mean?"

"You really should be more careful—of your health. Why don't you call a doctor?"

"Oh, it's not necessary. I'm not that bad. I'll be all right in a few days."

"Yes, I think so," said Victor, rising.

"Where are you going today, Victor?" Marisha asked.

"Why do you have to know?"

"Oh, nothing . . . I . . . well . . . You see, I thought if you weren't too busy, I'd like you to come over to my Club and say a few words about something. They've all heard about my prominent husband and I've promised to bring you to address them—you know, something on Electrification or modern airplanes or something."

"Sorry," said Victor, "some other time. I've got to see a man today. About a job. About that job on the dam."

"May I go with you, Victor?"

"Certainly not. What's this? Checking up on me? Jealous or something?"

"Oh, no, no, darling. No. Nothing."

"Well, then, shut up. I'm not going to have a wife tagging me around."

"Are you looking for a new job, Victor?" Vasili Ivanovitch asked.

"Well, what do you think? Think I'll settle down to a ration-card slave's drudgery for the rest of my life? Well, you'll see."

*

"Are you sure?" the official asked.

"I'm sure," said Victor.

"Who else is responsible?"

"No one. Just my sister."

"Who else lives in your apartment, Comrade Dunaev?"

"My wife, my father, and my little sister—she's just a child. My father doesn't suspect a thing. My wife is a scatter-brained creature who wouldn't notice anything right under her nose. And anyway, she's a member of the Komsomol. There are also tenants, but they never come in contact with our side of the apartment."

"I see. Thank you, Comrade Dunaev."

"I'm merely doing my duty."

The official rose and extended his hand. "Comrade Dunaev, in the name of the Union of Socialist Soviet Republics, I thank you for your courage. They are still few, those whose devotion to the State rises above all personal ties of blood and family. That is an attitude of the future, toward which we are trying to educate our backward people. That is the highest proof of loyalty a Party man can give. I shall see to it that your heroism does not remain unknown."

"I do not deserve this high praise, comrade," said Victor. "The only value of my example is in showing our Party that the family is an institution of the past, which should not be considered when judging a member's loyalty to our great Collective."

VIII

The door bell rang.

Irina shuddered and dropped her newspaper. Marisha lowered her book.

"I'll open it," said Victor, rising.

Irina looked at the dining-room clock. One hour was left before the train's departure. And Victor had not gone to the Party meeting; and he would not leave the house.

Vasili Ivanovitch was carving a paper knife, sitting by the window. Acia yelled from somewhere under the table, rustling old magazines: "Say, is this a picture of Lenin? I gotta cut out ten of them for the Nook and I can't find that many. Is this Lenin or is it a Czechoslovakian general? I'll be damned if I can . . ."

They heard the steps of many heavy boots in the lobby. The door was thrown open. A man in a leather jacket stood on the threshold, a slip of paper in his hand. Two soldiers in peaked caps stood behind him, their hands on the butts of the guns at their belts. A third one stood at the entrance door in the lobby, holding a bayonet.

They heard a scream; it came from Marisha. She jumped up, pressing both hands to her mouth. Vasili Ivanovitch rose slowly. Acia stared up from under the table, her mouth hanging open. Irina stood very straight, too straight, leaning back a little.

"Search warrant," said the man in the leather jacket, throwing the paper on the table, and motioning to his soldiers. "This way!"

They walked down the corridor to Irina's room.

They threw the closet door open. Sasha stood on the threshold, looking at them with a somber grin.

Vasili Ivanovitch gasped, in the corridor, behind the soldiers. Acia yelled: "Oh, God! That's why she wouldn't let me open . . ." Marisha kicked her ankles. A drawing on the edge of a table slid down, rustling, fluttering to the floor.

"Which one is the Citizen Irina Dunaeva?" asked the man in the leather jacket.

"I am," said Irina.

"Listen," Sasha jerked forward. "She had nothing to do with it . . . she . . . it's not her fault. . . . I threatened her and . . ."

"With what?" the man in the leather jacket asked, his voice expressionless.

A soldier ran his hands swiftly down Sasha's clothes. "No weapons," he reported.

"All right," said the man in the leather jacket. "Take him down to the car. The Citizen Dunaeva, too. And the old man. Search the apartment."

"Comrade," Vasili Ivanovitch approached the leader, his voice steady, his hands shaking. "Comrade, my daughter couldn't be guilty of . . ."

"You'll have a chance to talk later," said the man and turned to Victor. "Are you a Party member?"

"Yes," said Victor.

"Your card?" Victor showed his Party card. The man pointed to Marisha: "Your wife?"

"Yes."

"All right. These two can stay. Get your coats, citizens."

On the floor, melting snow trailed the soldiers' boots. A lamp with a shade that had slipped sidewise, threw a broken patch of light into the corridor, on Marisha's face, greenish-white, with sunken eyes staring at Victor.

The soldier on guard in the lobby opened the door to admit the Upravdom. The Upravdom's coat was thrown hurriedly over his shoulders, over a dirty, unbuttoned shirt. He wailed, clutching his fingers with a dry little crackle of stretched joints: "Oh, my God! Oh, my God! Oh, my God! . . . Comrade Commissar, I knew nothing about this. Comrade Commissar, I swear. . . ." The soldier slammed the door in the faces of curious neighbors gathered on the stair-landing.

Irina kissed Acia and Marisha. Victor approached her, his face frozen in anxious concern: "Irina, I'm so sorry. . . . I don't understand. . . . I'll see what I can do and . . ."

Her eyes stopped him; they were looking at him fixedly; they looked suddenly like the eyes of Maria Petrovna in the old portrait. She turned and followed the soldiers, without a word. She went first; Sasha and Vasili Ivanovitch followed.

*

Vasili Ivanovitch was released in three days.

Sasha Chernov was sentenced to ten years in a Siberian prison, for counter-revolutionary activity.

Irina Dunaeva was sentenced to ten years in a Siberian prison, for assisting a counter-revolutionary.

Vasili Ivanovitch tried to see officials. got a few letters of introduction to a few assistant secretaries, spent hours huddled in the corners of unheated waiting rooms, made telephone calls, trying to keep his voice from trembling. Nothing could be done and he knew it.

When he came home, he did not speak to Victor. He did not look at Victor. He did not ask for Victor's help.

Marisha, alone, greeted Vasili Ivanovitch when he came home. She said timidly: "Here, Vasili Ivanovitch, have some dinner. I cooked the noodle soup you like—for you, specially." She blushed, grateful and embarrassed, when he answered with a silent, absent-minded smile.

Vasili Ivanovitch saw Irina in a cell of the G.P.U. He locked himself in his room for many hours and cried silently, happily, on the day when he arranged for her last request to be granted. She had asked permission to marry Sasha before they were sent away.

The wedding was performed in a bare hall of the G.P.U. Armed guards stood at the door. Vasili Ivanovitch and Kira were the witnesses. Sasha's lips twitched. Irina was very calm. She had been calm ever since her arrest. She looked a little thinner, a little paler; her skin seemed transparent; her eyes too big; her fingers were steady on Sasha's arm. She raised her face for his kiss after the ceremony, with a tender, compassionate smile.

The official whom Vasili Ivanovitch saw on the following day said: "Well, you got what you wanted. Only I don't see what good that fool rigmarole will do them. Don't you know that their prisons are three hundred and fifty kilometers apart?"

"No," said Vasili Ivanovitch and sat down heavily. "I didn't know that."

But Irina had expected it. That had been the reason for the

wedding; she had hoped it would influence the decision. It had not.

*

It was Vasili Ivanovitch's last crusade. No one could appeal a sentence of the G.P.U. But a prison assignment could be changed; if he could get the proper influence, the proper connections. . . . Vasili Ivanovitch rose at dawn. Marisha forced him to swallow a cup of black coffee, stopping him in the lobby on his way out, pushing the mug into his hands, trembling in her long nightgown. Night found him in a casino lobby, pushing his way through a crowd, crumpling his hat in both hands, stopping an imposing figure he had been expecting for hours, saying softly: "Comrade Commissar . . . just a few words . . . please . . . Comrade Commissar . . ." He was thrown out by an attendant in uniform, once, and lost his hat.

He made appointments and obtained interviews. He entered a solemn office, his old, patched coat brushed thoroughly, his shoes shined, his white hair parted neatly. He stood before a desk, and his tall shoulders that had carried a heavy rifle through many dark nights, through many Siberian forests, many years ago, sagged helplessly. He looked into a stern face and said:

"Comrade Commissar, that's all I ask. Just that. It's not much, is it? Just send them to the same place. I know they've been counter-revolutionaries and you have a right to punish them. I'm not complaining, Comrade Commissar. It's ten years, you know, but that's all right. Only send them to the same place. What difference does it make to you? What difference does it make to the State? They're so young. They love each other. It's ten years, but you know and I know that they'll never come back—it's Siberia, and the cold and the hunger, and the conditions . . ."

"What's that?" a stern voice interrupted him.

"Comrade Commissar, I . . . I didn't mean anything . . . No . . . I didn't mean . . . Only suppose they get sick or something? Irina is not very strong. They're not sentenced to death. And while they're alive—couldn't you let them be together? It would mean so much to them—and so little to anyone else. I'm an old man, Comrade Commissar, and she's my daughter. I know Siberia. It would help me, if I knew that she wasn't alone—there—that she had a man with her, her husband. I'm not sure I know how to ask you, Comrade Commissar, but you must forgive me. You see, I've never asked a favor in my life. You probably think that I'm indignant and hate you all in my heart. But I don't. I won't. Just do that one thing—that last thing—send them to the same prison—and I'll bless you as long as I live."

He was refused.

*

"I heard the whole story," said Andrei, when Kira spoke to him about it. "Do you know who denounced Irina?"

"No," said Kira, and turned away, and added: "I suspect it, though. Don't tell me. I don't want to hear it."

"I won't."

"I didn't want to ask for your help, Andrei. I know I can't expect you to intercede for a counter-revolutionary, but couldn't you ask them to change her prison assignment and have them sent to the same place? It wouldn't be treason on your part, and it really makes no difference to your officials."

He held her hand and said: "Certainly. I'll try."

In an office of the G.P.U., the executive looked at Andrei coldly and asked:

"Pleading for a . . . relative, aren't you, Comrade Taganov?"

"I don't understand you, comrade," Andrei answered slowly, looking straight at him.

"Oh, yes, I think you do. And I think you should understand that keeping a mistress who is the daughter of a former factory owner, is not the best way to strengthen your Party standing. . . . Don't look startled, Comrade Taganov. You really didn't think it was unknown to us, did you? And you working in the G.P.U.! You surprise me."

"My personal affairs . . ."

"Your *what kind* of affairs, Comrade Taganov?"

"If you're speaking of Citizen Argounova . . ."

"I *am* speaking of Citizen Argounova. And I'd suggest that you use some of the methods and authority which your position gives you, to investigate Citizen Argounova a little—for your own sake, while we're on the subject."

"I know everything I have to know about Citizen Argounova. You don't have to bring her into this. She is absolutely blameless politically."

"Oh, *politically?* And in other respects?"

"If you're speaking as my superior, I refuse to listen to anything about Citizen Argounova except her political standing."

"Very well. I don't have to say anything. I was speaking merely as a friend. You should be careful, Comrade Taganov. You don't have many friends left—in the Party."

Andrei could do nothing to change Irina's sentence.

*

"Hell!" said Leo, dipping his head into a basin of cold water, for he had come home very late the night before, "I'm going to see that skunk Syerov. He has a big boy friend in the G.P.U. He'll have to do something if I tell him to."

"I wish you'd try, Leo," said Kira.

"The damned sadists! What difference should it make to them if the poor kids rot together in their infernal prison? They know they'll never come back alive."

"Don't tell him that, Leo. Ask him nicely."

"I'll ask him *nicely!*"

In Pavel Syerov's outer office, the secretary sat typing intently, biting her lower lip. Ten visitors were waiting before the wooden railing. Leo walked straight through the office, swung the little gate open and threw at the secretary:

"I want to see Comrade Syerov. At once."

"But, citizen," the secretary gasped, "you're not allowed to . . ."

"I said I want to see him at once."

"Comrade Syerov is very busy, citizen, and there are all these citizens here waiting, and he can't see you out of turn . . ."

"You go and tell him it's Lev Kovalensky. He'll see me fast enough."

The secretary rose and backed into Syerov's office, staring at Leo, as if she expected him to draw a gun. She returned, looking more frightened, and said, gulping: "Go right in, Citizen Kovalensky."

When the door closed and they were alone, Pavel Syerov jumped up and hissed at Leo, his voice a muffled roar: "You damn fool! Are you insane? How dare you come here?"

Leo laughed, his icy laughter that was like a master's hand slapping an insolent slave's face. "You're not speaking to me, are you?" he asked. "Particularly when you're worried about caution?"

"Get out of here! I can't talk to you here!"

"You don't have to," said Leo, sitting down comfortably. "I'll do the talking."

"Do you realize whom you're talking to? You're demented or else I've never seen insolence in my life!"

"Repeat that to yourself," said Leo, "with my compliments."

"Hell!" said Syerov, dropping into his chair. "What do you want?"

"You have a friend in the G.P.U."

"I'm glad you remember that."

"I do. That's why I'm here. I have two friends sentenced to ten years in Siberia. They've just been married. They're being sent to prisons hundreds of kilometers apart. I want you to see that they're sent together, to the same place."

"Uh-huh," said Pavel Syerov. "I've heard about the case. A beautiful example of Party loyalty on the part of Comrade Victor Dunaev."

"Don't you think it's slightly ludicrous, *you* talking of Party loyalty to *me?*"

"Well, what are you going to do, if I don't lift a finger about the case?"

"You know," said Leo. "I could do a lot."

"Sure," said Syerov complaisantly. "I know you could. I also know you won't. Because, you see, to drown me, you'd have to be the stone tied around my neck, and I don't think you'll go that far in your noble unselfishness."

"Listen," said Leo, "drop the official pose. We're both crooks, and you know it, and we hate each other, and we both know it, but we're in the same boat and it's not a very steady one. Don't you think it would be wiser if we helped each other as much as we could?"

"Yes, I sure do. And your part of it is to keep as far away from here as you can. And if you weren't so damn blinded by your old patrician arrogance, which it's about time to forget, you'd know better than to ask me to intercede for any cousins of yours, which would be as good as posting on a poster my exact connection with you."

"You damn coward!"

"Well, maybe I am. And maybe it would do you good to acquire some of the same quality. You'd better not come around demanding any favors from me. You'd better remember that even if we are chained together—for the time being—I have more opportunities than you to break the chain."

Leo rose. At the door he turned and said: "As you wish. Only it would have been wiser of you—in case the chain is ever in my hands. . . ."

"Yes. And it would have been wiser of you if you hadn't come here—in case it's ever in mine. . . . And listen," he lowered his voice, "you can do something for me and you'd better do it. Tell that hog Morozov to send the money. He's late again on the last deal. I told him I'm not to be kept waiting."

*

Marisha said hesitantly, trying not to look at Victor: "Listen, don't you think that if I saw someone and asked . . . You know, just to send them to the same prison . . . it wouldn't make any difference to anyone . . . and . . ."

Victor seized her wrist and swung her around so savagely that she squealed with pain. "Listen," he said through his teeth, "you keep as far out of it as your fool legs will carry you. It would be fine for me, wouldn't it? My wife begging for counter-revolutionaries!"

"But it's only . . ."

"Listen! You breathe only one word—understand?—just one to any friend of yours—and you'll get a divorce notice the next morning!"

That night, Vasili Ivanovitch came home, looking calmer than usual. He took off his coat and folded his gloves neatly, meticulously on the mirror-stand in the lobby. He did not look at the dinner Marisha had set out for him in the dining room. He said: "Victor, I want to speak to you."

Victor followed him reluctantly to his office.

Vasili Ivanovitch did not sit down. He stood, his hands hanging limply by his sides, and looked at his son.

"Victor," said Vasili Ivanovitch, "you know what I might say. But I won't say it. I won't ask any questions. It's a strange time we're living in. Many years ago, I felt sure of what I thought. I knew when I was right and I knew when to condemn. I can't do it now. I don't know whether I can condemn anyone for anything. There's so much horror and suffering around us that I don't want to brand anyone as guilty. We're poor, bewildered creatures—all of us—who suffer so much and know so little! I can't blame you for anything you might have done. I don't know your reasons. I won't ask. I know I won't understand. No one understands each other these days. You're my son, Victor. I love you. I can't help it, as you can't help being what you are. You see, I've wanted a son ever since I was younger than you are now. I've never trusted men. And so I wanted a man of my own, at whom I could look proudly, directly, as I'm looking at you now. When you were a little boy, Victor, you cut your finger, once, a deep cut, clear to the bone. You came in from the garden to have it bandaged. Your lips were blue, but you didn't cry. You didn't make a sound. Your mother was so angry at me because I laughed happily. But, you see, I was proud of you. I knew I would always be proud of you. . . . You know, you were so funny, when your mother made you wear a velvet suit with a big lace collar. You were so angry—and so pretty! You had curly hair . . . Well, all that doesn't matter. It's only that I can't say anything against you, Victor. I can't think anything against you. So I won't question you. I'll only ask you for one favor: you can't save your sister, I know it; but ask your friends—I know you have friends who can do it—just ask them to have her sent to the same prison with Sasha. Just that. It won't interfere with the sentence and it won't compromise you. It's one last favor to her—a death-bed favor, Victor, for you know you'll never see her again. Just do that—and the book will be closed. I'll never look back. I'll never try to read some of the pages which I don't want to see. That will settle all our accounts. I'll still go on having a son, and even if it's hard, sometimes, not to think, one can do it, these days, one has to, and you'll help me. Just one favor, in exchange for . . . in exchange for all that's past."

"Father," said Victor, "you must believe me, I'd do anything in my power, if I could. . . . I've tried, but . . ."

"Victor, we won't argue. I'm not asking whether you can do it. I know you can. Don't explain. Just say yes or no. Only, if it's no, Victor, then it's the end for you and me. Then I have no son any longer. There's a limit, Victor, to how much I can forgive."

"But, Father, it is thoroughly impossible, and . . ."

"Victor, I said if it's no, I have no son any longer. Think of how much I've lost these last few years. Now what is the answer?"

"I can do nothing."

Vasili Ivanovitch straightened his shoulders slowly, the two lines that cut his cheeks, from his nostrils to the corners of his mouth, looked set, firm, emotionless. He turned and walked to the door.

"Where are you going?" Victor asked.

"That," said Vasili Ivanovitch, "does not concern you any longer."

In the dining room, Marisha and Acia were sitting at the

table, staring at the plates of a cold dinner they had not touched.

"Acia," said Vasili Ivanovitch, "get your coat and hat."

"Father!" Marisha's chair clattered back as she leaped to her feet; it was the first time she had ever addressed that word to Vasili Ivanovitch.

"Marisha," Vasili Ivanovitch said gently, "I'll telephone you in a few days . . . when I find a place to live. Will you then send my things over . . . what's left of mine here?"

"You can't go!" said Marisha, her voice breaking. "With no job and no money and . . . This is your house."

"This is your husband's house," said Vasili Ivanovitch. "Come on, Acia."

"May I take my stamp collection along?" Acia muttered.

"Take your stamp collection along."

Marisha knelt on the window sill, her nose flattened against the glass, her back heaving in silent sobs, and watched them go. Vasili Ivanovitch's shoulders drooped and, under the street lantern, she could see the white patch of his bare neck, between the collar of his old coat and the black fur cap on his bowed head; he held Acia's hand, and her arm was stretched up to his, and she seemed very small next to his huge bulk; she shuffled obediently, heels first, through a brown slush, and clutched the big stamp album to her breast.

*

Kira saw Irina in a cell of the G.P.U. on the evening of her departure. Irina smiled calmly; her smile was soft, wondering; her eyes, in a face that looked like wax, stared at Kira gently, vaguely, as if fixed, with quiet astonishment, on something distant that she was struggling to understand.

"I'll send you mittens," said Kira, trying to smile, "woolen ones. Only I warn you, I'll knit them myself, so don't be surprised if you won't be able to wear them."

"No," said Irina, "but you can send me a snapshot. It will look nice: Kira Argounova knitting!"

"And you know," said Kira, "you've never given me that drawing you promised."

"That's right, I haven't. Father has them all. Tell him to let you select any that you want. Tell him I said so. Still, it's not what I promised you. I promised a real portrait of Leo."

"Well, we'll have to wait for that till you come back."

"Yes." Then she jerked her head and laughed. "It's nice of you, Kira, only you don't have to fool me. I'm not afraid.

But I know. Remember, when they sent those University students to Siberia? You don't hear of any of them coming back. It's the scurvy or consumption, or both. . . . Oh, it's all right. I know it."

"Irina . . ."

"Come on, we don't have to be emotional, even if it is the last time. . . . There's something I wanted to ask you, Kira. You don't have to answer, if you don't want to, it's just curiosity: what is there between you and Andrei Taganov?"

"I've been his mistress for over a year," said Kira. "You see, Leo's aunt in Berlin didn't . . ."

"It's just as I thought. Well, kid, I don't know which one of us needs more courage to face the future."

"I'll be afraid only on a day that will never come," said Kira. "The day when I give up."

"I've given up," said Irina, "and I'm not afraid. Only there's something I would like to understand. And I don't think anyone can explain it. You see, I know it's the end for me. I know it, but I can't quite believe it, I can't feel it. It's so strange. There's your life. You begin it, feeling that it's something so precious and rare, so beautiful that it's like a sacred treasure. Now it's over, and it doesn't make any difference to anyone, and it isn't that they are indifferent, it's just that they don't know, they don't know what it means, that treasure of mine, and there's something about it that they should understand. I don't understand it myself, but there's something that should be understood by all of us. Only what is it, Kira? What?"

*

Political convicts traveled in a separate car; men with bayonets stoods at its doors. Irina and Sasha sat facing each other on hard wooden benches; they had traveled together part of the way, but they were approaching a junction where Irina was to be transferred to another train. The car windows were black and lustrous, as if sheets of dusty patent leather had been pasted behind the glass panes; only the fluffy, wet stars of snow, smashing against the glass, showed that there was an earth beyond the panes, and wind, and a black sky. A lantern trembled high under the ceiling, as if every knock of the wheels under the floor kicked the yellow flame out, and it fluttered and came back again, shivering, clutching the little stub of candle. A boy in an old green student's cap, alone by a window, sang softly, monotonously, through his teeth, and his voice sounded as if he were grinning, although his cheeks were motionless:

> *"Hey, little apple*
> *Where are you rolling?"*

Sasha held Irina's hands. She was smiling, her chin buried in an old woolen scarf. Her hands were cold. A white vapor fluttered at her lips as she whispered: "We must not think of it as ten years. It sounds so long, doesn't it? But it really isn't. You know, some philosopher said that time is only an illusion or something like that. Who was it that said it? Well, it doesn't matter. Time can pass very quickly, if one stops thinking of it. We'll still be young, when we'll . . . when we'll be free. So let's promise each other not to think of anything else. Now, promise?"

"Yes," he whispered, looking at her hands. "Irina, if only I hadn't . . ."

"And that's something you've already promised me never to mention again, not even to yourself. Darling, don't you see that it's really easier for me—this way—than to have remained at home, with you sent here alone? This way, I'll feel that we have something in common, that we're sharing something. Aren't we?"

He buried his face in her hands and said nothing.

"And listen," she whispered, bending down to his blond hair, "I know it won't always be easy to remain cheerful. Sometimes one thinks: oh, what's the use of remaining brave just for one's pride's sake? So let's agree on this: we'll both be brave for each other. When you feel the worst, just smile —and think that you're doing something for me. And I'll do the same. That will keep us together. And you know, it's very important to remain cheerful. We'll last longer."

"What for?" he asked. "We won't last long enough anyway."

"Sasha, what nonsense!" She pulled his head up by a strand of hair, looking straight into his eyes, as if she believed her every word. "Two strong, healthy creatures like us! And, anyway, I'm sure those stories are exaggerated—if you mean the hunger and the consumption. Nothing is ever as bad as it's painted."

The wheels grated under the floor, slowing down.

"Oh, God!" Sasha moaned. "Is that the station?"

The car jerked forward and the wheels went on knocking under the floor, like a mallet striking faster and faster.

"No," Irina whispered breathlessly, "not yet."

The student by the window wailed, as if he were grinning, to the rhythm of the wheels:

> *"Hey, little apple,*
> *Where are you rolling?"*

And he repeated, slowly, biting into every word, as if the words were an answer to a question, and the question itself, and a deadly certainty of some silent thought of his own: "Hey . . . little . . . apple . . . where . . . are . . . you . . . rolling?"

Irina was whispering: "Listen, here's something we can do: we can look at the moon, sometimes—and, you know, it's the same moon everywhere—and we would be looking at the same thing together that way, you see?"

"Yes," said Sasha, "it will be nice."

"I was going to say the sun, but I don't suppose there will be much sun there, so . . ." A cough interrupted her; she coughed dully, shaking, pressing her hand to her mouth.

"Irina!" he cried. "What's that?"

"Nothing," she smiled, blinking, catching her breath. "Just a little cold I caught. Those G.P.U. cells weren't heated too well."

A lantern swam past the window. Then there was nothing but the silent snowflakes splattering against the glass, but they sat, frozen, staring at the window.

Irina whispered: "I think we're approaching."

Sasha sat up, erect, his face the color of brass, darker than his hair, and said, his voice changed, firm: "If they let us write to each other, Irina, will you . . . every day?"

"Of course," she answered gaily.

"Will you . . . draw things in your letters, too?"

"With pleasure. . . . Here," she picked a small splinter of coal from the window ledge, "here, I'll draw something for you, right now."

With a few strokes, swift and sure as a surgeon's scalpel, she sketched a face on the back of her seat, an imp's face that grinned at them with a wide, crescent mouth, with eyebrows flung up, with one eye winking mischievously, a silly, infectious, irresistible grin that one could not face without grinning in answer.

"Here," said Irina, "he'll keep you company after . . . after the station. . . ."

Sasha smiled, answering the imp's smile. And suddenly throwing his head back, clenching his fists, he cried, so that the student by the window shuddered and looked at him: "Why do they talk of honor, and ideals, and duty to one's country? Why do they teach us . . ."

"Darling, not so loud! Don't think useless thoughts. There are so many useless thoughts in the world!"

At the station, another train was waiting on a parallel track. Guards with bayonets escorted some of the prisoners out. Sasha held Irina, and her bones creaked in his huge arms, and he kissed her lips, her chin, her hair, her neck, and he made a sound that was not quite a moan and not quite a beast's growl. He whispered hoarsely, furiously, into her scarf, blushing, choking, words he had always been reluctant to utter: "I . . . I . . . I love you. . . ."

A guard touched her elbow; she tore herself away from Sasha and followed the guard down the aisle. At the door, Sasha pushed the guard aside, savagely, insanely, and seized Irina again, and held her, not kissing her, looking at her stupidly, his long hands crushing the body of the wife he had never possessed.

The guard tore her away from him and pushed her out through the door. She leaned back for a second, for a last look at Sasha. She grinned at him, the homely, silly grin of her imp, her nose wrinkled, one eye winking mischievously. Then the door closed.

The two trains started moving at once. Pressed tightly to the glass pane, Sasha could see the black outline of Irina's head in the yellow square of a window in the car on the next track. The two trains rolled together, iron mallets striking faster and faster under the floor, the glow of the station swimming slowly back over the dark floor of the car that Sasha was watching. Then the grayish patch of snow between them grew wider. He could still touch the other train with his outstretched arm if the window were open, he thought; then he could still touch it if he were to fling his whole body straight to the other train; then he could reach it no longer, even were he to leap out. He tore his eyes from that other window and watched the white stretch that was growing between them, his fingers on the glass, as if he wanted to seize that white stretch and hold it, and pull with his whole strength, and stop it. The tracks were flying farther and farther apart. At the level of his eyes he could now see the bluish, steely gleams of wheels whirling down narrow bands in the snow. Then he did not look at the snow any longer. His glance clung to the tiny yellow square with a black dot that was a human figure, far away. And as the yellow square shrank swiftly, his eyes would not let it go, and he felt his glance being pulled, stretched, with a pain as excruciating as a wrenched nerve. Across an endless waste of snow, two long caterpillars crawled apart; two thin, silvery threads preceded each; the threads led, disappearing, into a black void. Sasha lost sight of the window; but he could still see a string of yellow spots that still looked square, and above them something black moving against the sky, that looked like car roofs. Then there was only a string of yellow beads, dropping into a black well. Then, there was only the dusty glass pane with patent leather pasted behind it, and he was not sure whether he still saw a string of sparks somewhere or whether it was something burned into his unblinking, dilated eyes.

Then there was only the imp left, on the back of the empty seat before him, grinning with a wide, crescent mouth, one eye winking.

IX

Comrade Victor Dunaev, one of our youngest and most brilliant engineers, has been assigned to a job on the Volkhovstroy, the great hydroelectric project of the Soviet Union. It is a responsible post, never held previously by one of his years.

The clipping from *Pravda* lay in Victor's glistening new brief case, along with a similar one from the *Krasnaya Gazeta*, and, folded carefully between them, a clipping from the Moscow *Izvestia*, even though it was only one line about "Comrade V. Dunaev."

Victor carried the brief case when he left for the construction site on Lake Volkhov, a few hours ride from Petrograd. A delegation from his Party Club came to see him off at the station. He made a short, effective speech about the future of proletarian construction, from the platform of the car, and forgot to kiss Marisha when the train started moving. The speech was reproduced in the Club's Wall Newspaper on the following day.

Marisha had to remain in Petrograd; she had her course at the Rabfac to finish and her social activities; she had suggested timidly that she would be willing to give them up and accompany Victor; but he had insisted on her remaining in the city. "My dear, we must not forget," he had told her, "that our social duties come first, above all personal considerations."

He had promised to come home whenever he was back in the city. She saw him once, unexpectedly, at a Party meeting. He explained hurriedly that he could not come home with her, for he had to take the midnight train back to the construction site. She said nothing, even though she knew that there was no midnight train.

She had developed a tendency to be too silent. At the Komsomol meetings, she made her reports in a strident, indifferent voice. When caught off guard, she sat staring vacantly ahead, her eyes puzzled.

She was left alone in the big, empty rooms of the Dunaev apartment. Victor had talked intimately to a few influential officials, and no tenants had been ordered to occupy their vacant rooms. But the silence of the apartment frightened Marisha, so she spent her evenings with her family, in her old room, next to Kira's.

When Marisha appeared, her mother sighed and muttered some complaint about the rations at the co-operative, and bent silently over her mending. Her father said: "Good evening," and gave no further sign of noticing her presence. Her little brother said: "You here again?" She had nothing to say. She sat in a corner behind the grand piano, reading a book until late at night; then she said: "Guess I'll be going," and went home.

One evening, she saw Kira crossing the room hurriedly on her way out. Marisha leaped to her feet, smiling eagerly, hopefully, although she did not know why, nor what she hoped for, nor whether she had anything to say to Kira. She made a timid step forward and stopped: Kira had not noticed her and had gone out. Marisha sat down slowly, still smiling vacantly.

*

Snow had come early. It grew by Petrograd's sidewalks in craggy mountain ranges, veined with thin, black threads of soot, spotted with brown clods and cigarette stubs and greenish, fading rags of newspapers. But under the walls of the houses, snow grew slowly, undisturbed, soft, white, billowing, pure as cotton, rising to the top panes of basement windows.

Above the streets, window sills hung as white, overloaded shelves. Cornices sparkled, trimmed with the glass lace of long icicles. Into an icy, summer-blue sky little billows of pink smoke rose slowly, melting like petals of apple blossoms.

High on the roofs, snow gathered into menacing white walls behind iron railings. Men in heavy mittens swung shovels high over the city and hurled huge, frozen white clods, as rocks, down to the pavements below; they crashed with a dull thud and a thin white cloud. Sleighs whirled sharply to avoid them; hungry sparrows, their feathers fluffed, scattered from under the muffled, thumping hoofs.

On street corners, huge cauldrons stood encased in boxes of unpainted boards. Men with shovels swung the snow up into the cauldrons, and narrow streams of dirty water gurgled from under the furnaces, running by the curb, long black threads cutting white streets.

At night, the furnaces blazed open in the darkness, little purplish-orange fires low over the ground, and ragged men slipped out of the night, bending to extend frozen hands into the red glow.

Kira walked soundlessly through the palace garden. A narrow track of footprints, half-buried under a fresh white powder, led through the deep snow to the pavilion; Andrei's footprints, she knew; few visitors ever crossed that garden. Tree trunks stood bare, black and dead like telegraph poles. The palace windows were dark; but, far at the end of the garden, showing through the stiff, naked branches, a bright yellow square hung in the darkness and a little patch of snow was golden-pink under Andrei's window.

She rose slowly up the long marble stairway. There was no light; her foot searched uncertainly for every frozen, slippery step. It was colder than in the street outside, the dead, damp, still cold of a mausoleum. Hesitantly, her hand followed the broken marble rail. She could see nothing ahead; it seemed as if the steps would never end.

When she came to a break in the railing, she stopped. She called helplessly, with a little note of laughter in her frightened voice: "Andrei!"

A wedge of light split the darkness above as he flung the door open. "Oh, Kira!" He rushed down to her, laughing apologetically: "I'm so sorry! It's those broken electric wires."

He swung her up into his arms and carried her to his room, while she laughed: "I'm sorry, Andrei, I'm getting to be such a helpless coward!"

He carried her to the blazing fireplace. He took off her coat and hat, his fingers wet with snow melting on her fur collar. He made her sit down by the fire, removed her mittens and rubbed her cold fingers between his strong palms; he unfastened her new felt overshoes, and took them off, shaking snow that sizzled on the bright red coals.

Then he turned silently, took a long, narrow box, dropped it in her lap and stood watching her, smiling. She asked: "What is this, Andrei?"

"Something from abroad."

She tore the paper and opened the box. Her mouth fell open without a sound. The box held a nightgown of black chiffon, so transparent that she saw the flames of the fireplace dancing through its thin black folds, as she held it high in frightened, incredulous fingers. "Andrei . . . where did you get that?"

"From a smuggler."

"Andrei! *You*—buying from a smuggler?"

"Why not?"

"From an . . . illegal speculator?"

"Oh, why not? I wanted it. I knew you'd want it."

"But there was a time when . . ."

"There *was*. Not now." Her fingers wrinkled the black chiffon as if they were empty. "Well?" he asked. "Don't you like it?"

"Oh, Andrei!" she moaned. "Andrei! Do they wear things like that abroad?"

"Evidently."

"Black underwear? How—oh, how silly and how lovely!"

"That's what they do abroad. They're not afraid of doing silly things that are lovely. They consider it reason enough to do things because they're lovely."

She laughed: "Andrei, they'd throw you out of the Party if they heard you say that."

"Kira, would you like to go abroad?"

The black nightgown fell to the floor. He smiled calmly, bending to pick it up: "I'm sorry. Did I frighten you, Kira?"

"What . . . what did you say?"

"Listen!" He was kneeling suddenly by her side, his arms around her, his eyes intent with a reckless eagerness she had never seen in them before. "It's an idea I've had for some time . . . at first, I thought it was insane, but it keeps coming back to me. . . . Kira, we could . . . You understand? Abroad . . . forever. . . ."

"But, Andrei . . ."

"It can be done. I could still manage to be sent there, get an assignment, some secret mission for the G.P.U. I'd get you a passport to go as my secretary. Once across the border—we'd drop the assignment, and our Red passports, and our names. We'd run away so far they'd never find us."

"Andrei, do you know what you're saying?"

"Yes. Only I don't know what I'd do there. I don't know—yet. I don't dare to think about it, when I'm alone. But I can think of it, I can talk of it when you're here with me. I want to escape before I see too much of what I see around us. To break with all of it at once. It would be like starting again, from the beginning, from a total void. But I'd have you. The rest doesn't matter. I'd grow to understand what I'm just beginning to learn from you now."

"Andrei," she stammered, "you, who were the best your Party had to offer the world . . ."

"Well, say it. Say I'm a traitor. Maybe I am. And maybe I've just stopped being one. Maybe I've been a traitor all these years—to something greater than what the Party ever offered the world. I don't know. I don't care. I feel as if I were naked, naked and empty and clear. Because, you see, I feel certain of nothing in that involved mess they call existence, of nothing but you." He noticed the look in her eyes and asked softly: "What's the matter, Kira? Have I said anything to frighten you?"

She whispered without looking at him: "No, Andrei."

"It's only what I said once—about my highest reverence—remember?"

"Yes . . ."

"Kira, will you marry me?"

Her hands fell limply. She looked at him, silently, her eyes wide and pleading.

"Kira, dearest, don't you see what we're doing? Why do we have to hide and lie? Why do I have to live in this agony of counting hours, days, weeks between our meetings. Why have I no right to call you in those hours when I think I'll go insane if I don't see you? Why do I have to keep silent? Why can't I tell them all, tell men like Leo Kovalensky, that you're mine, that you're my . . . my wife?"

She did not look frightened any longer; the name he had pronounced had given her courage, her greatest, coldest battlefield courage. She said: "Andrei, I can't."

"Why?"

"Would you do something for me, if I asked you very urgently?"

"Anything."

"Don't ask me why."

"All right."

"And I can't go abroad. But if you want to go alone . . ."

"Let's forget it, Kira. I won't ask any questions. But as for my going alone—don't you think you shouldn't say that?"

She laughed, jumping up: "Yes, let's forget it. Let's have our own bit of Europe right here. I'm going to try your gift on. Turn around and don't look."

He obeyed. When he turned again, she was standing at the fireplace, her arms crossed behind her head, fire flickering behind the black silhouette of her body, through a thin, black mist.

He was bending her backward, so that the locks of her hair, tumbling down, looked red in the glow of the fire; he was whispering: "Kira . . . I wasn't complaining tonight . . . I'm happy . . . happy that I have nothing left but you. . . ."

She moaned: "Andrei, don't say it! Please, please, don't say it!"

He did not say it again. But his eyes, his arms, the body she felt against her body, cried to her without sound: "I have nothing left but you . . . nothing . . . but you. . . ."

*

She came home long after midnight. Her room was dark, empty. She sat wearily down on the bed, to wait for Leo. She fell asleep, exhausted, her hair spilled over the foot of the bed, her body huddled in her crumpled red dress.

The telephone awakened her; it was ringing fiercely, insistently. She jumped up. It was daylight. The lamp was still burning on the table; she was alone.

She staggered to the telephone, her eyes closing heavily, her eyelids leaden. "Allo?" she muttered, leaning against the wall, her eyes closed.

"Is that you, Kira Alexandrovna?" an unctuous masculine voice asked, drawling vowels meticulously, with an anxious note in the pleasant inflection.

"Yes," said Kira. "Who . . ."

"It's Karp Morozov speaking, Kira Alexandrovna. Kira Alexandrovna, soul of mine, can you come over and take that . . . that Lev Sergeievitch home? Really, he shouldn't be seen at my house so often. It seems there was a party and . . ."

"I'll be right over," said Kira, her eyes open wide, dropping the receiver.

She dressed hurriedly. She could not fasten her coat; her fingers would not slip the buttons through the buttonholes: her fingers were trembling.

It was Morozov who opened the door when she arrived. He was in his shirtsleeves, and a vest was fastened too tightly, pulled in taut little wrinkles, across his broad stomach. He bowed low, like a peasant: "Ah, Kira Alexandrovna, soul of mine, how are we today? Sorry I had to trouble you, but . . . Come right in, come right in."

The wide, white-paneled lobby smelled of lilac and moth balls. Behind a half-open door, she heard Leo laughing, a gay, ringing, carefree laughter.

She walked straight into the dining room, without waiting for Morozov's invitation. In the dining room, a table was set for three. Antonina Pavlovna held a teacup, her little finger crooked delicately over its handle; she wore an Oriental kimono; powder was caked in white patches on her nose; lipstick was smeared in a blot between her nose and chin; her eyes seemed very small without make-up, puffed and weary. Leo sat at the table in his black trousers and dress shirt, his collar thrown open, his tie loose, his hair disheveled. He was laughing sonorously, trying to balance an egg on the edge of a knife.

He raised his head and looked at Kira, astonished. His face was fresh, young, radiant as on an early spring morning, a face that nothing, it seemed, could mar or alter. "Kira! What are you doing here?"

"Kira Alexandrovna just happened to . . ." Morozov began timidly, but Kira interrupted bluntly:

"He called me."

"Why, you . . ." Leo whirled on Morozov, his face turned into a vicious snarl; then he shook his head and laughed again, as swiftly and suddenly: "Oh, hell, that's a good one! So they all think that I have a wet-nurse to watch me!"

"Lev Sergeievitch, soul of mine, I didn't mean to . . ."

"Shut up!" Leo ordered and turned to Kira. "Well, since you're here, take your coat off and sit down and have some breakfast. Tonia, see if you have another couple of eggs."

"We're going home, Leo," Kira said quietly.

He looked at her and shrugged: "If you insist . . ." and rose slowly.

Morozov picked up his unfinished cup of tea; he poured it into his saucer and held the saucer on the tips of his fingers and drank, sucking loudly. He said, looking at Kira, then at Leo, hesitantly, over the edge of the saucer: "I . . . you see . . . it was like this: I called Kira Alexandrovna because I was afraid that you . . . you weren't well, Lev Sergeievitch, and you . . ."

". . . were drunk," Leo finished for him.

"Oh, no, but . . ."

"I was. Yesterday. But not this morning. You had no business . . ."

"It was just a little party, Kira Alexandrovna," Antonina Pavlovna interrupted soothingly. "I suppose we did stay a little too late, and . . ."

"It was five o'clock when you crawled into bed," Morozov growled. "I know, because you bumped into my bed and upset the water pitcher."

"Well, Leo brought me home," Antonina Pavlovna continued, ignoring him, "and I presume he must have been a little tired. . . ."

"A little . . ." Morozov began.

". . . drunk," Leo finished for him, shrugging.

"Plenty drunk, if you ask me." Morozov's freckles disappeared in a red flush of anger. "Just so drunk that I get up this morning and find him sprawled on the davenport in the lobby, full dress and all, and you couldn't have awakened him with an earthquake."

"Well," Leo asked indifferently, "what of it?"

"It was a grand party," said Antonina Pavlovna. "And how Leo can spend money! It was thrilling to watch. Really, Leo darling, you were too reckless, though."

"What did I do? I don't remember."

"Well, I didn't mind it when you lost so much on the roulette, and it was cute when you paid them ten rubles for every cheap glass you broke, but really you didn't have to give the waiters hundred-ruble tips."

"Why not? Let them see the difference between a gentleman and the Red trash of today."

"Yes, but you didn't have to pay the orchestra fifty rubles to shut up every time they played something you didn't like. And then, when you chose the prettiest girl in the crowd, whom you'd never seen before, and you offered her any price she named to undress before the guests, and you stuck those hundreds down her décolleté . . ."

"Well," Leo shrugged, "she had a beautiful body."

"Let's go, Leo," said Kira.

"Wait a minute, Lev Sergeievitch," Morozov said slowly, putting his saucer down. "Just where did you get all that money?"

"I don't know," said Leo. "Tonia gave it to me."

"Antonina, where did you . . ."

"Oh?" Antonina Pavlovna raised her eyebrows and looked bored. "I took that package you had under the waste basket."

"Tonia!" Morozov roared, jumping up, so that the dishes rattled on the table. "You didn't take that!"

"Certainly I took it," Antonina Pavlovna tilted her chin defiantly. "And I'm not accustomed to being reproached about money. I took it and that's that, so what are you going to do about it?"

"My God! Oh, my God! Oh, my Lord in Heaven!" Morozov grasped his head and nodded, rocking like a toy with a broken spring. "What are we going to do? That was the money we owe Syerov. It was due yesterday. And we haven't got another ruble on hand . . . and Syerov . . . well, if I don't deliver it today, he'll kill me. . . . What am I going to do? . . . He won't be kept waiting and . . ."

"Oh, he won't, eh?" Leo chuckled coldly. "Well, he'll wait and he'll like it. Stop whining like a mutt. What are you afraid of? He can do nothing to us and he knows it."

"I'm surprised at you, Lev Sergeievitch," Morozov growled, his freckles drowned in red. "You get your fair share, don't you? Do you think it was honorable to take . . ."

"Honorable?" Leo laughed resonantly, his gaiest, lightest, most insulting laughter. "Are you speaking to me? My dear friend, I've acquired the great privilege of not having to worry about that word at all. Not at all. In fact, if you find something particularly dishonorable—you may be sure I'll do it. The lower—the better. I wish you a good day. . . . Come on, Kira." He looked around uncertainly: "Where the hell's my hat?"

"Don't you remember, Leo?" Antonina Pavlovna reminded him gently. "You lost it on the way home."

"That's right, I did. Well, I'll buy another one. Buy three of them. So long."

Kira called a sleigh and they rode home in silence.

When they were alone in their room, Leo said brusquely: "I won't have any criticism from you or anybody else. And you, particularly, have no complaints to make. I haven't slept with any other woman, if that's what you're worried about, and that's all you have to know."

"I wasn't worried, Leo. I have no complaints to make and no criticism. But I want to speak to you. Will you listen?"

He said: "Sure," indifferently, and sat down.

She knelt before him and slipped her arms around him and shook her hair back, her eyes wide, intent, her voice tense with the calm of a last effort: "Leo, I can't reproach you. I can't blame you. I know what you're doing. I know why you're doing it. But listen: it's not too late; they haven't caught you; you still have time. Let's make an effort, a last one: let's save all we can and apply for a foreign passport. Let's run to the point of the earth that's the farthest from this damned country."

He looked into her flaming eyes with eyes that were like mirrors which could not reflect a flame any longer. "Why bother?" he asked.

"Leo, I know what you'll say. You have no desire to live. You don't care any more. But listen: do it without desire. Even if you don't believe you'll ever care again. Just postpone your final judgment on yourself; postpone it till you get there. When you're free in a human country again—then see if you still want to live."

"You little fool! Do you think they give foreign passports to men with my record?"

"Leo, we have to try. We can't give up. We can't go on for one minute without that hope ahead of us. Leo, it can't get you! I won't let it get you!"

"Who? The G.P.U.? How are you going to stop it?"

"No! Not the G.P.U. Forget the G.P.U. There's something worse, much worse. It got Victor. It got Andrei. It got mother. It won't get you."

"What do you mean, it got Victor? Are you comparing me to that bootlicking rat, that . . ."

"Leo, the bootlicking and all those things—that's nothing. There's something much worse that it's done to Victor, underneath, deeper, more final—and the bootlicking, it's only a consequence. It does that. It kills something. Have you ever seen plants grown without sunlight, without air? I won't let it do that to you. Let it take a hundred and fifty million living creatures. But not you, Leo! Not you, my highest reverence . . ."

"What an exaggerated expression! Where did you get that?"
She stared at him, repeating: "Where did I . . ."

"Really, Kira, sometimes I wonder why you've never outgrown that tendency to be so serious about everything. Nothing is getting me. Nothing is doing anything to me. I'm doing what I please, which is more than you can say about anyone else these days."

"Leo, listen! There's something I want to do—to try. We have a lot of things to untangle, you and I both. And it's not easy. Let's try to slash it all off, at once."

"By doing what?"

"Leo, let's get married."

"Huh?" He stared at her incredulously.

She repeated: "Let's get married."

He threw his head back and laughed. He laughed resonantly, a clear, light, icy laughter, as he had laughed at Andrei Taganov, as he had laughed at Morozov. "What's this, Kira? The make-an-honest-woman-of-you nonsense?"

"No, it's not that."

"Rather late for the two of us, isn't it?"

"Why not, Leo?"

"What for? Do we need it?"

"No."

"Then why do it?"

"I don't know. But I'm asking it."

"That's not reason enough to do something senseless. I'm not in a mood to become a respectable husband. If you're afraid of losing me—no scrap of paper, scribbled by a Red clerk, is going to hold me."

"I'm not afraid of losing you. I'm afraid that you will lose yourself."

"But a couple of rubles at the Zags and the Upravdom's blessing will save my soul, is that it?"

"Leo, I have no reasons to offer. But I'm asking it."

"Are you delivering an ultimatum?"

She said softly, with a quiet smile of surrender and resignation: "No."

"Then we'll forget about it."

"Yes, Leo."

He slipped his hands under her armpits and pulled her up into his arms, and said wearily: "You crazy, hysterical child! You drive yourself into a fit over some weird fears. Now forget about it. We'll save every ruble from now on, if that's what you want. You can put it away for a trip to Monte Carlo or

San Francisco or the planet Jupiter. And we won't talk about it again. All right?"

He was smiling, his arrogant smile on a face that remained incredibly beautiful, a face that was like a drug to her, inexplicable, unconditional, consummate like music. She buried her head on his shoulder, repeating helplessly, hopelessly, a name as a drug: "Leo . . . Leo . . . Leo . . ."

X

Pavel Syerov had a drink before he came to his office. He had another drink in the afternoon. He had telephoned Morozov and a voice he knew to be Morozov's had told him that the Citizen Morozov was not at home. He paced up and down his office and smashed an inkstand. He found a misspelled word in a letter he had dictated, and threw the letter, crumpled into a twisted ball, at his secretary's face. He telephoned Morozov and got no answer. A woman telephoned him and her soft, lisping voice said sweetly, insistently: "But, Pavlusha darling, you promised me that bracelet!" A speculator brought a bracelet tied in the corner of a dirty handkerchief, and refused to leave it without the full amount in cash. Syerov telephoned Morozov at the Food Trust; a secretary demanded to know who was calling; Syerov slammed the receiver down without answering. He roared at a ragged applicant for a job that he would turn him over to the G.P.U. and ordered his secretary to throw out all those waiting to see him. He left the office an hour earlier than usual and slammed the door behind him.

He walked past Morozov's house on his way home and hesitated, but saw a militia-man on the corner and did not enter.

At dinner—which had been sent from a communal kitchen two blocks away, and was cold, with grease floating over the cabbage soup—Comrade Sonia said: "Really, Pavel, I've got to have a fur coat. I can't allow myself to catch a cold— you know—for the child's sake. And no rabbit fur, either. I know you can afford it. Oh, I'm not saying anything about anyone's little activities, but I'm just keeping my eyes open."

He threw his napkin into the soup and left the table without eating.

He called Morozov's house and let the telephone ring for five minutes. There was no answer. He sat on the bed and emptied a bottle of vodka. Comrade Sonia left for a meeting of the Teachers' Council of an Evening School for Illiterate Women House Workers. He emptied a second bottle.

Then he rose resolutely, swaying a little, pulled his belt tight across his fur jacket and went to Morozov's house.

He rang three times. There was no answer. He kept his finger on the bell button, leaning indifferently against the wall. He heard no sound behind the door, but he heard steps rising up the stairs and he flung himself into the darkest corner of the landing. The steps died on the floor below and he heard a door opening and closing. He could not let himself be seen waiting there, he remembered dimly. He reached for his note-book and wrote, pressing the notebook to the wall, in the light of a street lamp outside:

MOROZOV, YOU GOD-DAMN BASTARD!

If you don't come across with what's due me before tomorrow morning, you'll eat breakfast at the G.P.U., and you know what that means.

Affectionately,

PAVEL SYEROV.

He folded the note and slipped it under the door.

Fifteen minutes later, Morozov stepped noiselessly out of his bathroom and tiptoed to the lobby. He listened nervously, but heard no sound on the stair-landing. Then he noticed the faint blur of white in the darkness, on the floor.

He picked up the note and read it, bending under the dining-room lamp. His face looked gray.

The telephone rang. He shuddered, frozen to the spot, as if the eyes somewhere behind that ringing bell could see him with the note in his hand. He crammed the note deep into his pocket and answered the telephone, trembling.

It was an old aunt of his and she sniffled into the receiver, asking to borrow some money. He called her an old bitch and hung up.

Through the open bedroom door, Antonina Pavlovna, sitting at her dressing table, brushing her hair, called out in a piercing voice, objecting to the use of such language. He whirled upon her ferociously: "If it weren't for you and that damn lover of yours . . ."

Antonina Pavlovna shrieked: "He's not my lover—yet! If he were, do you think I'd be squatting around a sloppy old fool like you?"

They had a quarrel.

Morozov forgot about the note in his pocket.

*

The European roof garden had a ceiling of glass panes; it looked like a black void staring down, crushing those below more implacably than a steel vault. There were lights; yellow lights that looked dimmed in an oppressive haze which was cigarette smoke, or heat, or the black abyss above. There were white tables and yellow glints in the silverware.

Men sat at the tables. Yellow sparks flashed in their diamond studs and in the beads of moisture on their red, flushed faces. They ate; they bent eagerly over their plates; they chewed hurriedly, incredulously; they were not out on a carefree evening in a gay night spot; they were *eating*.

In a corner, a yellowish bald head bent over a red steak on a white plate; the man cut the steak, smacking his fleshy red lips. Across the table, a red-headed girl of fifteen ate hastily, her head drawn into her shoulders; when she raised her head, she blushed from the tip of her short, freckled nose to her white, freckled neck, and her mouth was twisted as if she were going to scream.

A fierce jet of smoke swayed by a dark window pane; a thin individual, with a long face that betrayed too closely its future appearance as a skull, rocked monotonously on the back legs of his chair, and smoked without interruption, holding a cigarette in long, yellow fingers, spouting smoke out of wide nostrils frozen in a sardonic, unhealthy grin.

Women moved among the tables, with an awkward, embarrassed insolence. A head of soft, golden waves nodded unsteadily under a light, wide eyes in deep blue rings, a young mouth open in a vicious, sneering smile. In the middle of the room, a gaunt, dark woman with knobs on her shoulders, holes under her collar-bones and a skin the color of muddy coffee, was laughing too loudly, opening painted lips like a gash over strong white teeth and very red gums.

The orchestra played "John Gray." It flung brief, blunt notes out into space, as if tearing them off the strings before they were ripe, hiding the gap of an uncapturable gaiety under a convulsive rhythm.

Waiters glided soundlessly through the crowd and bent over the tables, obsequious and exaggerated, and their flabby jowls conveyed expressions of respect, and mockery, and pity for those guilty, awkward ones who made such an effort to be gay.

Morozov did remember that he had to raise money before morning. He came to the European roof garden, alone. He sat at three different tables, smoked four different cigars and whispered confidentially into five different ears that belonged to corpulent men who did not seem to be in a hurry. At the end of two hours, he had the money in his wallet.

He mopped his forehead with relief, sat alone at a table in a dark corner and ordered cognac.

Stepan Timoshenko leaned so far across a white table cloth that he seemed to be lying on, rather than sitting at, the table. His head was propped on his elbow, his fingers on the nape of his broad neck; he had a glass in his other hand. When the glass was empty, he held it uncertainly in the air, wondering how to refill it with one hand; he solved the problem by dropping the glass with a sonorous crash and lifting the bottle to his lips. The maitre d'hotel looked at him nervously, sidewise, frowning; he frowned at the jacket with the rabbit fur collar, at the crumpled sailor cap sliding over one ear, at the muddy shoes flung out onto the satin train of a woman at the next table. But the maitre d'hotel had to be cautious; Stephan Timoshenko had been there before; everyone knew that he was a Party member.

A waiter slid unobtrusively up to his table and gathered the broken glass into a dust-pan. Another waiter brought a sparkling clean glass and slipped his fingers gently over Timoshenko's bottle, whispering: "May I help you, citizen?"

"Go to hell!" said Timoshenko and pushed the glass across the table with the back of his hand. The glass vacillated on the edge and crashed down. "I'll do as I please!" Timoshenko roared, and heads turned to look at him. "I'll drink out of a bottle if I please. I'll drink out of two bottles!"

"But, citizen . . ."

"Want me to show you how?" Timoshenko asked, his eyes gleaming ominously.

"No, indeed, citizen," the waiter said hastily.

"Go to hell," said Timoshenko with soft persuasion. "I don't like your snoot. I don't like any of the snoots around here." He rose, swaying, roaring: "I don't like any of the damn snoots around here!"

He staggered among the tables. The maitre d'hotel whispered gently at his lebow: "If you're not feeling well, citizen . . ."

"Out of my way!" bellowed Timoshenko, tripping over a woman's slippers.

He had almost reached the door, when he stopped suddenly and his face melted into a wide, gentle smile. "Ah," he said. "A friend of mine. A dear friend of mine!"

He staggered to Morozov, swung a chair high over some-one's head, planted it with a resounding smash at Morozov's table and sat down.

"I beg your pardon, citizen?" Morozov gasped, rising.

"Sit still, pal," said Timoshenko and his huge tanned paw pressed Morozov's shoulder down, like a sledge hammer, so that Morozov fell back on his chair with a thud. "Can't run away from a friend, Comrade Morozov. We're friends, you know. Old friends. Well, maybe you don't know me. Stepan Timoshenko's the name. Stepan Timoshenko. . . . Of the Red Baltfleet," he added as an after-thought.

"Oh," said Morozov. "Oh."

"Yep," said Timoshenko, "an old friend and admirer of yours. And you know what?"

"No," said Morozov.

"We gotta have a drink together. Like good pals. We gotta have a drink. Waiter!" he roared so loudly that a violinist missed a note of "John Gray.".

"Bring us two bottles!" Timoshenko ordered when a waiter bowed hesitantly over his shoulder. "No! Bring us three bottles!"

"Three bottles of what, citizen?" the waiter asked timidly.

"Of anything," said Timoshenko. "No! Wait! What's the most expensive? What is it that the good, fat capitalists guzzle in proper style?"

"Champagne, citizen?"

"Make it champagne and damn quick! Three bottles and two glasses!"

When the waiter brought the champagne, Timoshenko poured it and planted a glass before Morozov. "There!" said Timoshenko with a friendly smile. "Going to drink with me, pal?"

"Yes, co . . . comrade," said Morozov meekly. "Thank you, comrade."

"Your health, Comrade Morozov!" said Timoshenko, solemnly, raising his glass. "To Comrade Morozov, citizen of the Union of Socialist Soviet Republics!"

They clinked their glasses. Morozov glanced around furtively, helplessly, but no help was coming. He drank, the glass trembling at his lips. Then he smiled ingratiatingly: "This was very nice of you, comrade," he muttered, rising. "And I appreciate it very much, comrade. Now if you don't mind. I've got to be going and . . ."

"Sit still," ordered Timoshenko. He refilled his glass and raised it, leaning back, smiling, but his smile did not seem friendly any longer and his dark eyes were looking at Morozov steadily, sardonically. "To the great Citizen Morozov, the man who beat the revolution!" he said and laughed resonantly, and emptied the glass in one gulp, his head thrown back.

"Comrade . . ." Morozov muttered through lips he could barely force open, "comrade . . . what do you mean?"

Timoshenko laughed louder and leaned across the table toward Morozov, his elbows crossed, his cap far back on his head, over sticky ringlets of dark hair. The laughter stopped abruptly, as if slashed off. Timoshenko said softly, persuasively, with a smile that frightened Morozov more than the laughter: "Don't look so scared, Comrade Morozov. You don't have to be afraid of me. I'm nothing but a beaten wretch, beaten by you, Comrade Morozov, and all I want is to tell you humbly that I know I'm beaten and I hold no grudge. Hell, I hold a profound admiration for you, Comrade Morozov. You've taken the greatest revolution the world has ever seen and patched the seat of your pants with it!"

"Comrade," said Morozov with a blue-lipped determination, "I don't know what you're talking about."

"Oh, yes," said Timoshenko ruefully. "Oh, yes, you do. You know more about it than I do, more than millions of young fools do, that watch us from all over the world with worshipping eyes. You must tell them, Comrade Morozov. You have a lot to tell them."

"Honestly, comrade, I . . ."

"For instance, you know how you made us do it. I don't. All I know is that we've done it. We made a revolution. We had red banners. The banners said that we made it for the world proletariat. We had fools who thought in their doomed hearts that we made it for all those downtrodden ones who suffer on this earth. But you and me, Comrade Morozov, we have a secret. We know, but we won't tell. Why tell? The world doesn't want to hear it. We know that the revolution—it was made for you, Comrade Morozov, and hats off to you!"

"Comrade whoever you are, comrade," Morozov moaned, "what do you want?"

"Just to tell you it's yours, Comrade Morozov."

"What?" Morozov asked, wondering if he was going insane.

"The revolution," said Timoshenko pleasantly. "The revolution. Do you know what a revolution is? I'll tell you. We killed. We killed men in the streets, and in the cellars, and aboard our ships. . . . Aboard our ships . . . I remember . . . There was one boy—an officer—he couldn't have been more than twenty. He made the sign of the cross—his mother must've taught him that. He had blood running out of his mouth. He looked at me. His eyes—they weren't frightened any more. They were kind of astonished. About something his mother hadn't taught him. He looked at me. That was the last thing. He looked at me."

Drops were rolling down Timoshenko's jowls. He filled a glass and it tottered uncertainly in his hand, trying to find his mouth, and he drank without knowing that he was drinking, his eyes fixed on Morozov's.

"That's what we did in the year nineteen-hundred-and-seventeen. Now I'll tell you what we did it for. We did it so that the Citizen Morozov could get up in the morning and scratch his belly, because the mattress wasn't soft enough and it made his navel itch. We did it so that he could ride in a big limousine with a down pillow on the seat and a little glass tube for flowers by the window, lilies-of-the-valley, you know. So that he could drink cognac in a place like this. So that he could scramble up, on holidays, to a stand all draped in red bunting and make a speech about the proletariat. We did it, Comrade Morozov, and we take a bow. Don't glare at me like that, Comrade Morozov, I'm only your humble servant, I've done my best for you, and you should reward me with a smile, really, you have a lot to thank me for!"

"Comrade!" Morozov panted. "Let me go!"

"Sit still!" Timoshenko roared. "Pour yourself a glass and drink. Do you hear me? Drink, you bastard! Drink and listen!"

Morozov obeyed; his glass tinkled, shaking, against the bottle.

"You see," said Timoshenko, as if each word were tearing his throat on its way out, "I don't mind that we're beaten. I don't mind that we've taken the greatest of crimes on our shoulders and then let it slip through our fingers. I wouldn't mind it if we had been beaten by a tall warrior in a steel helmet, a human dragon spitting fire. But we're beaten by a louse. A big, fat, slow, blond louse. Ever seen lice? The blond ones are the fattest. . . . It was our own fault. Once, men were ruled with a god's thunder. Then they were ruled with a sword. Now they're ruled with a Primus. Once, they were held by reverence. Then they were held by fear. Now they're held by their stomachs. Men have worn chains on their necks, and on their wrists, and on their ankles. Now they're enchained by their rectums. Only you don't hold heroes by their rectums. It was our own fault."

"Comrade, for God's sake, comrade, why tell it all to me?"

"We started building a temple. Do we end with a chapel? No! And we don't even end with an outhouse. We end with a musty kitchen with a second-hand stove! We set fire under a kettle and we brewed and stirred and mixed blood and fire and steel. What are we fishing now out of the brew? A new humanity? Men of granite? Or at least a good and horrible monster? No! Little puny things that wiggle. Little things that can bend both ways, little double-jointed spirits. Little things that don't even bow humbly to be whipped. No! They take the lash obediently and whip themselves! Ever sat at a social-activity club meeting? Should. Do you good. Learn a lot about the human spirit."

"Comrade!" Morozov breathed. "What do you want? Is it money you want? I'll pay. I'll . . ."

Timoshenko laughed so loudly that heads turned and Morozov cringed, trying not to be noticed. "You louse!" Timoshenko roared, laughing. "You fool, near-sighted, demented louse! Who do you think you're talking to? Comrade Victor Dunaev? Comrade Pavel Syerov? Comrade . . ."

"Comrade!" Morozov roared, so that heads turned to him, but he did not care any longer. "You . . . you . . . you have no right to say that! I have nothing whatever to do with Comrade Syerov! I . . ."

"Say," Timoshenko remarked slowly, "I didn't say you had. Why the excitement?"

"Well, I thought . . . I . . . you . . ."

"I didn't say you had," Timoshenko repeated. "I only said you should have. You and he and Victor Dunaev. And about one million others—with Party cards and stamps affixed. The winners and the conquerors. Those who crawl. That, pal, is the great slogan of the men of the future: those who crawl.

Listen, do you know how many millions of eyes are watching us across lands and oceans? They're not very close and they can't see very well. They see a big shadow rising. They think it's a huge beast. They're too far to see that it's soft and brownish and fuzzy. You know, fuzzy, a glistening sort of fuzz. They don't know that it's made of cockroaches. Little, glossy, brown cockroaches, packed tight, one on the other, into a huge wall. Little cockroaches that keep silent and wiggle their whiskers. But the world is too far to see the whiskers. That's what's wrong with the world, Comrade Morozov: they don't see the whiskers!"

"Comrade! Comrade, what are you talking about?"

"They see a black cloud and they hear thunder. They've been told that behind the cloud, blood is running freely, and men fight, and men kill, and men die. Well, what of it? They, those who watch, are not afraid of blood. There's an honor in blood. But do they know that it's not blood we're bathed in, it's pus? Listen, I'll give you advice. If you want to keep this land in your tentacles, tell the world that you're chopping heads off for breakfast and shooting men by the regiment. Let the world think that you're a huge monster to be feared and respected and fought honorably. But don't let them know that yours is not an army of heroes, nor even of fiends, but of shriveled bookkeepers with a rupture who've learned to be arrogant. Don't let them know that you're not to be shot, but to be disinfected. Don't let them know that you're not to be fought with cannons, but with carbolic acid!"

Morozov's napkin was crumpled into a drenched ball in his fist. He wiped his forehead once more. He said, trying to make his voice gentle and soothing, trying to rise imperceptibly: "You're right, comrade. Those are very fine sentiments. I agree with you absolutely. Now if you'll allow . . ."

"Sit down!" roared Timoshenko. "Sit down and drink a toast. Drink it or I'll shoot you like a mongrel. I still carry a gun, you know. Here . . ." he poured and a pale golden trickle ran down the table cloth to the floor. "Drink to the men who took a red banner and wiped their ass with it!"

Morozov drank.

Then he put his hand in his pocket and took out a handkerchief to mop his forehead. A crumpled piece of paper fell to the floor.

It was the swift, ferocious jerk, with which Morozov plunged down for it, that made Timoshenko's fist dart out and seize Morozov's hand. "What's that, pal?" asked Timoshenko.

Morozov's foot kicked the paper out of reach and it rolled under an empty table. Morozov said indifferently, little damp beads sparkling under his wide nostrils: "Oh, that? Nothing, comrade. Nothing at all. Just some scrap of waste paper."

"Oh," said Timoshenko, watching him with eyes that were alarmingly sober. "Oh, just a scrap of waste paper. Well, we'll let it lie there. We'll let the janitor throw it in the waste basket."

"Yes," Morozov nodded eagerly, "that's it. In the waste basket. Very well put, comrade." He giggled, mopping his forehead. "We'll let the janitor throw it in the waste basket. Would you like another drink, comrade? The bottle's empty. The next one's on me. Waiter! Another bottle of the same."

"Sure," said Timoshenko without moving. "I'll have another drink."

The waiter brought the bottle. Morozov filled the glasses, leaning solicitously over the table. He said, regaining his voice syllable by syllable: "You know, comrade, I think you misunderstood me, but I don't blame you. I can see your motives and I sympathize thoroughly. There are so many objectionable —er—shall we say dishonorable?—types these days. One has to be careful. We must get better acquainted, comrade. It's hard to tell at a glance, you know, and particularly in a place like this. I bet you thought I was a—a speculator, or something. Didn't you? Very funny, isn't it?"

"Very," said Timoshenko. "What are you looking down at, Comrade Morozov?"

"Oh!" Morozov giggled, jerking his head up. "I was just looking at my shoes, comrade. They're sort of tight, you know. Uncomfortable. Guess it's because I'm on my feet so much, you know, in the office."

"Uh-huh," said Timoshenko. "Shouldn't neglect your feet. Should take a hot bath when you come home, a pan of hot water with a little vinegar. That's good for sore feet."

"Oh, indeed? I'm glad you told me. Yes, indeed, thank you very much. I'll be sure and try it. First thing when I get home."

"About time you were getting home, isn't it, Comrade Morozov?"

"Oh! . . . well, I guess . . . well, it's not so late yet and . . ."

"I thought you were in a hurry a little while ago."

"I . . . well, no, I can't say that I'm in any particular hurry, and besides, such a pleasant . . ."

"What the matter, Comrade Morozov? Anything you don't want to leave around here?"

"Who, me? I don't know what that could be, comrade . . . comrade . . . what did you say your name was, comrade?"

"Timoshenko. Stepan Timoshenko. It isn't that little scrap of waste paper down there under the table, by any chance?"

"Oh, that? Why, Comrade Timoshenko, I'd forgotten all about that. What would I want with it?"

"I don't know," said Timoshenko slowly.

"That's just it, Comrade Timoshenko, nothing. Nothing at all. Another drink, Comrade Timoshenko?"

"Thanks."

"Here you are, comrade."

"Anything wrong under the table, Comrade Morozov?"

"Why no, Comrade Timoshenko. I was just bending to tie my shoe lace. The shoe lace is unfastened."

"Where?"

"Well, isn't that funny? It really isn't unfastened at all. See? And I thought it was. You know how it is, these Soviet . . . these shoe laces nowadays. Not solid at all. Not dependable."

"No," said Timoshenko, "they tear like twine."

"Yes," said Morozov, "just like twine. Just, as you would say, like—like twine. . . . What are you leaning over for, Comrade Timoshenko? You're not comfortable. Why don't you move over here like this, you'll be more . . ."

"No," said Timoshenko, "I'm just fine here where I am. With a fine view of the table there. I like that table. Nice legs it has. Hasn't it? Sort of artistic, you know."

"Quite right, comrade, very artistic. Now on the other hand, comrade, there, on our left, isn't that a pretty blonde there, by the orchestra? Quite a figure, eh?"

"Yes, indeed, comrade. . . . It's nice shoes you have, Comrade Morozov. Patent leather, too. Bet you didn't get those in a co-operative."

"No . . . that is . . . to tell you the truth . . . well, you see . . ."

"What I like about them is that bulb. Right there, on the toes. Like a bump on someone's forehead. And shiny, too. Yep, those foreigners sure know how to make shoes."

"Speaking of the efficiency of production, comrade, take for instance, in the capitalistic countries . . . in the . . . in the . . ."

"Yes, Comrade Morozov, in the capitalistic countries?"

It was Morozov who leaped for the letter. It was Timoshenko who caught his wrist with fingers like talons, and for one brief moment they were on their hands and knees on the floor, and their eyes met silently like those of two beasts in deadly battle. Then Timoshenko's other hand seized the letter, and he rose slowly, releasing Morozov, and sat down at the table. He was reading the letter, while Morozov was still on his hands and knees, staring up at him with the eyes of a man awaiting the verdict of a court-martial.

MOROZOV, YOU GOD-DAMN BASTARD!

If you don't come across with what's due me before tomorrow morning, you'll eat breakfast at the G.P.U., and you know what that means,

Affectionately,

PAVEL SYEROV.

Morozov was sitting at the table when Timoshenko raised his head from the letter. Timoshenko laughed as Morozov had never heard a man laugh.

Timoshenko rose slowly, laughing. His stomach shook, and his rabbit fur collar, and the sinews of his bare throat. He swayed a little and he held the letter in both hands. Then his laughter died down slowly, smoothly, like a gramophone record unwinding, to a low, coughing chuckle on a single dry note. He slipped the letter into his pocket and turned slowly, his shoulders stooped, his movements suddenly awkward, humble. He shuffled heavily, uncertainly to the door. At the door, the maitre d'hotel glanced at him sidewise. Timoshenko returned the glance; Timoshenko's glance was gentle.

Morozov sat at the table, one hand frozen in mid-air in an absurd, twisted position, like the hand of a paralytic. He heard Timoshenko's chuckles dropping down the stairway; monotonous, disjoined chuckles that sounded like hiccoughs, like barks, like sobs.

He jumped up suddenly. "Oh my God!" he moaned. "Oh, my God!"

He ran, forgetting his hat and coat, down the long stairs, out into the snow. In the broad, white, silent street, Timoshenko was nowhere in sight.

*

Morozov did not send the money to Pavel Syerov. He did not go to his own office at the Food Trust. He sat all the following morning and all of the afternoon at home, in his room, and drank vodka. Whenever he heard the telephone or the door bell ringing, he crouched, his head in his shoulders, and bit his knuckles. Nothing happened.

At dinner time, Antonina Pavlovna brought the evening paper and threw it to him, snapping: "What the hell's the matter with you today?"

He glanced through the paper. There were news items on the front page:

In the village Vasilkino, in the Kama region, the peasants, goaded by the counter-revolutionary hoarder element, burned the local Club of Karl Marx. The bodies of the Club president and secretary, Party comrades from Moscow, were found in the charred ruins. A G.P.U. squad is on its way to Vasilkino.

In the village Sverskoe, twenty-five peasants were executed last night for the murder of the Village Correspondent, a young comrade from the staff of a Communist Union of Youth newspaper in Samara. The peasants refused to divulge the name of the murderer.

On the last page was a short item:

The body of Stepan Timoshenko, former sailor of the Baltic Fleet, was found early this morning under a bridge, on the ice of Obukhovsky Canal. He had shot himself through the mouth. No papers, save his Party card, were found on the body to explain the reason for his suicide.

Morozov wiped his forehead, as if a noose had been slipped off his throat, and drank two glasses of vodka.

When the telephone rang, he swaggered boldly to take the receiver, and Antonina Pavlovna wondered why he was chuckling.

"Morozov?" a muffled voice whispered over the wire.

"That you, Pavlusha?" Morozov asked. "Listen, pal, I'm awfully sorry, but I have the money and . . ."

"Forget the money," Syerov hissed. "It's all right. Listen . . . did I leave you a note yesterday?"

"Why, yes, but I guess I deserved it and . . ."

"Have you destroyed it?"

"Why?"

"Nothing. Only you understand what it could . . . Have you destroyed it?"

Morozov looked at the evening paper, grinned and said: "Sure. I have. Forget about it, pal."

He held the paper in his hand all evening long.

"The fool!" he muttered under his breath, so that Antonina Pavlovna looked at him inquisitively, chin forward. "The damn fool! He lost it. Wandered about all night, God knows where, the drunken fool. He lost it!"

Morozov did not know that Stepan Timoshenko had come home from the European roof garden and sat at a rickety table in his unheated garret and written painstakingly a letter on a piece of brown wrapping paper, in the light of a dying candle in a green bottle; that he had folded the letter carefully and slipped it into an old envelope and slipped another scrap of paper, wrinkled and creased, into the envelope, and written Andrei Taganov's address on it; that he had sealed the letter and had gone, steadily, unhurriedly, down the creaking stairs into the street.

The letter on the brown wrapping paper said:

DEAR FRIEND ANDREI,

I promised to say goodbye and here it is. It's not quite what I promised, but I guess you'll forgive. I'm sick of seeing what I see and I can't stand to see it any longer. To you—as my only legacy—I'm leaving the letter you will find enclosed. It's a hard legacy, I know. I only hope that you won't follow me—too soon.

Your friend,
STEPAN TIMOSHENKO.

XI

Pavel Syerov sat at the desk in his office, correcting the typewritten copy of his next speech on "Railroads and the Class Struggle." His secretary stood by the desk, watching anxiously the pencil in his hand. The window of his office opened upon one of the terminal platforms. He raised his head just in time to notice a tall figure in a leather jacket disappearing down the platform. Syerov jerked forward, but the man was gone.

"Hey, did you see that man?" he snapped at the secretary.

"No, Comrade Syerov. Where?"

"Never mind. It doesn't matter. I just thought it was someone I knew. Wonder what he's doing around here?"

An hour later, Pavel Syerov left his office, and—walking down the stairs, on his way to the street, chewing sunflower seeds and spitting out their shells—saw the man in the leather jacket again. He had not been mistaken: it was Andrei Taganov.

Pavel Syerov stopped, and his brows moved closer together, and he spit one more shell out of the corner of his mouth. Then he approached Andrei casually and said: "Good evening, Comrade Taganov."

Andrei answered: "Good evening, Comrade Syerov."

"Thinking of taking a trip, Andrei?"

"No."

"Hunting train speculators?"

"No."

"Been shifted to the G.P.U. transport section?"

"No."

"Well, I'm glad to see you. A rare person to see, aren't you? So busy you have no time for old friends any more. Have some sunflower seeds?"

"No, thank you."

"Don't have the dirty habit? Don't dissipate at all, do you? No vices, but one, eh? Well, I'm glad to see you taking an interest in this old station which is my home, so to speak. Been around for an hour or so, haven't you?"

"Any more questions to ask?"

"Who, me? I wasn't asking any questions. What would I be questioning you for? I was just being sociable, so to speak. One must be sociable once in a while, if one doesn't want to be branded as an individualist, you know. Why don't you drop in to see me while you're in these parts?"

"I may," said Andrei slowly. "Good-bye, Comrade Syerov."

Syerov stood, frowning, an unbroken sunflower seed between his teeth, and watched Andrei descending the stairs.

*

The clerk wiped his nose with his thumb and forefinger, wiped the linseed oil off the bottle's neck with his apron, and asked: "That all today, citizen?"

"That's all," said Andrei Taganov.

The clerk tore a piece of newspaper and wrapped the bottle, greasy stains spreading on the paper.

"Doing good business?" Andrei asked.

"Rotten," the clerk answered, shrugging his shoulders in an old blue sweater. "You're the first customer in three hours, I guess. Glad to hear a human voice. Nothing to do here but sit and scare mice off."

"That's too bad. Taking a loss, then?"

"Who, me? I don't own the joint."

"Then I guess you'll lose your job soon. The boss will be coming to do his own clerking."

"Who? My boss?" The clerk made a hoarse, cackling sound that was laughter, opening a wide hole with two broken, blackened teeth. "Not my boss, he won't. I'd like to see the elegant Citizen Kovalensky slinging herrings and linseed oil."

"Well, he won't be elegant long with such poor business."

"Maybe he won't," said the clerk, "and maybe he will."

"Maybe," said Andrei Taganov.

"Fifty kopeks, citizen."

"Here you are. Good night, citizen."

*

Antonina Pavlovna had tickets for the new ballet at the Marinsky Theater. It was a "profunion" show and Morozov had received the tickets at the Food Trust. But Morozov did not care for ballet and he had a school meeting to attend, where he was to make a speech on the "Proletarian Distribution of Food Products," so he gave the tickets to Antonina Pavlovna. She invited Leo and Kira to accompany her. "Well, of course, it's supposed to be a revolutionary ballet," she explained. "The first Red ballet. And, of course, you know my attitude on politics, but then, one should be broad-minded artistically, don't you think so? At least, it's an interesting experiment."

Kira refused the invitation. Leo left with Antonina Pavlovna. Antonina Pavlovna wore a jade green gown embroidered in gold, too tight across her stomach, and carried mother-of-pearl opera glasses on a long gold handle.

Kira had made a date with Andrei. But when she left the tramway and walked through the dark streets to the palace garden, she noticed her feet slowing down of their own will, her body tense, unyielding, fighting her, as if she were walking forward against a strong wind. It was as if her body remembered that which she was trying to forget: the night before, a night such as her first one in the gray and silver room she had shared with Leo for over three years. Her body felt pure and hallowed; her feet were slowing down to retard her progress toward that which seemed a sacrilege because she did desire it and did not wish to desire it tonight.

When she reached the top of the long, dark stairs and Andrei opened the door, she asked: "Andrei, will you do something for me?"

"Before I kiss you?"

"No. But right after. Will you take me to a motion picture tonight?"

He kissed her, his face showing nothing but the ever-incredulous joy of seeing her again, then said: "All right."

They walked out together, arm in arm, fresh snow squeaking under their feet. The three largest film theaters on Nevsky displayed huge cotton signs with red letters:

THE HIT OF THE SEASON!
NEW MASTERPIECE OF THE SOVIET CINEMA!
''RED WARRIORS''
A gigantic epic of the struggle of red heroes
in the civil war!
A SAGA OF THE PROLETARIAT!
A titanic drama of the heroic unknown masses
of Workers and Soldiers!

One theater also bore the sign:

COMRADE LENIN SAID: "OF ALL THE ARTS, THE MOST IMPORTANT ONE FOR RUSSIA IS THE CINEMA!"

The theater entrances blazed in streams of white light. The cashiers watched the passersby wistfully and yawned. No one stopped to look at the display of stills.

"You don't want to see that," said Andrei.

"No," said Kira.

The fourth and smaller theater played a foreign picture. It was an old, unknown picture with no stars, no actors' names announced; three faded stills were pasted in the show window, presenting a lady with too much make-up and a dress fashionable ten years ago.

"We might as well see that," said Kira.

The box office was closed.

"Sorry, citizens," said the usher, "no seats left. All sold out for this show and the next one. The foyer's jammed with people waiting."

"Well," said Kira, as they turned away with resignation, "it may as well be 'The Red Warriors.'"

The foyer of the huge, white-columned "Parisiana" was empty. The picture was on, and no one was allowed to enter in the middle of a show. But the usher bowed eagerly and let them enter.

The theater was dark, cold, and seemed silent under the roar of the orchestra, with the echoing silence of a huge, empty room. A few heads dotted the waste of grayish, empty rows.

On the screen, a mob of ragged gray uniforms ran through mud, waving bayonets. A mob of ragged gray uniforms sat around fires, cooking soup. A long train crawled slowly through endless minutes, open box cars loaded with a mob of ragged gray uniforms. "A MONTH LATER" said a title. A mob of ragged gray uniforms ran through mud, waving bayonets. A sea of arms waved banners. A mob of ragged gray uniforms crawled down trench tops, against a black sky. "THE BATTLE OF ZAVRASHINO" said a title. A mob in patent leather boots shot a mob in bast shoes lined again a wall. "THE BATTLE OF SAMSONOVO" said a title. A mob of ragged gray uniforms ran through mud, waving bayonets. "THREE WEEKS LATER" said a title. A long train crawled into a sunset. "THE PROLETARIAT STAMPED ITS MIGHTY BOOT DOWN THE TREACHEROUS THROAT OF DEPRAVED ARISTOCRATS" said a title. A mob in patent leather boots danced in a gaudy brothel, amid broken bottles and half-naked women who looked at the camera. "BUT THE SPIRIT OF OUR RED WARRIORS FLAMED WITH LOYALTY TO THE PROLETARIAN CAUSE" said a title. A mob of ragged gray uniforms ran through mud, waving bayonets. There was no plot, no hero. "THE AIM OF PROLETARIAN ART," a poster in the foyer had explained, "IS THE DRAMA AND COLOR OF MASS LIFE."

In the intermission before the second show, Andrei asked: "Do you want to see the beginning of that?"

"Yes," said Kira. "It's still early."

"I know you don't like it."

"I know you don't, either. It's funny, Andrei, I had a chance to go to the new ballet at the Marinsky tonight, and I didn't go because it was revolutionary, and here I am looking at this epic."

"You had a chance to go with whom?"

"Oh—a friend of mine."

"Not Leo Kovalensky?"

"Andrei! Don't you think you're being presumptuous?"

"Kira, of all your friends he's the one . . ."

". . . that you don't like. I know. Still, don't you think that you're mentioning it too often?"

"Kira, you're not interested in politics, are you?"

"No. Why?"

"You've never wanted to sacrifice your life senselessly, to have years torn out of it for no good reason, years of jail or exile? Have you?"

"What are you driving at?"

"Keep away from Leo Kovalensky."

Her mouth was open and her hand was lifted in the air and she did not move for a long second. Then she asked, and no words had ever been so hard to utter:

"What—do—you—mean—Andrei?"

"You don't want to be known as the friend of a man who is friendly with the wrong kind of people."

"What people?"

"Several. Our own Comrade Syerov, for one."

"But what has Leo . . ."

"He owns a certain private food store, doesn't he?"

"Andrei, are you being the G.P.U. agent with me and . . ."

"No, I'm not questioning you. I have nothing to learn from you. I'm just wondering how much you know about his affairs —for your own protection."

"What . . . what affairs?"

"That's all I can tell you. I shouldn't have told you even that much. But I want to be sure that you don't let your name be implicated, by chance, in any way."

"Implicated—in what?"

"Kira, I'm not a G.P.U. agent—*with* you or *to* you."

The lights went out and the orchestra struck up the "Internationale."

On the screen, a mob of dusty boots marched down a dry, clotted earth. A huge, gray, twinkling, shivering rectangle of boots hung before them, boots without bodies, thick, cobbled soles, old leather gnarled, warped into creases by the muscles and the sweat inside; the boots were not slow and they were not in a hurry; they were not hoofs and they did not seem to be human feet; they rolled forward, from heels to toes, from heels to toes, like gray tanks waddling, crushing, sweeping all before them, clots of earth crumbling into dust, gray boots, dead, measured, endless, lifeless, inexorable.

Kira whispered through the roar of the "Internationale": "Andrei, are you working on a new case for the G.P.U.?"

He answered: "No. On a case of my own."

On the screen, shadows in gray uniforms sat around fires under a black sky. Calloused hands stirred iron kettles; a mouth grinned wide over crooked teeth; a man played a harmonica, rocking from side to side with a lewd grin; a man twirled in a Cossack dance, his feet flashing, his hands clapping in time; a man scratched his beard; a man scratched his neck; a man scratched his head; a man chewed a crust of bread, crumbs rolling into the open collar of his tunic, into a black, hairy chest. They were celebrating a victory.

Kira whispered: "Andrei, do you have something to report to the G.P.U.?"

He answered: "Yes."

On the screen, a demonstration marched down a city street, celebrating a victory. Banners and faces swam slowly past the camera. They moved as wax figures pulled by invisible wires, young faces in dark kerchiefs, old faces in knitted shawls, faces in soldiers' caps, faces in leather hats, faces that looked alike, set and humorless, eyes flat as if painted on, lips soft and shapeless, marching without stirring, marching without muscles, with no will but that of the cobblestones pulled forward under their motionless feet, with no energy but that of the red banners as sails in the wind, no fuel but the stuffy warmth of millions of skins, millions of flaccid, doughy muscles, no breath but the smell of patched armpits, of warm, weary, bowed necks, marching, marching, marching in an even, ceaseless movement, a movement that did not seem alive.

Kira jerked her head with a shudder that ran down to her knees and gasped: "Andrei, let's go!"

He rose swiftly, obediently.

When he motioned to a sleigh driver in the street outside, she said: "No. Let's walk. Walk. With both feet."

He took her arm, asking: "What's the matter, Kira?"

"Nothing," she walked, listening to the living sound of her heels crunching snow. "I . . . I didn't like the picture."

"I'm sorry, dear. I don't blame you. I wish they wouldn't make those things, for their own sake."

"Andrei, you wanted to leave it all, to go abroad, didn't you?"

"Yes."

"Then why are you starting something . . . against someone . . . to help the masters you no longer want to serve?"

"I'm going to find out whether they're still worth serving."

"What difference would that make to you?"

"A difference on which the rest of my life may depend."

"What do you mean?"

"I'm giving myself a last chance. I have something to put before them. I know what they should do about it. I'm afraid I know also what they're going to do about it. I'm still a member of the Party. In a very short while, I'll know whether I'll remain a member of the Party."

"You're making a test, Andrei? At the cost of several lives?"

"At the cost of several lives that should be ended."

"Andrei!"

He looked at her white face, astonished: "Kira, what's the matter? You've never questioned me about my work. We've never discussed it. You know that my work deals with lives—and death, when necessary. It has never frightened you like this. It's something the two of us must keep silent about."

"Are you forbidding me to break that silence?"

"Yes. And there's something I have to tell you. Please listen carefully and don't answer me, because, you see, I don't want to know the answer. I want you to keep silent because I don't want to learn how much you know about the case I'm investigating. I'm afraid I know already that you're not quite ignorant about it. I'm expecting the highest integrity from the men I'm going to face. Don't make me face them with less than that on my part."

She said, trying to be calm, her voice quivering, a voice with a life and a terror of its own which she could not control: "Andrei, I won't answer. Now listen and don't question me. Please don't question me! I have nothing to tell you but this: I'm begging you—you understand—begging you with all there is in me, if I ever meant anything to you, this is the only time I want to claim it, I'm begging you, while it's still in your hands, to drop this case, Andrei! for one reason only, for me!"

He turned to her and she looked into a face she had never seen before, the implacable face of Comrade Taganov of the G.P.U., a face that could have watched secret executions in dark, secret cellars. He asked slowly: "Kira, what is that man to you?"

The tone of his voice made her realize that she could protect Leo best by remaining silent. She answered, shrugging: "Just a friend. We'll keep silent, Andrei. It's late. Will you take me home?"

But when he left her at her parents' house, she waited only to hear his steps dying around the corner. Then she ran through dark streets to the first taxi she could find and leaped in, ordering: "Marinsky Theater! As fast as you can go!"

In the dim, deserted lobby of the theater, she heard the thunder of the orchestra behind closed doors, a tuneless, violent jumble of sound.

"Can't go in now, citizen," said a stern usher.

She slipped a crumpled bill into his hand, whispering: "I have to find someone, comrade. . . . It's a matter of life and death . . . his mother is dying. . . ."

She slipped noiselessly between blue velvet curtains into a dark, half-empty theater. On the glittering stage a chorus of fragile ballerinas in short, flame-red tulle skirts fluttered, waving thin, powdered arms with gilded chains of papier-mâché, in a "Dance of the Toilers."

She found Leo and Antonio Pavlovna in comfortable armchairs in an empty row. They jumped up when they saw Kira slipping toward them down the long row of chairs, and someone behind them hissed: "Sit down!"

"Leo!" Kira whispered. "Come on! Right away! Something's happened!"

"What?"

"Come on! I'll tell you! Let's get out of here!"

He followed her up the dark aisle. Antonina Pavlovna waddled hurriedly after them, her chin pointing forward.

In a corner of the empty foyer, Kira whispered: "It's the G.P.U., Leo, they're after your store. They know something."

"What? How did you find out?"

"I just saw Andrei Taganov and he . . ."

"You saw Andrei Taganov? Where? I thought you were going to visit your parents."

"Oh, I met him on the street and . . ."

"What street?"

"Leo! Stop that nonsense! Don't you understand? We have no time to waste!"

"What did he say?"

"He didn't say much. Just a few hints. He told me to keep away from you if I didn't want to be arrested. He said you had a private food store, and he mentioned Pavel Syerov. He said he had a report to make to the G.P.U. I think he knows everything."

"So he told you to keep away from me?"

"Leo! You refuse to . . ."

"I refuse to be frightened by some jealous fool!"

"Leo, you don't know him! He doesn't joke about G.P.U. matters. And he's not jealous of you. Why should he be?"

"What department of the G.P.U. is he in?"

"Secret service department."

"Not the Economic Section, then?"

"No. But he's doing it on his own."

"Well, come on. We'll call Morozov and Pavel Syerov. Let Syerov call his friend of the Economic Section and find out what your Taganov's doing. Don't get hysterical. Nothing to be afraid of. Syerov's friend will take care of it. Come on."

"Leo," Antonina Pavlovna panted, running after them, as they hurried to a taxi outside, "Leo, I had nothing to do with the store! If there's an investigation, remember, I had nothing to do with it! I only carried money to Syerov and I knew nothing about where it came from! Leo, remember!"

An hour later, a sleigh drove noiselessly up to the back entrance of the store that carried the sign "Lev Kovalensky. Food Products." Two men slipped silently down frozen, unlighted stairs to the basement, where Leo and the clerk were waiting with a dim old lantern. The newcomers made no sound. Leo pointed silently to the sacks and boxes. The men carried them swiftly up the stairs to the sleigh. The sleigh was covered with a large fur blanket. In less than ten minutes the basement was empty.

"Well?" Kira asked anxiously, when Leo came home.

"Go to bed," said Leo, "and don't dream of any G.P.U. agents."

"What did you do?"

"It's all done. We got rid of everything. It's on its way out of Red Leningrad this very minute. We had another load coming from Syerov tomorrow night, but we've cancelled that. We'll be running a pure little food store—for a while. Till Syerov checks up on things."

"Leo, I . . ."

"You won't start any arguments again. I've told you once: I'm not going to leave town. That would be the most dangerous, the most suspicious thing to do. And we have nothing to worry about. Syerov's too strong at the G.P.U. for any . . ."

"Leo, you don't know Andrei Taganov."

"No, I don't. But you seem to know him too well."

"Leo, they can't bribe him."

"Maybe not. But they can make him shut up."

"If you're not afraid . . ."

"Of course I'm not afraid!"

But his face was paler than usual and she noticed his hands, unbuttoning his coat, trembling.

"Leo, please! Listen!" she begged. "Leo, please! I . . ."
"Shut up!" said Leo.

XII

The executive of the Economic Section of the G.P.U. called Andrei Taganov into his office.

The office was in a part of the G.P.U. headquarters' building which no visitors ever approached and into which few employees were ever admitted. Those who were admitted spoke in low, respectful voices and never felt at ease.

The executive sat at his desk. He wore a military tunic, tight breeches, high boots and a gun on his hip. He had close-cropped hair and a clean-shaved face that betrayed no age. When he smiled, he showed short teeth and very wide, brownish gums. His smile betrayed no mirth, no meaning; one knew it was a smile only because the muscles of his cheeks creased and his gums showed.

He said: "Comrade Taganov, I understand you've been conducting some investigations in a case which comes under the jurisdiction of the Economic Section."

Andrei said: "I have."

"Who gave you the authority to do it?"

Andrei said: "My Party card."

The executive smiled, showing his gums, and asked: "What made you begin the investigation?"

"A piece of incriminating evidence."

"Against a Party member?"

"Yes."

"Why didn't you turn it over to us?"

"I wanted to have a complete case to report."

"Have you?"

"Yes."

"You intend to report it to the chief of your department?"

"Yes."

The executive smiled and said: "I suggest that you drop the entire matter."

Andrei said: "If this is an order, I'll remind you that you are not my chief. If it is advice, I do not need it."

The executive looked at him silently, then said: "Strict discipline and a straightforward loyalty are commendable traits, Comrade Taganov. However, as Comrade Lenin said, a Communist must be adaptable to reality. Have you considered the consequences of what you plan to expose?"

"I have."

"Do you find it advisable to make public a scandal involving a Party member—at this time?"

"That should have been the concern of the Party member involved."

"Do you know my . . . interest in that person?"

"I do."

"Does the knowledge make any difference in your plans?"

"None."

"Have you ever thought that I could be of service to you?"

"No. I haven't."

"Don't you think that it is an idea worth considering?"

"No. I don't."

"How long have you held your present position, Comrade Taganov?"

"Two years and three months."

"At the same salary?"

"Yes."

"Don't you think a promotion desirable?"

"No."

"You do not believe in a spirit of mutual help and co-operation with your Party comrades?"

"Not above the spirit of the Party."

"You are devoted to the Party?"

"Yes."

"Above all things?"

"Yes."

"How many times have you faced a Party Purge Committee?"

"Three times."

"Do you know that there is another purge coming?"

"Yes."

"And you're going to make your report on that case you've investigated—to your chief?"

"Yes."

"When?"

"At four o'clock this afternoon."

The executive looked at his wristwatch: "Very well. In an hour and a half then."

"Is that all?"

"That's all, Comrade Taganov."

*

A few days later, Andrei's chief called him into his office. The chief was a tall, thin man with a pointed blond beard and a gold pince-nez on a high, thin nose. He wore the expensive, blondish-brown suit of a foreign tourist; he had the long, knotty hands of a skeleton and the appearance of an unsuccessful college professor.

"Sit down," said the chief, and rose, and closed the door. Andrei sat down.

"Congratulations, Comrade Taganov," said the chief.

Andrei inclined his head.

"You have done a valuable piece of work and rendered a great service to the Party, Comrade Taganov. You could not have chosen a better time for it. You have put into our hands just the case we needed. With the present difficult economic situation and the dangerous trend of public sentiment, the government has to show the masses who is responsible for their suffering, and show it in a manner that will not be forgotten. The treacherous counter-revolutionary activities of speculators, who deprive our toilers of their hard-earned food rations, must be brought into the full light of proletarian justice. The workers must be reminded that their class enemies are plotting day and night to undermine the only workers' government in the world. Our toiling masses must be told that they have to bear their temporary hardships patiently and lend their full support to the government which is fighting for their interests against such heavy odds, as the case you've discovered will display to the public. This, in substance, was the subject of my conversation with the editor of the *Pravda* this morning, in regard to the campaign we are starting. We shall make an example of this case. Every newspaper, every club, every public pulpit will be mobilized for the task. The trial of Citizen Kovalensky will be broadcast into every hamlet of the U.S.S.R."

"Whose trial, comrade?"

"The trial of Citizen Kovalensky. Oh, yes, of course, by the way, that letter of Comrade Syerov which you attached to your report on the case—was that the only copy of it in existence?"

"Yes, comrade."

"Who has read it besides yourself?"

"No one."

The chief folded his long, thin hands, the tips of his fingers meeting, and said slowly: "Comrade Taganov, you will forget that you've ever read that letter."

Andrei looked at him silently.

"This is an order from the committee which investigated your report. However, I shall take the time to explain, for I appreciate your efforts in the matter. Do you read the newspapers, Comrade Taganov?"

"Yes, comrade."

"Do you know what is going on in our villages at the present time?"

"Yes, comrade."

"Are you aware of the mood in our factories?"

"Yes, comrade."

"Do you realize the precarious equilibrium of our public opinion?"

"Yes, comrade."

"In that case, I do not have to explain to you why a Party member's name must be kept from any connection with a case of counter-revolutionary speculation. Is that clear?"

"Perfectly, comrade."

"You must be very careful to remember that you know nothing about Comrade Pavel Syerov. Am I understood?"

"Thoroughly, comrade."

"Citizen Morozov will resign from his position with the Food Trust—by reason of ill health. He will not be brought into the case, for it would throw an unfavorable light on our Food Trust and create a great deal of unnecessary comment. But the real culprit and dominant spirit of the conspiracy, Citizen Kovalensky, will be arrested tonight. Does that meet with your approval, Comrade Taganov?"

"My position does not allow me to approve, comrade. Only to take orders."

"Very well said, Comrade Taganov. Of course, Citizen Kovalensky is the sole legal, registered owner of that food store, as we've checked. He is an aristocrat by birth and the son of a father executed for counter-revolution. He has been arrested before—for an illegal attempt to leave the country. He is a living symbol of the class which our working masses know to be the bitterest enemy of the Soviets. Our working masses, justly angered by lengthy privations, by long hours of waiting in lines at our co-operatives, by lack of the barest necessities, will know who is to blame for their hardships. They will know who strikes deadly blows at the very heart of our economic life. The last descendant of a greedy, exploiting aristocracy will pay the penalty due every member of his class."

"Yes, comrade. A public trial with headlines in the papers and a radio microphone in the courtroom?"

"Precisely, Comrade Taganov."

"And what if Citizen Kovalensky talks too much and too near the microphone? What if he mentions names?"

"Oh, nothing to fear, Comrade Taganov. Those gentlemen are easy to handle. He'll be promised life to say only what he's told to say. He'll be expecting a pardon even when he hears his death sentence. One can make promises, you know. One doesn't always have to keep them."

"And when he faces the firing squad—there will be no microphone on hand?"

"Precisely."

"And, of course, it won't be necessary to mention that he was jobless and starving at the time he entered the employ of those unnamed persons."

"What's that, Comrade Taganov?"

"A helpful suggestion, comrade. It will also be important to explain how a penniless aristocrat managed to lay his hands on the very heart of our economic life."

"Comrade Taganov, you have a remarkable gift for platform oratory. Too remarkable a gift. It is not always an asset to an agent of the G.P.U. You should be careful lest it be appreciated and you find yourself sent to a nice post—in the Turkestan, for instance—where you will have full opportunity to display it. Like Comrade Trotzky, for instance."

"I have served in the Red Army under Comrade Trotzky."

"I wouldn't remember that too often, Comrade Taganov, if I were you."

"I won't, comrade. I shall do my best to forget it."

"At six o'clock tonight, Comrade Taganov, you will report for duty to search Citizen Kovalensky's apartment for any additional evidence or documents pertaining to this case. And you will arrest Citizen Kovalensky."

"Yes, comrade."

"That's all, Comrade Taganov."

"Yes, comrade."

*

The executive of the Economic Section of the G.P.U. smiled, showing his gums, at Comrade Pavel Syerov and said coldly: "Hereafter, Comrade Syerov, you will confine your

literary efforts to matters pertaining to your job on the railroad."

"Oh, sure, pal," said Pavel Syerov. "Don't worry."

"I'm not the one to worry in this case, I'll remind you."

"Oh, hell, I've worried till I'm seasick. What do you want?
One has only so many hairs to turn gray."

"But only one head under the hair."

"What . . . what do you mean? You have the letter,
haven't you?"

"Not any more."

"Where is it?"

"In the furnace."

"Thanks, pal."

"You have good reason to be grateful."

"Oh, sure. Sure, I'm grateful. A good turn deserves another. An eye for an eye . . . how does the saying go? I
keep my mouth shut about some things and you keep others
shut for me about my little sins. Like good pals."

"It's not as simple as that, Syerov. For instance, your aristocratic playmate, Citizen Kovalensky, will have to go on trial
and . . ."

"Hell, do you think that will make me cry? I'll be only
too glad to see that arrogant bum get his white neck twisted."

*

"Your health, Comrade Morozov, requires a long rest and
a trip to a warmer climate," said the official. "That is why, in
acknowledgment of your resignation, we are giving you this
assignment to a place in a House of Rest. You understand?"

"Yes," said Morozov, mopping his forehead, "I understand."

"It is a pleasant sanatorium in the Crimea. Restful and
quiet. Far from the noise of the cities. It will help your health
a great deal. I would suggest that you take full advantage of
the privilege for, let us say, six months. I would not advise
you to hurry back, Comrade Morozov."

"No," said Morozov, "I won't hurry."

"And there's another advice I would like to give you, Comrade Morozov. You are going to hear a great deal, from the
newspapers, about the trial of a certain Citizen Kovalensky
for counter-revolutionary speculation. It would be wise to let
your fellow patients in the sanatorium understand that you
know nothing about the case."

"Of course, comrade. I don't know a thing about it. Not a thing."

The official bent toward Morozov and whispered bluntly, confidentially: "And if I were you, I wouldn't try to pull any wires for Kovalensky, even though he's going to the firing squad."

Morozov looked up into the official's face and drawled, his soft vowels blurring, trailing off into a whine, his wide, vertical nostrils quivering: "Who, me, pull any wires? For him? Why should I, comrade? Why should I? I had nothing to do with him. He owned that store. He alone. You can look up the registration. He alone. He can't prove I knew anything about . . . about anything. He alone. Sole owner. Lev Kovalensky—you can look it up."

*

Lavrov's wife opened the door.

She made a choked sound, like a hiccough, somewhere in her throat, and clamped her hand over her mouth, when she saw Andrei Taganov's leather jacket and the holster on his hip, and behind him—the steel blades of four bayonets.

Four soldiers entered, following Andrei. The last one slammed the door shut imperiously.

"Lord merciful! Oh, my Lord merciful!" wailed the woman, clasping a faded apron in both hands.

"Keep still!" ordered Andrei. "Where's Citizen Kovalensky's room?"

The woman pointed with a shaking finger and kept on pointing, foolishly, persistently, while the soldiers followed Andrei. She stared stupidly at the clothes rack in the lobby, at the old coats that seemed warm and creased to the lines of human bodies, hanging there while three thin, steel blades moved slowly past, and six boots stamped heavily, the floor sounding like a muffled drum. The soldier with the fourth bayonet remained standing at the door.

Lavrov jumped up when he saw them. Andrei crossed the room swiftly, without looking at him. A short, sharp movement of Andrei's hand, brusque and imperious as a lash, made one of the soldiers remain stationed at the door. The others followed Andrei into Leo's room.

Leo was alone. He sat in a deep armchair by the lighted fireplace, in his shirt sleeves, reading a book. The book was the first thing to move when the door was flung open; it descended slowly to the arm of the chair and a steady hand closed it. Then, Leo rose unhurriedly, the glow of the fire flickering on the white shirt on his straight shoulders.

He said, smiling, his smile a scornful arc: "Well, Comrade Taganov, didn't you know that some day we would meet like this?"

Andrei's face had no expression. It was set and motionless like a passport photograph; as if lines and muscles were hardened into something which had no human meaning, something which was a human face in shape only. He handed to Leo a paper bearing official stamps; he said, in a voice which was a human voice only because it made sounds that were of the human alphabet: "Search warrant, Citizen Kovalensky."

"Go ahead," said Leo, bowing sternly, graciously, as if to a guest at a formal reception. "You're quite welcome."

Two swift movements of Andrei's hand sent one soldier to a chest of drawers and the other to the bed. Drawers clattered open; white stacks of underwear fell to the floor, from under huge, dark fists that dug swiftly, expertly and slammed the drawers shut with a bang, one after the other. A white pile grew on the floor, around black boots glistening with melting snow. A quick hand ripped the satin cover off the bed, then the quilt and the sheets; the thrust of a bayonet split the mattress open and two fists disappeared in the cut.

Andrei opened the drawers of a desk. He went through them swiftly, mechanically, his thumb running the pages of books in a quick, fan-shaped whirl, with a swishing rustle like the shuffling of a pack of cards; he threw the books aside, gathering all notes and letters, shoving them into his brief case.

Leo stood alone in the middle of the room. The men took no notice of his presence, as if their actions did not concern him, as if he were only a piece of furniture, the last one to be torn open. He was half-sitting, half-leaning against a table, his two hands on the edge, his shoulders hunched, his long legs sliding forward. The logs creaked in the silence, and things thudded against the floor, and the papers rustled in Andrei's fingers.

"I'm sorry I can't oblige you," said Leo, "by letting you find secret plans to blow up the Kremlin and overthrow the Soviets, Comrade Taganov."

"Citizen Kovalensky," said Andrei, as if they had never met before, "you are speaking to a representative of the G.P.U."

"You didn't think I had forgotten that, did you?" said Leo.

A soldier stuck a bayonet into a pillow, and little white lakes of down fluttered up like snowdrops. Andrei jerked the door of a cabinet open; the dishes and glasses tinkled, as he piled them swiftly, softly on the carpet.

Leo opened his gold cigarette case and extended it to Andrei. "No, thank you," said Andrei.

Leo lighted a cigarette. The match quivered in his fingers for an instant, then grew steady. He sat on the edge of the table, swinging one leg, smoke rising slowly in a thin, blue column.

"The survival," said Leo, "of the fittest. However, not all philosophers are right. I've always wanted to ask them one question: the fittest—for what? . . . You should be able to answer it, Comrade Taganov. What are your philosophical convictions? We've never had a chance to discuss that—and this would be an appropriate time."

"I would suggest," said Andrei, "that you keep silent."

"And when a representative of the G.P.U. suggests," said Leo, "it's a command, isn't it? I realize that one should know how to respect the grandeur of authority under all circumstances, no matter how trying to the self-respect of those in power."

One of the soldiers raised his head and made a step toward Leo. A glance from Andrei stopped him. The soldier opened a wardrobe and took Leo's suits out, one by one, running his hand through the pockets and linings.

Andrei opened another wardrobe.

The wardrobe smelled of a fine French perfume. He saw a woman's dresses hanging in a row.

"What's the matter, Comrade Taganov?" asked Leo.

Andrei was holding a red dress.

It was a plain red dress with a patent leather belt, four buttons, a round collar and a huge bow.

Andrei held it spread out in his two hands and looked at it. The red cloth spurted in small puffs between his fingers.

Then his eyes moved, slowly, a glance like a weight grating through space, to the line of clothes in the wardrobe. He saw a black velvet dress he knew, a coat with a fur collar, a white blouse.

He asked: "Whose are these?"

"My mistress's," Leo answered, his eyes fixed on Andrei's face, pronouncing the word with a mocking contempt that suggested the infamy of obscenity.

Andrei's face had no expression, no human meaning. He looked down at the dress, his lashes like two black crescents on his sunken cheeks. Then he straightened the dress slowly and, cautiously, a little awkwardly, as if it were of breakable glass, hung it back in the wardrobe.

Leo chuckled, his eyes dark, his mouth twisted: "A disappointment, isn't it, Comrade Taganov?"

Andrei did not answer. He took the dresses out slowly, one by one, and ran his fingers through the pockets, through the soft folds that smelled of a French perfume.

"I say you can't, citizen!" The guard's voice roared suddenly behind the door. "You can't go in now!"

There was the sound of a struggle behind the door, as if an arm had pushed a body aside.

A voice screamed, and it was not a woman's voice, it was not a female's voice, it was the ferocious howl of an animal in mortal agony: "Let me in there! Let me in!"

Andrei looked at the door and walked to it slowly and threw it open.

Andrei Taganov and Kira Argounova stood face to face.

He asked slowly, evenly, the syllables falling like measured drops of water: "Citizen Argounova, do you live here?"

She answered, her head high, her eyes holding his, the sound of her voice like his: "Yes."

She stepped into the room; the soldier closed the door.

Andrei Taganov turned very slowly, his right shoulder drooping, every tendon of his body pulled to the effort of the motion, very cautiously, as if a knife had been thrust between his shoulder blades and he had to move carefully, not to disturb it. His left arm hung unnaturally, bent at the elbow, his fingers half-closed as if holding something they could not spill.

He turned to the soldiers and said: "Search that cabinet—and the boxes in the corner."

Then he walked back to the open wardrobe; his steps and the logs of the fireplace creaked in the silence.

Kira leaned against the wall, her hat in her hand. The hat slipped out of her fingers and fell to the floor, unnoticed.

"I'm sorry, dearest," said Leo. "I hoped it would be over before you came back."

She was not looking at Leo. She was looking at the tall figure in a leather jacket with a holster on his hip.

Andrei walked to her dresser, and opened the drawers, and she saw her underwear in his hands, white batiste nightgowns, lace ruffles crumpled in his steady, unhurried fingers.

"Look through the davenport pillows," Andrei ordered the soldiers, "and lift that rug."

Kira stood pressed against the wall, her knees sagging, her hips, arms and shoulder blades holding her upright.

"That will be all," Andrei ordered the soldiers. He closed the last drawer, evenly, without sound.

He took his brief case from the table and turned to Leo. He said, his mouth opening strangely, his upper lip motionless and only the lower one moving to form the sounds: "Citizen Kovalensky, you're under arrest."

Leo shrugged and reached silently for his coat. His mouth was drooping contemptuously, but he noticed that his fingers were trembling. He threw his head up, and flung his words at Andrei: "I'm sure this is the most pleasant duty you've ever performed, Comrade Taganov."

The soldiers picked up their bayonets, kicking aside the things on the cluttered floor.

Leo walked to the mirror and adjusted his tie, his coat, his hair, with the meticulous precision of a man dressing for an important social engagement. His fingers were not trembling any longer. He folded his handkerchief neatly and slipped it into his breast pocket.

Andrei stood waiting.

Leo stopped before Kira on his way out. "Aren't you going to say good-bye, Kira?" he asked.

He took her in his arms and kissed her. It was a long kiss. Andrei stood waiting.

"I have only one last favor to ask, Kira," Leo whispered. "I hope you'll forget me."

She did not answer.

A soldier threw the door open. Andrei walked out and Leo followed. The soldier closed the door behind them.

XIII

Leo had been locked in a cell at the G.P.U. Andrei had come home. At the gate of the palace garden, a Party comrade, hurrying into the Club, had stopped him.

"You're giving us a report on the agrarian situation tonight, Comrade Taganov, aren't you?" he had asked.

"Yes," Andrei had answered.

"At nine o'clock, isn't it? We're all looking forward to it, Comrade Taganov. See you at nine."

"Yes," Andrei had answered.

He had walked slowly through the deep snow of the garden, up the long stairs, to his dark room.

A Club window was lighted in the palace and a yellow square fell across the floor. Andrei took off his cap, his leather jacket, his gun. He stood by the fireplace, kicking gray coals with his toe. He threw a log on the coals and struck a match.

He sat on a box by the fire, his hands hanging limply between his knees, his hands and his forehead pink in the darkness.

He heard steps on the landing outside, then a hand knocking sharply. He had not locked the door. He said: "Come in."

Kira came in. She slammed the door behind her and stood in the archway of his room. He could not see her eyes in the darkness; black shadows swallowed her eyes and forehead; but the red glow fell on her mouth, and her mouth was wide, loose, brutal.

He rose and stood silently, looking at her.

"Well?" she threw at him savagely. "What are you going to do about it?"

He said slowly: "If I were you, I'd get out of here."

She leaned against the archway, asking: "And if I don't?"

"Get out of here," he repeated.

She tore her hat off and flung it aside, she threw her coat off and dropped it to the floor.

"Get out, you—"

"—whore?" she finished for him. "Certainly. I just want to be sure you know that that's what I am."

He asked: "What do you want? I have nothing to say to you."

"But I have. And you'll listen. So you've caught me, haven't you, Comrade Taganov? And you're going to have your revenge? You came with your soldiers, with a gun on your hip, Comrade Taganov of the G.P.U., and you arrested him? And now you're going to use all your influence, all your great Party influence, to see that he's put before the firing squad, aren't you? Perhaps you'll even ask for the privilege of giving the order to fire? Go ahead! Have your revenge. And this is mine. I'm not pleading for him. I have nothing to fear any more. But, at least, I can speak. And I'll speak. I have so much to say to you, to all of you, and I've kept silent for so long that it's going to tear me to pieces! I have nothing to lose. But you have."

He said: "Don't you think it's useless? Why say anything? If you have any excuses to offer . . ."

She laughed, a human laughter that did not sound human, that did not sound like laughter: "You fool! I'm proud of what I've done! Hear me! I don't regret it! I'm proud of it! So you think I loved you, don't you? I loved you, but I was unfaithful to you, on the side, as most women are? Well, then, listen: all you were to me, you and your great love, and your kisses, and your body, all they meant was only a pack of crisp, white, square, ten-ruble bills with a sickle and hammer printed in the corner! Do you know where those bills went? To a tubercular sanatorium in the Crimea. Do you know what they paid for? For the life of a man I loved long before I ever saw you, for the life of a body that had possessed mine before you ever touched it—and now you're holding him in one of your cells and you're going to shoot him. Why not? It's fair enough. Shoot him. Take his life. You've paid for it."

She saw his eyes, and they were not hurt, they were not angry. They were frightened. He said: "Kira . . . I . . . I . . . I didn't know."

She leaned back, and crossed her arms, and rocked softly, laughing: "So you loved me? So I was the highest of women, a woman like a temple, like a military march, like a god's statue? Remember who told me that? Well, look at me! I'm only a whore and you're the one who made the first payment! I sold myself—for money—and you paid it. Down in the gutter, that's where I belong, and your great love put me there. I thought you'd be glad to know that. Aren't you? So you think I loved you? I thought of Leo when you held me in your arms! When I spoke of love—I was speaking to him. Every kiss you got, every word, every hour was given to him, for him. I've never loved him as I loved him in your bed! . . . No, I won't leave you your memories. They're his. I love him. Do you hear me? I love him! Go ahead! Kill him. Nothing you can do to him will compare with what I've done to you. You know that, don't you?"

She stood, swaying, and her shadow rose to the ceiling, and the shadow rocked as if it were going to crash down.

He repeated helplessly, as if she were not present, as if he were hanging on to the syllables for support: "I didn't know. . . ."

"No, you didn't know. But it was very simple. And not very

unusual. Go through the garrets and basements where men live in your Red cities and see how many cases like this you can find. He wanted to live. You think everything that breathes can live? You've learned differently, I know. But he was one who could have lived. There aren't many of them, so they don't count with you. The doctor said he was going to die. And I loved him. You've learned what that means, too, haven't you? He didn't need much. Only rest, and fresh air, and food. He had no right to that, had he? Your State said so. We tried to beg. We begged humbly. Do you know what they said? There was a doctor in a hospital and he said he had hundreds on his waiting list."

She leaned forward, her voice soft, confidential, she spread her hands out, trying to explain, suddenly gentle and business-like and childishly insistent, her lips soft and a little bewildered, and only her eyes fixed and in her eyes, alone, a horror that did not belong in a room where human beings lived but only in a morgue:

"You see, you must understand this thoroughly. No one does. No one sees it, but I do, I can't help it, I see it, you must see it, too. You understand? Hundreds. Thousands. Millions. Millions of what? Stomachs, and heads, and legs, and tongues, and souls. And it doesn't even matter whether they fit together. Just millions. Just flesh. Human flesh. And they —it—had been registered and numbered, you know, like tin cans on a store shelf. I wonder if they're registered by the person or by the pound? And they had a chance to go on living. But not Leo. He was only a man. All stones are cobble-stones to you. And diamonds—they're useless, because they sparkle too brightly in the sun, and it's too hard on the eyes, and it's too hard under the hoofs marching into the proletarian future. You don't pave roads with diamonds. They may have other uses in the world, but of those you've never learned. That is why you had sentenced him to death, and others like him, an execution without a firing squad. There was a big com-missar and I went to see him. He told me that a hundred thousand workers had died in the civil war and why couldn't one aristocrat die—in the face of the Union of Socialist Soviet Republics? And what is the Union of Socialist Soviet Republics in the face of one man? But that is a question not for you to answer. I'm grateful to that commissar. He gave me permission to do what I've done. I don't hate him. You should hate him. What I'm doing to you—he did it first!"

He stood looking down at her. He said nothing. He did not move. He did not take his eyes off hers.

She walked toward him, her legs crossing each other, with a slow, unsteady deliberation, her body slouching back. She stood looking at him, her face suddenly empty and calm, her eyes like slits, her mouth a thin incision into a flesh without color. She spoke, and he thought that her mouth did not open, words sliding out, crushed, from between closed lips, a voice frightening because it sounded too even and natural:

"That's the question, you know, don't you? Why can't one aristocrat die in the face of the Union of Socialist Soviet Republics? You don't understand that, do you? You and your great commissar, and a million others, like you, like him, that's what you brought to the world, that question and your answer to it! A great gift, isn't it? But one of you has been paid. I paid it. In you and to you. For all the sorrow your comrades brought to a living world. How do you like it, Comrade Andrei Taganov of the All-Union Communist Party? If you taught us that our life is nothing before that of the State—well then, are you really suffering? If I brought you to the last hell of despair—well then, why don't you say that one's own life doesn't really matter?" Her voice was rising, like a whip, lashing him ferociously on both cheeks. "You loved a woman and she threw your love in your face? But the proletarian mines in the Don Basin have produced a hundred tons of coal last month! You had two altars and you saw suddenly that a harlot stood on one of them, and Citizen Morozov on the other? But the Proletarian State has exported ten thousand bushels of wheat last month! You've had every beam knocked from under your life? But the Proletarian Republic is building a new electric plant on the Volga! Why don't you smile and sing hymns to the toil of the Collective? It's still there, your Collective. Go and join it. Did anything really happen to you? It's nothing but a personal problem of a private life, the kind that only the dead old world could worry about, isn't it? Don't you have something greater—greater is the word your comrades use—left to live for? Or do you, Comrade Taganov?"

He did not answer.

Her arms were thrown wide, and her breasts stood out under her old dress, panting, and he thought he could see every muscle of her body, a female's body in the last convulsion of rage. She screamed:

"Now look at me! Take a good look! I was born and I knew I was alive and I knew what I wanted. What do you think is alive in me? Why do you think I'm alive? Because I have a stomach and eat and digest the food? Because I breathe and work and produce more food to digest? Or because I know what I want, and that something which knows how to want —isn't that life itself? And who—in this damned universe— who can tell me why I should live for anything but for that which I want? Who can answer that in human sounds that speak for human reason? . . . But you've tried to tell us what we should want. You came as a solemn army to bring a new life to men. You tore that life you knew nothing about, out of their guts—and you told them what it had to be. You took their every hour, every minute, every nerve, every thought in the farthest corners of their souls—and you told them what it had to be. You came and you forbade life to the living. You've driven us all into an iron cellar and you've closed all doors, and you've locked us airtight, airtight till the blood vessels of our spirits burst! Then you stare and wonder what it's doing to us. Well, then, look! All of you who have eyes left—look!"

She laughed, her shoulders shaking, stepping close to him. She screamed at his face:

"Why do you stand there? Why don't you speak? Are you wondering why you've never known what I was? Well, here I am! Here's what's left after you took him, after you reached for the heart of my life—and do you know what that is? Do you know what it meant when you reached for my highest reverence . . ."

She stopped short. She gasped, a choked little sound, as if he had slapped her. She slammed the back of her hand against her mouth. She stood in silence, her eyes staring at something she had seen suddenly, clearly, fully for the first time.

He smiled, very slowly, very gently. He stretched out his hands, palms up, shrugging sadly an explanation she did not need.

She moaned: "Oh, Andrei! . . ."

She backed away from him, her terrified eyes holding his.

He said slowly: "Kira, had I been in your place, I would have done the same—for the person I loved—for you."

She moaned, her hand at her mouth: "Oh, Andrei, Andrei, what have I done to you?"

She stood before him, her body sagging, looking suddenly like a frightened child with eyes too big for its white face.

He approached her and took her hand from her mouth and held it in his steady fingers. He said, and his words were like the steps of a man making an immense effort to walk too steadily: "You're done me a great favor by coming here and telling me what you've told. Because, you see, you've given me back what I thought I'd lost. You're still what I thought you were. More than I thought you were. Only . . . it's not anything you've done to me . . . it's what you had to suffer and I . . . I gave you that suffering, and all those moments were to you . . . to you . . ."

His voice broke. Then he shook his head, and his voice was firm as a doctor's: "Listen, child, we won't talk any more. I want you to keep silent for a little while, quite silent, even silent inside, you understand? Don't think. Try not to think. You're trembling. You have to rest. Here. I want you to sit down and just sit still for a few minutes."

He led her to a chair, and her head fell on his shoulder, and she whispered: "But . . . Andrei . . . You . . ."

"Forget that. Forget everything. Everything will be all right. Just sit still and don't think."

He lifted her gently and put her down on a chair by the fire. She did not resist. Her body was limp; her dress was pulled high above her knees. He saw her legs trembling. He took his leather jacket and wrapped it around her legs. He said: "This will keep you warm. It's cold here. The fire hasn't been on long enough. Now sit still."

She did not move. Her head fell back against the edge of the chair; her eyes were closed; one arm hung limply by her side, and the pink glow of the fire twinkled softly on her motionless hand.

He stood in the darkness by the fireplace and looked at her. Somewhere in the Club someone was playing the "Internationale."

He did not know how long he had stood there, when she stirred and raised her head. He asked: "Do you feel better now?"

Her head moved feebly, trying to nod.

He said: "Now let's put your coat on and I'll take you home. I want you to go to bed. Rest and don't think of anything."

She did not resist. Her head bent, she watched his fingers buttoning her coat. Then she raised her head, and her eyes looked into his. His eyes smiled at her, in quiet understanding, as he had smiled on their first meetings at the Institute.

He helped her down the long, frozen stairs. He called a sleigh at the garden gate and gave the address of her home,

Leo's home. He buttoned the fur blanket over her knees, and his arm held her as the sleigh tore forward. They rode in silence.

When the sleigh stopped, he said: "Now I want you to rest for a few days. Don't go anywhere. There's nothing you can do. Don't worry about . . . him. Leave that to me."

The snow was deep at the curb by the sidewalk. He lifted her in his arms and carried her to the door and up the stairs. She whispered, and there was no sound, but he saw the movements of her lips: ". . . Andrei. . . ."

He said: "Everything will be all right."

He returned to the sleigh, alone. He gave the driver the address of the Party Club, where his comrades were waiting for a report on the agrarian situation.

*

". . . and you've locked us airtight, airtight till the blood vessels of our spirits burst! You've taken upon your shoulders a burden such as no shoulders in history have ever carried! You said that your end justified your means. But your end, comrades? What is your end?"

The chairman of the Club struck his desk with his gavel. "Comrade Taganov, I'm calling you to order!" he cried. "You will kindly confine your speech to the report on the agrarian situation."

A wave of motion rippled through the crowded heads, down the long, dim hall, and whispers rose, and somewhere in the back row someone giggled.

Andrei Taganov stood on the speaker's platform. The hall was dark. A single bulb burned over the chairman's desk. Andrei's black leather jacket merged into the black wall behind him. Three white spots stood out, luminous in the darkness: his two long, thin hands and his face. His hands moved slowly over a black void; his face had dark shadows in the eyesockets, in the hollows of the cheekbones. He said, his voice dull, as if he could not hear his own words:

"Yes, the agrarian situation, comrades . . . In the last two months, twenty-six Party members have been assassinated in our outlying village districts. Eight clubhouses have been burned. Also three schools and a Communal Farm storehouse. The counter-revolutionary element of village hoarders has to be crushed without mercy. Our Moscow chief cites the example of the village Petrovshino where, upon their refusal to surrender their leaders, the peasants were lined in a row and every third one was shot, while the rest stood waiting. The peasants had locked three Communists from the city in the local Club of Lenin and boarded the windows on the outside and set fire to the house. . . . The peasants stood and watched it burn and sang, so they would hear no cries. . . . They were wild beasts. . . . They were beasts run amuck, beasts crazed with misery. . . . Perhaps there, too—in those lost villages somewhere so far away—there, too, they have girls, young and straight and more precious than anything on earth, who are driven into the last hell of despair, and men who love them more than life itself, who have to stand by and see it and watch it and have no help to offer! Perhaps they too . . ."

"Comrade Taganov!" roared the chairman. "I'm calling you to order!"

"Yes, Comrade Chairman. . . . Our Moscow chief cites the . . . What was I saying, Comrade Chairman? . . . Yes, the hoarders' element in the villages . . . Yes . . . The Party has to take extraordinary measures against the counter-revolutionary element in the villages, that threatens the progress of our great work among the peasant masses. . . . Our great work. . . . We came as a solemn army and forbade life to the living. We thought everything that breathed knew how to live. Does it? And aren't those who know how to live, aren't they too precious to be sacrificed in the name of any cause? What cause is greater than those who fight for it? And aren't those who know how to fight, aren't they the cause itself and not the means?"

"Comrade Taganov!" roared the chairman. "I'm calling you to order!"

"I'm here to make a report to my Party comrades, Comrade Chairman. It's a very crucial report and I think they should hear it. Yes, it's about our work in the villages, and in the cities, and among the millions, the living millions. Only there are questions. There are questions that must be answered. Why should we be afraid if we can answer them? But if we can't . . . ? If we can't? . . . Comrades! Brothers! Listen to me! Listen, you consecrated warriors of a new life! Are we sure we know what we are doing? No one can tell men what they must live for. No one can take that right— because there are things in men, in the best of us, which are above all states, above all collectives! Do you ask: what things? Man's mind and his values. Look into yourself, honestly and fearlessly. Look and don't tell me, don't tell anyone, just tell yourself: what are you living for? Aren't you living for yourself and only for yourself? Call it your aim, your love, your cause—isn't it still *your* cause? Give your life, die for your ideal—isn't it still *your* ideal? Every honest man lives for himself. Every man worth calling a man lives for himself. The one who doesn't—doesn't live at all. You cannot change it. You cannot change it because that's the way man is born, alone, complete, an end in himself. No laws, no Party, no G.P.U. will ever kill that thing in man which knows how to say 'I.' You cannot enslave man's mind, you can only destroy it. You have tried. Now look at what you're getting. Look at those whom you allow to triumph. Deny the best in men—and see what will survive. Do we want the crippled, creeping, crawling, broken monstrosities that we're producing? Are we not castrating life in order to perpetuate it?"

"Comrade Ta . . ."

"Brothers! Listen! We have to answer this!" The two luminous white hands flew up over a black void, and his voice rose, ringing, as it had risen in a dark valley over the White trenches many years ago. "We have to answer this! If we don't—history will answer it for us. And we shall go down with a burden on our shoulders that will never be forgiven! What is our goal, comrades? What are we doing? Do we want to feed a starved humanity in order to let it live? Or do we want to strangle its life in order to feed it?"

"Comrade Taganov!" roared the chairman. "I deprive you of speech!"

"I . . . I . . ." panted Andrei Taganov, staggering down the platform steps. "I have nothing more to say. . . ."

He walked out, down the long aisle, a tall, gaunt, lonely figure. Heads turned to look at him. Somewhere in the back row someone whistled through his teeth, a long, low, sneering triumphant sound.

When the door closed after him, someone whispered:

"Let Comrade Taganov wait for the next Party purge!"

XIV

Comrade Sonia sat at the table, in a faded lavender kimono, with a pencil behind her ear. The kimono did not meet in front, for she had grown to proportions that could not be concealed any longer. She bent under the lamp, running through the pages of a calendar; she seized the pencil once in a while, jotting hurried notes down on a scrap of paper, and bit the pencil, a purple streak spreading on her lower lip, for the pencil was indelible.

Pavel Syerov lay on the davenport, his stocking feet high on its arm, reading a newspaper, chewing sunflower seeds. He spat the shells into a pile on a newspaper spread on the floor by the davenport. The shells made a little sizzling sound, leaving his lips. Pavel Syerov looked bored.

"Our child," said Comrade Sonia, "will be a new citizen of a new state. It will be brought up in the free, healthy ideology of the proletariat, without any bourgeois prejudices to hamper its natural development."

"Yeah," said Pavel Syerov without looking up from his newspaper.

"I shall have it registered with the Pioneers, the very day it's born. Won't you be proud of your living contribution to the Soviet future, when you see it marching with other little citizens, in blue trunks and with a red kerchief around its neck?"

"Sure," said Pavel Syerov, spitting a shell down on the newspaper.

"We'll have a real Red christening. You know, no priests, only our Party comrades, a civil ceremony, and appropriate speeches. I'm trying to decide on a name and . . . Are you listening to me, Pavel?"

"Sure," said Syerov, sticking a seed between his teeth.

"There are many good suggestions for new, revolutionary names here in the calendar, instead of the foolish old saints' names. I've copied some good ones. Now what do you think? If it's a boy, I think Ninel would be nice."

"What the hell's that?"

"Pavel, I won't tolerate such language and such ignorance! You haven't given a single thought to your child's name, have you?"

"Well, say, I still have time, haven't I?"

"You're not interested, that's all, don't you fool me, Pavel Syerov, and don't you fool yourself thinking I'll forget it!"

"Aw, come on, now, Sonia, really, you know, I'm leaving the name up to you. You know best."

"Yes. As usual. Well, Ninel is our great leader Lenin's name —reversed. Very appropriate. Or we could call him Vil— that's for our great leader's initials—Vladimir Ilyitch Lenin. See?"

"Yeah. Well, either one's good enough for me."

"Now, if it's a girl—and I hope it's a girl, because the new woman is coming into her own and the future belongs, to a greater extent than you men imagine, to the free woman of the proletariat—well, if it's a girl, I have some good names here, but the one I like best is Octiabrina, because that would be a living monument to our great October Revolution."

"Sort of . . . long, isn't it?"

"What of it? It's a very good name and very popular. You know, Fimka Popova, she had a Red christening week before last and that's what she called her brat—Octiabrina. Even got a notice in the paper about it. Her husband was so proud— the blind fool!"

"Now, Sonia, you shouldn't insinuate . . ."

"Listen to the respectable moralist! That bitch Fimka is known as a . . . Oh, to hell with her! But if she thinks she's the only one to get a notice in the paper about her litter I'll . . . I've copied some other names here, too. Good modern ones. There's Marxina, for Karl Marx. Or else Communara. Or . . ."

Something clattered loudly under the table.

"Oh, hell!" said Comrade Sonia. "Those damn slippers of mine!" She wriggled uncomfortably on her chair, stretching out one leg, her foot groping under the table. She found the slipper and bent painfully over her abdomen, pulling the slipper on by a flat, wornout heel. "Look at the old junk I have to wear! And I need so many things, and with the child coming . . . You would choose a good time to write certain literary compositions and ruin everything, you drunken fool!"

"Now we won't bring that up again, Sonia. You know I was lucky to get out of it as I did."

"Yeah! Well, I hope your Kovalensky gets the firing squad

and a nice, loud trial. I'll see to it that the women of the Zhenotdel stage a demonstration of protest against Speculators and Aristocrats!" She fingered the pages of the calendar and cried: "Here's another good one for a girl: Tribuna. Or—Barricada. Or, if we prefer something in the spirit of modern science: Universiteta."

"That's too long," said Syerov.

"I prefer Octiabrina. More symbol to that. I hope it's a girl. Octiabrina Syerova—the leader of the future. What do you want it to be, Pavel, a boy or a girl?"

"I don't care," said Syerov, "so long as it isn't twins."

"Now I don't like that remark at all. It shows that you . . ."

They heard a knock at the door. The knock seemed too loud, too peremptory. Syerov, his head up, dropped the newspaper and said: "Come in."

Andrei Taganov entered and closed the door. Comrade Sonia dropped her calendar. Pavel Syerov rose slowly to his feet.

"Good evening," said Andrei.

"Good evening," said Syerov, standing, watching him fixedly.

"What's the big idea, Taganov?" Comrade Sonia asked, her voice low, husky, menacing.

Andrei did not turn to her. He said: "I want to speak to you, Syerov."

"Go ahead," said Syerov without moving.

"I said I want to speak to you alone."

"I said go ahead," Syerov repeated.

"Tell your wife to get out."

"My husband and I," said Comrade Sonia, "have no secrets from each other."

"You get out of here," said Andrei, without raising his voice, "and wait in the corridor."

"Pavel! If he . . ."

"You'd better go, Sonia," said Syerov slowly, without looking at her, his eyes fixed on Andrei.

Comrade Sonia coughed out a single chuckle from the corner of her mouth: "Comrade Taganov still going strong, eh? Well, we shall see what we shall see and we don't have long to wait."

She gathered her lavender kimono, pulling it tightly across her abdomen, stuck a cigarette into her mouth and walked out, the slippers flapping against her heels.

"I thought," said Pavel Syerov, "that you had learned a lesson in the last few days."

"I have," said Andrei.

"What else do you want?"

"You'd better put your shoes on while I'm talking. You're going out and you haven't much time to lose."

"Am I? Glad you let me in on the little secret. Otherwise I might have said that I had no such intention. And maybe I'll still say it. Where am I going, according to Comrade Mussolini Taganov?"

"To release Leo Kovalensky."

Pavel Syerov sat down heavily and his feet scattered the pile of sunflower-seed shells over the floor. "What are you up to, Taganov? Gone insane, have you?"

"You'd better keep still and listen. I'll tell you what you have to do."

"You'll tell me what I have to do? Why?"

"And after that, I'll tell you why you will do it. You'll dress right now and go to see your friend. You know what friend I mean. The one at the G.P.U."

"At this hour?"

"Get him out of bed, if necessary. What you'll tell him and how you'll tell it, is none of my business. All I have to know is that Leo Kovalensky is released within forty-eight hours."

"Now will you let me in on the little magic wand that will make me do it?"

"It's a little paper wand, Syerov. Two of them."

"Written by whom?"

"You."

"Huh?"

"Photographed from one written by you, to be exact."

Syerov rose slowly and leaned with both hands on the table. "Taganov, you God-damn rat!" he hissed. "It's a rotten time to be joking."

"Am I?"

"Well, I'll go to see my friend all right. And you'll see Leo Kovalensky all right—and it won't take you forty-eight hours, either. I'll see to it that you get the cell next to his and then we'll find out what documents . . ."

"There are two photostats of it, as I said. Only I don't happen to have either one of them."

"What . . . what did you . . ."

"They're in the possession of two friends I can trust. It would be useless to try to find out their names. You know me well enough to discard any idea of the G.P.U. torture chamber, if that idea occurs to you. Their instructions are that if anything happens to me before Leo Kovalensky is out—the photostats go to Moscow. Also—if anything happens to him after he's out."

"You God-d . . ."

"You don't want those photostats to reach Moscow. Your friend won't be able to save your neck, then, nor his own, perhaps. You don't have to worry about my becoming a nuisance. All you have to do is release Leo Kovalensky and hush up this whole case. You'll never hear of those photostats again. You'll never see them, either."

Syerov reached for his handkerchief and wiped his forehead. "You're lying," he said hoarsely. "You've never taken any photostats."

"Maybe," said Andrei. "Want to take a chance on that?"

"Sit down," said Syerov, falling on the davenport.

Andrei sat down on the edge of the table and crossed his legs.

"Listen, Andrei," said Syerov. "Let's talk sense. All right, you're holding the whip. Still, do you know what you're asking?"

"No more than you can do."

"But, good Lord in Heaven, Andrei! It's such a big case and we're all set with a first-class propaganda campaign and the newspapers are getting headlines ready to . . ."

"Stop them."

"But how can I? How can I ask him? What am I going to tell him?"

"That's none of my business."

"But after he's already saved my . . ."

"Don't forget it's in his interests, too. He may have friends in Moscow. And he may have some who aren't friends."

"But, listen . . ."

"And when Party members can no longer be saved, they're the ones who get it worse than the private speculators, you know. Also a good occasion for first-class propaganda."

"Andrei, one of us has gone insane. I can't figure it out. Why do you want Kovalensky released?"

"That's none of your business."

"And if you've appointed yourself his guardian angel, then why the hell did you start the whole damn case? You started it, you know."

"You said that I had learned a lesson."

"Andrei, haven't you got any Party honor left? We need a good smashing bang at the speculators right now, with food conditions as they are and all the . . ."

"That doesn't concern me any longer."

"You damn traitor! You said it was the only copy of the letter in existence, when you turned it in!"

"Maybe I was lying then."

"Listen, let's talk business. Here—have a cigarette."

"No, thank you."

"Listen, let's talk as friend to friend. I take back all those things I said to you. I apologize. You can't blame me, you know how it is, you can see it's enough to make a fellow lose his mind a little. All right, you have your own game to play, I had mine and I made a misstep, but then we're both no innocent angels, as I can see, so we can understand each other. We used to be good friends, childhood friends, remember? So we can talk sensibly."

"About what?"

"I have an offer to make to you, Andrei. A good one. That friend of mine, he can do a lot if I slip a couple of words to him, as you know, I guess. I guess you know that I have enough on him for a firing squad, too. You're learning the same game, I see, and doing it brilliantly, I must hand it to you. All right, we understand each other. Now I can talk plain. I guess you know that your spot in the Party isn't so good any more. Not so good at all. And particularly after that little speech you made tonight—really, you know, it won't be so easy on you at the next Party purge."

"I know it."

"In fact, you're pretty sure to get the axe, you know."

"I do."

"Well, then, what do you say if we make a bargain? You drop this case and I'll see to it that you keep your Party card and not only that, but you can have any job you choose at the G.P.U. and name your own salary. No questions asked and no ill feeling. We all have our own way to make. You and I —we can help each other a lot. What do you say?"

"What makes you think that I want to remain in the Party?"

"Andrei! . . ."

"You don't have to worry about helping me at the next purge. I may be kicked out of the Party or I may be shot or I may be run over by a truck. That won't make any difference to you. Understand? But don't touch Leo Kovalensky. See that no one touches him. Watch him as you would watch your own child, no matter what happens to me. I am not his guardian angel. You are."

"Andrei," Syerov moaned, "what is that damned aristocrat to you?"

"I've answered that question once."

Syerov rose unsteadily and drew himself up for a last, desperate effort: "Listen, Andrei, I have something to tell you. I thought you knew it, but I guess you don't. Only pull yourself together and listen, and don't kill me on the first word. I know there's a name you don't want to be mentioned, but I'll mention it. It's Kira Argounova."

"Well?"

"Listen, we're not mincing words, are we? Hell, not now we aren't. Well, then, listen: you love her and you've been sleeping with her for over a year. And. . . . Wait! Let me finish. . . . Well, she's been Leo Kovalensky's mistress all that time. . . . Wait! You don't have to take my word for it. Just check up on it and see for yourself."

"Why check up on it? I know it."

"Oh!" said Pavel Syerov.

He stood, rocking slowly from heels to toes, looking at Andrei. Then he laughed. "Well," he said, "I should have known."

"Get your coat," said Andrei, rising.

"I should have known," laughed Syerov, "why the saint of the Comm-party would go in for blackmail. You fool! You poor, virtuous, brainless fool! So that's the kind of grandstand you're playing! I should have known that the lofty heroics are a disease one never gets cured of! Come on, Andrei! Haven't you any sense left? Any pride?"

"We've talked long enough," said Andrei. "You seem to know a lot about me. You should know that I don't change my mind."

Pavel Syerov reached for his overcoat and pulled it on slowly, his pale lips grinning.

"All right, Sir Galahad or whatever it's called," he said. "Sir Galahad of the blackmail sword. You win—this time. It's no use threatening you with any retaliation. Fellows like you get theirs without any help from fellows like me. In a year— this little mess will be forgotten. I'll be running the railroads of the U.S.S.R. and buying satin diapers for my brat. You'll be standing in line for a pot of soup—and maybe you'll get it. But you'll have the satisfaction of knowing that your sweetheart is being . . . by a man you hate!"

"Yes," said Andrei. "Good luck, Comrade Syerov."

"Good luck, Comrade Taganov."

*

Kira sat on the floor, folding Leo's underwear, putting it back into the drawer. Her dresses were still piled in a heap before her open wardrobe. Papers rustled all over the room when she moved. Down from the torn pillows fluttered like snow over the furniture.

She had not been out for two days. She had heard no sound from the world beyond the walls of her room. Galina Petrovna had telephoned once and wailed into the receiver; Kira had told her not to worry and please not to come over; Galina Petrovna had not come.

The Lavrovs had decided that their neighbor was not shaken by her tragedy; they heard no tears; they noticed nothing unusual in the frail little figure whom they watched sidewise when they crossed her room on their way to the bathroom. They noticed only that she seemed lazy, for her limbs fell and remained in any position, and it took her an effort to move them; and her eyes remained fixed on one spot and it took a bigger effort to shift her glance, and her glance was like a forty-pound sack of sand being dragged by a child's fist.

She sat on the floor and folded shirts neatly, creasing every pleat, slipping them cautiously into the drawer on the palms of her two hands. One shirt had Leo's initials embroidered on the breast pocket; she sat staring at it, without moving.

She did not raise her head when she heard the door opening.

"Allo, Kira," said a voice.

She fell back against the open drawer and it slammed shut with a crash. Leo was looking down at her. His lips drooped, but it was not a smile; his lips had no color; the circles under his eyes were blue and sharp, as if painted on by an amateur actor.

"Kira . . . please . . . no hysterics . . ." he said wearily.

She rose slowly, her arms swinging limply. She stood, her fingers crumpling the hair on her right temple, looking at him incredulously, afraid to touch him.

"Leo . . . Leo . . . you're not . . . free, are you?"

"Yes. Free. Released. Kicked out."

"Leo . . . how . . . how could it . . . happen . . . ?"

"How do I know? I thought you knew something about that."

She was kissing his lips, his neck, the muscles exposed by

his torn shirt collar, his hands, his palms. He patted her hair and looked indifferently over her head, at the wrecked room.

"Leo . . ." she whispered, looking up into his dead eyes, "what have they done to you?"

"Nothing."

"Did they . . . did they . . . I heard they sometimes . . ."

"No, they didn't torture me. They say they have a room for that, but I didn't have the privilege. . . . I had a nice cell all to myself and three meals a day, although the soup was rotten. I just sat there for two days and thought of what last words I could say before the firing squad. As good a pastime as any."

She took his coat off; she pushed him into an armchair; she knelt, pulling off his overshoes; she pressed her head to his knees for a second and jerked it away, and bent lower, to hide her face, and tied his unfastened shoestring with trembling fingers.

He asked: "Have I any clean underwear left?"

"Yes . . . I'll get it . . . only . . . Leo . . . I want to know . . . you haven't told me . . ."

"What is there to tell? I guess it's all over. The case is closed. They told me to see that I don't get into the G.P.U. for a third time." He added indifferently: "I think your friend Taganov had something to do with my release."

"He . . ."

"You didn't ask him to?"

"No," she said, rising. "No, I didn't ask him."

"Did they ruin the furniture completely, and the bed, too?"

"Who? . . . Oh, the search . . . No . . . Yes, I guess they have. . . . Leo!" she cried suddenly, so that he shuddered and looked at her, lifting his eyelids with effort. "Leo, have you nothing to say?"

"What do you want me to say?"

"Aren't you . . . aren't you glad to see me?"

"Sure. You look nice. Your hair needs combing."

"Leo, did you think of me . . . there?"

"No."

"You . . . didn't?"

"No. What for? To make it easier?"

"Leo, do you . . . love me?"

"Oh, what a question. . . . What a question at what a time. . . . You're getting feminine, Kira. . . . Really, it's not becoming. . . . Not becoming at all. . . ."

"I'm sorry, dear. I know it's foolish. I don't know why I had to ask it just then. . . . You're so tired. I'll get your underwear and I'll fix your dinner. You haven't had dinner, have you?"

"No. I don't want any. Is there anything to drink in the house?"

"Leo . . . you're not going . . . again . . . to . . ."

"Leave me alone, will you? Get the hell out, please could you? Go to your parents . . . or something . . ."

"Leo!" She stood, her hands in her hair, staring down at him incredulously. "Leo, what have they done to you?"

His head was leaning back against the chair and she looked at the quivering white triangle of his neck and chin; he spoke, his eyes closed, only his lips moving, his voice even and flat: "Nothing. . . . No one's going to do anything to me any more. . . . No one. . . . Not you nor anyone else. . . . No one can hurt me but you—and now you can't either. . . . No one. . . ."

"Leo!" She seized his limp, white-faced head and shook it furiously, pitilessly. "Leo! It can't get you like this! It won't get you!"

He seized her hand and flung it aside. "Will you ever come down to earth? What do you want? Want me to sing of life with little excursions to the G.P.U. between hymns? Afraid they've broken me? Afraid they'll get me? Want me to keep something that the mire can't reach, the more to suffer while it sucks me under? You're being kind to me, aren't you, because you love me so much? Don't you think you'd be kinder if you'd let me fall into the mire? So that I'd be one with our times and would feel nothing any longer . . . nothing . . . ever . . ."

A hand knocked at the door.

"Come in," said Kira.

Andrei Taganov came in. "Good evening, Kira," he said and stopped, seeing Leo.

"Good evening, Andrei," said Kira.

Leo raised his head with effort. His eyes looked faintly startled.

"Good evening," said Andrei, turning to him. "I didn't know you were out already."

"I'm out. I thought you had reason to expect it."

"I did. But I didn't know they'd hurry. I'm sorry to intrude like this. I know you don't want to see any visitors."

"It's all right, Andrei," said Kira. "Sit down."

"There's something I have to tell you, Kira." He turned to Leo: "Would you mind if I took Kira out—for a few minutes?"

"I certainly would," Leo answered slowly. "Have you any secrets to discuss with Kira?"

"Leo!" Her voice was almost a scream. She added, quietly, her voice still trembling: "Come on, Andrei."

"No," said Andrei calmly, sitting down. "It isn't really necessary. It's not a secret." He turned to Leo. "I just wanted to spare you the necessity of . . . of feeling indebted to me, but perhaps it would be better if you heard it, too. Sit down, Kira. It's perfectly all right. It's about his release from the G.P.U."

Leo was looking at him fixedly, silently, leaning forward. Kira stood, her shoulders hunched, her hands clasped behind her back, as if they were tied. She looked at Andrei; his eyes were clear, serene.

"Sit down, Kira," he said almost gently.

She obeyed.

"There's something you should know, both of you," said Andrei, "for your own protection. I couldn't tell you sooner, Kira. I had to be sure that it had worked. Well, it has. I suppose you know who's really behind your release. It's Pavel Syerov. I want you to know what's behind him—in case you ever need it."

"It's you, isn't it?" asked Leo, a faint edge of sharpness in his voice.

"Leo, keep quiet. Please!" said Kira, turning away not to see his eyes watching her.

"It's a letter," Andrei continued calmly. "A letter he wrote and you know what that was. The letter had been sent to me . . . by someone else. Syerov has powerful friends. That saved him. But he's not very brave. That saved you. The letter had been destroyed. But I told him that I had photostats of it and that they were in the possession of friends who would send them to higher authorities in Moscow—unless you were released. The case is killed. I don't think they'll ever bother you again. But I want you to know this, so that you can hold it over Syerov's head—if you need it. Let him think that you know the photostats are in good hands—and on their way to Moscow, if he makes one step in your direction. That's all. I don't think you'll ever need it. But it's a useful protection to have, in these times—and with your social record."

"And . . . the photostats?" Kira whispered. "Where are they actually?"

"There are no photostats," said Andrei.

A truck thundered in the street below and the window panes trembled in the silence.

Andrei's eyes met Kira's. Their eyes met and parted swiftly, for Leo was watching them.

It was Leo who spoke first. He rose and walked to Andrei, and stood looking down at him. Then he said: "I suppose I should thank you. Well, consider me grateful. Only I won't say that I thank you from the bottom of my heart, because in the bottom of my heart I wish you had left me where I was."

"Why?" Andrei asked, looking up at him.

"Do you suppose Lazarus was grateful when Christ brought him back from the grave—if He did? No more than I am to you, I think."

Andrei looked at him steadily; Andrei's face was stern; his words were a threat: "Pull yourself together. You have so much to live for."

Leo shrugged and did not answer.

"You'll have to close that store of yours. Try to get a job. Better not a very prominent one. You'll hate it. But you'll have to stick to it."

"If I can."

"You can. You have to."

"Do I?" said Leo, and Kira saw his eyes watching Andrei closely.

She asked: "Andrei, why did you want to tell us about Syerov's letter?"

"So that you'd know in case . . . in case anything happened to me."

"What is going to happen to you, Andrei?"

"Nothing . . . Nothing that I know of." He added, rising: "Except that I'm going to be thrown out of the Party, I think."

"It . . . it meant a lot to you, didn't it . . . your Party?"

"It did."

"And . . . and when you lose something that meant a lot to you, does it . . . make any difference?"

"No. It still means a lot to me."

"Will you . . . hate them for it . . . for throwing you out?"

"No."

"Will you . . . forgive them . . . some day?"

"I have nothing to forgive. Because, you see, I have a lot to be grateful for, in the past, when I belonged to—to the Party. I don't want them to feel that they had been . . . unjust. Or that I blame them. I can never tell them that I understand. But I would like them to know it."

"Perhaps they may be worried . . . although they have no right to question you any longer . . . about a life they may have broken . . ."

"If I could ask a favor—when they throw me out—I'd ask them not to worry about me. So that . . . in the Party annals . . . I won't become a wound, but a bearable memory. Then, my memories will be bearable, too."

"I think they'd grant you that . . . if they knew."

"I'd thank them . . . if I could."

He turned and took his cap from the table and said, buttoning his jacket: "Well, I have to go. Oh, yes, another thing: keep away from Morozov. I understand he's leaving town, but he'll be back and starting some new scheme. Keep away. He'll always get out of it and leave you to take the blame."

"Shall we . . . see you again, Andrei?" asked Kira.

"Sure. I'll be very busy—for a while. But I'll be around. . . . Well, good night."

"Good night, Andrei."

"Wait a minute," said Leo suddenly. "There's something I want to ask you."

He walked to Andrei, and stood, his hands in his pockets, his lips spitting the words out slowly: "Just why did you do all this? Just what is Kira to you?"

Andrei looked at Kira. She stood, silent, erect, looking at them. She was leaving it up to him. He turned to Leo and answered: "Just a friend."

"Good night," said Leo.

The door had closed, and the door in Lavrov's room, and in the silence they heard the door in the lobby opening and closing behind Andrei. Then Kira tore forward suddenly. Leo could not see her face. He heard only a sound that was not a moan and not quite a cry. She ran out of the room, and the door slammed shut behind her, and the crystals of the chandelier tinkled softly.

She ran down the stairs, out into the street. It was snowing. She felt the air like a scalding jet of steam striking her bare neck. Her feet felt very light and thin in their open slippers in the snow. She saw his tall figure walking away and she ran after him, calling: "Andrei!"

He wheeled about and gasped: "Kira! In the snow without a coat!"

He seized her arm and jerked her back into the house, into the dim little lobby at the foot of the stairs.

"Go back! Immediately!" he ordered.

"Andrei . . ." she stammered. "I . . . I . . ."

In the light of a lamp post from across the street, she saw him smiling slowly, gently, and his hand brushed the wet snow-flakes off her hair. "Kira, don't you think it's better—like this?" he whispered. "If we don't say anything—and just leave it to . . . to our silence, knowing that we both understand, and that we still have that much in common?"

"Yes, Andrei," she whispered.

"Don't worry about me. You've promised that, you know. Go back now. You'll catch cold."

She raised her hand, and her fingers brushed his cheek slowly, barely touching it, from the scar on his temple to his chin, as if her trembling finger tips could tell him something she could not say. He took her hand and pressed it to his lips and held it for a long time. A car passed in the street outside; through the glass door, the sharp beam of a headlight swept over their faces, licked the wall and vanished.

He dropped her hand. She turned and walked slowly up the stairs. She heard the door opening and closing behind her. She did not look back.

When she returned to her room, Leo was telephoning. She heard him saying: "Allo, Tonia? . . . Yes, I just got out. . . . I'll tell you all about it. . . . Sure, come right over. . . . Bring some. I haven't got a drop in the house. . . ."

*

Andrei Taganov was transferred from the G.P.U. to the job of librarian in the library of the Lenin's Nook of the Club of Women Houseworkers in the suburb Lesnoe.

The clubhouse was a former church. It had old wooden walls that let the wind through, to rustle the bright posters inside; a slanting beam of unpainted wood in the center, supporting a roof ready to cave in; a window covered with boards over the dusty remnants of a glass pane; and a cast-iron "Bourgeoise" that filled the room with smoke. There was a banner of red calico over the former altar, and pictures of Lenin on the walls, pictures without frames, cut out of magazines: Lenin as a child, Lenin as a student, Lenin addressing the Petrograd Soviet, Lenin in a cap, Lenin without a cap, Lenin in the Council of People's Commissars, Lenin in his coffin. There were shelves of books in paper covers, a sign that read:

"Proletarians of the World, Unite!" and a plaster bust of Lenin with a scar of glue across his chin.

Andrei Taganov tried to hold on.

At five o'clock, when store windows made yellow squares in the snow and the lights of tramways rolled like colored beads high over the dark streets, he left the Technological Institute and rode to Lesnoe, sitting at the window of a crowded tramway, eating a sandwich, for he had no time to eat dinner. From six to nine, he sat alone in the library of the Lenin's Nook of the Club of Women Houseworkers, wrote card indexes, glued torn covers, added wood to the "Bourgeoise," numbered books, dusted shelves, and said when a woman's figure in a gray shawl waddled in, shaking snow off her heavy felt-boots:

"Good evening, comrade. . . . No, 'The A B C of Communism' is not in. I have your reservation, comrade. . . . Yes, this is a very good book, Comrade Samsonova, very instructive and strictly proletarian. . . . Yes, Comrade Danilova, it is recommended by the Party Council as indispensable to the political education of a conscientious worker. . . . Please, comrade, do not draw pictures on library books in the future. . . . Yes, I know, comrade, the stove isn't very good, it always smokes this way. . . . No, we don't carry any books on birth-control. . . . Yes, Comrade Selivanova, it is advisable to get acquainted with all of Comrade Lenin's works in order to understand our great leader's ideology. . . . Please close the door, comrade. . . . Sorry, comrade, we have no rest-room. . . . No, we have no books by Mussolini. . . . No, we carry no love stories, Comrade Ziablova. . . . No, Comrade Ziablova, I can't take you to the Club dance Sunday. . . . No, 'The A B C of Communism' is not in, comrade. . . ."

In the offices of the G.P.U. they whispered: "Let Comrade Taganov wait for the next Party purge."

Comrade Taganov did not wait for the next Party purge.

On a Saturday evening, he stood in line at the district co-operative for his food rations. The co-operative smelled of kerosene and rotted onions. There was a barrel of sauerkraut by the counter, a sack of dried vegetables, a can of linseed oil, and bars of bluish Joukov soap. A kerosene lamp smoked on the counter. A line of customers stretched across the long, bare room. There was only one clerk; he had a sty over his left eye and he looked sleepy.

A little man stood in line ahead of Andrei. His coat collar was loose, with a greenish, greasy patch at the nape of his neck. His neck was thin and wrinkled, with an Adam's apple

like a chicken's craw. He fingered his ration card nervously
and fidgeted, peering past the line at the counter. He sniffled
sonorously, for he had a cold, and scratched his Adam's apple.

He turned and grinned amicably up at Andrei. "Party comrade?" he asked, pointing a gnarled finger at the red star on
Andrei's lapel. "Me, too, comrade. Sure, Party member. Here's
my star, too. Cold weather we're having, comrade. Awfully
cold weather. I hope the dried vegetables aren't all gone before
our turn comes, comrade. They're wonderful for making soup
Julienne. Really should have meat for it, though, but I'll tell
you a nice little trick: just let them soak overnight, then boil
them in plain water, and when it's almost ready drop in a
spoonful of sunflower-seed oil, just one spoonful, and it makes
such nice grease spots float on the surface, just the same as if
you had meat, never tell the difference. Yes, I sure like soup
Julienne. Hope they're not all gone before our turn comes.
He's not very fast, that clerk. Only I'm not complaining. No,
please, don't think I'm complaining, comrade."

He peered at the counter, fingered his card, counted the
coupons, scratched his Adam's apple, and whispered confidentially: "Only I hope the vegetables aren't all gone. And
another thing: I wish they would give us all the stuff in the
same place. We wait for the general products here, and tomorrow two hours at the bread store, and day after-tomorrow
here again for kerosene. Still, I don't mind. Next week, they
say, we're going to get lard. That will be a holiday, won't it?
That's something to look forward to, isn't it?"

When Andrei's turn came, the clerk shoved the rations at
him, seized his card impatiently and growled: "What the hell's
the matter, citizen? Your coupon's half torn off."

"I don't know," said Andrei. "I must have torn it accidentally."

"Well, I could have refused to accept it, you know. Not
supposed to be half torn off. I got no time to check on all of
you mugs. See that it's right, next month."

"Next . . . month?" said Andrei.

"Yeah, and next year, too, or else go empty-bellied. . . .
Next!"

Andrei walked out of the co-operative with a pound of
sauerkraut, a pound of linseed oil, a bar of soap and two
pounds of dried vegetables for soup Julienne.

He walked slowly, and the streets were white with a hard,
polished snow, and men's heels cut sharp ridges, creaking.
Snow sparkled like salt crystals in the white circles of lamp

posts; and in the yellow cones of light at store windows, snow twinkled like splinters of powdered fire. Under a soft, glassy fuzz of frost, a poster showed a husky giant in a red blouse, raising two arms imperiously, triumphantly to the red letters:

WE ARE THE BUILDERS OF A NEW HUMANITY!

Andrei's steps were steady, calm. Andrei Taganov was always calm when he had reached a decision.

He turned on the light, when he entered his room, and put his packages on the table. He took off his cap and jacket, and hung them on a nail in the corner. A strand of hair fell across his forehead; he brushed it back with a long, slow movement. He had left a few coals smouldering in the fireplace and the room was hot. He took off his coat and straightened the wrinkled sleeves of his shirt.

He looked around slowly. He saw some books on the floor, and picked them up, and put them neatly into a pile on the table.

He lighted a cigarette and stood in the middle of the room, his elbow pressed to his side, like a wax figure in a store window, motionless but for the slow movement of one forearm with a hand tracing an even line in the air, carrying to his lips a cigarette held in two long, straight fingers. Nothing moved in the room but that arm with a motionless hand, and the smoke rising slowly, at his lips, then at his shoulder, then at his lips again, the ashes falling to the floor.

When he felt a hot breath on his fingers and saw that the cigarette had burned, he threw the stub into the fireplace and walked to his table. He sat down and opened the drawers, one by one, and looked through their contents. He took out a few papers and gathered them into a pile on the table.

Then he rose and walked to the fireplace. He knelt and stuffed newspapers into the coals and blew at them until bright orange tongues leaped up. He threw two logs into the fire and stood, watching them until he saw white flames spurt from the creaking bark. Then he walked to the table, took the pile of papers he had selected and threw it into the fire.

Then he opened the old boxes that served as his wardrobe. There were the things he did not want to be found in his room. He took a girl's black satin robe and threw it into the fire. He watched the cloth shriveling slowly in red, glowing, flameless patches, with long, thin columns of smoke, with a heavy, acrid odor. He watched it, his eyes quiet, astonished.

Then he threw in a pair of black satin slippers, and a little lace handkerchief, and a lace jacket with white ribbons. A sleeve of the jacket rolled out on the blackened bricks by the fireplace; he bent and, lifting it delicately, placed it back over the flames.

Then he found "The American Resident," the little glass toy with a black imp in a red liquid. He looked at it, and hesitated, and put it cautiously down into the smouldering lace. The glass tube cracked, and the liquid sizzled on the coals with a sharp little puff of steam, and "The Resident" rolled into a crack among the coals.

Then he took out the black chiffon nightgown.

He stood at the fireplace and held the gown in both hands, and his fingers crumpled slowly, softly the light silk that felt like a handful of smoke. He held it on his two palms, and looked at his fingers through the thin black film, and moved his fingers slowly.

Then he knelt and spread it over the fire. For a second, the red coals were dimmed as under a clouded black glass; then the gown shuddered, as in a gust of wind, and a corner of the hem curled up, and a thin blue flame shot out of a fold at the neckline.

He rose and stood watching it; he watched glowing red threads running down the black cloth, and the black film twisting, as if it were breathing, curling, shrinking slowly into a smoke light as the cloth.

He stood for a long time, looking at the motionless black thing with twinkling red edges, that still had the shape of a gown, but it was not transparent any longer.

Then he touched it softly with his foot. It crumbled almost before it was touched, and little black flakes fluttered up into the chimney.

He turned away and sat down at the table. He sat with one forearm resting on the table and the other on his knee, his hands hanging down, ten fingers motionless, straight, broken only by the small angles of the joints, so still that they seemed grown fast to the air. An old alarm clock ticked on a shelf. His face was grave, quiet. His eyes were gentle, astonished, wondering. . . .

Then he turned, and took a piece of paper from the drawer, and wrote: "No one is to be held responsible for my death." And signed: "Andrei Taganov."

There was only one shot, and because the frozen marble

stairway was long and dark and led to a garden buried in deep snow, no one came up to investigate.

XV

On the front pages of the *Pravda,* a square in a heavy black frame carried the words:

The Central Committee of the All-Union Communist Party expresses its profound grief at the death of a heroic fighter of the Revolution, former member of the Red Army, member of the Party since 1915,

COMRADE ANDREI TAGANOV

Under it, another square in a heavy black frame said:

The Leningrad Committee of the All-Union Communist Party sorrowfully announces the death of

COMRADE ANDREI TAGANOV

The funeral will take place tomorrow, on the Field of Victims of the Revolution. The procession will start from the Smolny Institute at 10 o'clock in the morning.

An editorial of the *Pravda* said:

Another name has been added to the glorious list of victims fallen on the field of honor of the Revolution. That name may not be known to many, but it represents and symbolizes the common ranks of our Party, the unsung heroes of our weekdays. In the person of Comrade Andrei Taganov, we pay a last tribute to the unknown warriors of the Army of the Proletariat. Comrade Taganov is dead. He committed suicide under the strain of a nervous collapse caused by overwork. His health and body were broken by the demanding, ceaseless task which his Party membership imposed upon him. Such was his sacrifice to the Revolution. Such is the sacrifice of a Party that rules, not for the sake of personal loot and fame, like the rulers of capitalistic countries, but for the sake of assuming the hardest work, the most pitiless tasks in the service of the Collective. And if, in these days of struggle and privation, some of us may weaken in spirit, let us look up to the great All-Union Communist Party that leads us, that spares not its strength, its energy, its lives. Let us make the Red funeral of a Party hero an occasion of tribute to our leaders. Let all toilers of Leningrad join in the procession that will escort Comrade Taganov to his last place of rest.

In an office of the G.P.U., a man with a smile that showed his gums, said to Pavel Syerov: "Well, he gave us a good opportunity for a lot of useful noise, after all. You making the opening speech?"

"Yeah," said Syerov.

"Don't forget his Red Army record and all that. Well, I hope this will shut them up, those damn fools, some of those old dotards of the 1905 vintage, who showed an inclination to talk too much about his pre-October Party card and other things, the Kovalensky case among other things."

"Forget it," said Pavel Syerov.

*

The toilers of Leningrad marched behind a red coffin.

Row after row, like walls, like the rungs of an endless ladder, they moved forward, swallowing Nevsky in the slow, rumbling, growing tide of bodies and banners, thousands of feet stepping in time, as if one gigantic pair of boots made Nevsky shudder in rhythm, from the statue of Alexander III to the columns of the Admiralty. Thousands of human bodies marched gravely, flaming banners raised high in a last salute.

Soldiers of the Red Army came as khaki ramparts, row after row of straight, husky shoulders, of boots firm and steady in the snow, of peaked caps with a red star on each forehead, and over them—a red banner with gold letters:

GLORY ETERNAL TO A FALLEN COMRADE

Workers of the Putilovsky factory came in gray, unbroken ranks, moving slowly under a red banner held high in sturdy fists:

HE CAME FROM THE WORKERS' RANKS.
HE GAVE HIS LIFE TO THE WORKERS OF THE WORLD.
THE PROLETARIAT THANKS ITS FALLEN FIGHTER.

Students of the Technological Institute followed, rows of young, earnest faces, of grave, clear eyes, of straight, taut bodies, of boys in black caps and girls in red kerchiefs, red as the banner that said:

THE STUDENTS OF THE TECHNOLOGICAL INSTITUTE ARE PROUD
OF THEIR SACRIFICE TO THE CAUSE OF THE REVOLUTION

Members of his Party Collective, rows of black leather jackets, marched gravely, austere as monks, stately as warriors, their banner spread high and straight, without a wrinkle, a narrow red band with black letters, as sharp and plain as the men who carried it:

THE ALL-UNION COMMUNIST PARTY OFFERS ALL AND EVERY ONE
OF ITS LIVES TO THE SERVICE OF THE WORLD REVOLUTION

Every factory of Petrograd, every club, every office, every Union, every small, forgotten Cell rolled in a single stream, gray, black and red, through a single artery of the great city, three miles of caps and red kerchiefs and feet crunching snow and banners like red gashes in the mist. And the gray walls of Nevsky were like the sides of a huge canal where human waves played a funeral dirge on a snow hard as granite.

It was cold; a piercing, motionless cold hung over the city, heavy as a mist that cut into the walls, into the cracks of sealed windows, into the bones and skins under the heavy clothes. The sky was torn into gray layers of rags, and clouds were smeared on, like patches of ink badly blotted, with a paler ink under them, and a faded ink beneath, and then a water turbid with soap suds, under which no blue could ever have existed. Smoke rose from old chimneys, gray as the clouds, as if that smoke had spread over the city, or the clouds had belched gray coils into the chimneys and the houses were spitting them back, and the smoke made the houses seem unheated. Snowflakes fluttered down lazily, once in a while, to melt on indifferent, moving foreheads.

An open coffin was carried at the head of the procession. The coffin was red. A banner of scarlet, regal velvet was draped over a still body; a white face lay motionless on a red pillow, a clear, sharp profile swimming slowly past the gray walls, black strands of hair scattered on the red cloth, black strands of hair hiding a dark little hole on the right temple. The face was calm. Snowflakes did not melt on the still, white forehead.

Four honorary pall-bearers, his best Party comrades, carried the coffin on their shoulders. Four bowed heads were bared to the cold. The coffin seemed very red between the blond hair of Pavel Syerov and the black curls of Victor Dunaev.

A military band followed the coffin. The big brass tubes were trimmed with bows of black crêpe. The band played "You fell as a victim."

Many years ago, in secret cellars hidden from the eyes of the Czar's gendarmes, on the frozen roads of Siberian prison camps, a song had been born to the memory of those who had fallen in the fight for freedom. It was sung in muffled, breathless whispers to the clanking of chains, in honor of nameless heroes. It traveled down dark sidelanes; it had no author, and no copy of it had ever been printed. The Revolution brought it into every music store window and into the roar of every band that followed a Communist to his grave. The Revolution brought the "Internationale" to its living and "You fell as a victim" to its dead. It became the official funeral dirge of the new republic.

The toilers of Leningrad sang solemnly, marching behind the open red coffin:

> *"You fell as a victim*
> *In our fateful fight,*
> *A victim of endless devotion.*
> *You gave all you had to the people you loved,*
> *Your honor, your life and your freedom."*

The music began with the majesty of that hopelessness which is beyond the need of hope. It mounted to an ecstatic cry, which was not joy nor sorrow, but a military salute. It fell, breaking into a pitiless tenderness, the reverent tenderness that honors a warrior without tears. It was a resonant smile of sorrow.

And feet marched in the snow, and the brass tubes thundered, and brass cymbals pounded each step into the earth, and gray ranks unrolled upon gray ranks, and scarlet banners swayed to the grandeur of the song in a solemn farewell.

> *"The tyrant shall fall and the people shall rise,*
> *Sublime, almighty, unchained!*
> *So farewell, our brother,*
> *You've gallantly made*
> *Your noble and valiant journey!"*

Far beyond the rows of soldiers and students and workers, in the ranks of nameless stragglers that carried no banners, a girl walked alone, her unblinking eyes fixed ahead, even though she was too far away to see the red coffin. Her hands hung limply by her sides; above the heavy woolen mittens, her wrists were bare to the cold, frozen to a dark, purplish red. Her face had no expression; her eyes had: they seemed astonished.

Those marching around her paid no attention to her. But at the start of the demonstration, someone had noticed her. Comrade Sonia, leading a detachment of women workers from the Zhenotdel, had hurried past to take her place at the head of the procession, where she had to carry a banner; Comrade Sonia had stopped short and chuckled aloud: "Really, Comrade Argounova, you—here? I should think you'd be the one person to stay away!"

Kira Argounova had not answered.

Some women in red kerchiefs had passed by. One had pointed at her and whispered something, eagerly, furtively, to her comrades; someone had giggled.

Kira walked slowly, looking ahead. Those around her sang "You fell as a victim." She did not sing.

A red banner said:

PROLETARIANS OF THE WORLD, UNITE!

A freckled woman with strands of rusty hair under a man's cap, whispered to her neighbor: "Mashka, did you get the buckwheat at the co-operative this week?"

"No. They giving any?"

"Yeah. Two pounds per card. Better get it before it's all gone."

A red banner said:

FORWARD INTO THE SOCIALISTIC FUTURE UNDER THE
LEADERSHIP OF LENIN'S PARTY!

A woman hissed through blackened stumps of teeth: "Oh,

hell! They would choose a cold day like this to make us march in another one of their cursed parades!"

> *"You fell a-a-as a vic-ti-i-im*
> *Inour fate— fullfight,*
> *A vic-tim of e-end-less de-vo-o-otion. . . ."*

". . . stood in line for two hours yesterday, but best onions you ever hope to see. . . ."

"Dounka, don't miss the sunflower-seed oil at the co-operative. . . ."

"If they don't get shot by someone, they shoot themselves— just to make us walk. . . ."

> *"Yougave a-a-all you had fo-o-or the people you loved . . ."*

A red banner said:

TIGHTEN THE BONDS OF CLASS SOLIDARITY UNDER THE
STANDARD OF THE COMMUNIST PARTY!

"God! I left soup cooking on the Primus. It will boil all over the house. . . ."

"Stop scratching, comrade."

> *"Your ho-nor, yourli-ife and your free-ee-ee-edom. . . ."*

"Comrade, stop chewing sunflower seeds. It's disrespectful. . . ."

"It's like this, Praskovia: you peel the onions and add a dash of flour, just any flour you can get, and then a dash of linseed oil and . . ."

"What do *they* have to commit suicide about?"

A red banner said:

THE COMMUNIST PARTY SPARES NO VICTIMS IN ITS FIGHT
FOR THE FREEDOM OF MANKIND

"There's a little closet under the back stairs and some straw and no one can hear us in there. . . . My husband? The poor sap will never get wise. . . ."

"Let the millet soak for a coupla hours before cooking. . . ."

"God! It's the seventh month, it is, and you can't expect me to have a figure like a match stick, and here I have to walk like this. . . . Yeah, it's my fifth one. . . ."

*"Thety-rant shall fall and thepeo-ple shallrise,
Sublime, al-mighty, unchai-ai-ai-ned! . . ."*

"Lord Jesus Christ! I bet the newspaper's grown fast to my skin. Ever use newspapers to keep your feet warm, comrade? Under the socks?"

"Makes your feet stink."

"Cover your mouth when you yawn like that, comrade."

"Damn these demonstrations! Who the hell was he, anyway?"

"Yougave a-a-all youhad fo-o-or thepeople you loved . . ."

The Field of Victims of the Revolution was a huge square in the heart of the city, on the shore of the Neva, a vast, white desert, stretching for half a mile, like a bald spot on the scalp of Petrograd. The iron lances of the Summer Garden fence stood on guard at one side of the Field, and behind them lay the white desolation of a park with bare trees that seemed made of black iron like the lances.

Before the revolution, it had been called the Field of Mars and long ranks of gray uniforms had crossed it in military drills. The revolution had erected a small square of rose granite slabs, a little island lost in the center of the Field. Under the slabs were buried the first victims fallen in the streets of Petrograd in February of 1917. The days since February of 1917 had added more granite slabs to the little island. The names carved on the granite had belonged to those whose death had been the occasion for a demonstration, whose last reward had been the honor of the title of "The Revolution's Victim."

Pavel Syerov mounted a block of red granite over a red coffin. His slender figure in a tight, new leather jacket and breeches and tall military boots stood sharply, proudly against the gray sky, his blond hair waved in the wind, and his arms rose solemnly, in blessing and exhortation, over a motionless sea of heads and banners.

"Comrades!" Pavel Syerov's voice thundered over the solemn silence of thousands. "We are here, united by a common sorrow, by the common duty of paying a last tribute to a fallen hero. We have lost a great man. We have lost a great fighter. Perhaps, I may be permitted to say that I feel the loss more keenly than many who join me in honoring his death, but who knew him not while he lived. I was one of his closest friends—

and it was a privilege which I must share with all of you. Andrei Taganov was not a famous man, but he bore, proudly and gallantly, one title: that of a Communist. He came from the toilers' ranks. His childhood was spent at the proletarian work bench. He and I, we grew up together, and together we shared the long years of toil in the Putilovsky factory. We joined the Party together, long before the Revolution, in those dark days when a Party card was a ticket to Siberia or a mark for the Czar's hangman's noose. Side by side, Comrade Taganov and I fought in the streets of this city in the glorious days of October, 1917. Side by side, we fought in the ranks of the Red Army. And in the years of peace and reconstruction that followed our victory, the years which are harder and, perhaps, more heroic than any warfare, he did more than his share of the silent, modest, self-sacrificing work which your Party carries on for you, toilers of the U.S.S.R.! He fell as a victim to that work. But our sorrow at his death shall also be joy at his achievement. He is dead, but his work, our work, goes on. The individual may fall, but the Collective lives forever. Under the guidance of the Soviets, under the leadership of the great All-Union Communist Party, we are marching into a radiant tomorrow when the honest toil of free toilers will rule the world! Then labor will no longer be slavery, as it is in capitalistic countries, but a free and happy duty to that which is greater than our petty concerns, greater than our petty sorrows, greater than our very lives—the eternal Collective of a Proletarian Society! Our glorious dead shall be remembered forever, but we are marching on. Andrei Taganov is dead, but we remain. Life and victory are ours. Ours is the future!"

The applause rolled like a dull thunder to the houses of the city far away, to the snow of the Summer Garden, and red banners waved in the roar of clapping hands, rising to the gray sky. When the hands dropped and the heads turned their eyes to the red granite slab, Comrade Syerov was gone—and against the gray sky stood the trim, proud, resolute figure of Victor Dunaev, black curls waving in the wind, eyes sparkling, mouth open wide over lustrous white teeth, throwing into the silence the clear, ringing notes of a young, powerful voice:

"Comrade workers! Thousands of us are gathered here to honor one man. But one man means nothing in the face of the mighty Proletarian Collective, no matter how worthy his achievements. We would not be here, if that man were not more than a single individual, if he were not a symbol of something greater, which we are gathered here to honor. This is not a funeral, comrades, but a birthday party! We are not celebrating the death of a comrade, but the birth of a new humanity. Of that new humanity, he was one of the first, but not the last. The Soviets, comrades, are creating a new race of men. That new race terrifies the old world, for it brings death to all its outworn standards. What, then, are the standards of our new humanity? The first and basic one is that we have lost a word from our language, the most dangerous, the most insidious, the most evil of human words: the word 'I.' We have outgrown it. 'We' is the slogan of the future. The Collective stands in our hearts where that old monster—'self'— had stood. We have risen beyond the worship of the pocketbook, of personal power and personal vanity. We do not long for gold coins and gold medals. Our only badge of honor is the honor of serving the Collective. Our only aim is the honest toil which profits not one, but all. What is the lesson we are to learn here today and to teach our enemies beyond the borders? The lesson of a Party comrade dying for the Collective. The lesson of a Party that rules but to sacrifice itself to those it rules. Look at the world around you, comrades! Look at the fat, slobbering ministers of the capitalistic countries, who fight and stab one another in the back in their bloody scramble for power! Then look at those who rule you, who consecrate their lives to the unselfish service of the Collective, who carry the tremendous responsibility of the Dictatorship of the Proletariat! If you do, you will understand me when I say that the All-Union Communstic Party is the only honest, fearless, idealistic body of men in the politics of the world today!"

The applause thundered as if the old cannons of the Peter-Paul Fortress across the river had been fired all at once. And it thundered again when Victor's black curls disappeared in the crowd, and the straight, stubby mane of Comrade Sonia waved high in the air, while she roared with all the power of her broad chest about the new duties of the new woman of the Proletariat. Then another face rose over the crowd, a thin, consumptive, unshaved face that wore glasses and opened a pale mouth wide, coughing words which no one could hear. Then another mouth spoke, and it could be heard far beyond the crowd, a mouth that bellowed sonorously through a thick, black beard. A freckled boy from the Communist Union of Youth spoke, stuttering, scratching his head. A tall spinster in a crumpled, old-fashioned hat spoke ferociously, opening her small mouth as if she were at the dentist's, shaking her thin finger at the crowd as at a school-room of disobedient pupils. A tall sailor spoke, his fists on his hips, and those in the back rows laughed occasionally when they heard the front rows laughing, even though the words did not reach them.

Thousands stood, fidgeting nervously, knocking their heels together to keep them warm, burying their hands in their armpits, in their sleeves, in their fur lapels, breathing little wet icicles on the old scarfs high under their noses. They took turns in holding the red banners, and those who held them pressed the poles tightly to their sides with their elbows, blowing on their frozen fingers. A few sneaked away, hurrying furtively down side streets.

Kira Argounova stood without moving and listened attentively. She listened to every word. Her eyes held a question she hoped the words could answer.

Over the vast field, the sky was turning a dark, dirty, grayish blue, and in a window far away the first little yellow spark of light twinkled, greeting the early winter dusk. The voice of the last speaker had died, smothered in the thick mist of frost which one could not see, but felt flowing down heavily from the darkness above. The red coffin had been closed and had disappeared in the earth, and the grave had been filled, and a slab of red granite had risen over it. And suddenly the gray sea had shuddered, and the ranks were broken, and dark streams of men rolled swiftly into side streets, as if a dam had burst open. And far away, dying in the frozen twilight, the military band struck up the "Internationale," the song of the living, like the marching of thousands of feet, measured and steady, like soldiers' feet drumming a song upon the earth.

Then Kira Argounova walked slowly toward the new grave.

The Field was empty. The sky was descending, locking a frozen blue vault over the city. Through a crack in the vault, a single steely dot twinkled feebly. The houses far away were not houses any longer but flat, broken shadows of thin black paper pasted in a narrow strip against a brownish glow that had been red. Little lights trembled in little holes pierced through the paper. The Field was not in a city. The empty, quiet silence of a countryside hung over a white desert where whirls of snow rose in the wind, melting into thin white powder.

A lonely little figure stood over a granite tombstone.

Snowflakes fluttered lazily down on her bowed head, on the lashes of her eyes. Her lashes glistened with snowflakes, but without tears. She looked at the words cut into the red granite:

GLORY ETERNAL TO THE VICTIMS OF THE REVOLUTION

ANDREI TAGANOV

1896-1925

She wondered whether she had killed him, or the revolution had, or both.

XVI

Leo sat alone by the fireplace, smoking. A cigarette hung limply in his hand, then slipped out of his fingers; he did not notice it. He took another cigarette and held it unlighted for a long time, not noticing it. Then he glanced around for a match, and could not find it, even though the box lay on the arm of his chair. Then he picked up the match box and stared at it, puzzled, for he had forgotten what he wanted.

He had spoken little in the past two weeks. He had kissed Kira violently, once in a while, too violently, and she had felt his effort, and she had avoided his lips and his arms.

He had left home often and she had never asked him where he went. He had been drinking too often and too much, and she had not said whether she noticed it. When they had been alone together, they had sat silently, and the silence had spoken to her, louder than any words, of something which was an end. He had been spending the last of their money and she had not questioned him about the future. She had not questioned him about anything, for she had been afraid of the answer she knew: that her fight was lost.

When Kira came home from the funeral, Leo did not rise to his feet, but sat by the fireplace, not moving. He looked at her with a slow, curious, heavy glance between heavy eyelids.

Silently, she took off her coat and hung it in her wardrobe.

She was taking off her hat when a sound made her turn: Leo was laughing; it was a hard, bitter, brutal laughter.

She looked at him, her eyes wide: "Leo, what's the matter?"

He asked her fiercely: "Don't you know?"

She shook her head.

"Well, then," he asked, "do you want to know how much I know?"

"How much . . . you know . . . about what, Leo?"

"I don't suppose this is a good time to tell you, is it? Right after your lover's funeral?"

"My . . ."

He rose and approached her, and stood, his hands in his pockets, looking down at her with the arrogantly contemptuous look she worshipped, with the scornful, drooping smile; but his arched lips moved slowly to form three words: "You little bitch!"

She stood straight, without moving, her face white. "Leo . . ."

"Shut up! I don't want to hear a sound out of you! You rotten little . . . I wouldn't mind it, if you were like the rest of us! But you, with your saintly airs, with your heroic speeches, trying to make me walk straight, while you were . . . you were rolling under the first Communist bum who took the trouble to push you!"

"Leo, who . . ."

"Shut up! . . . No! I'll give you a chance to speak. I'll give you a chance to answer just one word. Were you Taganov's mistress? Were you? Yes or no?"

"Yes."

"All the time I was away?"

"Yes."

"And all the time since I came back?"

"Yes. What else did they tell you, Leo?"

"What else did you want them to tell me?"

"Nothing."

He looked at her; his eyes were suddenly cold, clear, weary.

"Who told you, Leo?"

"A friend of yours. Of his. Our dear comrade, Pavel Syerov. He dropped in on his way back from the funeral. He just wanted to congratulate me on the loss of my rival."

"Was it . . . was it a hard blow to you, Leo?"

"It was the best piece of news I'd heard since the revolution. We shooks hands and had a drink together, Comrade Syerov and I. Drank to you and your lover, and any other lovers you may have. Because, you see, that sets me free."

"Free . . . from what, Leo?"

"From a little fool who was my last hold on self-esteem! A little fool I was afraid to face, afraid to hurt! Really, you know, it's funny. You and your Communist hero. I thought he had died, making a great sacrifice by saving me for you. And he was just tired of you, he probably wanted to get you off his hands, for some other whore. So much for the sublime in the human race."

"Leo, we don't have to discuss him, do we?"

"Still love him?"

"That doesn't make any difference to you—now—does it?"

"None. None whatever. I won't even ask whether you had ever loved me. That, too, doesn't make any difference. I'd rather think you hadn't. That will make it easier for the future."

"The future, Leo?"

"Well, what did you plan it to be?"

"I . . ."

"Oh, I know! Get a respectable Soviet job and rot over a Primus and a ration card, and keep holy something in your fool imagination—your spirit or soul or honor—something that never existed, that shouldn't exist, that is the worst of all curses if it ever did exist! Well, I'm through with it. If it's murder— well—I don't see any blood. But I'm going to have champagne, and white bread, and silk shirts, and limousines, and no thoughts of any kind, and long live the Dictatorship of the Proletariat!"

"Leo . . . what . . . are you going to do?"

"I'm going away."

"Where?"

"Sit down."

He sat down at the table. His one hand lay in the circle of light under the lamp, and she noticed how still and white it was, with a net of blue veins that did not seem alive. She stood, watching it, until one finger moved. Then she sat down. Her face was expressionless. Her eyes were a little wide. He noticed her lashes—little needles of shadow on her cheeks—and the lashes were dry.

"Citizen Morozov," said Leo, "has left town."

"Well?"

"He's left Tonia—he wants no connections that could be investigated. But he's left her a nice little sum of money—oh, quite nice. She's going for a rest and vacation in the Caucasus.

She has asked me to go with her. I've accepted the job. Leo Kovalensky, the great gigolo of the U.S.S.R.!"

"Leo!"

She stood before him—and he saw terror in her eyes, such naked, raw terror that he opened his mouth, but could not laugh.

"Leo . . . not that!"

"She's an old bitch. I know. I like it better that way. She has the money and she wants me. Just a business deal."

"Leo . . . *you* . . . like a . . ."

"Don't bother about the names. You can't think of any as good as the ones I've thought of myself."

He noticed that the folds of her dress were shivering and that her hands were flung back unnaturally, as if leaning on space, and he asked, rising: "You're not going to be fool enough to faint, are you?"

She said, drawing her shoulders together: "No, of course not. . . . Sit down. . . . I'm all right. . . ."

She sat on the edge of the table, her hands clutching it tightly, and she looked at him. His eyes were dead and she turned away, for she felt that those eyes should be closed. She whispered: "Leo . . . if you had been killed in the G.P.U. . . . or if you had sold yourself to some magnificent woman, a foreigner, young and fresh and . . ."

"I wouldn't sell myself to a magnificent woman, young and fresh. I couldn't. Not yet. In a year—I probably will."

He rose and looked at her and laughed softly, indifferently: "Really, you know, don't you think it's not for you to express any depths of moral indignation? And since we both are what we are, would you mind telling me just why you kept me on while you had him? Just liked to sleep with me, like all the other females? Or was it my money and his position?"

Then she rose, and stood very straight, very still, and asked: "Leo, when did you tell her that you'd go with her?"

"Three days ago."

"Before you knew anything about Andrei and me?"

"Yes."

"While you still thought that I loved you?"

"Yes."

"And that made no difference to you?"

"No."

"If Syerov had not come here today, you'd still go with her?"

"Yes. Only then I'd have to face the problem of telling you.

He spared me that. That's why I was glad to hear it. Now we can say good-bye without any unnecessary scenes."

"Leo . . . please listen carefully . . . it's very important . . . please do me a last favor and answer this one question honestly, to the best of your knowledge: if you were to learn suddenly—it doesn't matter how—but if you were to learn that I love you, that I've always loved you, that I've been loyal to you all these years—would you still go with her?"

"Yes."

"And . . . if you *had* to stay with me? If you learned something that . . . that bound you to stay and . . . and to struggle on—would you try it once more?"

"If I were bound to—well, who knows? I might do what your other lover did. That's also a solution."

"I see."

"And why do you ask that? What is there to bind me?"

She looked straight at him, her face raised to his, and her hair fell back off a very white forehead, and only her lips moved as she answered with the greatest calm of her life: "Nothing, Leo."

He sat down again and clasped his hands and stretched them out, shrugging: "Well, that's that. Really, I still think you're wonderful. I was afraid of hysterics and a lot of noise. It's ended as it should have ended. . . . I'm leaving in three days. Until then—I can move out of here, if you want me to."

"No. I'd rather go. Tonight."

"Why tonight?"

"I'd rather. I can share Lydia's room, for a while."

"I haven't much money left, but what there is, I want you to . . ."

"No."

"But . . ."

"Please, don't. I'll take my clothes. That's all I need."

She was packing a suitcase, her back turned to him, when he asked suddenly: "Aren't you going to say anything? Have you nothing to say?"

She turned and looked at him calmly, and answered: "Only this, Leo: it was I against a hundred and fifty million people. I lost."

When she was ready to go, he rose and asked suddenly, involuntarily: "Kira . . . you loved me, once, didn't you?"

She answered: "When a person dies, one does not stop loving him, does one?"

"Do you mean Taganov or . . . me?"

"Does it make any difference, Leo?"

"No. May I help you to carry the suitcase downstairs?"

"No, thank you. It's not heavy. Good-bye, Leo."

He took her hand, and his face moved toward hers, but she shook her head, and he said only: "Good-bye, Kira."

She walked out into the street, leaning slightly to her left, her right arm pulled down by the weight of the suitcase. A frozen fog hung like cotton over the street, and a lamp post made a sickly, yellow blot spilled in the fog. She straightened her shoulders and walked slowly, and the white earth creaked under her feet, and the line of her chin was parallel with the earth, and the line of her glance parallel with her chin.

To her family, three silent, startled faces, Kira explained quietly and Galina Petrovna gasped: "But what happened to . . ."

"Nothing. We're just tired of each other."

"My poor, dear child! I . . ."

"Please don't worry about me, Mother. If you'll forgive me the inconvenience, Lydia, it will be only for a little while. I couldn't have found another room for just a few weeks."

"Why certainly! Why, I'll be only too glad to have you, Kira, after all you've done for us. But why for a few weeks? Where are you going after that?"

She answered, and her voice had the intensity of a maniac's: "*Abroad.*"

*

On the following morning, Citizen Kira Argounova filed an application for a foreign passport. She had several weeks to wait for an answer.

Galina Petrovna moaned: "It's insanity, Kira! Sheer insanity! In the first place, they won't give it to you. You have no reasons to show why you want to go abroad, and with your father's social past and all. . . . And even if you do get the passport—then what? No foreign country will admit a Russian and I can't say that I blame them. And if they admit you—what are you going to do? Have you thought of that?"

"No," said Kira.

"You have no money. You have no profession. How are you going to live?"

"I don't know."

"What will happen to you?"

"I don't care."

"But why are you doing it?"

"I want to get out."

"But you'll be all alone, lost in a wide world, with not a . . ."

"I want to get out."

". . . with not a single friend to help you, with no aim, no future, no . . ."

"I want to get out."

On the evening of his departure, Leo came to say good-bye. Lydia left them alone in her room.

Leo said: "I couldn't go, Kira, after parting as we did. I wanted to say good-bye and . . . Unless you'd rather . . ."

She said: "No. I'm glad you came."

"I wanted to apologize for some of the things I said to you. I had no right to say them. It's not up to me to blame you. Will you forgive me?"

"It's all right, Leo. I have nothing to forgive."

"I wanted to tell you that . . . that . . . Well, no, there's nothing to tell you. Only that . . . we have a great deal to . . . remember, haven't we?"

"Yes, Leo."

"You'll be better off without me."

"Don't worry about me, Leo."

"I'll be back in Petrograd. We'll meet again. We'll meet when years have passed, and years make such a difference, don't they?"

"Yes, Leo."

"Then we won't have to be so serious any more. It will be strange to look back, won't it? We'll meet again, Kira. I'll be back."

"If you're still alive—and if you don't forget."

It was as if she had kicked a dead animal in the road and saw it jerking in a last convulsion. He whispered: "Kira . . . don't . . ."

But she knew it was only a last convulsion and she said: "I won't."

He kissed her and her lips were soft and tender and yielding to his. Then he went.

*

She had several weeks to wait.

In the evenings, Alexander Dimitrievitch came home from work and shook snow off his galoshes in the lobby, and wiped them carefully with a special rag, for the galoshes were new and expensive.

After dinner, when he had no meeting to attend, he sat in

a corner with an unpainted wooden screen frame and worked
patiently, pasting match box labels on the frame. He collected
the labels and guarded them jealously in a locked box. At
night, he spread them cautiously on the table, and moved
them slowly into patterns, trying out color combinations. He
had a whole panel completed, and he muttered, squinting at
it appraisingly: "It's a beauty. A beauty. I bet no one in Petrograd has anything like it. What do you think, Kira, shall I use
two yellow ones and a green one in this corner, or just three
yellows?"

She answered quietly: "The green one will be nice, Father."

Galina Petrovna thundered in, at night, and flung a heavy
brief case on a chair in the lobby. She had had a telephone
installed, and she tore the receiver off the hook and spoke
hurriedly, still removing her gloves, unbuttoning her coat:
"Comrade Fedorov? . . . Comrade Argounova speaking. I have
an idea for that number in the Living Newspaper, for our
next Club show. . . . Now when we present Lord Chamberlain crushing the British Proletariat, we'll have one of the
pupils, a good husky one, wearing a red blouse, lie down on
the floor and we'll put a table on him—oh, just the front legs
—and we'll have the fat one, playing Lord Chamberlain, in a
high silk hat, sit at the table and eat steak. . . . Oh, it doesn't
have to be a real steak, just papier-mâché. . . ."

Galina Petrovna ate her dinner hurriedly, reading the evening paper. She jumped up, looking at the clock, before she
had finished, dabbed a smear of powder on her nose and, seiz-
ing her brief case, rushed out again to a Council meeting.
On the rare evenings when she stayed at home, she spread
books and newspaper clippings over the dining-room table,
and sat writing a thesis for her Marxist Club. She asked, raising her head, blinking absent-mindedly: "Kira, do you happen
to know, the Paris Commune, what year was that?"

"Eighteen seventy-one, Mother," Kira answered quietly.

Lydia worked at night. In the daytime, she practiced the
"Internationale" and "You fell as a victim" and the Red
Cavalry song on her old grand piano that had not been tuned
for over a year. When she was asked to play the old classics
she loved, she refused flatly, her mouth set in a thin, foolish,
stubborn line. But once in a while, she sat down at the piano
suddenly and played for hours, fiercely, violently, without
stopping between pieces; she played Chopin and Bach and
Tchaikovsky, and when her fingers were numb she cried,
sobbing aloud in broken hiccoughs, senselessly, monotonously,

like a child. Galina Petrovna paid no attention to it, saying: "Just another one of Lydia's fits."

Kira was lying on her mattress on the floor, when Lydia came home from work. Lydia took a long time to undress and a longer time to whisper endless prayers before the ikons in her corner. Some evenings, she came over to Kira and sat down on the mattress, and shivering in the darkness, in her long, white nightgown, her hair falling in a thick braid down her back, whispered confidentially, a ray of the street lamp beyond the window falling on her tired face with swollen eyes and dry little wrinkles in the corners of the mouth, on her dry, knotty hands that did not look young any longer: "I had a vision again, Kira, a call from above. Truly, a prophetic vision, and the voice told me that salvation shall not be long in coming. It is the end of the world and the reign of the Anti-Christ. But Judgment Day is approaching. I know. It has been revealed to me."

She whispered feverishly, she expected nothing but a peal of laughter from her sister, she was not looking at Kira, she was not certain whether Kira heard it; but she had to talk and she had to think that some human ears were listening.

"There is an old man, Kira, God's wanderer. I've been to see him. Please don't mention this to anyone, or they'll fire me from the Club. He is the Chosen One of the Lord and he knows. He says it has been predicted in the Scriptures. We are punished for our sins, as Sodom and Gomorrah were punished. But hardships and sorrows are only a trial for the soul of the righteous. Only through suffering and long-bearing patience shall we become worthy of the Kingdom of Heaven."

Kira said quietly: "I won't tell anyone, Lydia. And now you'd better go to bed, because you're tired and it's so cold here."

In the daytime, Kira led excursions through the Museum of the Revolution. In the evening, she sat in the dining room and read old books. She spoke seldom. When anyone addressed her, she answered evenly, quietly. Her voice seemed frozen on a single note. Galina Petrovna wished, uncomfortably, to see her angry, at least once; she did not see it. One evening, when Lydia dropped a vase in the silence of the dining room, and it broke with a crash, and Galina Petrovna jumped up with a startled little scream, and Alexander Dimitrievitch shuddered, blinking—Kira raised her head slowly, as if nothing had happened.

But there was a flicker of life in her eyes when, on her way home from the Excursion Center, she stopped at the window of a foreign book store on Liteiny, and stood looking thoughtfully at the bright covers with gay, broken, foreign letters, with chorus girls kicking long, glistening legs, with columns and searchlights and long, black automobiles. There was a jerk of life in her fingers when, every evening, as methodically as a bookkeeper, with a dull little stub of a pencil, she crossed another date off an old calendar on the wall over her mattress.

*

The foreign passport was refused.

Kira received the news with a quiet indifference that frightened Galina Petrovna, who would have preferred a stormy outbreak.

"Listen, Kira," said Galina Petrovna vehemently, slamming the door of her room to be left alone with her daughter, "let's talk sense. If you have any insane ideas of . . . of . . . Now, I want you to know that I won't permit it. After all, you're my daughter. I have some say in the matter. You know what it means, if you attempt . . . if you even dare to think of leaving the country illegally."

"I've never mentioned that," said Kira.

"No, you haven't. But I know you. I know what you're thinking. I know how far your foolish recklessness can . . . Listen, it's a hundred to one that you don't get out. And you'll be lucky if you're just shot at the border. It will be worse if you're caught and brought back. And if you're lucky enough to draw the one chance and slip out, it's a hundred to one that you'll die in a blizzard in those forests around the border."

"Mother, why discuss it?"

"Listen, I'll keep you here if I have to chain you. After all, one can be allowed to be crazy just so far. What are you after? What's wrong with this country? We don't have any luxuries, that's true, but you won't get any over there, either. A chambermaid is all you can hope to be, there, if you're lucky. This is the country for young people. I know your crazy stubbornness, but you'll get over it. Look at me. I've adapted myself, at my age, and, really, I can't say that I'm unhappy. You're only a pup and you can't make decisions to ruin your whole life before you've even started it. You'll outgrow your foolish notions. There is a chance for everyone in this new country of ours."

"Mother, I'm not arguing, am I? So let's drop the subject."

Kira returned home later than usual from her excursions. There were people she had to see in dark side streets, slipping furtively up dark stairs through unlighted doorways. There were bills to be slipped into stealthy hands and whispers to be heard from lips close to her ear. It would cost more than she could ever save to be smuggled out on a boat, she learned, and it would be more dangerous. She had a better chance if she tried it alone, on foot, across the Latvian border. She would need white clothes. People had done it, dressed all in white, crawling through the snow in the winter darkness. She sold her watch and paid for the name of the station and the village, and for a square inch of tissue paper with the map of the place where a crossing was possible. She sold the fur coat Leo had given her and paid for a forged permit to travel.

She sold her cigarette lighter, her silk stockings, her French perfume. She sold all her new shoes and her dresses. Vava Milovskaia came to buy the dresses. Vava waddled in, shuffling heavily in wornout felt boots. Vava's dress had a greasy patch across the chest, and her matted hair looked uncombed. Her face was puffed, a coarse white powder had dried in patches on her nose, and her eyes were encircled in heavy blue bags. When she took off her clothes, slowly, awkwardly, to try on the dresses, Lydia noticed the swelling at her once slender waistline.

"Vava, darling! What, already?" Lydia gasped.

"Yes," said Vava indifferently, "I'm going to have a baby."

"Oh, darling! Oh, congratulations!" Lydia clasped her hands.

"Yes," said Vava, "I'm going to have a baby. I have to be careful about eating and I take a walk every day. When it's born, we're going to register it with the Pioneers."

"Oh, no, Vava!"

"Oh, why not? Why not? It has to have a chance, doesn't it? It has to go to school, and to the University, maybe. What do you want me to do? Bring it up as an outcast? . . . Oh, what's the difference? Who knows who's right? . . . I don't know any more. I don't care."

"But, Vava, your child!"

"Lydia, what's the use? . . . I'll get a job after it's born, I'll have to. Kolya is working. It will be the child of Soviet employees. Then, later, maybe they'll admit in into the Communist Union of Youth. . . . Kira, that black velvet dress—it's so lovely. It looks almost . . . almost foreign. I know it's too tight for me now . . . but afterwards . . . maybe I'll get my figure back. They say you do. . . . Of course, you know, Kolya isn't making very much, and I don't want to take anything from father, and . . . But father gave me a present for my birthday, fifty rubles, and I think I should . . . I could never buy anything like it anywhere."

She bought the velvet dress and two others.

To Galina Petrovna, Kira had explained: "I don't need those dresses. I don't go anywhere. And I don't like to keep them."

"Memories?" Galina Petrovna had asked.

"Yes," Kira had said. "Memories."

She did not have much money after everything was sold. She knew that she would need every ruble. She could not buy a white coat. But she had the white bear rug that she had bought from Vasili Ivanovitch long ago. She took it secretly to a tailor and ordered it made into a coat. The coat came out as a short jacket that did not reach down to her knees. She would need a white dress. She could not buy one. But she still had Galina Petrovna's white lace wedding gown. When she was alone at home, she took her old felt boots into the kitchen and painted them white with lime. She bought a pair of white mittens and a white woolen scarf. She bought a ticket to a town far out of the way, far from the Latvian border.

When everything was ready, she sewed her little roll of money into the lining of the white fur jacket. She would need it there—if she crossed the border.

On a gray winter afternoon, she left the house when no one was at home. She did not say good-bye. She left no letter. She walked down the stairs and out into the street as if she were going to the corner store. She wore an old coat with a matted fur collar. She carried a small suitcase. The suitcase contained a white fur jacket, a wedding gown, a pair of boots, a pair of mittens, a scarf.

She walked to the station. A brownish mist hung over the roof tops, and men walked, bent to the wind, huddled, their hands in their armpits. A white frost glazed the posters, and the bronze cupolas of churches were dimmed in a silvery gray. The wind whirled little coils in the snow, and kerosene lamps stood in store windows, melting streaks on the frozen white panes.

"Kira," a voice called softly on a corner.

She turned. It was Vasili Ivanovitch. He stood under a lamp post, hunched, the collar of his old coat raised to his red ears, an old scarf twisted around his neck, two leather straps slung over his shoulders, holding a tray of saccharine tubes.

"Good evening, Uncle Vasili."

"Where are you going, Kira, with that suitcase?"

"How have you been, Uncle Vasili?"

"I'm all right, child. It may seem a strange business to find me in, I know, but it's all right. Really, it's not as bad as it looks. I don't mind it at all. Why don't you come to see us, sometimes, Kira?"

"I . . ."

"It's not a grand place, ours, and there's another family in the same room, but we're getting along. Acia will be glad to see you. We don't have many visitors. Acia is a nice child."

"Yes, Uncle Vasili."

"It's such a joy to watch her growing, day by day. She's getting better at school, too. I help her with her lessons. I don't mind standing here all day, because then I go home, and there she is. Everything isn't lost, yet. I still have Acia's future before me. Acia is a bright child. She'll go far."

"Yes, Uncle Vasili."

"I read the papers, too, when I have time. There's a lot going on in the world. One can wait, if one has faith and patience."

"Uncle Vasili . . . I'll tell them . . . over there . . . where I'm going . . . I'll tell them about everything . . . it's like an S.O.S. . . . And maybe . . . someone . . . somewhere . . . will understand. . . ."

"Child, where are you going?"

"Will you sell me a tube of saccharine, Uncle Vasili?"

"Why, no, I won't sell it to you. Take it, child, if you need it."

"Certainly not. I was going to buy it anyway from someone else," she lied. "Don't you want me for a customer? It may bring you luck."

"All right, child."

"I'll take this nice big one with the big crystals. Here you are."

She slipped the coin into his hand and the tube of saccharine into her pocket.

"Well, good-bye, Uncle Vasili."

"Good-bye, Kira."

She walked away without looking back. She walked through the dusk, through gray and white streets, under grayish ban-

ners bending down from old walls, grayish banners that had
been red. She walked through a wide square where the tramway lights twinkled, springing out of the mist. She walked
up the frozen steps of the station, without looking back.

XVII

The train wheels knocked as if an iron chain were jerked
twice, then rumbled dully, clicking, then gave two sharp broken jerks again. The wheels tapped like an iron clock ticking
swiftly, knocking off seconds and minutes and miles.

Kira Argounova sat on a wooden bench by the window.
She had her suitcase on her lap and held it with both hands,
her fingers spread wide apart. Her head leaned back against
the wooden seat and trembled in a thin little shudder, like the
dusty glass pane. Her lids drooped heavily over her eyes fixed
on the window. She did not close her eyes. She sat for hours
without moving, and her muscles did not feel the immobility,
or she did not feel her muscles any longer.

Beyond the window, nothing moved in the endless stretches
of snow but black smears of telegraph poles, as if the train
were suspended, stationary, between two slices of white and
gray, and the wheels shrieked as if grating in a void. Once in
a while, a white blot on a white desert, a blot with black edges
shaped as fir branches, sprang up suddenly beyond the window
and whirled like lightning across the pane.

When she remembered that she had not eaten for a long
time, dimly uncertain whether it was hours or days, dimly
conscious that she had to eat, even though she had forgotten
hunger, she broke a chunk off a stale loaf of bread, which she
had bought at the station, and chewed it slowly, with effort,
her jaws moving monotonously, like a machine.

Around her, men left the car, when the train stopped at
stations, and came back with steaming tea kettles. Once, someone put a cup into her hand, and she drank, the hot tin edge
pressed to her lips.

Telegraph wires raced the train, crossing and parting and
crossing again, thin black threads flying faster, faster than
the shuddering car could follow.

In the daytime, the sky seemed lighter than the earth, a pale stretch of translucent gray over a heavy white. At night, the earth seemed lighter than the sky, a pale blue band under a black void.

She slept, sitting in her corner, her head on her arms, her arms on her suitcase. She tied the suitcase handle to her wrists, with a piece of string, at night. There were many moans around her about stolen luggage. She slept, her consciousness frozen on a single thought—of her suitcase. She awakened with a jolt whenever the motion of the car made the suitcase slip a little.

She had no thoughts left. She felt empty, clear and quiet, as if her body were only an image of her will, and her will—only an arrow, tense and hard, pointing at a border that had to be crossed. The only living thing she felt was the suitcase on her lap. Her will was knocking with the wheels of the train. Her heart beat there, under the floor.

She noticed dimly, once, on the bench before her, a woman pressing a cold white breast into a child's lips. There still were people and there still were lives. She was not dead. She was only waiting to be born.

At night, she sat for hours, staring at the window. She could see nothing but the dim reflection of the candle-glow and benches and boarded walls shuddering in space, and the tousled shadow of her own head. There was no earth, no world beyond the window. Only far down, by the track, yellow squares of snow raced the train in the glow of the windows, and black clots whirled past as long, thin streaks. Once in a while, a spark of light pierced the darkness, somewhere far away, at the edge of the sky, and brought suddenly into existence a blue waste of snow beyond the glass. The light died and the earth went with it, leaving nothing in the window but the boarded walls and the candle and the tousled head.

There were stations where she had to get out, and stand at a ticket window on a windswept platform, and buy a new ticket, and wait for another train to come rumbling through the dusk, a black engine spewing showers of red sparks.

Then there were wheels again, knocking under the floor, and another station, and another ticket, and another train. There were many days and nights, but she did not notice them. The men in khaki peaked caps, who examined the tickets, could not know that the girl in the old coat with the matted fur collar was going toward the Latvian border.

The last station, where she did not buy another ticket, was

a dark little platform of rotted wooden planks, the last stop before the train's terminal, before the border town.

It was getting dark. Brown wheel-tracks in the snow led far away into a glowing red patch. A few sleepy soldiers on the platform paid no attention to her. A large wicker hamper rattled as husky fists lowered it to the ground from a baggage car. At the station door, someone begged loudly for hot water. Lights twinkled in the car windows.

She walked away, clutching her suitcase, following the wheel tracks in the snow.

She walked, a slender black figure, leaning faintly backward, alone in a vast field rusty in the sunset.

It was dark when she saw the village houses ahead and yellow dots of candles in windows low over the ground. She knocked at a door. A man opened it; his hair and beard were a bushy blond tangle from which two bright eyes peered inquisitively. She slipped a bill into his hand and tried to explain as fast as she could, in a choked whisper. She did not have to explain much. Those in the house knew and understood.

Behind a low wooden partition, her feet in the straw where two pigs slept huddled together, she changed her clothes, while those in the room sat around a table, as if she were not present, five blond heads, one of them in a blue kerchief. Wooden spoons knocked in the wooden bowls on the table, and the sound of another spoon came from the shelf of a brick stove in the corner, where a gray head bent, sighing, over a wooden bowl. A candle stood on the table, and three little red tongues flickered before a bronze triangle of ikons in a corner, little glimmers of red in the bronze halos.

She put on the white boots and took off her dress; her naked arms shuddered a little, even though the room was hot and stuffy. She put on the white wedding gown, and its long train rustled in the straw, and a pig opened one slit of an eye. She lifted the train and pinned it carefully to her waistline, with big safety-pins. She wound the white scarf tightly about her hair, and put on the white fur jacket. She felt cautiously the little lump in the lining over her left breast, where she had sewn the bills; it was the last and only weapon she would need.

When she approached the table, the blond giant said, his voice expressionless: "Better wait for an hour or so, till the moon sets. The clouds ain't so steady."

He moved, making room for her on the bench, pointing to it silently, imperatively. She raised the lace dress, stepped over the bench and sat down. She took off the jacket and held it over her arm, pressed tightly to her body. Two pairs of feminine eyes stared at her high lace collar, and the girl in the blue kerchief whispered something to the older woman, her eyes awed, incredulous.

Silently, the man put a steaming wooden bowl before the guest.

"No, thank you," she said. "I'm not hungry."

"Eat," he ordered. "You'll need it."

She ate obediently a thick cabbage soup that smelled of hot lard.

The man said suddenly in the silence, without looking at her: "It's pretty near a whole night's walk."

She nodded.

"Pretty young," said the woman across the table, shaking her head, and sighed.

When she was ready to go, the man opened the door to a cold wind whining over an empty darkness, and muttered in his blond beard: "Walk as long as you can. When you see a guard—crawl."

"Thank you," she said, as the door closed.

*

Snow rose to her knees, and each step was like a fall forward, and she held her skirt high, clutched in her fist. Around her, a blue that did not seem blue, a color that was no color, that had never existed in the world she had known, stretched without end, and sometimes she thought she was standing alone, very tall, very high over a flat circle, and sometimes she thought the bluish whiteness was a huge wall closing in over her head.

The sky hung low, in grayish patches, and black patches, and streaks of a blue that one could never remember in the daytime; and blots of something which was not a color and not quite a light ray, flowed from nowhere, trickling once in a while among the clouds, and she bent her head not to see it.

There were no lights ahead; she knew that the lights behind her had long since vanished, even though she did not look back. She carried nothing: she had left her suitcase and her old clothes in the village; she would need nothing—there—ahead —but the little roll in the lining of her jacket, and she touched it cautiously, once in a while.

Her knees hurt with the piercing pain of stretched sinews, as if she were climbing a long stairway. She watched the pain, a little curiously, like an outsider. Scalding needles pierced

her cheeks, and they itched, and she scratched them once in a
while with a white mitten, but it did not help.

She heard nothing but the rustle of the snow under her
boots, and she tried to walk faster, not to listen beyond the
sound of her feet, not to notice the slurred shadows of sounds
hanging around her, floating from nowhere.

She knew she had been walking for hours, that which she
had once called hours. There were no hours here; there were
only steps, only legs rising and falling deep into the snow,
and a snow that had no end. Or had it an end? That, really,
did not matter. She did not have to think of that. She had to
think only that she had to walk. She had to walk west. That was
the only problem, that was the total of all the problems. Had
she any problems? Had she any questions to be answered?
If she had—they would be answered—there. She did not have
to think. She had to get out. She would think—then—if there
were thoughts to be faced. Only she had to get out. Only to
get out.

In the white mittens, her fingers ached, her bones drawn
tight, her joints squeezed as in a vise. She must be cold, she
thought; she wondered dimly whether it was a very cold night.

Before her, the blue snow was luminous, the snow lighting
the sky. There was nothing but a haze, ahead of her, where
the earth was smeared into the clouds, and she was not sure
whether the clouds were close to her face and she would knock
against them, or many miles away.

She had left nothing behind. She was walking out of a void,
a void white and unreal as that earth around her. She could not
give up. She still had them—those two legs that could move—
and something lost somewhere within her, that told them to
move. She would not give up. She was alive; alive and alone
in a desert which was not a living earth. She had to walk, because she was still alive. She had to get out.

Long spirals of snow rose in the wind, brushing the low
sky, far ahead. She saw strips of a sharp black above her and
specks of bright dust twinkling at her from between the clouds.
She huddled tighter, hunching her shoulders; she did not want
to be seen.

Something hurt in her waistline, as if each step jerked her
spine forward, and something throbbed, rising up her back.
She pressed her fingers to the roll in her jacket. She had to
watch that. She could not lose it. She had to watch that and
her legs. The rest did not matter.

She stopped short when she saw a tree, the long white pyramid of a giant fir, rising suddenly out of the snow, and she stood without breath, her knees bent, crouching like an animal, listening. She heard nothing. Nothing moved behind the low branches. She went on. She did not know how long she had waited.

She did not know whether she was moving forward. Perhaps she was only stamping her feet, up and down, on the same spot. Nothing changed in that white immensity around her. Would it ever change? She was like an ant crawling over a white table, a hard, bright, lustrous, enameled table. She threw her arms wide, suddenly feeling the space around her. She looked up at the sky. She looked, her head and shoulders thrown back. Those twinkling splinters above—they were endless worlds, people said. Wasn't there room for her in the world? Who was mowing her feet off the small space they held in that vast universe? Who were they and why were they doing it? She had forgotten. She had to get out.

Those legs were not hers any longer. They moved like a wheel, like levers, rising, bending, falling, up and down, down with a jerk that reverberated up to her scalp.

She felt, suddenly, that she was not tired, she had no pain, she was light and free, she was well, too well, she could walk like this through years to come. Then, a sudden jolt of pain shot through her shoulder blades, and she wavered, and she felt as if hours went by while a motionless leg rose, rose the space of an atom at a time and fell down again, cutting the snow, and she was walking again. She bent, her arms huddled over her stomach, drawing herself into a little ball, so that her legs would have less to carry.

Somewhere there was a border and it had to be crossed. She thought, suddenly, of a restaurant she had seen, for the flash of a second, in a German film. It had a sign over the door, with plain, thin letters, nickel-plated letters, insolent in their simplicity, on dull white glass—"Café Diggy-Daggy." They had no signs like that in the country she was leaving. They had no pavements lustrous as a ball-room floor. She repeated senselessly, without hearing the sounds, as a charm, as a prayer: "Café Diggy-Daggy . . . Ca . . . fé . . . Dig . . . gy . . . Dag . . . gy . . ." and she tried to walk in rhythm with the syllables.

She did not have to tell her legs to move any longer. She thought they were running. An instinct was driving her, the instinct of an animal, whipping her blindly into the battle of self-preservation.

She was whispering through frozen lips: "You're a good soldier, Kira Argounova, you're a good soldier. . . ."

*

Ahead of her, the blue snow billowed dimly against the sky. The waves did not change as she came closer; they stood out, sharper, harder, low hills undulating in the darkness. White cones rose to the sky, with black edges of branches.

Then she saw a black figure. The figure was moving. It was moving in a straight line across the hills, across the horizon. She saw the legs, like scissors, opening and closing. She saw a small black spike on his shoulder, and it gleamed sharply, once, against the sky.

She fell down on her stomach. She felt, dimly, as through an anesthetic, snow biting the wrists under her sleeves, rolling into her boots. She lay still, her heart pounding against the snow.

Then she raised her head a little and crawled slowly forward, on her stomach. She stopped and lay still, watching the black figure in the distance, and crawled again, and stopped, and watched, and crawled again.

Citizen Ivan Ivanov was six feet tall. He had a wide mouth and a short nose, and when he was puzzled, he blinked, scratching his neck.

Citizen Ivan Ivanov was born in the year 1900, in a basement, in a side street of the town of Vitebsk. He was the ninth child of the family. At the age of six, he started in as apprentice to a shoemaker. The shoemaker beat him with leather suspenders and fed him buckwheat gruel. At the age of ten, he made his first pair of shoes, all by himself, and he wore them proudly down the street, the leather squeaking. That was the first day Citizen Ivan Ivanov remembered all through his life.

At the age of fifteen, he lured the neighborhood grocer's daughter into a vacant lot and raped her. She was twelve years old, with a chest as flat as a boy's, and she whined shrilly. He made her promise not to tell anyone, and he gave her fifteen kopeks and a pound of sugar candy. That was the second day he remembered.

At the age of sixteen, he made his first pair of military boots for a real general, and he polished them thoroughly, spitting on the flannel rag, and he delivered them to the general himself, who patted him on the shoulder and gave him a tip of a ruble. That was the third day he remembered.

There was a gay bunch of fellows around the shoemaker's

shop. They rose at dawn and they worked hard and their shirts stuck to their backs with sweat, but they had a good time at night. There was a saloon on the corner of the street, and they sang gay songs, their arms about one another's shoulders. There was a house around the corner, where a wizened little man played the piano, and Ivan's favorite was a fat blonde in a pink kimono; she was a foreigner called Gretchen. And those were the nights Citizen Ivan Ivanov remembered.

He served in the Red Army, and, shells roaring overhead, made bets on lice races with the soldiers in the bottom of the trench.

He was wounded and told he would die. He stared dully at the wall, for it did not make any difference.

He recovered and married a servant girl with round cheeks and round breasts, because he had gotten her in trouble. Their son was blond and husky, and they named him Ivan. They went to church on Sundays, and his wife cooked onions with roasted mutton, when they could get it. She raised her skirt high over her fat legs, and knelt, and scrubbed the white pine floor of their room. And she sent him to a public bath once every month. And Citizen Ivan Ivanov was happy.

Then he was transferred to the border patrol, and his wife went back to live with her parents in the village, and took their son with her.

Citizen Ivan Ivanov had never learned to read.

Citizen Ivan Ivanov was guarding the border of the Union of Socialist Soviet Republics.

He walked slowly through the snow, his rifle on his shoulder, blowing at his frozen fingers, cursing the cold. He did not mind going down hill, but going up hill was hard, and he scrambled up, groaning, to stand there alone on the summit, with the wind biting his nose, and not a living soul for miles around.

Then, Citizen Ivan Ivanov saw something moving in the snow, far away.

He was not sure it had moved. He peered into the darkness, but the wind raised whirls of snow dust over the plain and he thought he might have been mistaken; only it had seemed as if something had moved, which was not snow dust. He yelled, cupping his hands over his mouth: "Who goes there?"

Nothing answered. Nothing moved in the plain under the hill.

He yelled: "You'd better come out or I'll shoot!"

There was no answer.

He hesitated, scratching his neck. He stared far out into the night. But he had to be safe.

Citizen Ivan Ivanov raised his rifle to his shoulder and fired.

A blue flame streaked through the darkness and a dull echo rolled in the distance, far away. There was no sound after the echo had died, no movement in the white plain under the hill.

Citizen Ivan Ivanov scratched his neck. He should go down there and investigate, he thought. But it was too far, and the snow was too deep, and the wind was too cold. He waved his hand and turned away. "Just a rabbit, most likely," he muttered, descending the hill to continue his route.

Kira Argounova lay very still in the snow, on her stomach, her arms thrown forward, and only a lock of hair moved, falling from under the white scarf, and her eyes followed the black figure walking away across the hills, disappearing in the distance. She lay still for a long time, watching a red spot widening slowly under her in the snow.

She thought, clearly, sharply, in words she could almost hear: "Well, I'm shot. Well, that's how it feels to be shot. It's not so frightful, is it?"

She rose slowly to her knees. She took off a mitten and slipped her hand into her jacket to feel the roll of bills over her left breast. She hoped the bullet had not gone through the bills. It hadn't. The little hole in the jacket was just under them. And her fingers felt something hot and sticky.

It did not hurt much. It felt like a sharp little burn in her side, with less pain than in her tired legs. She tried to stand up. She swayed a little, but she could stand. There was a dark patch on her jacket and the fur was drawn into red, warm clusters. It did not bleed much; just a few drops she could feel slithering down her skin.

She could walk. She would keep her hand on it and it would not bleed. She was not far from the border now. Over there, beyond, she would have it bandaged. It was not serious and she could stand it. She had to go on.

She staggered forward and wondered at the weakness in her knees. She whispered to herself through lips that were turning blue: "Of course, you're wounded and you're a little weak. That's to be expected. Nothing to worry about."

Swaying, her shoulders drooping forward, her hand at her side, she went on, through the snow, stumbling, her knees meeting, faltering as if she were drunk. She watched little dark drops falling off the hem of her lace gown, slowly, once in a while. Then the drops stopped falling. She smiled.

She felt no pain. The last of her consciousness had gone into one will into two legs that were growing weaker and weaker. She had to go on. She had to get out. She had to get out.

She whispered to herself, as if the sound of her voice were a living fluid giving her strength: "You're a good soldier, Kira Argounova, you're a good soldier and now's the time to prove it. . . . Now. . . . Just one effort. . . . One last effort. . . . It's not so very bad yet, is it? . . . You can make it. . . . Just walk. . . . Please, walk. . . . You have to get out . . . get out . . . get out . . . get out . . ."

She pressed her hand to the roll of bills in her jacket. She could not lose that. She had to watch that. She could not see things clearly any longer. She had to remember that.

Her head was drooping forward. She closed her eyes, leaving slits open between her lashes to watch her legs, her legs that should not stop.

She opened her eyes suddenly to find herself lying in the snow. She raised her head slowly, wondering, for she did not remember having fallen.

She must have fainted, she thought, wondering curiously how it felt to faint, for she did not remember.

It took a long time to rise. She noticed a red spot in the snow where she had fallen. She must have lain there for some time. She staggered forward, then stopped, some thought forming itself slowly in her dull eyes, and she came back and covered the red spot with snow, with her foot.

She went on, wondering dimly why the weather had become so hot and why the snow did not melt when it was so hot, so hot that she could hardly breathe, and what if the snow did melt? She would have to swim, then, well, she was a good swimmer and that would be easier than walking, for her legs could rest, then.

She went reeling forward. She did not know whether she was walking in the right direction. She had forgotten that she had to think of a direction. She remembered only that she had to walk.

She did not notice that the hill ended sharply on the edge of a ravine, and she fell and rolled down the white slope in a whirl of legs, arms and snow.

She could move nothing but one hand, at first, to rub the wet snow off her face, off her lips, off her frozen lashes. She lay huddled in a white heap on the bottom of a white gulch. The time it took to rise again seemed like hours, like years: just to draw her hands to her body, at first, palms down, to press her elbows to her body, turn her legs, push her feet out, then rise to her knees, leaning on tense, trembling arms, and breathe, with a breath like a knife inside, then rise a little further, leaning on one hand, then tear that hand, too, off the snow, and rise, and stand erect, panting.

She made a few steps. But she could not walk up the other side of the gulch. She fell and crawled up the hill on her hands and knees, dipping her burning face into the snow to cool her cheeks.

She rose to her feet again on the top of the hill. She had lost her mittens. She felt something in the corners of her mouth and she rubbed her lips and looked at her fingers: her fingers were pink with froth.

She felt too hot. She tore the white scarf off her hair and threw it down into the gulch. The wind was a relief, blowing her hair back in a straight, shivering line.

She went on, raising her face to the wind.

She felt too hot and it was so difficult to breathe. She tore off her fur jacket and dropped it into the snow, and went on, without looking back.

In the sky, the clouds were rolling away in whirls of blue and gray and dark green. Ahead of her, above the snow, a pale line glowed, rising, and it was a transparent white, but above the snow it looked like a very pale green.

She pitched forward, and jerked back again, brushing the hair out of her eyes, and faltered, and went on, a trembling, swaying, reeling, drunken figure in a long wedding gown of lace white as the snow around her.

The train was torn off her waistline and it dragged behind her, her legs getting tangled in the long lace. She staggered blindly, the wind waving her hair, her arms swinging, as if they, too, were loose in the wind. She leaned back and her breasts stood out under the white lace, and from under her left breast a little stream of red trickled down slowly, and long dark patches spread down to the train, and delicate flowers of lace were red on the white satin.

And suddenly her dry lips, caked and sealed with froth, opened again, and she called softly, one name, as a plea for help from over there, from across the border, as a caress, her voice tender and almost joyous:

"Leo! . . ."

She repeated, louder and louder, without despair, as if the sound, that one sound in the world, were giving her life: "Leo! . . . Leo! . . . Leo! . . ."

She was calling him, the Leo that could have been, that would have been had he lived there, where she was going, across the border. He was awaiting her there, and she had to go on. She had to walk. There, in that world, across the border, a life was awaiting her to which she had been faithful her every living hour, her only banner that had never been lowered, that she had held high and straight, a life she could not betray, she would not betray now by stopping while she was still living, a life she could still serve, by walking, by walking forward a little longer, just a little longer.

Then she heard a song, a tune not loud enough to be a human sound, a song as a last battle-march. And it was not a funeral dirge, it was not a hymn, it was not a prayer. It was a tune from an old operetta, the "Song of Broken Glass."

Little notes of music trembled in hesitation, and burst, and rolled in quick, fine waves, like the thin, clear ringing of glass. Little notes leaped and exploded and laughed, laughed with a full, unconditional, consummate human joy.

She did not know whether she was singing. Perhaps she was only hearing the music somewhere.

But the music had been a promise; a promise at the dawn of her life. That which had been promised then, could not be denied to her now. She had to go on.

She went on, a fragile girl in the flowing, medieval gown of a priestess, red stains spreading on the white lace.

At dawn, she fell on the edge of a slope. She lay very still, for she knew that she could not rise again.

Far down, below her, an endless snow plain stretched into the sunrise. The sun had not come. A band of pink, pale and young, like the breath of a color, like the birth of a color, rose over the snow and glowed, trembling, flowing up into a pale blue, a blue immensity of sparks twinkling under a thin veil, like the faint, fading ghost of a lake in a summer sun, like the still surface of a lake with a sun drowned far in its depths. And the snow, at the rise of that liquid flame, seemed to quiver, breathing, glittering softly. Long bands stretched across the plain, shadows that seemed light itself, a heavier, bluer light with edges ready to burst into dancing fires.

A lonely little tree stood far away in the plain. It had no leaves. Its slim, rare twigs had gathered no snow. It stretched, tense with the life of a future spring, thin black branches, like arms, into the dawn rising over an endless earth where so much had been possible.

She lay on the edge of a hill and looked down at the sky. One hand, white and still, hung over the edge, and little red drops rolled slowly in the snow, down the slope.

She smiled. She knew she was dying. But it did not matter any longer. She had known something which no human words could ever tell and she knew it now. She had been awaiting it and she felt it, as if it had been, as if she had lived it. Life had been, if only because she had known it could be, and she felt it now as a hymn without sound, deep under the little hole that dripped red drops into the snow, deeper than that from which the red drops came. A moment or an eternity —did it matter? Life, undefeated, existed and could exist.

She smiled, her last smile, to so much that had been possible.

THE END

THE VIRTUE OF SELFISHNESS:

A New Concept of Egoism

by Ayn Rand

With additional articles by Nathaniel Branden

Ayn Rand is one of the most widely discussed figures on the contemporary intellectual scene. She advocates a new morality, an ethics of rational self-interest, that stands in complete opposition to the political, social, and religious attitudes of our day. Her unique philosophy, known as *Objectivism*, is the underlying theme of her famous novels.

Now for the first time, articles on ethics from *The Objectivist Newsletter*, a periodical published and edited by Ayn Rand and Nathaniel Branden, have been gathered together in a single volume. Here are the basic tenets of a new ethics that challenges the accepted standards of our age.

Signet T2791—75¢

ATLAS SHRUGGED
by *Ayn Rand*

Tremendous in scope, breath-taking in its suspense, this is the story of a man who said that he would stop the motor of the world—and did.

Is he a destroyer or a liberator? Why does he have to fight his battle not against his enemies but against those who need him most—including the woman he loves?

Ayn Rand says about this book, "To all the readers who discovered *The Fountainhead* and asked me many questions about the wider application of its ideas, I want to say that I am answering these questions in the present novel, and that *The Fountainhead* was only an overture to *Atlas Shrugged*. I trust that no one will tell me that men such as I write about don't exist. That this book has been written—and published—is my proof that they do."

Signet W3170—$1.50